P9-BHS-609

PATTERNS OF ABUSE

JOHN H. TAYLOR

PATTERNS OF ABUSE

WYNWOOD™ Press
New York, New York

Library of Congress Cataloging-in-Publication Data

Taylor, John H. (John Harvey).
Patterns of abuse.

I. Title.
PS3570.A9415P38 1988 813'.54 88-20763
ISBN 0-8007-7208-3

Published by WYNWOOD™ Press
New York, New York
Printed in the United States of America

For
Lily Sharley
and
Lily Richardson

Author's Note

This novel is a work of fiction. Names, characters, places, and incidents are either the product of the author's imagination or are used fictitiously. Any resemblance to actual events, locales, or persons, living or dead, is entirely coincidental.

Because the setting of this book is Washington, D.C., the real names of certain long-established institutions, publications, agencies, and public offices are mentioned. However, to repeat: this book's story, incidents, and characters are entirely fictional and imaginary. Likewise, the actions and motivations of the characters (including the institutions, publications, agencies, and public offices in Washington, D.C.) are entirely fictitious and imaginary and should not be considered real or factual. This is a novel, nothing more.

Prologue

WHEN ALI RAHMI WALKED INTO HIS MOTHER-IN-LAW'S kitchen, his wife's female relatives were at the pink Formica table wearing their formless *chadors,* sitting like seven black candles around a birthday cake. His wife was squatting against the wall, her hands clasped between her knees and her chin pressed against her chest as she cried quietly. The stale smell of cooking hung in the air. It was an ancient tableau of shame and doom.

Ali did not yet know exactly what had happened, but he was certain what would happen soon. He'd known instinctively the moment his brother called him out of his meeting at the foreign ministry. He'd driven as fast as he could through the crowded streets of Teheran, gasping from dread and the heat and dirt that blew in the car windows. The lie he had been living had finally been exposed, and he knew there would be no happiness for him for the rest of his life. He also knew his wife was going to die.

Her aunt, the grim old hag, announced the specifications: His wife had been discovered committing an abomination with his own brother Abol. From the kitchen, Ali could see Abol in the parlor, pacing back and forth and smoking. *Wasn't he just glancing at his watch? The bastard is impatient to get back to work already, back to kissing the asses of the mullahs.* Ali looked back at the aunt. She was saying they were found by his eleven-year-old niece when she came home early from school. "She was on all fours on the floor," spat the aunt, who grinned when she added, "He was at her from behind, like a Bedouin."

The finality of the circumstances hadn't permitted even a instant of anger at Soraya, who was now convulsed with sobbing. He yearned to go to her and embrace her and let her dry her eyes on his shoulder, but he couldn't. She was defiled, untouchable. The scheming shit Abol, who'd just been caught with his pants around his knees, was now watching *him,* probably hoping to be able to report to their superiors that in this moment of judgment Ali had disobeyed the law of Allah. Ever since the revolution, Ali had been under suspicion because his education had been paid for by the Shah and because of his legendary affection for the ways of the West. They would need little pretext to strike at him. So he stood before this council of savagery looking silently at his shoes as his brother's vengeful, gloating eyes bore into him. In a moment he left, knowing he would never see her again.

That night, while she slept, the women decided they didn't want to invite the ridicule and humiliation of a public trial for adultery, especially since the outcome was already assured. They crept to her room, bent over her, and in a quiet flurry of black muslin smothered her with a pillow. From the doorway the eleven-year-old watched in horror and wonder. She had always been told that the world of Islam was a man's world, but what man commanded power such as this?

He never knew for certain why she'd done it. *But I know why he did.*

In 1979, when the Shah fled and the ayatollahs came, Ali and Abol had been in the University of Teheran, where their father was a respected member of the faculty of engineering. Ali was in an advanced program in public administration, being groomed for the Pahlavis' elite corps of civil servants. Abol was just as bright as his brother but less content to study and work. *The lazy bastard always had an eye peeled for the easy score.* When the campus erupted in

Islamic primitivism, Ali kept to his books, attending only enough meetings of the Revolutionary Student Council to avoid attracting suspicion. But Abol was on the front lines, shouting slogans and burning American flags and joining the mobs that boiled through the streets for the benefit of American TV. One afternoon as Abol and some other students were laboring to topple the Shah's statue at the university gate, a jittery police sergeant opened fire. Abol was hit in the arm, and for days afterwards he strutted around the most modern city in the Mideast with a filthy, blood-soaked rag wrapped around his arm like Che Guevara among the *campesinos*.

As Ali looked back, he realized both he and his brother had been hypocrites, paying lip service to the revolution for different reasons. What he saw as an episode of mass insanity to be survived, Abol saw as an opportunity to be ruthlessly exploited. Both tactics worked. The ignorant farm boys who had rushed to Teheran to join the mobs were fine for stoning embassies, but Shah or no Shah the mullahs needed people who could read and write to run the country. The brothers entered the foreign service bureaucracy together. Abol's battle scars won him a place on the fast track. For his part, Ali felt he was under constant surveillance by a regime that considered him only a temporarily necessary evil. But Abol's satisfaction at getting a leg up on his bookworm brother turned to outrage when Ali courted and married the sixteen-year-old apple of Abol's eye, the daughter of a deeply religious Teheran soap merchant.

Abol had been hanging around Soraya's house for months, pouring his syrupy, reverential charm over her while her family's females clucked approvingly. She liked him well enough, but when Ali met her one day, she never looked at his brother again. Though her parents violently disapproved of Abol's odd, French-speaking brother, they were soon married. His unimaginative superiors believed that by choosing a pious woman, Ali had shed his peculiar ambivalence about Islam, and they sent him to work in the ambassador's office in the Paris embassy. He took his wife with him and left behind a brother who brooded about the indignity he had suffered even as he rose steadily as a trusted Revolutionary Guard *apparatchik* in the foreign ministry's secretariat.

When diplomatic ties between Iran and France were temporarily ruptured over a terrorist who was hiding in the basement of the Paris embassy, the foreign ministry grudgingly decided that one key to more placid relations with Western countries whose assistance it valued was to permit diplomats to live outside the bleak residence it had maintained for them on Avenue d'Iena. With his parents' help Ali was able to afford an apartment in the Rue d'Orsel, in the shadow of the Sacre Coeur.

In the beginning, Soraya found the West impenetrably strange, but with Ali's guidance she learned its charms were not necessarily inconsistent with a life of devotion. Without advertising their behavior to the other Iranians in Paris, they explored the gamut of its sordid secular diversions—*Madama Butterfly* and the Talking Heads, the razzle-dazzle of the Pompidou Center and the quiet of the gardens of Giverny. When they were alone at home, Ali liked to tug at the multitudinous layers of clothing Soraya wore indoors and out and joke that since the Imam had been married when his bride was only ten, he had sent them to Paris so that *someone* in the Islamic Republic would have a passionate honeymoon. *She was so shocked when I said such things!* But soon she lost her shyness and let him remove the coarse cotton gown she'd always worn at night. And one Saturday afternoon—*in broad daylight!*—he took her to bed, and they made love with the windows open and let the warm breeze dry the sweat from their naked bodies.

Then they were called home for six weeks. It was a chance for his wife to see her family. But something wicked happened. He never knew exactly what. Abol did, but since his wife's murder, he had not spoken to his brother. *No matter;* he could guess easily enough. When they had left Iran, Soraya had been steeped in complacent ignorance about the world and works of nonbelievers, and yet in Paris she had never felt happier, freer, or more enriched. When she returned home, the cold contempt her friends and family showed when she tried to share her experiences left her torn and unhappy. She was young and impressionable. Ali blamed himself for neglecting her for endless meetings at the foreign ministry during what he realized only too late had been a moment of profound spiritual crisis for her. In his place, Abol had somehow insinuated himself with her again, encouraging the guilt she felt for living and relishing a life so different from the drudgery for which she'd been bred.

That afternoon he must have come around wheedling, manipulating, frightening, threatening. He'd seen they were alone in the house; all the hens had gone to market. *Come on, little flower,* he had murmured. *You missed me, didn't you?* He pushed her to the floor. *Do you want to feel the hard touch of a real man, not that Paris faggot?* He leaned against her from behind, holding her down and putting his foul lips close to her ear as he lifted the folds of her clothing. *Do you read the Koran in Paris?* he hissed. *Have you forgotten its lessons? Righteous women are obedient! You have lost the path of righteousness!*

Ali swore quietly. Islam had punished one malefactor. Who would punish the other?

"Are you lost on the Plain of Arafat again, Ali?"

He looked up at his malodorous colleague Mahdi, the civilian military attaché who had been so solicitous since Ali had returned to Paris from his home leave the year before. Home leave! What an appalling joke. What he had left at home was his heart and soul, burned out of him by the fires of cant that had scarred his homeland beyond recognition. But it wasn't good that Mahdi had found him so thoroughly preoccupied. He must again act the bereaved widower. He smiled wanly and shrugged. "I'm sorry, my friend. I sometimes daydream about the past too much."

Madhi dropped into the chair in front of Ali's desk. "You do indeed. How long will you mourn a woman who betrayed you?"

A curse caught in Ali's throat. *Be calm!* he thought. *Remember you are the proud Islamic idiot whose confused wife had to die for the sake of his honor.* "I was thinking about the happier times, before her treachery," he said.

"Exactly!" said Mahdi, smacking his palms authoritatively on the arms of the chair. "And now you deserve some happiness again." He stood and walked to the door and motioned Ali to follow him. "We live in a city full of wicked Western pleasures and almost every night you go home and sit alone in your apartment. To defeat the devil we must study his weaknesses! You must do your job and come out dancing, or I'll report you to Teheran!"

Ali didn't think Mahdi was necessarily joking. Why had he had to suffer these attentions for the last year? As he looked at Mahdi's grimy open-necked shirt, he remembered something he had read about how to recognize a *Hezbollahi,* a true believer: He doesn't wear cologne or a tie, and he doesn't smoke American cigarettes. Was this one assigned to watch him? After taking his wife from him, did the mullahs trust him even less than before? If he went out rutting with the pig would he be signing his own death warrant? Or would it be better to go, to show that he wasn't obsessed with the past? Still: Not tonight.

He stood up, smiling as broadly as he could. "When you file your report," he said, "say that Ali Rahmi walked home through the streets of Paris, miraculously immune to the lure of their evil, and then spent the evening reading the Koran by candlelight." He took his raincoat from a hook on the back of the door and put his hand on Mahdi's shoulder. "And that he promised to go out on the town with his worried friend the next evening." They left the embassy together, then Ali waved good-bye and wandered off along the Seine toward home. Mahdi stood and watched him go.

It was a cool May evening, but Ali began to sweat at the thought of what he was about to do.

At the Place de l'Alma he glanced over his shoulder and entered the Metro. As he walked down the stairs a pack of boisterous Japanese tourists was coming up, on their way to gawk at the bare breasts at the Crazy Horse. Doing his best to get lost in the rush hour crowds, Ali walked across the station and back up the stairs on the other side. He hurried up to the Champs Elysees, caught another train at the FDR station, and got off at the Etoile, then walked counterclockwise around the Arc until he was back on the Champs. Outside a pharmacy he looked at himself in a mirrored column, elaborately brushing his hair with his hands and then reaching into his back pockets as if he were searching for a comb. He slipped inside, darting around the densely packed shoppers and out a side door. By now he felt thoroughly flustered and ridiculous.

I wouldn't make a good spy! Ali thought as he continued down a side street. *Of course even our spies aren't good spies.* Khomeini's secret agents had no style, no finesse; their stupid pride kept them from mastering the deceptive arts. Occasionally he saw them skulking around the embassy. Inept fools! Even if they shaved and put on a clean shirt, they couldn't keep the gleam of insufferable moral superiority from their eyes. Let an operative of the SAVAMA in a linen suit and Italian leather shoes approach a Paris maître d' and ask for a table and in two minutes the place would be full of police and bomb-sniffing dogs. They weren't like Communists; they couldn't hide who they were. A Communist revolutionary so convincingly buried his true feelings under layers of bourgeois affectations that he even developed the capacity to enjoy them. An Islamic revolutionary was like a pervert who couldn't help taking his pecker out and shaking it at people. In the end they would all rather be martyrs than moles.

Ali had reached the Place de la Concorde, the scene of the demise of Louis XVI and his young queen and now the address of the Crillon, home away from home for visiting royalty and rock stars. *Our own revolution was an orgy of dim-witted religious exhibitionism, and we have not yet gotten over it.* His anxious expression turned angry as he realized that the question of whether Iran would ever emerge from the first savage throes of its revolution had become purely academic for him. He would never return there again.

It was dark by the time he turned from the Rue de Rivoli up the Rue St. Denis, where there were several blocks of pornography shops and bright, festive cafés. Farther along, the business was more serious. There were no streetlights, just dimly backlit figures in doorways. He was looking for a certain girl. Not one in tight jeans, hot pants, or a leather skirt. No black fishnet stockings or red spiked heels. The girls could look but could not speak; only when a customer sought them out could they state particulars. He was sick to his stomach from fear, and his legs and arms felt stiff and thick, as if all the blood were being drained out of them. Was this how faithful French husbands felt when they came here for the first time? Ali was near the end of the strip when he saw a gleam in a doorway on the left. A dress of white satin with a crinoline underneath, white stockings, white shoes, one foot crossed daintily over the other. She was leaning against the doorjamb, smiling faintly.

He spoke in English, the international language of license and debauchery. "How much?"

When she shook her head he repeated the question in French. "Three hundred francs," she said, tracing the numbers on the wall with her finger.

"I feel generous this evening. I will pay you four hundred. Where shall we go?"

"We shall go up."

She turned around and walked through the doorway; Ali followed. He watched her as she led him up narrow wooden stairs, her hips swaying no more than necessary. She had already made the sale. She was taller than Soraya. Her waist was slimmer. She was about the same age. He wasn't a romantic about whores, but he couldn't imagine wishing her dead for the sake of a principle.

On the top floor was a dingy room with a bed, toilet, and sink. Next to the bed was an aluminum roasting pan full of prophylactics. He looked inquiringly at the girl, who smiled again and stepped out of the room. In a moment the American came in.

Ali didn't feel like a traitor as he walked down the stairs with $250,000 stuffed into the lining of his coat. The theocrats were the ones who had betrayed his country by hurling it back into the Middle Ages to fight a 1,300-year-old feud between Islamic Hatfields and McCoys. *So now we send our children to kill Iraqi Sunnis and our pilgrims to start riots in Mecca to kill Saudi Arabian Sunnis*. The Koran was a compact of fellowship and charity, the most enlightened religious code in the history of man. Where did it justify the slaughter of other Moslems and the loving wives of Moslems? How better to outshine the Sunnis than the Shah's way? While the Saudis grew fat on oil, ruling their people like sleepy benevolent cartoon kings, the Shah's father built houses and schools, imported technology from the West, freed the women. While King Faisal scratched his hemorrhoids the Shah built a mighty army and air force. Even today Saudi Arabia couldn't defend itself against a single Iranian division marching backwards!

No. And it's too bad. Today he would take no pride in a Persian army on the march. The twentieth century had proven to be too demanding for his country, so it had buggered out and taken his sweet wife with it. So let Iran sputter and burn, howling against the Soviets and the Americans and the Saudis and the Iraqis and the Kuwaitis and the Jews. They said seven thousand just men had held off three hundred thousand Persians at Thermopylae. He would see what he could do alone against fifty million. As he stepped into the dark his face was grim, resolute. There was one Persian he knew would feel his wrath. Ali was a civilized man, but to avenge the murder of his wife he would strike down his brother in hate and rage.

He looked down the street each way and then across the

street, where he saw Mahdi standing smoking in a doorway. Ali knew he was a dead man. *They make lousy spies, but they made a fool out of me!* His mind ordered him to run, but he could only wander listlessly across the narrow street toward his enemy.

The mean bastard was smiling. "You devil!" said Mahdi. "Our untrusting friends in Teheran were afraid that in your grief you'd do something foolish. They were right, but this wasn't what they had in mind."

Could it be he doesn't know? Ali mustered a weak burst of outrage. "You've been following me, Mahdi? Don't you have anything better to do than harass an unhappy man during a brief moment of companionship far away from home?" He had to be careful; the man could ruin him just by reporting him for whoring. He needed a few more days.

Mahdi shrugged. "They want me to look after you. But I see now that all you need is instruction. An important diplomat with francs in his pocket can find much prettier girls than the ones in the Rue St. Denis." He offered Ali a cigarette. "You're hungry now, I suppose? Let's get some supper."

Ali reached out for the cigarette—*Careful about the money!*—as Mahdi struck a match. It was a Marlboro. Ali stooped cautiously for the light, and they walked away together.

PART ONE

ONE

"HE THINKS HE'S DOUGLAS MACARTHUR," WHISPERED one National Security Council staffer to another as the vision in crisp khaki materialized in the West Wing.

"He's *better* than Douglas MacArthur," the other whispered back, "because O'Brien works for a president who would *let* him nuke China. All he's got to do is ask. The old man would say, 'Fine, Bob, fine. Anything you want. You go right ahead.' "

Major General Robert J. O'Brien, Chief of Special Operations, was not highly regarded in the United States government. White House aides disliked him for wearing mirrored sunglasses and an open-necked shirt and for prowling their sacred domain so freely, calling on the President's national security advisor, Parker DuBois, whenever the mood struck him. Pentagon officials disliked him for visiting the White House, too, because it meant he was conducting business with civilians in person instead of in writing, which meant they would have even less of an idea what he was doing than they usually did. Members of Congress disliked him because so few of them knew precisely how much money he had or how he was spending it, since at considerable political cost the President had carved out a shadowy niche of semiaccountability for him such as used to be enjoyed only by the intelligence services. People who did not have some specific institutional grudge disliked him for being a hard-hearted killer of men, women, children, and small animals.

In short, O'Brien was one one of those phenomena that made life in Washington so grand: a focus of public calumny and secret envy, of unceasing speculation, of columns and Sunday morning talk shows and coy, cutesy Style section profiles in the *Post,* of fund-raising mailings praising him by Richard Viguerie and fund-raising mailings denouncing him by Norman Lear. At the mention of his name, liberals were appalled and conservatives transfixed, while Ripon Republicans and other moderates pronounced themselves sympathetic to his *goals* but deeply concerned about some of the *specific remedies* he contemplated.

None of which would have mattered so much if Washington's favorite son of a bitch was not also widely known to be the President's favorite son of a bitch.

O'Brien arrived outside DuBois's office. "Good afternoon, young lady," he said to the secretary with a smile, sliding his sunglasses up into his salt-and-pepper crewcut and putting his hands on his trim hips. "I believe I have an appointment with your Mr. *Do*-boys."

"Yes, sir, general. One moment, please, general." She was a bit flustered as she reached for the intercom. O'Brien sat down by her desk to wait, crossing his long, spidery legs and balancing his sunglasses on his knee. O'Brien's patience infuriated DuBois's staff even more. They would have preferred him to pace back and forth impatiently or just barge in unannounced, maybe after raping the secretary or biting off and swallowing her head. As it was, when they caucused in the White House Mess some new arrival or habitual party pooper never failed to mention that he had met the guy and he had seemed . . . well, *pleasant.*

In a moment, DuBois collected O'Brien and motioned him into his office. As his door closed, the first NSC aide spoke portentously to the second, in the manner of a latter-day Theodore Sorenson addressing a twenty-first-century documentary producer: "I vividly recall the day in May when

Bobby O'Brien—that's what I used to call him, *Bobby*—visited Parker DuBois at the White House. Of course none of us realized it then, but the world would never again be the same."

The boilerplate bio distributed by the press office disclosed that President Eugene Hoskins was a clean-desk man. *Only technically true,* DuBois thought the next morning as he watched the President manhandle his paperwork. DuBois observed the drill most days when he arrived at seven for the national security briefing. The President would wave him in whether he had finished or not. When the President was done shuffling papers, his desk was indeed empty. But the junk piled onto the long Louis XIV table behind the desk would have reached the ceiling of the Oval Office if Irene did not purge it six times a year, taking care to remove only the longest-forgotten books from the bottom out of the thoroughly unwarranted fear that Hoskins might someday want to examine something he had deposited there.

Some presidents liked to govern by talking to people, others by reading memos. *Gene's still searching for a more efficient option,* DuBois thought. *Probably telepathy.* The President abhorred windy, inconclusive Cabinet meetings, yet he loved chewing over knotty issues for hours with his closest aides. He read ceaselessly and then railed about how nobody knew how to write short and get to the point anymore.

Hoskins approached paperwork grimly, like war. Personal letters or memos demanding a dictated response were shuttled to a neat pile to his left. These included notes from friends and relatives who were apt to send him steamy historical novels in hopes he might curl up with them and thus ease the burdens of state from his shoulders. First he would set the note aside so he and Irene could conspire on an effusive thank-you letter that would end up in the recipient's scrapbook and occasionally as a promotional blurb on the paperback edition of the book. Then he would pivot smoothly on the balls of his feet and plop the volume down in the purgatory of good intentions behind his desk.

What the President really liked to curl up with was the *Economist, Asia Week,* and his political office's 120-page weekly summaries of White House-commissioned public-opinion polls. DuBois had seen him read fiction only once, aboard *Air Force One* en route home after spending a grueling week briefing Western Europe's prime ministers and chancellors on his arms control breakthrough. It was a novel about a president who was sleeping with his official photographer, a perky, comely blonde. Hoskins read about a third of it and then sent it back to the staff compartment for his potbellied, cigar-smoking, sixty-three-year-old official photographer with a note: "Lose a few pounds and I might think about it. *Gene.*"

He handled domestic policy reports on the spot by reading the three-page cover memo, scanning the attachments, scrawling a few comments or instructions, and then checking one of the options listed by the staff before dumping it in his out box. An assistant scored extra points if the President flipped his memo across the room in the direction of his briefcase, which lay open on the floor next to his overstuffed easy chair. This meant it would be carefully read that evening in the residence—and that it was probably about the new Soviet MiG or the extent of Nicaraguan aid to antigovernment guerrillas in Peru.

DuBois grimaced. The domestic guys envied his command of the President's attention. He envied the amount of time they spent playing tennis.

"Now Park, I know it's early. Maybe I'm missing something. So could you please tell me what the hell this is?"

DuBois had been waiting for that question since the night before, when he had personally placed the report from the embassy in Paris on the President's desk. The President was waving the black binder in the air. "Why am I now getting intelligence reports from twenty-eight-year-old foreign service punks? This guy isn't CIA, is he?"

DuBois shook his head. "Mr. President, he is in fact a twenty-eight-year-old foreign service punk whose information is one hundred percent solid. I wouldn't have given it to you otherwise."

The President harrumphed and tossed the report into his out box. Then he stood and picked it up again, smirking as he paged through it. "You don't believe this is legit, do you, Park?" he said, baiting his friend. "Do the Iranians think we would act on the basis of a story this preposterous? I may be crazy, but I'm not stupid." He closed the folder and dropped it on his desk, then looked at DuBois.

DuBois looked back and took a deep breath. "Sir, when we got this yesterday afternoon from Paris, we compared it to bits of intelligence from our assets in Lebanon." He quickly raised his hand to forestall a presidential interruption. "Yes, we still have some. And it checks out completely, down to the last dit and twiddle. We don't think the Iranians or the Shi'ites are aware of our sources, which means the only reason their information would jibe with this is because it's genuine." He waited a moment. Hoskins didn't speak. *He's listening*. "Mr. President, we can run with this." DuBois thought about saying he staked his job on it, but the old man hated that Kissinger stuff.

"Check it again, okay?" the President said, sitting down behind the desk. "You talk to O'Brien yet?"

"Yesterday."

"What's he think?"

"He's not about to vouch for the intelligence. He did say that if it *is* genuine, it's plenty good enough for him."

The President's gray eyes drifted up and his chair squeaked back until he was gazing vaguely at the Great Seal of the President of the United States that was carved in the ceiling. "Bobby never said that before, did he?"

"Never has."

He focused on DuBois again. "Tell me about this foreign service kid."

Here we go. "Deerfield, Yale . . ." The President rolled his eyes and reached for the report again. ". . . but he's fine, Gene. His father's an oilman who made him put in a couple of years on a rig in the Gulf before he sent him to college." The old man leaned back. *Ivy League crisis over*. "He took Mideast studies at Fletcher and speaks Persian, but since there's not much call for Persian speakers these days, he's the deputy political officer in Paris. Joe Morris says he's discreet and buttoned-down, and his analysis is some of the best we get from Europe."

"You're suggesting our loudmouthed ambassador is an accurate judge of a man's sense of discretion?" The President shook his head and glanced through the French doors into the Rose Garden. "Park, this smells worse and worse." He looked back. "Who approved the payment, incidentally? Morris?" DuBois nodded. The President shook his head again and smiled weakly. "Where did he get it, the entertainment fund?" He didn't wait for an answer. "You've of course told him to shut up?"

"Mr. President, you know Joe means well. He'll be all right. As a matter of fact, you should know he had the good sense to send this straight to us, rather than through State."

"Wheeler won't like that," the President said with some satisfaction.

Over the last day and a half, DuBois had, despite his equable nature, grown increasingly excited about what could be done with the information the President was batting around Woodrow Wilson's antique desk. He risked a note of bravado. "I'll take care of the secretary of state, Mr. President. You take care of the Iranians."

"Yeah. Right." Hoskins was not in the mood. "Park, these bastards kicked Carter's and Reagan's asses around the world, and I'd rather be a one-term president than have that happen to us. And I'll be damned if I'll send two hundred kids into an ambush." It occurred to DuBois that the President was one of the few men on earth for whom that expression might not be simply a figure of speech. He said nothing.

Hoskins sighed. "Okay. But get him over here, Park. I want to talk to him myself."

"Morris?"

The President looked up in horror. "Hell no! Why do you think I made him an ambassador? You keep him away from me, I mean it. We've got enough trouble." He leaned back. "I want to see the kid. Tomorrow morning, here. Eight-thirty."

"Yes, sir," DuBois said, adding a discreet reminder, "from Paris."

The President reconsidered briefly. "Tell him we'll give him some coffee."

As the next day's 6:45 A.M. Pan Am shuttle from La Guardia unloaded its passengers at National Airport and Russell J. Wolcott III shuffled down the ramp into the terminal, he suddenly remembered seeing a newspaper story about some California fraternity brothers who had gone into business designing the world's most elaborate practical jokes. A man in a tux arrives at your door with a TV crew and says you won the lottery, only to take a phone call, snatch the check back, say "Wrong guy. Sorry, pal!" and leave. A fourteen-year-old girl announces to the receptionist in your office that she is the illegitimate daughter you left behind after a mad weekend in Puerto Vallarta. A man calls and says the President wants to see you at the White House the next morning at 8:30.

He would have confirmed it with Ambassador Morris, but Parker DuBois—it had *sounded* like DuBois's mild Louisiana drawl, anyway—had said, "Tell no one. Be at the northwest gate at 8:25 and ask for my office. You can take the 1:00 A.M. Air France flight to Kennedy, get a cab to La Guardia, and hop an early shuttle. Understood? *Don't tell anybody*. Just get here. See you tomorrow." He assumed at first that old Joe had sent the report up the line. But after a cold, sleepless night in tourist class, he wasn't so sure. *It was all a setup, the Iranian and his crazy story, the ambassador's money—damn, it was counterfeit!* One of his Yale buddies who went to work at Treasury got it from the Secret Service! All so he would show up one morning at the White House smelling like a sewer and saying he had an appointment with the President of the United States. *I will find the son of a bitch that did this and—*

"Mr. Wolcott?" Glancing up from his scuffed shoes, Wolcott beheld a vision of executive-branch suavity: a solid six-feet-two in a pinstripe suit, white Oxford button-down shirt, and red and green silk rep tie, complete with gold lapel pin, plastic earplug, and steely gaze. He did not seem to require confirmation of Wolcott's identity. "I've got a car waiting," he said. He reached for Wolcott's garment bag and let him keep his briefcase. The blue Chrysler New Yorker, its engine already running, was curbside with regular D.C. plates and a driver. The man held the door for him, hit the lock, and slammed it closed. As the agent took the shotgun position in front, Wolcott glanced out the window and saw two of his fellow passengers from the Paris flight—he remembered them sitting in the row right behind him—trot out of the terminal and climb into another sedan parked in front of the Chrysler. Its driver reached out his window, put a plainclothesman's portable flashing bubble on the roof, and swung into traffic with the Chrysler six feet behind his rear bumper.

Holy shit, thought Russell J. Wolcott III.

DuBois dialed his own home number. The phone rang four times before Carole answered.

"Hey."

"Hey yourself," said DuBois. "Get your butt out of the sack. It's eight in the morning."

She brushed the sheet aside, rolled over, and reached for

his pillow, tucking it under her breasts and propping herself up on her elbows. "After your morning dose of the big guy you are somewhat less than the southern gentleman I have come to love and respect. What's his problem today?"

"He was just fine."

"Loquacious as usual, Parker."

"Miss Nelson, hadn't you better get to work for your daily debriefing about whether I disclosed any state secrets last night during sexual intercourse?"

She frowned. "That's a real sore subject."

He sighed. "I know. Sorry."

Carole rolled onto her back and smiled at the cracks in the ceiling of DuBois's Connecticut Avenue studio apartment. Her long brown hair flared over the sheet. "What would that crab patch think about your sitting in his West Wing talking on his telephones about sexual intercourse with a naked woman twenty years your junior?"

"He'd love it. In fact, he's probably listening in. Anyhow, you're not naked. You're wearing one of my twelve-year-old sleeveless undershirts. Which, as I think about it, brings a not-unpleasant picture to mind. Come on. Get to work. See if you can get that stubborn bastard at the Fed to print a little more money so we can get reelected and I can continue to get us Redskins tickets."

"Drink tonight?"

"Maybe even dinner. Eight at Duke's?"

"Done. Thanks for the wake-up."

"Oh, and Carole?"

"Yep?"

"Pawn takes knight."

She hung up, hopped off the bed, and in two strides reached the chessboard on the coffee table. The evening before, he had blundered into permitting a forked check by her knight that threatened a rook. He had studied the board for a moment and then, without a word, had moved the table aside, lifted the cushions out of the couch they had been sitting on, and folded out the bed. *And that was that. Typical Parker tactical move: Refocus the point of attack.*

But what's he up to here? He still loses the rook to my queen's bishop. She moved the pawn and saw that DuBois was offering an exchange of queens that would save the rook but after which he would be unable to castle his king out of danger. *A more than usually adventurous maneuver for the cagey old Cajun. We'll have to see about this!*

After starting a pot of coffee in the kitchenette, Carole wandered over to DuBois's dresser, gathering her hair into a ponytail. Ever since she had begun dating DuBois, George Stevens, her editor, had been teasing her savagely. "You're probably screwing the guy," he said, in keeping with his one concession to feminism, which was to display absolutely no class to anybody without regard to gender. Carole had reminded him that she covered the Federal Reserve Board. "And Bob Woodward was on the night police beat until something better came along. Just keep your eyes and ears open, honey—or whatever," he'd said, leering.

Still holding her hair back she opened the top dresser drawer to look for a rubber band. Didn't anyone give Parker anything besides cuff links? There was a green velvet pouch with his medals from Vietnam and a leather cigarette holder he'd taken off the body of an enemy soldier. She poked around some more. Pounds, pennies, handkerchiefs, stamps, francs, unmatched socks, paper clips, yuans, keys to doors in the house in Baton Rouge he'd sold six years before, when Debbie died. Three buffalo-head nickels. But no rubber bands. She turned over a yellowed black and white snapshot of a smiling young couple. "Deborah and Parker, Mardi Gras '62." She turned it back. It was a nightclub scene, and the handsome young officer's grin was wide and affectionate as he looked down at his pretty wife. *What do you suppose was on his mind?* As she shut the drawer, she smiled at the thought of DuBois and the President, two middle-aged widowers, sitting around the White House every morning talking about reforms in the Argentine military and thinking about girls. She let her hair fall around her shoulders and turned away, catching her profile in the mirror over the dresser. *I can see what he means.* The undershirt revealed more than it covered, when viewed from the proper angle. She resolved to arrange the proper angle that evening. She was pretty sure Parker would, too.

She hadn't put on the undershirt to tantalize him, just to get warm on a brisk night. Only in the last few months, as they grew more comfortable with each other and she grew less worried about making a bad impression—something *he* never worried about at all—had she begun to sleep over a night or two a week. But she didn't keep a nightgown here, or anything else. So after he'd fallen asleep last night, she had slid from under his arm, gone to his bureau, and put on the first garment she could find in the darkness.

If I put it on tonight, he won't let me take it off. Carole's imagination drifted twelve hours ahead. He had become so predictable in his keen manipulation of the visual stimuli her body provided that once, after they'd made love, she had joked that he made her feel like a copy of *Playboy.* After an embarrassed pause, he had said lightly that he might apply for a lifetime subscription. *Isn't a man who* always *says the right thing dangerous? Not to mention* does *the right things.* Tonight he'd pull her down onto his lumpy hideabed and pull the shirt up, surveying the unveiled, smooth, dusky territory, stroking the long muscles that ran along the inside of her thighs, lingering at their apex, making her ache for him to linger there longer. Instead, he would stretch a thin shoulder strap toward the center of her chest so he could bare a breast and cup it in his hand and then bend to kiss it as well. Later he would rise over her with his weight on one arm, now letting her enjoy the sight of his powerful chest and the thick, soft brown hair that covered it, smiling at her rapt face as he covered her up again with the shirt, only to stretch the cloth tight so he could see the spur and shadow of her nipples.

Shivering with anticipatory pleasure, she crossed her bare arms to rub the gooseflesh that was spreading over them. For a man *Cosmo* would say had probably reached his sexual peak at seventeen, Parker was managing to sustain quite a satisfactory pace at fifty-five.

Arms still crossed, she wandered languidly back to the kitchen. *Think pure thoughts, Nelson. It's time to get to work.* She poured some coffee and looked at her watch. Eight-fifteen. She would still be at the office at 7:30 that evening finishing her story for the morning paper, but one of her eager-beaver young sources was already at his desk checking the printouts from the European currency markets. She grabbed her notebook, sat on the edge of the bed, and reached for the phone. *Let's see what Sammy will tell me about tomorrow's board of governors' agenda.*

DuBois left his office and passed through the crowded clerks' area, receiving somewhat broader smiles and brighter greetings from his assistants than usual this early in the morning. *Maybe* they *had been listening. But what a girl!* In a year and a half she had never violated a confidence, asked an untoward question, or published one of his few unintended indiscretions. Helluva reporter, though. Last year Hoskins had learned the names of his top five candidates for Greenspan's job at the Fed at 6:30 A.M. from Carole's story in the *Post* and again at 8:30 from Don Hendricks, his chief of staff. DuBois was even further out of that particular loop than the President, but the old man had nonetheless cocked an eyebrow at him and asked where he thought that pretty little girl was getting her information. DuBois had answered, "I'm sorry, Mr. President, but I want you to know I'd do it again. And again." *Damn George Stevens for giving her such a hard time.*

The marine guard at the main entrance to the West Wing pulled the door open and saluted as DuBois passed into the sunshine. The two cars were just pulling up. Wolcott was still combing his hair when the Secret Service agent opened the door. He climbed out and blinked.

"Good morning, Mr. Wolcott," he said, extending his

hand. "I'm Parker DuBois. Hope you didn't mind the reception, but I didn't want to bother you with a lot of details. The President is waiting."

DuBois announced him and left. Wolcott must have let his eyes linger on the door as it closed behind the national security advisor, because the President said, "Parker is one of the rare White House staff members who isn't afraid to let a president have a substantive conversation in private. I'll teach him yet." Wolcott turned back to Hoskins, who had risen from behind his desk and was coming around to shake his hand. His tightly packed, barrel-chested mass was moving so fast that Wolcott almost stepped backward. "Good to meet you, Russ. Notice you played ball for Yale the last time they had a winning season. Atta boy. How was the flight? You pick up the six hours coming this way, of course, but you'll be a mess tomorrow. Try to get a few winks this afternoon. Don't eat a lot, but drink plenty of liquids. No alcohol. You don't want any coffee, do you?"

"Fine, Mr. President. Uh—no. No thank you, sir."

The President had not stopped moving. He let go of Wolcott's hand and grabbed him by the elbow, propelling him toward a couch in front of the fireplace. He sat in an armchair to the younger man's left, crossed his legs, pressed his palms together next to his knees, and produced a constricted smile. "So, Russ," he said. "When did you get into the intelligence business?"

"I beg your pardon, sir?" *Does he think I'm in the CIA? What a colossal screwup!*

"What are you doing giving a quarter of a million dollars of taxpayers' money to Iranians in whorehouses? We've got a whole separate agency for that kind of stupid bullshit."

"Mr. President, if you've read my memo—"

"I have. That's why you're here. But I was wondering whether you might just spin the whole tale from the top." Wolcott was reaching for his briefcase when the President said, "You won't need any notes, or to take any. Just tell me what happened. I know, it's all in the report. Humor your commander-in-chief and run through it again—keeping in mind, of course, that many lives may well hang on your every word." The President sat back and beamed.

Wolcott swallowed and cleared his throat. "About a week ago—" Hoskins glared at him. He began again. "On May twenty-first, last Thurday evening, at a reception at the Mexican embassy, an Iranian diplomat approached me and said that he wished to propose selling information that would permit us to mount a rescue operation to free our hostages, plus the two Germans, in Lebanon."

"His name?"

"Ali Rahmi."

"Why do you think he picked you? Because you speak Farsi?"

Wolcott shook his head. "I don't think he knew that. Anyway, he spoke to me in English. I've spent a lot of time trying to figure out the answer to that question, and all I've come up with is simply that I was there. I don't think I'm particularly known around Paris for being approachable or gullible. I believe he saw me and impulsively decided to act."

"His age? Appearance? Background?"

"About thirty-two or thirty-three. Well groomed. Sharper looking than most of their crew. Wore a tie and a well-pressed, tailored suit. Cosmopolitan. Cultured." He paused. "And nervous. He wasn't a professional."

Hoskins grinned with genuine pleasure. "You, of course, would have recognized a *real* spy."

"Mr. President, your point's certainly well taken. It just appeared to me—if from nothing else than that he was sweating heavily and showed the bad sense to approach me at a crowded cocktail party—that he was probably what he appeared to be: an inept amateur."

"Thank you, son," the President said, almost gently. "That's the kind of detail I'm looking for. Now, you wrote that you had been aware of him before and had wondered about his allegiance to Khomeini."

"Yes, sir. I had seen him at a number of diplomatic functions, and a couple of times I saw him and his wife around town participating in activities one would not expect of the Ayatollah's loyalists, who as you know are a pretty austere bunch."

"Exactly where?"

"Once in a brasserie, once at a concert. They were dancing."

"Dancing in the restaurant?"

"Dancing at the concert. It was . . . the Fabulous Thunderbirds, Mr. President. A rock and roll band." He added helpfully, "From Texas."

Hoskins nodded microscopically. "Are you suggesting, Mr. Wolcott, that this fellow is—to coin a phrase—an Iranian moderate?"

Wolcott was beginning to sense the peril and majesty of the moment to which he had brought his nation. *He's going to do it! But only if he decides his information—my information—is good enough. Is it?* He swallowed hard and continued.

"He's not a moderate, sir. He's a traitor, and he's committed treason because of a degree of alienation far more profound than anything existing between different governmental factions."

Hoskins waved his hand dismissively. "I know all about the poor dead wife. We'll get to that later."

Wolcott persisted. "It's more than the wife. Their bureaucracy, and especially their foreign services, are full of people—some of whom are nonreligious, others who are believers but not fanatics—who are biding their time until the hard edge comes off the revolution. Some of them are genuinely appalled at the direction their country is taking. With Rahmi, the death of his wife was probably only the last straw."

The President nodded. "Parker just sent in a cable you did on the subject a while ago. It was damn good. Now tell me what you did with this scoop. You took it to the ambassador, right? And what did he say? Obviously not that the matter should be turned over to one of the eight fully trained and licensed intelligence professionals sitting down the hall."

"No, sir. The ambassador felt . . . he thought Rahmi might be frightened off if we changed his contact."

Hoskins leaned forward and stared at Wolcott. "Please level with me, Mr. Wolcott. I like Joe Morris as much as you do. He is one of my oldest and richest friends, but at the moment I have more to worry about than friendship. And so do you."

Wolcott shifted in his chair and noticed his trousers were getting sticky. "The ambassador doesn't get along well with the intelligence guys," he said reluctantly. "He resents their autonomy and secretiveness. To be frank, they treat him like a boob, and it was pretty obvious to me that he wanted to show you what he could do by himself."

The President sank wearily into his chair and gazed through the windows behind his desk. "Poor dumb Joe," he said softly. Then he looked back at Wolcott and said sharply, "But he's a good and loyal American who has served his country and me magnificently in peace and war."

"Yes, sir."

"Go on."

"Well, Rahmi and I had established that we would both be at a lawn party the following Saturday afternoon at the British embassy."

"You characters go to a lot of parties, don't you? They play croquet, I imagine."

"Yes, sir, we do. They do. But I didn't. We met, and I told him that I was authorized to meet him a third time at a location of my choosing, examine the information, and then pay him if I believed it worthwhile. He told me that he wanted half a million dollars and that the information, which he said described circumstances that changed from week to week, would come in two installments. The first I would get at the meeting in exchange for half the money.

That's what you have now. He said we could check the accuracy of the first installment and then decide if we wanted to pay for the second."

"So you set the meeting. Why the whorehouse?"

Wolcott hesitated.

The President said, "Russ, I'm not your den mother. You'd been to the place before?"

Wolcott gulped and nodded.

"All right. Big deal. So you paid one of the girls to bring him upstairs?"

"Yes, sir. And before we went any further, I asked him how he had come by the information and why he was taking such an enormous risk by giving it to us. I told him the money couldn't be enough incentive. We had to have more."

"What'd he say?"

"He said that it was none of my damned business. So I stood up and started to leave."

The President was impressed. "This was Joe's idea?"

"It was."

"Not bad. What happened?"

"He stopped me. And then he told me the money was entirely incidental. He needed the resources to travel a long way quickly, if necessary. The real reason, he said, was that he wanted his brother dead for seducing his wife and causing her murder. His brother is the man in the foreign ministry in Teheran who coordinates the movements of the hostages. If we free them, Rahmi is certain his brother will lose his head." He hesitated a moment before he went on. "When he talked about his wife, there were tears in his eyes, and as he described what his brother did, he was livid—literally quivering with anger. If you can find out, sir, whether his wife—"

Hoskins interrupted. "We have. She is. Then what?"

"I asked him why we were supposed to believe that the Iranian embassy in Paris would have the kind of information he was peddling. God knows they don't need it. Rahmi said that his predecessor in the ambassador's office once worked in Teheran handling the hostages. When he was posted to Paris, he had his name added to the distribution list for the schedules so he could keep his nose in it. When Rahmi came the copies kept coming too, as copies will, and they were routinely put in Rahmi's slot. Then he got out the document and showed me the guy's name on the bottom."

The President grunted. "I'm glad to learn that their bureaucrats are just as bush-league as ours. So now you've got the piece of paper in your mitts. What was it?"

"Mr. President, it was a list of the names of the twenty-nine Western hostages being held by the Shi'ites in Beirut. Under each name was the location of their hiding places in the city and the Bekaa Valley and the exact dates, times, and routes for moving the hostages between the various locations. He said it was the list for last week. When we want to move, we get in touch with him, and he'll provide the list for the week we want."

"What did you do?"

"I gave him the money."

The President was silent for a moment. His brow tightened in concentration. Then he leaned forward and smacked Wolcott on the knee. "Good move, son." He poked a button on the telephone next to his chair and said, "Irene, please see if Parker can come in here."

Three hours later, Wolcott was munching on pâté and wheat crackers as the Air France *Concorde* cleared Newfoundland and accelerated to Mach 2. For an additional $2,500 the United States government had purchased the seat next to his for his briefcase, which contained the rest of Rahmi's money. He was insulated from the other passengers by five Secret Service agents, two of them women, to whom he had not been introduced and had not spoken. DuBois had told him to go about his business; they would go about theirs.

While giving Wolcott his instructions, the President had asked Parker if the Iranian embassy was sophisticated enough to monitor its diplomats' home telephones in a foreign capital. "You kidding?" Parker had said with a grin. So on a radiophone aboard the navy helicopter that had flown him from Andrews Air Force Base to Kennedy, Wolcott had called Rahmi and asked if he had the following week's schedule with him. Rahmi had said he did, and Wolcott arranged another meeting that evening at eleven. With the information in hand, Wolcott would again catch the red-eye to New York, where he would be met Friday morning by Parker DuBois. Wolcott did not know it yet, but when he handed DuBois the document, DuBois would hand him back a ticket for a flight leaving in 45 minutes for Rio de Janeiro and $2,000 in Brazilian cruzeiros, then instruct him to have a great time and not report or communicate in any way with Paris for two weeks. There would also be a handwritten note from Hoskins:

THE WHITE HOUSE
Washington

28 May '92

Russ:

You've done good work, which is a shame in a way, since you can't tell a single living soul about it for as long as you live, or at least for as long as I do. If you do say anything, I will personally bring the full weight of what's left of the imperial presidency right down on your ass.

You might console yourself by thinking how much this piece of paper will be worth in 30 years.

Best,
Gene Hoskins

In the twenty minutes he had before a Rose Garden photo opportunity with the new chairman of the Consumer Products Safety Council, the President was enjoying the all-too-brief contented glow he felt before the pleasure from some satisfactory development was engulfed and erased by the next inevitable crisis.

DuBois hated to intrude, but he had to. He steeled himself and said, "What about Morris?"

Hoskins looked up sharply. "What about him? You had better not tell him a thing, Parker."

"I'm sorry, but he's going to be wondering where Wolcott is, and if he doesn't hear anything about the intelligence report, he's going to start calling and asking what happened to it."

The President brooded for a moment and said, "Fine. You call him and. . . . No, I've got to, damn it all." He poked the intercom again. "Irene, please, and bring in Joe Morris's direct dial." In five seconds she glided in and went to the phone at the President's desk. After reaching Paris and telling the ambassador's secretary that the President was calling, she nodded to Hoskins, who picked up the phone next to his chair. She knew he wanted to be waiting on the line when Morris came on.

"Joe? Gene. Fine, fine. How's Beverly? Joe, you two have got to get out of there for a couple of weeks. No, I mean it. You don't know how hard you're working because you never slow down long enough to realize how tired you are. I know, believe me; I'd rather sit through a two-hour Cabinet meeting than a half-hour cocktail party." He glanced at DuBois and winked; DuBois winced and held his nose. The President continued, "Joe, Parker showed me that report your young man Wolcott did, and it was damn good. You've done an excellent job bringing him along. I need to borrow him for a couple of weeks. No, he's already here. Right. But it's important that you let it be for now, all right? When you see him again, don't mention it to him. It would put him in an awkward position. Just keep in mind that whatever may happen, you have once again served your country with distinction, and I thank you for it. I don't know what we would have done without you these last three years. I mean it.

"Listen, why don't you two book a flight to Palm Springs or somewhere and stop off here for dinner on the way?" Irene was already on the way over with his leather appointment book, which she held open in front of him. He glanced at it and said, "How about a week from next Monday? No, I insist. I want to have a little dinner for you. And then you can take a little vacation. Fine. See you then."

He hung up and said to Irene, "Make it for seven o'clock in the residence. Invite Parker, Billy Wheeler, whatever other Cabinet secretaries haven't been in for a while, and a couple of movie stars. Joe loves that sort of thing." He looked at his watch, stood up, and walked toward the door. "Gotta go, Park. When can you get back here from New York tomorrow?"

"I meet the kid at four in the morning. I can be here by six and have the schedule vetted by eight."

"Fine. I want to see O'Brien in the sit room at eight and the NSC at nine. How many in your shop know about this?"

"Three. Me and the top two Mideast officers."

"Let's keep it that way. If this leaks. . . ."

DuBois opened the door for him. "It won't." As the President passed through the doorway, DuBois could see Ned Flach, head of the Presidental Protective Detail of the Secret Service, waiting to escort Hoskins to the ceremony, together with three other agents and a klatch of the President's painfully serious younger aides. DuBois nodded at Flach; Flach nodded back. Hoskins looked over his shoulder and said, "You free to strike a blow for freedom at about 6:30?" DuBois smiled at the anachronism—*None of these pompous kids knows what the hell he's talking about*—and nodded yes. The President swept through the outer office, enveloped by Flach, the agents, and the aides, and was gone.

Carole kissed him lightly outside Duke Zeibert's and said, "I see you've already had a drink. Come on, Parker, who is she?"

"The old man served me one of his patented bruised martinis on the Truman Balcony after work tonight," he said, holding the door for her. He tried to ignore the sudden hush and frantic whispering that attended their arrival in virtually any public place inside the District of Columbia. He always resisted the impulse to take her to more secluded spots. He had known her before either of them had come to Washington, and he planned on knowing her for a long time after they left. *Damned if I'll sneak around like an adulterous senator.*

They were shown to a table overlooking Connecticut Avenue. Carole slid into her chair, reached for a complimentary half-sour pickle, and said, "As I recall, the last time he served you a drink in the White House was the day you got the word from Geneva about the arms deal."

DuBois glanced over affectionately while Carole arranged her napkin in her lap. The pearls he had brought from Hong Kong were ravishing against her antique black velvet blouse and her smooth, graceful neck. Her gleaming hair was bound back with Deb's ivory barrettes. "Give Carole anything she wants, so long as she promises to wear it," Deb had whispered about her beloved young friend the night before she died. "Then sell this house and every other thing in it." *What a relief it would be to share my misgivings. But what a burden they would be for her. Stevens doesn't deserve her being honest, but she shouldn't have to lie. So I will.* With practiced nonchalance he said, "Honey, when Gene and I were in the statehouse we used to toast appropriations for highway interchanges. Neither of us can handle quite as much of the stuff as we used to. To be honest, I'm not sure why he was so exuberant tonight." He opened his menu.

Carole reached across the table and ran her fingers along the knuckles of his left hand. He put down the menu, let his fingers entwine with hers, and smiled.

"Hi, baby," she said.

"Hi."

"Can you envision a normal life? Normal jobs—me editing the town weekly, you bringing your calming influence to bear on various community disputes? A normal house? Not being stared at in restaurants?"

"Indeed I can. I envision it daily. For one thing, we'd have substantially more to talk about than at present."

She tightened her grip on his hand and leaned forward. Close enough to smell her perfume and her hair. Close enough to kiss. *Hold your horses, DuBois. The Chief Justice is watching.*

"So how about you be a one-term national security advisor? I'll blow this town if you will."

"That may well occur, whether we want it to or not. But if it doesn't, I've got to stick with him as long he feels he needs me."

She let go of his hand and sat back. "Ever the loyal aide, right, Parker? The problem is, you're not honest about how much *you* need *him*. You revel in this geostrategic stuff. It animates you; it makes you whole. Without it, you'd be adrift. You're either one year or five years from oblivion, and you know it."

He shook his head. "Five years ago, I suppose that was true. I was unhappy. . . . No, I was desperate without Deb, and without Gene and the campaign and the job I probably would have been dead. I admit it. But not now. Sure I like it. I like you better, and I think *you* know it. So what the hell do you want to eat?" With some impatience, he whipped the menu open again. Actually he wanted to get Carole out of Washington so much that it hurt. *Maybe we* will *lose in November. But damn it all! If this operation succeeds we* can't *lose. If it fails, we can't win. For their sake, for Gene's, I pray it works. For mine, I wish it wouldn't.*

She was still looking at him with shining brown eyes. "Are you really hungry?"

She was suggesting a different kind of nourishment. "I can wait," he said. "How about you?"

"Let's go."

"Fine, but try not to look too lascivious when we walk past the Chief Justice. Mumble something about a deadline."

"Why me? You mumble something about Pakistan."

Eleven miles away, in a Mexican restaurant in Alexandria, Chuck Sampson of the *Washington Post* dipped a tortilla chip into a bowl of green tomatillo sauce and stuffed it into his mouth. "Why are you telling me this?" he mumbled skeptically to the NSC staffer.

"None of your business," said Pat Robinson. "Since when do you care about motives? You want the rest of the story or not?"

"I want it, I want it," he said. "Calm down. Have another margarita."

"I don't want another margarita," Robinson said. "I do want you to understand that you can have this only on the condition that you tell everyone you try to confirm it with that your source is at the Pentagon, whether they ask you or not—and that you find some way to indicate as much in your article."

Sampson shrugged; the ruse would be useful to him, as well. "Fine," he said. "When's the raid planned for?"

"O'Brien is meeting with the NSC first thing in the morning. If Hoskins hears what he wants to hear, probably Sunday."

"No shit?" Sampson said, reaching behind his chair for his jacket. "That soon? How big?"

"The details are still being worked out. Probably at least two hundred of O'Brien's hellions plus air cover—F-16s and maybe even bombers." Robinson chuckled wryly. "The old man's got a thing about the Bay of Pigs and air cover."

"I've got to boogie, pal," Sampson said. "Thanks a lot. I owe you one."

Robinson downed the dregs of the margarita and watched the reporter hurry out of the restaurant. "There goes an extraordinary American," she said, reaching for the check.

TWO

TO PLAY ON BOB O'BRIEN'S BLOCK A MAN NEEDED precision, stealth, speed, and cold, intelligent hate, hard as iron and hammered into a weapon for killing reflexively but judiciously. Every operation was a little Pearl Harbor intended to annihilate the enemy while he was in repose—washing out his black pj's, playing cards, sleeping, boasting, banging—and as a bonus to leave the good guys more or less without a scratch. A savage stroke by civilized men against savage men. *My life's work,* mused O'Brien as he gazed at the map of Beirut and the Bekaa Valley on the wall of his Pentagon office. *A neutron bomb kills people and leaves buildings. I leave people and kill assholes.*

In Vietnam whatever actual pleasure he had gotten from it, as opposed to mere professional satisfaction, came from putting the mean little VC bastards in the same position they liked to find South Vietnamese and Americans: shivering in the corner and shitting their pants as sudden death spat out of the jungle in the middle of the night. *Tit for tat.* Beyond that basic moral equation, O'Brien left the big issues to the wiser heads in Hollywood and on the editorial pages of *The New York Times.* To him the American failure in Vietnam was a simple tactical failure, like the settlers vs. the Indians and the Brits vs. the settlers, as frustrating as it was correctable. Earlier wars proved that you couldn't win while riding on horses or scampering across open fields at fortified positions. In Vietnam the communists proved that the best place to shoot a man was in the back or the sack, and that the one sure way to get men out of a place they didn't want to be was to go in fast and mean, collect them, and leave no living souls behind.

To those who didn't want America to sink to the level of its enemies, O'Brien liked to point out that in the waning days of the century we had precious few enemies willing to rise to ours. In the last war he felt we had sunk too little too late—which was not to say we hadn't been capable of the occasional bolt of evil inspiration. The idea one hot night in 1970 was to liberate seven pro-Saigon local officials from a VC village before Charlie could catch his breath and then nail his prisoners to trees and choke them with their own viscera, one of Charlie's standard methods of interrogation. O'Brien had needed a single piece of intelligence: Where were the good guys? Watching with his thirty commandos from the thick brush around the village, he saw there was one hut no one entered or left in the course of two hours. They could have sat there all night; communists didn't expect this kind of behavior from Americans, so the VC hadn't posted a guard. The information was passed, the word was given, and in forty-five seconds every hut but one and every Vietnamese but seven were ablaze. *Didn't even get my hands dirty!*

Trouble was, this time he'd have at least three widely separated sites spread over two hundred square miles, some in the city and others in the desert. The sites from Rahmi's list for the current week were marked on the map. Some would still be in use Sunday, or so the CIA's sketchy corroborative intelligence indicated, but he had to account for the possibility that there might be fewer locations, or more. *Wish the old man wasn't in such a hurry.* If he had two weeks' worth of data in hand, O'Brien could do much more exact planning. But he wouldn't have the second report until 0600 Friday. *Only six more hours,* he thought, surprised, after glancing at his watch. He'd been awake for a day and a half, and the operation was scheduled to begin at 0200 Sunday, Beirut time. That left fewer than thirty-six hours for final planning and briefings.

"Better than nothing," the general mused aloud. His eyes stayed on the map as he leaned against his gray government-issue desk. In fact, it was the first real break he'd had since taking the job. He already knew how many men he'd need and more or less where they would have to go and how long they would have to stay. He'd get them out. It might not be as pretty as Entebbe—civilians would say "surgical," which O'Brien found inappropriate, since he planned to send every non-Western soul within firing range well beyond the reach of medical science—but it would be pretty enough. Especially for Hoskins's purposes.

The saving grace is the Iranians wouldn't figure we'd have the balls for this kind of exercise in a million years. They've been waiting patiently until there was a market for hostages again, just like Hanoi has kept a few American POWs shoveling pig shit in Laos so they can fork them over as a dowry when Uncle Sam finally decides to come courting. The Japanese shot at us in World War II and are our best friends in Asia; the Chinese shot at us in Korea, and they're our second-best friends. A few more years and we'll be cozying up to the Vietnamese. The Ayatollah's got to figure he'll get the next available teat.

O'Brien muttered under his breath and reached behind him for a Styrofoam cup, tearing his eyes from the map just in time to see a cigarette butt floating in his hour-old coffee. "Lieutenant, cuppa mud please," he yelled at one of his aides. In a moment he turned to see Captain Mayberry, who handed him a fresh cup.

"General, a reporter from the *Post*'s on the line."

"What the hell's he want?"

"Wouldn't say, sir. What should I tell him?"

With tired blue eyes, O'Brien grinned at Mayberry over the edge of his cup as he took a sip. "Probably wants to do another big feature story about 'The President's Real-Life Rambo.' Tell him anything you want." He looked back at the map, and Mayberry went to take a message, stepping around his boss's duffel bag, which was packed and sitting by the door. O'Brien reached for the phone and dialed a five-digit number.

A quarter of a mile away, on the other side of the building, the Secretary of the Navy picked up the phone on its first ring. "Morning, Bobby."

"Morning, Rich. Got me a carrier yet?"

The secretary grunted. "You always were a pushy son of a bitch. The *John F. Kennedy*'s currently in the western Med, and she'll make her very nonchalant way to a position one hundred miles off Lebanon by 2100 local time tomorrow. It's a routine enough pattern for us lately that nobody should pay much attention."

"You managed to avoid any, ah, JCS entanglements?"

"Don't you worry about the Joint Chiefs, my friend. All I need to do is murmur your name. When they find out Eugene's magic genie is finally out of the bottle they'll hit the deck faster than shit through a goose. They've been waiting for three years for you to fall on your butt so they can get up to the Hill to lecture the Armed Services Committee about chain of command and all that nonsense."

O'Brien smiled wearily. "I assume you share their touching confidence in me."

Rich said, "You just get the people and especially the boat home. If you don't, all it means is that nobody can."

Since DuBois hated to get up in the middle of the night, at times like this he usually climbed out of the hideabed, tucked the blanket around Carole, and pulled one of the Danish modern chairs from his dinette set over by the bed. Sitting with his feet up, he would read his briefing materials with the miniature book light Carole had given him for this precise purpose. But tonight he sat in the dark and brooded about Bob O'Brien.

The Hoskins administration's first act of war was a day

and a half away. For three days, O'Brien had been functioning on coffee and sheer cussedness, bad-mouthing the politicians and plotting the swift demise of several hundred Shi'ite Moslems. Meanwhile, DuBois was romping with his girlfriend the newspaper reporter.

The previous year's arms control fight had been different. Then the White House had called the shots. *Damn if we didn't muscle the soldiers into line!* Gene had finally called in the Secretary of Defense and *ordered* him to tell his mice to stop squealing to George Will and the *Washington Times* about the limits on SDI deployment. But in this operation, civilian authority had been rendered extraneous the moment the President made his decision about the scope of the raids: "Go in and get 'em all. If we screw up, we'll take the same hit for sending two hundred men as we'd take if we sent twenty."

In these circumstances, civilian authority barely knew how to frame an intelligent question. DuBois's avocation, history and international affairs, had helped him avoid the predicament of one of Reagan's early State Department appointees who couldn't tell the Senate who the ruler of Zimbabwe was. But a few dimly remembered lectures on irregular warfare at West Point didn't give him the vaguest idea how to sneak two hundred men, based at four different installations in three Mideast countries, into Beirut in the middle of the night under the noses of the Soviets, Iranians, and Israelis, much less how to guide them out again without getting them and twenty-nine half-dead civilians massacred. Nor had his own Vietnam experience prepared him for an operation that demanded such delicacy.

DuBois had come home from Indochina in 1971, when he was thirty-four. They didn't give him a parade, but they threw him and Debbie one hell of a Cajun dinner-dance at the Lions hall. For the nine-times-decorated officer and Central High School's star fireballer, it was as flamboyant a homecoming as a warrior of that era could expect. Afterwards, the safe, logical place for him was in his father's small but profitable offshore operation. Oil had become the new ancestral industry in south Louisiana, what selling bowls of crawfish etouffee by the roadside had been in his grandparents' day. But the war had taught him, among many other things, that life was neither safe nor logical. Morgan City was way too small for a man who had seen how large the world was and how hostile to those civic qualities that made most of his neighbors in Morgan City so content. His proud papa was counting on him, so he set to work. But Parker DuBois had already set his sights far beyond the swamplands of Terrebonne Parish. He had seen Vietnam, and in that faraway swamp his distant French cousins had abandoned seventeen years before, he feared he'd seen the future.

By the end of his six-year tour, DuBois had realized the war had to end. It was taking too long and too much, and had long since taken on the smell of defeat. But then he returned home and got a whiff of Indochina's acrid stateside stench. It was a different smell, and it was the wrong smell. In Vietnam the war was a war. In the United States it had become some kind of anti-heroic cardboard metaphor, a purgative for the moral hypochondria of the most affluent and pampered generation in history. In addition to having to nurse the seen and unseen wounds of battle, Vietnam veterans had the additional burden of having to explain to family, friends, co-workers, and nameless interrogators in the streets exactly what they thought they'd been doing over there. Many veterans reported sheer abuse. DuBois felt from those around him only sympathy and the occasional furtive, searching glance, as if he were the lone survivor of a midair collision and they were looking over his torso or into his eyes for the scars they knew had to be there someplace.

DuBois's practical mind toyed with but soon rejected the simple anti-war verities. He knew he hadn't been part of a corrupt enterprise, just a clumsy one. His heart rejected them, too, forbidding him to believe a score of his friends had been crippled or blown to pieces for nothing. Those who would later marvel at Parker DuBois's subtle skill at edging warring factions toward uneasy agreements would have been surprised at how simple his calculus had been. His country was neither immoral nor absurd and therefore incapable of the immoral absurdity that Vietnam appeared to so many to be. Partly as justification for his own role there, he became a Vietnam hobbyist, a scholar of Dienbienphu, Geneva, the deceits of Ho, and the betrayal of Diem. Most of these events had unfolded when Parker was still studying arithmetic or first practicing the art of negotiation and gazing at its loveliest rewards in the still-pure light of the southern moon. Back then and while in-country, he'd had little time for the big picture. Once at home, when it was probably too late, it began to consume him.

His friends, mostly conservative Democrats, had supported the White House war policy through Kennedy and Johnson and into Nixon. But when he sat over coffee with them one morning, defending the invasion of Cambodia, explaining its obvious tactical rationale, he found there was no give anymore, on any side. One or two still stubbornly supported the president, as they would have if he'd vaporized Hanoi. This didn't satisfy DuBois, who wanted them to understand exactly how many hostiles had just been chased from their cozy nooks in the Parrot's Beak. But the rest just stared with tired eyes and, if he was lucky, gave him a weak smile and a pat on the arm before changing the subject. Nobody was listening anymore. They knew too much. The collective hypnosis that gave meaning to war had never been induced for Vietnam, which by now just seemed to be a conspiracy of insane mistakes. At the end of the American century, America was getting tired.

That was what scared him. Anyone who had faced the Vietnamese Communists in war knew what they would make out of Indochina in peace. When Saigon fell, their fears began to come true. DuBois realized the United States couldn't permit such horrors against those it called friends without eventually inviting them against itself. Once an indifferent student of history, he now felt he had personally been grappling with its most elemental forces and that they were shoving him and his country into a deep shadow of self-loathing. He felt himself being propelled toward some form of public service by anxiety alone. But what could he do? He had already bored Debbie to distraction with his dinnertime pontificating. His friends were starting to guffaw at all his table pounding and silver rattling, making him feel like a pompous zealot, telling him he ought to run for office or something.

Luckily, Eugene Hoskins, under whom he had served in Vietnam, already was. One day in 1978, DuBois went to hear him at Rotary. It was a tough, solid speech calling on the United States to "fill the post-Vietnam vacuum with a vigorous post-Vietnam vision" in the practice of foreign policy. The post-lunch audience was polite, sleepy, and indifferent. But by the time DuBois got back to his office, he had reenlisted, as the local coordinator of his ex-superior's foolhardy and hopeless effort to capture the Democratic nomination from the Third District's popular incumbent congressman. Two years later, Hoskins announced for governor, wisely talked about the sanctity of the oil depletion allowance instead of the increased pace of Soviet ICBM production, and won. He appointed Parker DuBois his chief of staff. Parker's father threw up his hands, his brother took over the oil business, and he and Deborah, who was showing the first signs of the blood disease that would take six more years to kill her, moved to her hometown of Baton Rouge.

DuBois uncrossed and recrossed his legs, trying not to jostle the bed and waken Carole. Now here he and Gene were in Washington, groomed to battle Communists and preparing to battle Moslem fundamentalists. Either way, Robert Jerome O'Brien was the man they needed for the job. They had made him the most watched behind-the-scenes operator in history, and there would be no denying him if he failed.

It had taken three years of international sweet-talking and interagency head knocking to equip and position the bureaucratic and technological apparatus that was now slouching toward Beirut. It had begun as the fulfillment of a campaign promise. In 1988 Hoskins had waxed eloquent about the $2 trillion Reagan defense buildup that left the navy so ill equipped that its antimine capability in the Persian Gulf had at first consisted of seventeen-year-old sailors posted with rifles on the bows of their frigates. After the election, Hoskins had quietly begun to beef up the United States' capacity for low-grade warfare. In the 1980s special operations had fallen victim to petty infighting. Hoskins ended it in a hurry by making it clear by word and deed that O'Brien, who'd also served under him in Vietnam, had his full confidence and that anyone who crossed him risked the President's wrath. The appointment of a Tulsa high school buddy of O'Brien as Secretary of the Navy eliminated one of the two obstacles to conducting a special ops raid quickly and secretly: the hassle-free availability of air and sea power. In the matter of the Lebanon hostages, Ali Rahmi had removed the other obstacle.

DuBois decided to call the maniac, just so he wouldn't forget whom he worked for. *And also to let him know I'm awake, too!* He got up, took his bulky secure telephone into the bathroom, and sat on the side of the tub. First he called the Secret Service command post at the White House to confirm that Wolcott was wheels up from Paris, because that was the first thing O'Brien would ask. *Who works for whom?* Then he had the switchboard connect him with the direct line in the general's office.

"Yo."

"It's Parker, Bobby."

"Hiya, Parker. Where's my intelligence?"

DuBois closed his eyes and rubbed his left eyelid with his thumb. "On the way. Where are we?"

"Up shit creek if the boss doesn't keep the Syrians off my ass."

"He's calling Assad again tomorrow. Today." DuBois ran his hand through his hair and stared at his toes. "I'd like him to call the Israelis, too."

"We've been all over that, my friend," O'Brien replied.

"It's a military decision, not a political one. The A-rabs need to think the air strike is coming from Israel. Give the Israelis two days to decide they don't like the A-rabs thinking that, and I guarantee you they'll foul this up. Besides, did they tell Ron when they hit the nuke plant in Iraq or took out PLO headquarters in Tunisia and violated the sovereign territory of our old buddy Bourguiba?"

DuBois chuckled. "If they did Ron wouldn't have remembered anyhow. Bobby, it's not a question of etiquette. What if somebody retaliates?"

"Except for the Syrians, there's nobody *to* retaliate. Besides, the misconception is going to last about seven minutes. We'll explain it to them personally."

DuBois had to admit the man had a certain style about him. "Buy you breakfast in my office before you give the President his final instructions?" he said.

"It'd be a pleasure. See you about seven. Oh, Park. I got a call from a *Post* reporter a couple of hours ago."

DuBois gripped the phone harder. "What did he want?"

"Wouldn't say. It's not the first time. Bastards know I keep funny hours, and sometimes I've been known to answer at night, in which case they ask me what I'm doing with all the funding they're not supposed to know I have. I thought you might know about it."

"Nope. I wouldn't worry." *Gene will kill me if this leaks!*

"I wasn't. See you."

Before he turned off the bathroom light, DuBois noticed that Carole had pushed the covers off. She was lying on her side with the undershirt hiked up over her hips. The shoulder straps had fallen off. Her long, handsome legs were stretched out, bent a little at the knees and crossed at the calves. *Ye gods.* He could wake her gently and they could make love again and whisper in the darkness until dawn. Or he could get dressed and go downstairs and ride with his grumpy White House driver to Andrews and then fly to Kennedy Airport in a draughty, rattletrap navy transport. He imagined Nixon calling Henry: "I don't care if it's Jill St. John or Betty Boop. Get your ass to Peking. I made you a blind date with Chou En-lai." Hoskins would never be quite that direct. As a matter of fact, he seemed genuinely happy for DuBois, albeit envious, because his friend was having the second chance that living in the world's largest fishbowl prevented him from having himself.

As DuBois dressed he tried not to think about the fact that he was starting another eighteen-hour day. He didn't bother to check to see if the car was waiting. He kissed Carole on the forehead, patted her smooth warm hip, and slipped out the door.

No matter how quietly he closed the door on the way out at night, Carole always awoke. Their understanding was that he stayed when he could and left when he had to, without having to explain. He rarely disrupted their plans because their schedules didn't permit any plans beyond their few hours together a few nights a week. But when he was gone, she always felt a momentary disruption in her gut.

She got out of bed and wrapped the blanket around her as she walked to the window and looked down to the street. His car was just pulling away, with the Country Squire wagon containing the follow-up agents right behind it. She had known since dinner that something was going on. She didn't wonder what. She wondered only whether DuBois was in danger.

She turned and sat in his chair, momentarily amused thinking of the paroxysms of speculation she could provoke by calling the night desk at the *Post* and mentioning that the national security advisor had left his apartment at one in the morning. Then she imagined George Stevens's howls if he knew she regularly possessed such information and withheld it from him. As it was, he regularly lectured her about the higher authority to which she owed her allegiance. He loved to tell the story about how Bob Woodward—*will he ever stop talking about Bob Woodward?*—had let his personal loyalty to his old roomie Gary Hart cloud his usually keen judgment and prevent him from filing a lurid story about all the babes the senator used to bring home.

She longed to tell the old hypocrite to stuff it. She knew he considered her weak for putting humanity above power. Because power was what was at stake. Stevens didn't care about the fate of great nations anymore than she did. He cared about gigging Eugene Hoskins and advancing the political fortunes of Marshall Brandon, the silver-tongued, empty-headed Pennsylvania Republican who was chairman of the Senate Foreign Relations Committee. Every reporter in town knew that from the moment Stevens first sat at Kissinger's knee as a diplomatic correspondent during those famous backgrounders en route hither and thither, he had imagined himself as Secretary of State someday. *And he knows Brandon's the only man in the country stupid enough to put him there.*

She slid off the chair and climbed back into bed. She was worried about Parker, but at least her conscience was clear. "I'd rather be a slave to passion than a shill for George," she said aloud, wondering in the instant before she fell asleep whether he had the place bugged.

Sampson sat in his boxer shorts with his feet on the coffee table, the Trinitron remote control balanced on one knee and a soggy slice of cold pizza draped over the other. He took a pull at his Michelob and punched the channel changer.

"No Klingons in sensor range, Captain."

Punch.

"I'm Bob Dylan, and if you liked my hits from the sixties, you'll love this new collection. . . ."

Punch.

". . . the value of the yen, which at ninety to the dollar has spurred GM and Ford to reopen abandoned plants in Ohio and California and retool them for Cavaliers and Escorts destined for export to Japan. Mr. Chairman, these developments. . . ."

Punch.

"He's *dead,* Jim."

Punch.

"Some of us have got to be at work before ten-thirty. You want to keep it down?"

Sampson looked up and saw Amanda squinting at him as she made her sleepy, crooked way out of the bedroom. She stretched out on the couch and put her feet in his lap. He hit the mute button. "Sorry, babe. I just can't get over catching the Neanderthal man in his office in the middle of the night."

"Can't you call somebody, preferably from a phone booth so I can get some sleep?"

"No one to ask until morning. But when I call DuBois's office, they'll shit. I wish I could see their faces."

"You told Stevens, yet?"

Sampson bit into his pizza and wiped the tomato sauce off his mouth with the back of his hand. He shook his head. "Can't. He always wants to know your sources."

"So?"

"So I don't want to tell him on this story, at least not until I get it pinned down." He let his hand fall on her and applied pressure against her crotch through the fabric of her nightgown.

Amanda brushed his hand away. "I was interested two hours ago, but *you* had to call the Pentagon."

He shrugged and stroked her ankles. "So I called. We're both up now, right?"

She rolled her eyes and struggled to her feet. "Anything to get you to go to sleep. But at least take your socks off, okay?"

The Air France 747 was an hour out of New York. Russ Wolcott discreetly checked to see how his bodyguards were holding up.

The cute blonde across the aisle was reading the *International Herald Tribune.* Her partner was fast asleep, his chin resting on his chest and the tip of his tie floating in the plastic glass of Bloody Mary mix he was holding in his lap. In the row in front of him, the laconic Italian was playing cards with the brunette. He looked behind him. The former New York City vice detective with the brush cut grinned and winked. *Four awake and accounted for. Not bad.* Actually he was surprised at their endurance. They had gone the whole way without a shift change, no doubt to reduce the number of agents who might casually mention in the gym that the NSC had conscripted them for some kind of a spook operation in Paris's red-light district. For them, this was a typical though lengthy day's work. But not for Wolcott, who was wide-eyed and wired.

Rahmi had bristled with defiance, as if he had been forced into a course of action he had in fact freely initiated. He had needled Wolcott about staging meetings in bordellos and said that he doubted the United States was competent enough to do anything with the information it was buying. Wolcott shivered, thinking of the Iranian holy men cackling like witches over the fried body parts of the men who died at Desert One in 1980. But everyone knew Hoskins had pumped billions into special operations. He was pretty sure there'd be a good show.

But why was Rahmi so hostile?

Probably because it had dawned on him that a man without a country was a man without friends.

After their transaction, Wolcott had said, "I am instructed to advise you that your position at the embassy is likely to become untenable within a few days."

"Do you think I haven't realized that?" Rahmi spat back.

"If you're going anywhere, you had better go now. I am also instructed to say that if you wish to come to the United States, your safety will be guaranteed by the President."

"As I recall, the guarantee of your president earned the Shah the right to languish in a rented house in Mexico and die in Egypt."

Wolcott had replied calmly. "This president is different from that president. And even if he weren't, you are different from the Shah. We appreciate the risks you are taking to enable us to get our people out of Beirut. We appreciate why you are taking these risks—*all* the reasons why. As an expression of our appreciation, we offer you permanent safe haven in the United States if you want it."

Rahmi had given him a surprised look. "I will consider your offer," he said finally.

Wolcott gave him a telephone number he could call in Paris and a code name to use. For a moment they stood awkwardly in the cramped garret. "Heloise will show you out," Wolcott said finally with an uncomfortable smile. Rahmi watched him for a moment and then smiled back, and for the first time, they shook hands.

THREE

THE NEXT MORNING, CAROLE NELSON WAS READING THE paper at her desk when she looked up and saw Chuck Sampson zigzagging toward her across the newsroom. She took a sip of coffee, winced, and reflected for a moment on the subtle interplay of reality and fantasy.

When she had first walked into the *Post* newsroom two and a half years before, she had exclaimed to the assistant business editor, who was showing her around, "It looks just like the movie!" Immediately she had feared she'd said something utterly insipid. A former statehouse reporter from Baton Rouge wishing to cut a wide swath in the big time should not be making spastic references to things she had seen in movies. A dry allusion to something on that day's op-ed page would have been better. But her new colleague said, "Well, yes and no. Of course we didn't have the computers then."

"We?"

She must have looked bemused, because he had said sheepishly, "They needed somebody to get them authentic stuff for the set. You know, banged-up old typewriters, dictionaries, copy paper, trash, and so on."

"Trash?"

"They wanted some typical newspaper trash. I volunteered to fly it out to LA, and they gave me a bit part."

Aware that she might not have noticed him, he added helpfully, "I'm in the background watching the AP ticker when Redford tries to call Howard Hunt at the White House."

The thirst for authenticity was strictly limited to inanimate objects, thought Carole as Sampson came closer. Robert Redford he was not. He had the sloppy, patrician mien of what had been called a preppie before the characteristics metastasized throughout the population of upwardly mobile baby boomers—a pasty, unblemished complexion, unkempt hair, tortoise-shell glasses, and a size forty Brooks Brothers blazer on a size thirty-eight frame. His tie was loose and his collar button undone, it being widely accepted in the newspaper business that people who tightened their ties all the way were less creative than people who did not. His hands were stuffed up to the brass buttons into the pockets of his wrinkled, cuffed chinos, and his chin jutted forward with youthful arrogance. He probably edited the *Andoverian* or the *Exeterian* or whatever they were called and then comped on the *Harvard Crimson.* He rarely paid much attention to her. Carole sensed an impending Parker attack. *What's he working on?* She quickly flipped to page two of the front section to scan "The *Washington Post* Index," which had always irritated her. *What the hell other paper would it be an index of?*

"Hey, Nelson," Sampson said. "Good piece today."

"Thanks." The *Post* that morning had revealed a plan by the new Fed chairman to propose a quarter-point reduction in the prime rate. It was indeed a good piece—by the time its author had decided to risk a second cup of coffee, the Dow had gone up twenty-five points—but since national desk reporters spent more time knitting than reading the business page, she doubted Sampson had done more than scan the headline and lead.

He took her paper and leafed through it as he sat on the edge of her desk. "How about that bozo Hoskins is sending to Tokyo? He's continuing to populate the great capitals of the world with his rich fishing buddies."

Carole knew she was being baited. Would she mouth the party line, extruding the breezy antiauthoritarianism that passed for small talk in the newsroom? Or would she mount an awkward defense of an appointment her lover had doubtlessly been involved in making? Too many happy words about the Hoskins administration, she realized, and she would finally, irrefutably confirm the unsuitability for her chosen trade that Sampson and most of her co-workers had suspected ever since the *Washingtonian*'s gossip columnist first spotted her during a chance encounter with Parker DuBois at an exhibit of Russian Late Impressionists at the Hirshhorn.

When they met that rainy Sunday, they had not seen each other for over five years. Carole had been a friend of Debbie DuBois's family in Baton Rouge and therefore a casual acquaintance of the governor's chief of staff. DuBois had been a source on a couple of stories, and she saw him on Thanksgiving and at cocktail parties. When Debbie fell ill for the last time, Carole visited her at the hospital and, as her illness advanced toward its painful end, sat and read to her for hours or just held her hand.

People had talked, as people talked now, and the talk had a decidedly ugly timbre because of the mutual professional benefit everyone knew would obtain if she and DuBois shared anything more profound than sex. *The hell with them,* she had thought, though she had been surprised by the sudden jolt of attraction she'd felt when he took her to a thank-you lunch one day. She resisted it. Had it seemed he was resisting, too? When their fingers touched while reaching simultaneously for the coffee creamer, they both reacted as if they had stuck their hands into a bucket of cold baked beans. Of course nothing had happened. That would have been an unconscionable betrayal of Debbie. After she died, Parker had smothered his grief in fourteen-hour days of spouselike devotion to his Washington-bound boss, and they lost touch.

When she landed the *Post* job, it occurred to her to give Parker a call, but how do you give a call to the President's national security advisor? While still on the horns of that procedural dilemma she saw him near the entrance to the exhibit under the beneficent gaze of a jumbo bust of Armand Hammer. At the first sight of him plunging through the crowds she had thought his wavy, grayish-brown hair was a little thinner than before and his pleasingly broad shoulders a little more stooped. But what she took to be the effects of lugging around the weight of the world was actually the turtlelike impulse of highly recognizable people to wrap their shoulders as tightly as possible around their chins to keep from being discovered. He turned to face her when she said his name, and as his expression of mild irritation softened, she saw that his eyes were as warm and reassuring as she had remembered.

Nervous "How are you?"s and "I'm doing fine"s and "Got to run"s were exchanged, and then they realized they were rushing away from each other in the same direction. After a half-hour of animated conversation and distracted glances at Korovins and Kuprins, they arrived at the coat check.

Carole said, "Maybe we could have lunch one day."

DuBois put on his raincoat, helped her with hers, and took his plaid hunter's cap from the attendant. "Can't get away for lunch. Usually can't get away at all. I am quite proud about managing to liberate myself this afternoon."

She had felt supremely foolish. How could she even have imagined having lunch with the closest friend of the President of the United States? "Well, then. We'll see each other around town, I suppose."

DuBois touched her lightly in the small of the back as they walked toward the door. "Please don't mistake my dull speech about my logistical difficulties for a complete answer. You free for dinner?"

"Tonight?"

"Heck yes. You have to get me while you can."

Many stolen hours of warmth and fellowship had followed, and also three instances of coitus interruptus owing to sudden crises, one of which DuBois had later confided was a computer glitch at NORAD that had brought United

States strategic forces to DEFCON 2. "You always have some excuse," Carole had complained, only half-facetiously. Their occasional games of coffeehouse-quality chess helped her gird for far more frequent games of cat and mouse with fellow reporters who felt she was giving aid and comfort to the enemy and yet refusing to exploit her access to his camp.

After months of tangling with sarcastic newspaper people, she had found honesty to be the most effective ploy. She glanced up at Sampson, who was still chuckling over the mug shot of the jolly new ambassador, and shrugged. "He does seem to be a turkey, doesn't he? I liked the quote about his 'many fine Japanese friends.' But isn't that the same old saw about political appointments? Every president does it." She got in a dig of her own. "If he overcomes the handicap of not having gone to Groton and Princeton and does all right, fine. If not, how much damage can he do?"

"Yeah. Maybe." Sampson had not trudged 120 arduous feet to argue the genetic superiority of career foreign service ambassadors. "Say, you're not free for lunch, are you?"

What a gentleman. I should say yes just to put him through the expense account paperwork. "Thanks, but I can't. I've got to cover a speech. What's on your mind, Chuck?"

He tried to look nonchalant as he asked, "Anything special cooking with DuBois?"

"Cooking?" She arched an eyebrow.

"Going on," he said quickly. "I mean at the office. The White House."

She smiled. "Right. No, not that I know of, though I never know when there is. What do you hear?" It was better to play the see-no-evil sex kitten than say she was not at liberty to violate a confidence, especially since in this instance she had none to violate. She decided to try to find out what he knew before she sent him packing. *Of course now he'll clam up out of the ridiculous fear that at this late date I might steal his tip and try to file a White House story.*

But he didn't. "I haven't tied it down yet," he said, "but it's something military and something big."

"How big?" She figured this might explain Parker's midnight ride.

"Bigger than Grenada."

Carole grinned. "That big, huh?"

He looked impatient. "There are no more recent points of comparison."

"You've got that right."

"DuBois just denied it to me, but I think he's lying."

Wouldn't you?

"I thought you might give him a call."

This is new. "Why would I?"

"To see if he'll reconsider his statement to me," he said with elaborate patience.

She shook her head. "I'm sorry if I failed to make myself clear. What I meant was why *should* I call him?"

"Because you're a reporter and the newspaper needs you to help follow a lead."

"Chuck, he's my friend."

"So? This is important."

"So is he. So are he and I. And besides, it would be wrong."

Sampson looked bewildered.

Carole shifted in her chair and leaned forward. She would give it a try. "Chuck, you have a wife? A girlfriend?"

"Yeah. Amanda. You've met, I think."

"Of course. I'm sorry. So what if Amanda's best friend is in PR and wants to sell us a story about a nonsexist day-care center or a new hybrid of kiwi fruit? She asks Amanda to talk to you. What does Amanda do?"

"She tells her friend to screw off. Which has nothing to do with the matter at hand."

"Why not?"

"Because this a question of the impending use of American military power. Lives are at stake."

"Right. Mine and Parker's. And yours, especially if you win the Pulitzer Prize or get promoted to deputy managing editor or somesuch, which is a factor you failed to mention. I'm sorry, but if you can't get the story without my violating the trust of someone I care about, maybe there's no story."

Sampson stood up. "There's a story, Nelson, despite what your boyfriend says. I just thought that when push came to shove, you might realize what side of town you lived on."

"Chuck—" She caught herself. "Have a nice day, all right?" He whirled and strode off, and she reached for the paper and stared unseeing at the classified ads.

"Irene," said DuBois, "I've got a problem. Who's in there?"

He was surprised that the President's longtime personal secretary did not need to look at the typed schedule on her desk. "The children's choir of St. Xavier Church." She flushed with humiliation. "From Thibodeaux, Louisiana."

Although he felt as though he were riding two greased skids to hell, DuBois could not help smirking. "Irene, you are an evil woman," he said. "There are twenty-seven people in the EOB whose job it is to make sure these little audiences get dispensed in a politically efficacious way among the lesser forty-nine states."

"Parker DuBois, it was his idea, not mine," she said with expertly calculated peevishness. "I just happened to mention the other morning that they were coming to town on a tour. Little dears sold cookies for twelve weeks to pay the bus fare."

"How many boxes did we buy?" She glared at him. "They finish singing yet?"

"Ten minutes ago." She motioned toward the door.

As he reached for the knob, the door flew open and the President's official photographer burst forth, dragging his handkerchief across his forehead. "You going in there, Parker? Abandon all hope."

Inside the Oval Office a little girl was holding one of Mrs. Boehm's limited-edition porcelain eastern brown pelicans over her head and running laps around the coffee table. A little boy was standing on the hearth juggling a one-of-a-kind Steuben glass magnolia that had been presented to Hoskins on his inauguration day by the Daughters of the American Revolution. The teacher who should have been keeping the children from busting the place up was fused to her spot, worrying the handle of her pocketbook and gazing at the President with a look of rapturous supplication.

The rest of the choir had Hoskins surrounded. He had finished his three-minute speech about how each of them might one day become the president. There was a boy squirming on Hoskins's knee as he frantically shuffled through his desk drawers, pulling out small presentation boxes and prying their lids open with one hand to see whether there was anything to send the youngsters on their way with. Presidential cuff links, collar stays, thimbles, tie bars, and coasters were scattered over the top of the desk. The children were busy looking askance at these items when DuBois approached the aide who was beaming unctuously over the chaos and whispered, "They've got to go."

The aide cleared his throat and said, "Mr. President? I'm sorry, sir, but that call from Mrs. Thatcher is coming through from London."

This was a code that was used when the President had asked to be interrupted or when something came up that the White House did not want described to every living acquaintance of the adult visitors in the room. Mrs. Thatcher was selected over leaders such as Chancellor Strauss or President Bongo because her name was immediately recognizable. It was used instead of General Secretary Gorbachev because it would not help the President's political fortunes if it were widely believed he was chatting regularly with the leader of the Soviet Union. Sometimes the President left instructions for an interruption and then brushed it aside because he found he was enjoying himself more than he had expected. On one such occasion, rather than saying, "Mr. President, it really *is* Mrs. Thatcher," the aide had told her he would return the call in a few moments.

This time the President stood up so fast that the boy in his lap nearly slid onto the floor. "Sorry, kids," he yelled. "Got to talk to Maggie."

The teacher finally piped up. "Oh, I'm sure that would be fascinating!"

The President looked menacingly at the aide, who said, "Oh, no, ma'am. It's a very private matter." He began to herd the children toward the door. As they left, the President promised to send each an autographed photo. Soon they were gone, and the room was characteristically, momentarily quiet.

DuBois walked to the front of the desk. "Mr. President," he said, "the *Post* knows about the raid."

A presidential aide with bad news is an alchemist who operates in reverse, turning the golden silence of the Oval Office into a lead balloon. Hoskins was still standing behind his desk. "Say what?" he whispered.

"They called fifteen minutes ago. I denied it."

Hoskins's face evinced disbelief, then astonishment, and finally rage. Through clenched teeth he said, "What exactly did he say? I want to know *every damned word!*"

DuBois had taken notes on a yellow legal pad. "He said, 'Mr. DuBois, I understand from the Defense Department that this weekend the United States will mount a rescue mission, including air strikes, to get hostages out of Lebanon. Will you confirm this?' "

"What did you say?"

"I categorically denied it. He asked twice more, and I denied it twice more."

"He said Defense? You didn't ask?"

"No, he offered."

"They don't usually do that, do they?"

"Usually no, though sometimes they will describe the source rather than identify it, but only after you ask."

"I didn't think their precious code of honor permitted them to go that far."

DuBois managed a thin smile. "It'll stretch from here to the moon and back, if necessary. If you can make them think you'll tell them something in exchange, they might give you a little peek at their source, but that's only if they need your help for the story. This guy says he's ready to go."

"Maybe he's lying. Maybe he doesn't have enough yet but was trying to lead you to believe otherwise."

"A perfectly reasonable possibility, although if he makes enough calls at the Pentagon, he will have enough pretty damn fast. Most people don't know how to talk to reporters. They try to be honest and finesse the question. But if you deny something the wrong way, you've confirmed it. You've preserved your honor and sunk the ship."

The President was still trying to find the leak. "On the Defense thing. Maybe he's covering for someone at the White House."

DuBois replied quickly. "No. Nobody knows but you, me, Robinson, and Mendez. I vouch for them both without reservation."

"Could they have just seen O'Brien hanging around here?"

"He's in all the time. Besides, the reporter's information is too detailed to be guesswork."

Hoskins wandered from behind his desk, sat on the arm the couch, and stroked his chin. DuBois turned around to face him. "So it *must* be Defense," Hoskins said. "Some jealous old lady on the Joint Chiefs of Staff?"

"Doubtful."

"Then O'Brien's operation. How many possibilities there?"

"I haven't talked to him, but I'd say at least two dozen. It's impossible—"

Hoskins interrupted him with a wave of his hand. "I've heard it all before, Parker. In any military operation you need at least three thousand people involved or there won't be enough jet fuel and toilet paper. We've both been there, and it's just not true. There has got to be a way to keep a secret in this town." He shook a finger at DuBois. "I swear to you, Park, I am going to tap every telephone in the executive branch if I have to, and that means you and your patootie."

DuBois looked at the rug.

The President covered his eyes with his hand. "Parker, I'm sorry." The hand fell away. "But you realize if this thing is in the paper, I've got to call it off. We'll look like fools. And we'll energize those shits in Beirut, who'll either kill all the hostages and send us their nuts in a grocery bag or just hold onto them for another ten years."

"Not necessarily. If we—"

"Two straight administrations ran aground on Iran. Vietnam lasted ten years. The Iranians have been screwing us for thirteen, and *not once* have we even had the pleasure of giving them a proper, fair pop in return." The President was on the move again, shifting from the couch to his easy chair in the corner. He put one foot on the ottoman and motioned to DuBois to sit in a chair facing him. "When is the axe going to fall?" he said.

"Tomorrow or Sunday. He wouldn't say for sure. Either way, we're sunk. The early Sunday edition is in circulation late Saturday afternoon, and besides, there are bound to be rumors about the story once it's written that could be picked up on radio and TV."

"So what do you suggest, Parker? Any way to kill the story short of killing the reporter? By the way, who the hell is it?"

"Kid named Charles W. Sampson. Assigned to the national desk." He skipped a beat. "I don't know him."

"Parker, please—I know it's not you. Who else do you figure knows besides him?"

"We can safely assume no one does," DuBois said. "Sampson's not assigned to the White House, and the reporters who are protect their turf like a pussycat guarding its supper dish. If he had told his editors, they would be swarming all over us by now. All my fellows would be getting calls from the writers who regularly cultivate them. Instead I just hear from Sampson. I'll bet this story just fell into his lap somehow, and he's tracking it down by himself so they don't take it away from him."

The President shoved the ottoman away with both feet, stood, and walked to the window. "What if you give him a call? Tell him what's at stake. See if there's something we can do for him. Maybe O'Brien will take him along to observe."

"I can try, Mr. President."

Hoskins turned and eyed him quizzically. "You don't sound hopeful."

"I'm just not sure there's a market anymore for that kind of appeal. The more that's at stake, the more the little bastard's going to want to run the story. He's holding the key to fame and fortune in his hand. Why should he give it back to us?"

Hoskins squared his shoulders. "Because the President of the United States is going to tell him to," he said.

Seated in his office just off the newsroom, George Stevens, the senior editor of the *Washington Post,* turned to his desktop computer terminal and called up the list of editorials scheduled for Sunday's paper. He chose the one slugged "Arms treaty," and in two seconds it scrolled silently onto his screen.

> While this newspaper has never been an enthusiastic advocate of the Reagan administration's Strategic Defense Initiative, we have found ourselves equally ambivalent about the Hoskins administration's sudden decision to delay SDI deployment for ten years as a part of its election-year arms control campaign. The cuts Hoskins was able to obtain in strategic and Warsaw Pact conventional forces appear dramatic enough, but given the drain on Moscow's resources from these commitments we wonder whether the President's men could have gotten the cuts without making concessions on SDI. In recent years there have been significant advances that have made space-based strategic defense appear far more practical than scientists first believed. Before trading

SDI away we would have thought the President would insist upon even stiffer cuts by the Soviets in both offensive weapons systems and also in its own substantial Star Wars program. Instead, when the Senate begins consideration of Hoskins's proposed treaty next month it will be passing judgment on an agreement that calls for Soviet offensive reductions some experts believe are inadequate and for virtually no cutbacks in Soviet space defense research.

Stevens cleared the screen and composed a message to the editorial page editor:

ABE—SUNDAY LEAD EDIT EXCELLENT. WOULD HOWEVER SUGGEST REF BE ADDED TO BRANDON COMMITTEE'S ANALYSIS OF TREATY. CREDIT WHERE CREDIT IS DUE AND ALL THAT. GEORGE.

He punched in his colleague's terminal number and hit the transmit button. Then he rose, stretched, and walked to the window.

The reporters could see their diminutive editor—in his wrinkled tropical suit, with his sleeves rolled up along skinny, hairless arms and tangled gray hair hanging an inch over his collar—whenever they wanted to, through a curtainless picture window that faced the newsroom. More to the point, he could see them. Like a video camera in a bank lobby, he never blinked and made everyone feel vaguely guilty. In his office by eight-thirty and rarely out before seven, he was the kind of editor reporters both admired and despised. He was a blessing because he was a font of good instinctual advice when they were stumped, a trial because he refused to leave them in peace when they weren't. As well-trained professionals, they felt they were entitled at least to get a story researched and written before their editors began to rip it to pieces.

Today he was watching the Harvard kid. He had been at his desk when Stevens arrived and was still there, making phone call after phone call and typing notes onto his terminal. This morning he'd had some kind of an embroglio with Nelson, with whom he was neither professionally nor socially close. When he stormed off, she looked like she'd suddenly gotten the curse. It had to have something to do with DuBois.

The incoming message beeper on his terminal sounded. Stevens went to his desk and called it up.

GEORGE—WILL DO, THOUGH MARSHALL'S GOING TO HAVE HIS NAME AND HIS PRETTY PUSS IN THE PAPER SO MUCH AFTER THE HEARINGS BEGIN WE THOUGHT WE'D GIVE THE FOLKS A REST. ABE.

Stevens replied:

ABE—YOU'RE A SWEETHEART. GEORGE.

Of course it was a damned waste of time, since he could have simply ordered the change made or typed it in himself. But in a building full of prima donnas, he had to avoid stepping on their dainty toes when he could.

He typed another message, this one to the national editor:

HERB—WHAT'S SAMPSON WORKING ON?

The reply came back in ten seconds:

MEDICARE SERIES. LAST I KNEW. WHY? YOU GOT SOMETHING IN MIND?

Stevens replied:

NOPE. JUST CURIOUS. HE'S WORKING LIKE A FIEND.

Nobody worked that hard on a Medicare series. He was reaching for the phone to summon Sampson when his intercom buzzed. "Mr. Stevens," said the operator, "we have a call from the White House for Charles Sampson. Would you like to listen in, as usual?"

Stevens lifted the receiver, whose voice pickup was automatically disabled in situations such as this, and looked out the window at Sampson. A second later the reporter picked up.

"Sampson."

"Mr. Sampson, this is Parker DuBois."

Sampson spun in his chair to face his terminal, his fingers flying over the keyboard to clear the screen so he could take notes.

"This conversation is off the record. Unless you agree, this conversation is over."

The hick's no fool. Stevens resolved to talk to somebody about muffling the clickety-clack of these keyboards. Sampson pushed the keyboard away and reached for a pencil and a piece of copy paper. Stevens smiled into the receiver. *The kid's not bad, either.*

"Agreed," said Sampson as he furiously scribbled what had been said so far. "Mr. DuBois, are you prepared to revise the statement you made to me this morning?"

"Young man, I am prepared only to invite you to stop by this evening for a private conversation with my employer."

Sampson's head jerked up. "You mean—"

"Will you still be at work at seven?"

"Yes." Sampson had stopped taking notes.

"There will be a car for you at the Fifteenth Street entrance at seven. Is that all right?"

"Yes, but—"

"We'll see you then."

Sampson put the receiver down and slumped into his chair. Stevens hung up, too, and looked down at the paperwork on his desk. The kid would probably look in his direction, and he didn't want their eyes to meet. In a few moments Stevens looked out again. Sampson was on the way to the coffee machine.

That explained it. He was running down some juicy and completely inadvertent White House tip and hadn't gone to his editors with it because he was afraid they would assign it to a White House reporter. He figured if he finished it and turned it in as a *fait accompli,* he would get the glory.

Sampson arrived back at his desk and set his coffee next to the cup he already had. After daydreaming for another few minutes, he began to copy his notes onto the computer. Stevens had to admire his balls, but this could end up being a pain in the ass. It would have to be a pretty good story to justify all the editorial conferences he would have to sit through while his subeditors and the lazy handout collectors at the White House complained about Sampson's interloping. But there must be something to it if Hoskins was going to see him. At least *somebody* on the paper was hustling!

Stevens decided to wait and see what Sampson came up with. If it was any good, it would be worth the trouble. *If it's not, I'll kick his ass out of here so hard his head'll land back in Harvard-f------ -Yard before his feet leave the ground!*

FOUR

FROM THEIR SOUND- AND MICROWAVE-PROOF OFFICE ON the third floor of the Old Executive Office Building, Parker DuBois's Mideast specialists could look through a stand of trees and see the West Basement entrance of the White House. Those whose visits Hoskins wanted to keep quiet arrived there, on the opposite side of the wing from the press room. That was how the Russian ambassador always went in, but by now DuBois's crew was fairly blasé about him. What they really wanted to see was a little blonde number in a little black dress. Rumors to that effect had been circulating since inaugural evening, but in three and a half years of discreet peeking, they had not spotted anybody fitting the description.

On Friday evening Pat Robinson was gazing out the window into the dusk. Behind her a computer was receiving a lengthy message in a series of quarter-second bursts relayed by satellite from the U.S. embassy in Damascus, and she was waiting for the synthesized tones that would tell her the full text was in. A nondescript sedan pulled up to the entrance, and she squinted through the leaves, curious about the identity of any caller who would arrive at the White House so unostentatiously.

As the passenger got out, she stiffened. It was Sampson. *And who's that with him? My God . . . no. No, it's not. It's another one. They all look the same. But Sampson coming here must mean they're trying to impress the hell out of him.* She smiled to herself. *Sampson wouldn't sit on a hot story if the fate of the Free World depended on it.*

The computer beeped, and Felix Mendez said, "Is it soup yet?"

Robinson turned from the window and sat at the keyboard. "Very funny. It's long enough, though." She called the document onto the screen and executed a decoding program. In ten seconds she was looking at a cable detailing the sizes of the Syrian army units stationed in Lebanon and their positions for the next seventy-two hours. She entered a command to send the document to the dot matrix printer next to her desk. "Assad is certainly being helpful," she said to Mendez, raising her voice so he could hear her over the sound of the printer and through the cushioned partition that separated them.

"Why not?" he said. "We're about to solve his principal foreign policy problem."

Guess again. Her mind drifted as she watched the print head fly back and forth, forming thousands of spots of ink into letters and numerals on the paper. She suddenly wondered how it might feel if it were writing on her skin instead. Like getting an injection? A tattoo? NO—more like the cold spasms she felt each time her brother had touched her, as if her flesh were contracting and recoiling to escape him. The memory focused her thoughts again, and a wave of revulsion made her stomach turn over. They hadn't spoken in nearly twenty years, and she saw him strutting around town only now and then. But she could still imagine his cold, powerful hands against her throat. She was always aware that he was nearby, polluting hallowed space just as he did her sleep. Ever since she learned he had been brought to Washington—at the President's personal request, it was said—she had been waking up at night to find herself up on her knees on the bed, sweating and shivering, the shadow of his taunting face melting away, his sour flavor lingering.

He'll get his, she had always thought. He'll get what he deserves. So what did he get? A position of absolute trust at the right hand of the President. Was that justice? She knew if she didn't get away from him again she would eventually go out of her mind. But why should *she* leave? She had run away once before. She had put herself in hock to pay for college, worked hard, and finally salvaged a career from the empty, ugly ruin he made out of her.

She wouldn't leave again. He should leave instead. She'd *make* him leave! When Sampson's story broke Hoskins would look like an inept amateur, just as Carter had when his own rescue mission failed. A foreign policy blunder plus the mild recession that had begun the previous winter would mean that the President would be sent home to Baton Rouge and his hand-picked boy wonder would be sent . . . *anywhere. Anywhere but here.*

She was sorry that to attack him she had to attack the administration they both served. But what choice did she have? His fortunes were tied to Hoskins's, but as a foreign service officer, hers were not. She had vowed never to give up another thing because of him. In fact, she had very little left. She had never managed a healthy, lasting relationship with a man. She had no friends from home, and few of her Washington friendships had grown any deeper than lunch-hour superficiality. People became wary when they confided intimacies and she offered nothing in return. Real friends wanted to know where you came from and who your family was and what they did. But her only family was her half brother, and they probably would not like her much anymore if she told them what he did to her, night after desolate night, for almost six months after her parents died.

The printout was finished. Startled out of her reverie by the sudden silence, she tore the paper off the machine, bursted it, and tucked it into her briefcase. "I'm out of here, Felix," she said. "You have anything more for O'Brien?"

"Thanks, Pat. I'm all set."

She closed her case, spun the combination locks, and

walked toward the door, waving at Mendez as she walked by his cubicle. He was engrossed in a report and didn't see.

An agent pointed to the door and said to go right in. Sampson looked at him quizzically, the moment striking him as overly prosaic. The focal point of the world's greatest civil authority throbbed with all the excitement of a Sears credit office after hours. No drums or trumpets, no guards in gaudy uniforms, not even an aide to announce him, rolling his tongue sensuously over the words, "Mr. President, Mr. Sampson is here." He didn't know that Hoskins had asked everyone, including Parker DuBois, to take the evening off.

He wondered where the President would be when he went in. Perhaps walking through the center of the room with his suit coat buttoned like Nixon, who had always wanted to be striding toward his guests as they entered. Or seated at his desk writing. *Just changing the course of history here, boy. Be right with you.* Or leaning over a table with his back to the door, like those gauzy photographs of Kennedy so artfully calculated to project the sense of the awful weight that rested on such youthful shoulders. Like all leaders, presidents pondered the impression they gave when entering a room or receiving a caller. *They've all got a gimmick,* Sampson thought. Patting the pocket of his blazer to make sure he had his spiral reporter's notebook, he opened the door and entered the Oval Office.

Hoskins had a new gimmick: He wasn't there. Sampson stood staring at the empty room as the door closed behind him.

"That you? In here."

He looked to his left, through a doorway and anteroom at the far end of the office. The President was in the Cabinet room, seated in front of the fireplace with his feet up on the long mahogany table. Sampson walked to the end of the table opposite Hoskins and wondered whether he should go around and shake his hand or just sit down where he was, like the duke's wife in a *New Yorker* cartoon. Then Hoskins tossed the book he was reading onto the table and pointed at the chair to his right. "Have a seat," he said.

Sampson walked along the wall, past the portraits Hoskins had chosen during his first week in office. Reagan's dour Coolidge had been shipped back to Worcester, Massachusetts, and his Ike had been moved back to the second floor. The new President substituted Lincoln, Wilson, FDR, and Nixon—two wartime presidents from each party. In his remarks at the unveiling ceremony, Hoskins had said that only the men who had led their nation in war could have fully appreciated the blessings of peace. "As we take our places for the first time under watchful eyes filled with the sadness of sending men to their deaths," the new President said to his Cabinet and the nation, "let us resolve to heed their silent counsel and conduct the nation's affairs with prudence and forbearance but also, when necessary, resoluteness. When we must spill blood, let it be on the hands of our adversaries."

The widespread misunderstanding this gesture evoked had been the first PR crisis of the Hoskins administration, proving once again that pictures spoke louder than words. George Stevens had been so delighted by the miscalculation that he wrote an editorial headlined THE MANY FACES OF WAR for the next day's edition. The editorial's rhetoric was mild, as befitted a honeymoon, but the real message was unmistakable: Ex-Colonel Hoskins was another of those presidents who would rather squeak America's rusty saber than grapple with the more nettlesome but more urgent domestic problems facing the country.

It was true that in the years since he had been less adventuresome than his critics had expected. They chalked it up to either a lack of guts or an inability to get the military to risk scratching the paint on any of its precious hardware. In its fickle way Washington, which had suspected Hoskins was a warmonger when he first hit town, now glanced archly up Pennsylvania Avenue and whispered "wimp." New York Governor Jack Kemp was now breathing down his neck, telling packed GOP audiences about Hoskins's "arms control sellout" and piling up most of the delegates needed to win the 1992 Republican nomination. In the upcoming California primary, Kemp was expected to go over the top. Hoskins needed a corrective before going head to head with him in the fall election.

Or so Charles Sampson figured as he took his seat. Hoskins did not offer his hand or introduce himself, only glancing at his guest. Their eyes locked for an instant before the younger man looked down, ostensibly to pull up his sagging left sock and cross his legs. When he looked back, Hoskins had turned away again.

The President, like his predecessor, was a throwback to an era before the appearance of moisture on the hair of a man under sixty-five was considered a lapse of etiquette at best and at worst a sign of unsuitability for the responsibilities of high office. His hair was thick, nearly white, and molded into the hint of a pompadour, which in editorial cartoons was more pronounced than Jerry Lee Lewis's. He wore gray suits (instead of navy blue and in spite of his media advisors), white shirts (instead of blue) and striped ties (never red). His face was rough, lined, and ruddy, and his eyes gleamed like onyx and could cut like diamonds.

As he spoke, Hoskins kept his eyes trained on a spot in the center of the room. He said, "Young man, I hope you'll excuse me if I cut the crap."

"Sure. Ah—fine. Yes, sir," Sampson said.

Hoskins continued. "You and I represent two practically infinite forces that can function only when voluntarily held in check. A president commands enormous destructive power, and yet I have given this country three peaceful years in a violent world. I have negotiated the first reductions in strategic nuclear weapons. And for the first time we have an effective way to fight terrorism directed against Americans abroad. I have resisted—*manfully* resisted—using it until I could guarantee a reasonable chance of success." He finally turned to face Sampson. "And now I find you have learned enough about a carefully planned and critical operation to destroy it in one thoughtless stroke.

"So now you must practice self-restraint, just as I have. By using your power unwisely, you will prevent me from being able to use mine when it can be applied most profitably in the interests of the country to which we both owe our first allegiance."

Sampson cleared his throat and answered, "So I take it, Mr. President, that you confirm you have ordered this raid."

Hoskins glared at him for a few seconds without speaking or moving. Then he slowly lifted his feet off the table and planted them on the floor, leaning forward toward the reporter with his forearms on his knees. "I guess you didn't hear me, Mr. Sampson," he said in a gruff near-whisper. "I'm asking you not to screw up this operation." He leaned back. "You can go along as the only representative of the press, and I'll announce that you knew all about it beforehand, owing to your exemplary reportorial skills, but heeded the pleas of your grateful President. If you want, I'll have you in for lunch and give you a damn medal. Just don't run the story now."

The last two things Sampson wanted were to be in Lebanon in the middle of World War III and afterward to suffer the professional humiliation of being thanked by the United States government. "Of course I'm going to run it," he said. "If I know, then the people have a right to know."

The President's brow darkened. "The people *elected* me, son," he said, "and they have a right to have me act in their interest without interference."

Sampson was awed. The most powerful man in the world was actually *arguing* with him. One of his political science professors had once written that a president's power was the power to persuade. *He might as well roll up his tent and take this medicine show back to Louisiana.* He barely suppressed a smile before saying, "Whether you're elected or not, the press also represents the interests of the people."

Hoskins grinned. "Chuck—may I call you Chuck?" Sampson nodded, nonplussed. "Chuck, there are five hundred and thirty-seven elected officials in this town, and we employ about two million more to do our bidding. *We* are the ones who represent the people, and as a matter of fact there's so much representing going on around here that it's a miracle we get anything done."

"You insult my intelligence if you suggest that our system doesn't demand an independent, aggressive press," Sampson shot back. "If your job is representing the people, then ours is seeing that you do it honestly."

"Don't make me laugh," the President said. "Honesty is no more a priority for you than for anyone else. The way you keep public figures honest is to print what other public figures say about them behind their backs, most of which is either lies or information calculated to boost the fortunes of one player at the expense of another."

"That's an absolutely astonishing oversimplification," Sampson said.

"The hell it is. I know of Democratic presidential candidates whose campaigns were destroyed by Republicans peddling information for the purpose of tilting the race to the guy the Republican would rather run against. The Democrat that was sunk blamed the other Democrats, who strenuously denied it, even though *they* fed the poop to the Republicans to begin with. Meanwhile the guy who wrote the story smiles like the cat that swallowed the canary. He gets a promotion, the people get one less choice, and *Time* magazine gets to do an analysis about the poor guy's 'fatal flaw' or his 'self-destructive impulses'." Hoskins joined his hands over his stomach and crossed his legs, jiggling his foot. "If you didn't exist, son, we'd have to invent you."

Sampson was distracted by the thought that this was an argument he had damn well better be able to win. "Mr. President," he said quickly, "that's the standard antimedia rap, and it's . . . it's pure bullshit." Hoskins's eyes narrowed. *Shit. No more cussing,* Sampson promised himself. "Our techniques tend to be unorthodox," he continued carefully, "because government uses all its power to manipulate information in its favor. We are lied to every day—by the

White House, the Pentagon, by everybody. We serve an indispensable role as the only people in this town who present information without coloring it to promote some personal or institutional agenda."

Hoskins, glowering, said, "Three-quarters of leaks are intended precisely to promote the leaker's personal agenda, and the fact of the leak promotes yours. I remember one guy used to get his stories off the wall of the boomer. Some discontented soul would go down and write a message under the tissue dispenser. Somehow you journalists have sold the idea that these little exercises in self-promotion and score settling serve the larger public good."

"You say they don't?"

"They primarily serve the interests of the people who leak and the people who write about it. It's important for you to at least admit this much, or we won't get anywhere. The media *do* have an institutional agenda, namely maintaining the political power and prerogatives of the media."

"I'll admit no such thing," Sampson replied, pouting.

The President shook his head and tsked. "Chuck, you are a piece of work," he said. "I've been sucking up to newspapermen for over ten years, and I can assure you it's the hardest job in politics. Every one of them acts like he is Jesus Christ and Ernest Hemingway rolled into one, the sentinel at the Republic's last outpost of justice and good taste." The President paused, reflected, and continued with even greater enthusiasm. "But I would even go so far as to say that the most corrupt relationships in Washington are between reporters and their sources. The reporter gets the coin of the realm, information. The leaker gets a cowardly potshot plus most-favored treatment himself. When I look in the newspaper and see a long, friendly profile of a member of my administration, I say to myself, 'There's a son of a bitch who talks to too many reporters.' Guys who don't talk to the press never get an even break. What's that got to do with truth and justice, Chuck? You use the free press for bribes, payoffs, and rubouts."

Sampson, feeling sweat starting to dampen the seat of his

pants, shifted his weight in his chair. *I've got to get the bastard off broad strokes and onto brass tacks.* "Mr. President," he said, thumping his forefinger against the edge of the table for emphasis, "my story came out of *your* administration, not out of whole cloth and *not* out of the men's room. You can be quite sure about that. Nobody forced my sources to talk to me. Your own house is obviously not in order. We don't make the news; we just report it."

Hoskins' already florid complexion reddened, and though his other features did not show it, Sampson sensed he was angering a man who rarely lost his equanimity in public. Hoskins stood, put his hands in his pockets, walked behind his chair, and turned to face Sampson again. He spoke in a hush. "We're not talking about news," he said. "We're talking about a state secret you're going to put in the damn newspaper. You found some lazy colonel who doesn't want his long weekend spoiled. Congratulations. But government shouldn't be a crapshoot where we only get to finish the jobs you guys don't stumble onto."

"Disagreement with the President is not *prima facie* proof of high treason," Sampson answered. "You want a town full of yes-men?"

"*Yes*-men?" Hoskins said, gesturing at the empty chairs around them with a dramatic sweep of both arms. "I got seven urgent staff memos when I switched to three-button suits last year. I have aides who feud over who gets credit for being the first to think of why a policy suggestion of mine stinks." He laid his hands on the back of the chair and spoke more slowly. "But an honest man who disagrees fundamentally on a major matter of national security policy ought to come to me and resign—quietly and anonymously. Since I am the one who got the votes, I'm entitled to that degree of loyalty, don't you think? No, I suppose not. You'd rather he stayed on the payroll and kept leaking." He paused, gazing reflectively over Sampson's head. "But what I can't figure out is, who's going to differ with me on this one? All we're doing is bringing home twenty-nine innocent victims of terrorism."

"How many of their rescuers will come home in Baggies?"

Hoskins gripped the back of the chair until his knuckles turned white. "Substantially fewer than if you print your story," he said, taking the tone of a father whose patience with a stubborn child was wearing dangerously thin.

"If I print my story," Sampson said, unable to prevent the self-satisfaction he felt from coloring his voice, "there won't be any raid." He added a somewhat more pious afterthought: "And lives will probably be saved. Anyway, you may thank me someday. As you well know, Kennedy said he wished the press had exposed the Bay of Pigs beforehand. *The New York Times* had it but didn't run it. If the press had covered Vietnam more aggressively in the early sixties, we also might have avoided that disaster."

"Every president for thirty years has had that Kennedy quote spooned at him by the press," said Hoskins. "The man was in the flush of a humiliating, unnecessary failure. I don't blame him for wishing you'd exposed it, because it didn't work. But you take his statement as a hunting license for all covert operations. Would Nixon have thanked you for exposing the secret early stages of the opening to China? Hell no—but if you'd been around and learned about it you would have printed it." Hoskins reached up and punched the air in front of him, setting a banner headline in imaginary type. " 'President in Bungled Bid for China Ties Despite Communist Giant's Aid to Our Enemies in Vietnam.' Wouldn't *that* have been a delicious story? A Pulitzer for sure, right, Chuck?"

"There's a difference," Sampson said. "Nobody died on the way to Peking."

"So answer the question."

Sampson waved his hand dismissively. "It's ridiculously hypothetical."

Hoskins smiled. "Right. You mentioned Vietnam. That was a disaster only because we lost. How in hell does that justify disclosure of a mission such as this beforehand?"

"Because you propose to use American military power and risk American lives," Sampson said. "Vietnam proved that the people with the power cannot always be trusted with it."

The reporter was shocked by the contempt in the President's stare. "Young man," he said in a harsh voice, "I was there, and I've got no patience for blithe remarks from people whose only experience of it came at the knee of their government professors at Harvard." He paused and looked away for a moment, and when he turned back his expression was calmer. "Vietnam proved only that ten years is too long for a democracy to fight a war. If World War II had lasted that long without an Allied breakthrough the Nazis' heirs would still be in power, probably even in Paris."

"But it didn't," said Sampson. "We won. That we lost in Vietnam automatically raises the question of whether we should've been there in the first place. In the future the press can help answer that question up front and not after the fact and after the carnage."

Hoskins cocked his head and said, "I'm beginning to understand you. Because you don't trust me with my power to command our armed forces, you're usurping it."

"It's simple vigilance," replied Sampson. "In the last twenty years, the press has learned to harbor a healthy skepticism about the public pronouncements and private plots of public officials."

"That's one way to put it," said the President. "As usual, you emphasize the public service and soft pedal your own self-interest. The way *I'd* put it would be that the press uses Vietnam and Watergate as excuses for its rash, haphazard, and self-serving disclosures of sensitive information and operations. It's like the circus coming to town for you but it makes success even more difficult for those who actually bear the responsibility for running the country."

Sampson grunted. "By *sensitive* you mean secret, which is what most government bureaucrats will stamp on their grocery lists if the mood strikes them."

"I agree," said the President, "that more is kept secret than needs to be. But much that should be isn't. Occasionally you will see some news guru concede that the government has to do some things secretly. The problem is that his definition of what documents should be kept secret always excludes the one he's about to ventilate. If someone in the press gets his mitts on it, that means it doesn't need to be secret. You refuse to apply any objective standard of national security, ostensibly because of the 'public's right to know' but actually because you've got it and you want to run it because it's hot," Hoskins grinned. "Dammit, Sampson, it wouldn't bother me half as much if you'd only admit it. You're human, you're selfish, and you're ambitious, just like me. Let your hair down, boy."

Sampson, who knew a rhetorical seduction when he heard one, kept every lock demurely in place. "You suggest that most journalists would publish truly sensitive information for the sake of doing so," he said. "But you're wrong. Of course we're not selfless. But we care about our country every bit as much as you do." He shifted in his chair again so he could reach his notebook, which he placed on the table as nonchalantly as he could.

Hoskins's head snapped around. "This is off the record," he said.

Sampson said airily, "From here on in? Fine."

The President barked, "From word one, pal!"

"You should have told me. It's too late now."

"Parker *told* you it was off the record."

Sampson shook his head. "He said his call to me was. He didn't say anything about the meeting."

Until now, Sampson had felt that all Hoskins's physical and forensic maneuvers—even the flashes of anger—had been precisely managed. But Hoskins had suddenly lost control of the situation. He was speaking not to one but one million—one hundred million when the report was picked up, as it inevitably would be. Sampson was shocked by the change in Hoskins's demeanor. He jerked to his feet, pushing his chair back so hard that it nearly rolled into the fireplace. He stood stolidly, gracelessly, his arms dangling at his side. "Do you think I would talk like this for publication?" he said in anguish.

"You already have, Mr. President."

Hoskins began to drift along the wall, keeping his face toward Sampson. "You had better think twice about what you're doing, boy," he said in a ragged, threatening voice. When he had completed a full circuit of the table, he stood over the reporter and stared down at him with sheer malice.

As Sampson looked over his shoulder at Hoskins, his face registered unease, but his tone was defiant. He lifted himself off the chair and edged it around so he could face Hoskins. "I intend to do my job, and that means reporting this story," he said, putting his notebook back in his pocket. "As a member of this nation's free press, my standing in this matter is as solid as yours. No president is above the law, and no president's actions should be beyond public scrutiny."

Hoskins's face gradually lost its manic expression. "There's only one man in this room who's above the law, and it isn't me," he said. "He's the one the framers left out of the picture in producing the miracle of checks and balances. Before I act, I have to think about the Congress, the courts, and God knows what else. To whom are you accountable, save the statesmanlike George Stevens?"

"To whom *should* I be? You? DuBois? Wheeler? The Ministry of Truth?"

The President tugged playfully at his lower lip. "It's got a nice ring to it, doesn't it?"

Sampson continued to resist Hoskins's spell. "I've never heard so much bitter media bashing in my life," he said. "You're at war with the Bill of Rights. The system is what it is. It's got some rough edges, sure. We're not perfect, you're not perfect. What would you propose as an alternative?"

Hoskins sat down next to Sampson. "I would propose only that journalists learn to practice some of the restraint they expect of the leaders of this country. Beginning right now," he said, leaning forward and looking beseechingly at the reporter. His words took on the balanced cadence of speech-making. "Mr. Sampson, this isn't just my operation. It's also yours. Those twenty-seven men aren't just my countrymen; they're also yours. I am sworn to protect them. Why do you want to prevent me from doing my job?"

Sampson blurted out, "What you're protecting is your right flank. Jack Kemp says you sold out to the Russians, and the Republicans and even some of your cracker Democrats are listening. I can just see you and DuBois sitting around the White House thinking, 'How about a little fireworks to show the folks we're tough guys?' "

The President seemed astonished. "Do you seriously think this operation is being undertaken for political purposes?" he asked softly.

"The timing's right, isn't it? Why haven't you done it before? Some of those poor bastards have been rotting in Lebanon for seven years."

Hoskins stood up, buttoned his coat, and said, calmly enough, "I order you to kill this story."

Sampson stood, too, and spoke a little uncertainly. "I refuse."

The President sighed and said, "Well, then, we have an unpleasant situation here, don't we?"

Eugene Hoskins's first major initiative as President was convincing the stewards in the White House residence to leave his butter dish on the kitchen counter rather than stow it in the refrigerator. His favorite snack was peanut butter and butter on raisin bread. He liked his butter soft and spreadable, but the stewards were understandably reluctant to risk letting the President poison himself. Rather than mention it to his staff and create a bureaucratic incident involving fourteen people and ending with the stewards being reprimanded by an imperious deputy assistant usher, he had taped a piece of White House notepaper to the dish with the note: "Please leave out. E.H." It worked the first day, and he removed the note. The following evening the butter was back in the refrigerator. The following morning, he mustered the stewards in the kitchen. He thanked them for their service to their country, said he would take full responsibility for the butter and its effects, and gave each an autographed picture. Bingo.

As he made a sandwich Friday night, Hoskins wished Charles Sampson had been as easy to handle as the stewards. He got a beer from the refrigerator and walked into his darkened sitting room. It was decorated as the Reagans had left it, though they had taken the giant wide-eyed portrait of Nancy that had hung over the mantel. During the transition between administrations, Hoskins had considered closing off most of the third-floor family quarters and living in two or three rooms, but his staff had bucked him. "The leader of the Free World," said one memo, "should not live in a cramped bachelor's apartment." The aide raised the specter of invidious comparisons in the press with former California governor Jerry Brown, rumored to have slept on a mattress on the floor of his $325-a-month Sacramento apartment. The President-elect had not remembered saying anything about a mattress on the floor, but for once he acquiesced to his exercised imagemeisters, keeping the entire suite open but using only two or three rooms.

It was lonely without a First Lady. But there were also advantages. The trouble with a First Lady was that the President always had to worry about what she was doing in the way of good works, whether the public and the press considered it worthwhile or just a cynical exercise in public relations, whether his West Wing staff was on speaking terms with her East Wing staff, and whether she was spending too much on clothes and silverware. Someday soon the problem would be a First Lady's understandable refusal to give up her law practice or corporate position for the sake of avoiding the appearance of a conflict of interest. Hoskins's troubles would've been more traditional. He dearly wished he had them. *Meg would have loved every single minute of this,* he thought, smiling sadly to himself at the memory of the way his wife had thrown herself into her duties as Louisiana's First Lady before she was killed in a small-plane crash six months into their first term in Baton Rouge. Their two grown children valued their privacy and stayed as far away from Washington as they could, visiting Hoskins only on holidays.

He dropped wearily into his reading chair and set his snack on a side table, flipping on the lamp. He sat motionless for a moment in the tear-shaped bubble of light. It *was* lonely, all the more so because it didn't have to be.

Gene Hoskins, the most eligible bachelor since Prince Charles, was surrounded by beautiful, ambitious, talented, exciting women. He was the white-hot center of a galaxy of shining faces and soulful, highly charged glances—secretaries, staff assistants, network correspondents, and deputy secretaries of state, all skilled professionals, many of whom made it abundantly clear by way of shy smiles and silky, downcast eyelashes that they were willing to bear the additional burden of ministering to the chief's emotional well-being.

Some presidents, installed in the White House without a wife, would have indulged themselves to the point of mental and physical collapse. But in Gene Hoskins's Washington, not a few social observers were remarking sotto voce how seldom the President appeared to embrace such opportunities. In the era when Gary Hart had gone down the tubes because he couldn't keep his zipper up, Hoskins had the opposite problem. Should a starving man still be hungry after being locked up all night in a Dunkin' Donuts? And who would blame him for pinching a dozen crullers? People wanted their presidents to be good, but they also expected them to be human. The consensus of his aides was that—assuming they could put the right spin on the story—Hoskins's approval rating would shoot up five points if he would only get himself laid. But it was not a subject any of them felt comfortable raising with him. One who did in the early weeks of the administration—a speech writer who proposed in a memo that it wouldn't hurt if Hoskins was "seen" in public with a woman now and then—found himself spending the next six months drafting congratulatory letters to Eagle Scouts.

During his first year in office, he had an occasional, purely sexual encounter, just as he had as governor after Margaret's death. But oh! the complexities of illicit sex in the modern White House! While he had plenty of energy for the act itself, he had neither energy nor time for the emotional exertions that went along with it. Dating was problematical, since he could not very well take a female assistant to sit in the presidential box at the Kennedy Center, and soon he came to believe that it would also be improper. Sleeping with aides led to an ambiguity in his relations with them while awake that interfered with the efficient operation of the staff command structure. And he could not abide having women call on him formally. After eight years of a nine-to-five presidency, the American people had voted for a worker bee, not a social butterfly. So Hoskins resolved to save himself for retirement, or at least for his second term, and to find whatever comfort he could in the solitude and quiet of the residence when he returned there each evening.

Tonight he found very little. He picked up the telephone and asked the operator to get Parker DuBois.

"Hello?"

"Park."

"Mr. President."

"Carole there?"

"She's still at work."

"Oh," said Hoskins, sounding disappointed. "She's a good kid, Parker. Pretty, too."

"I know, sir. Thank you." DuBois paused, waiting for Hoskins to state the reason for the call. "You need anything?" he said finally. "Want me to come down?"

"Hell no. You two go out. Have a quiet dinner somewhere."

"All right." DuBois paused again. Hoskins did not speak. "Mr. President, how'd it go with Sampson?"

Hoskins stared into the empty room. He had a tense, joyless smile on his face as he answered. "Could've gone a lot better," he said. "But I don't expect he'll be writing the story."

"Why not?"

"Because I locked him up."

FIVE

SPECIAL AGENT BILLY WORTLEY, DRIVING HIS BLUE Fairmont, followed the blue Fairmont containing Ned Flach and his mysterious passenger past the Lincoln Memorial, over Memorial Bridge, and into Virginia. His partner, Al DeMarco, was dozing, and Wortley was sulking about the overtime.

They'd worked the ten-to-six shift together at the White House, a wild and woolly day of standing on post outside the Oval Office, standing on post in the Rose Garden, standing on post in the residence, and standing on post outside the Cabinet room. By now he should have been at home watching "Dallas" while his wife put the kids to sleep with their Captain Choco-Chunks action figures, seized during the family's regular Friday evening raid on McDonald's. Normally by ten he was wrapped around two cold ones, and by eleven Gloria was wrapped around him. Instead he was hunched over the wheel, glowering through scratchy eyes at Flach's taillights as the two-car motorcade, traveling in the right-hand lane at a stately fifty-three miles per hour, passed National Airport and Mount Vernon on the George Washington Parkway and then picked up I-95 south. With luck he'd be home by before midnight, but after an evening spent herding the little monsters around by herself, Gloria was sure to suspend his grazing privileges.

She thought he had it easy, loitering at the White House eight hours a day for forty-five grand a year. Damn straight he did, and he'd earned every stultifying minute. Presidential Protective Detail was boring and therefore brutally exhausting, but it was a lot easier on his nerves than finding old corpses in hot apartments or exploring alleyways splattered with the red-slick human detritus of unconsummated drug deals. He was especially glad to be through with trying to put asunder men and women who were united in holy matrimony and trying to kill each other. He and every other police officer in the world would have preferred disarming a pipe bomb with a Q-tip to calling on quarreling taxpayers.

On a midsummer's evening nine years before, Patrolman Wortley had been dispatched to a drab bungalow in south Houston after the neighbors complained about a noisy fight. He entered slowly and carefully and identified himself to the couple, who stood exchanging murderous glares over the coffee table. An evaporative cooler had lowered the temperature in the house to a subtropical 95 degrees. As his last official act as a policeman, Wortley had touched the man's naked, sweaty shoulder and opened his mouth to say, "Mellow out, sir." The lady promptly heaved a cheap, lead-crystal jigger at Wortley, who woke up the next day in the hospital with a concussion, twelve stitches, and a month's disability during which to ponder other avenues of law enforcement. Someone gave him a Secret Service brochure, and he read about the travel, the contact with the high and mighty, the state-of-the art equipment, the regular hours. . . .

Damn. If there was a right way to ask a man to give up the beginning of his weekend, his boss, the blandly officious Ned Flach, didn't know it. "Will you and Al stand by," he had said, saving the question mark for later. "I may have to take a civilian to the safe house in Nokesville, and I'll need a follow-up." DeMarco just shrugged and said, "Sure thing, chief," and Wortley couldn't help but smile, pissed off as he was. Al could head home, eat a pound and a half of pasta, and go to sleep in front of the tube, or he could go to sleep in the car now and eat later. Same difference. But Wortley had his end of the vestige of a human sexual relationship to hold up. He figured he had about 250 Friday nights left before one or the both of them said the hell with it.

They had left the interstate for a dark two-lane road that ran near the northern bank of Bull Run in central Virginia. There were no more trucks behind him bearing down with their high beams. In fact, there was no one behind him at all. As he began to slow down to ease into a sharp curve, Wortley looked up for a moment and flipped his rearview mirror off the bright setting. Just then, there was a crash. At the sound, Wortley slammed on the brakes and DeMarco woke up. In three seconds, both agents had opened their doors and rolled out, crouching low and reaching for weapons in their ankle holsters.

"Holy Mother." Wortley heard DeMarco's horrified incantation from the other side of the car. Their headlights showed Flach's car crunched into a pine tree. Wortley reached into the car for the high-powered flashlight mounted in a charger pack under the dashboard, and DeMarco used his keys to open the trunk and pull out a first aid kit and a portable respirator. They ran together to the accident.

The door on the driver's side had popped open, and as he ran, Wortley shined his light toward the car. Flach's right hand lay motionless in his lap while he reached across his chest with his left to release the shoulder belt. He winced at the effort of holding the broken arm still.

"Damn," exclaimed Wortley. "What happened, Ned? Are you all right?"

DeMarco helped Flach ease out of the car. "You been on the radio yet?" Flach asked.

Wortley went to the front of the car and pointed the light through the shattered windshield. The passenger was on his back, his body bent into a right angle the wrong way. His feet rested on the floor, his head on the hood, and his wide eyes pointed straight up, frozen in a final moment of agony. Brains oozed and blood flowed from a jagged crack in the top of his head. "Oh, my God," Wortley gasped, pounding against the car with the butt of his flashlight.

"I said, have you been on the radio?" Flach said. He was leaning on DeMarco and hobbling around to make sure his legs were all right.

Fighting for breath, Wortley burst out, "Shit no we haven't been on the radio! It's only been thirty seconds."

"Good," said Flach. "Good." He pushed DeMarco away, walked unsteadily to the car, and leaned against it, cradling his broken arm in his healthy one. "Maybe we can fix this mess yet. Al, check these trees for paint. Then go turn off the lights and see if the passenger's got ID on him. Billy, pull yourself together and fish out your badge. Anybody that comes along, wave it and tell them to keep driving."

After the President's call, DuBois had hung up the phone, put on his jacket, and left the apartment, taking a cab to the White House rather than waiting for his car. He was in the family quarters in fifteen minutes, where he and Hoskins sat fidgeting, fuming, and mute while the steward poured coffee. Once they had openly discussed the most sensitive aspects of national security policy in front of the unfailingly discreet White House help. But they couldn't discuss this. DuBois had pulled a straight chair over and set it opposite the President. Hoskins was still slumped in his easy chair, his hands stuffed awkwardly into his pockets. Their eyes roamed over the room, fixing everywhere but on each other. They never touched the coffee.

When the steward left, the President spoke peremptorily. "It's done, Park, and it can't be undone. So let's please not agonize."

The utter perplexity of the situation impelled DuBois to make a detailed accounting of the utterly obvious. "For the first time I am aware of in the history of the United States," he said, "a president has thrown a newspaper reporter in the pokey with no warrant, no charges, no nothing." He shook his head, lost in the sheer horror of it all. "I really can't believe this is happening, Gene. We're deader than Kelsey's nuts."

"Parker, would you stop dramatizing?" Hoskins said. "Lincoln suspended habeas corpus during the Civil War."

"You're not Lincoln. This isn't the Civil War. He got away with it. We won't."

Hoskins reached for a book lying on his side table. "This is Sherman—"

"We're from Louisiana, Gene," DuBois said with heightened alarm. "You're going to call a press conference and quote *Sherman?*"

Hoskins ignored the interruption and opened the book. "—General Sherman talking about reporters who put his positions and plans in the Yankee papers, which Confederate agents bought for two cents and smuggled to Richmond." He read aloud: " 'I know the enemy received from the press notice of our intended attack on Vicksburg and thwarted our well laid schemes,' " he said, the stentorian tones he used for speeches to the Democratic national convention sounding enormous in the small, still room. " 'I *know* that the principal northern papers reach the enemy regularly and I know that all the vigilance of our army cannot prevent it, and I know that by this means the enemy can defeat us to the end of time.' " He cast a pleased glance over the top of the book at DuBois, turned the page, and continued. " 'Who can carry on a war thus? A day will come when the press must surrender some portion of its freedom to save the rest else it too will perish in the general wreck.' " The President closed the book and put it down with an authoritative smack. *"He* threatened to *hang* reporters who endangered his army and country," Hoskins said, jabbing his forefinger at the book.

"He was nuts," DuBois said. "A certifiable head case. Besides, who'd he hang?"

Hoskins shrugged. "Nobody," he said, adding significantly, "as far as we know."

"Which puts us back to square one," DuBois said.

"Namely the political crime of the twentieth century without even a crude nineteenth-century precedent."

The President looked irritated. "Answer me this," he said. "Is this operation critical to the long-term security of the United States?"

"Virtually, yes."

"What would've happened if I'd been forced to abort it because of a press leak?"

DuBois was silent for a brief moment. "O'Brien would have been discredited, perhaps fatally," he said. "Our counterterrorism efforts would be crippled, and our still shaky international reputation further damaged. I'd worry about the prospects for getting the START treaty ratified. In sum, we'd be the laughingstock of the world, again. Plus we would lose the election."

"Isn't curtailing the freedom of one unpatriotic shithead for a few hours worth avoiding all that?"

DuBois's head bobbed in agreement and exasperation. "I've no doubt about it," he said. "Personally, I wouldn't care if you dropped him head first off the Washington Monument. You've sold me, but you won't sell the country, because Sampson's colleagues are not going to view this with scholarly detachment. They are going to chew our butts but good, and you know it. This is going to make the Saturday Night Massacre look like the White House Easter egg roll." He shook his head again and chuckled without pleasure. "I can't wait to see what Stevens will say in the *Post*. He'll write an editorial on the front page and put a big red, white, and blue border around it."

"Screw the *Post,*" the President said petulantly.

DuBois eyed Hoskins to see whether he was being teased again. Satisfied he was not, he said, "An admirable sentiment. But it won't just be the *Post*. The story will play the same way everywhere, from the networks to the *Bangor Bugle,* and our justifications will be lost in the self-righteous din. No matter how much we talk about Lincoln and Sherman, no matter if we reenact Second Manassas on the

Ellipse, we're going to lose in the court of public opinion. The media aren't going to call our witnesses."

"Parker, you underestimate me," Hoskins said. "If the raid fails, then the action I took to protect it will appear unconscionable. It is then," he said, rapping the Sherman book with his knuckles, "that I will take some personal comfort from the bluebelly's wisdom as I'm being hauled off to a minimum security prison farm somewhere. But if we succeed, I think the American people will accept putting one preppie on ice for thirty-six hours in order to free twenty-seven guys who've been in jail for as long as seven years." The President grinned. "Hell, Parker, when they come home under the protection of the United States Marines you won't be able to see Chuck Sampson for the bands, balloons, and pretty girls."

"Maybe," said DuBois defiantly. "Maybe not. In any case, it's a damned cynical calculation."

"It's also a necessary one," Hoskins said, looking stern, "made by a president who decided this military operation was necessary."

"I'm not lecturing you," DuBois said. "I've no right to."

"Sure you do," Hoskins said generously, the clouds passing as quickly as they came.

"But I just don't see how it's going to fly."

Hoskins smirked. "Rare indeed is the White House advisor who underestimates the President and overestimates the people. I saw a poll that said sixty percent of our citizens don't know the Constitution protects freedom of assembly and religion. This is not exactly a nation of dyed-in-the-wool civil libertarians."

"Social science doubletalk," DuBois said. "Pollsters and professors love to demonstrate how much smarter they are than the American people. But smart or stupid, folks have a vague but nagging feeling that politicians aren't supposed to arrest reporters."

"I didn't arrest him," said Hoskins. "Needless to say I didn't run this one by the White House counsel's office, but what I believe I have committed is a kidnapping." He looked away from DuBois for a moment. "Which brings me to a subject I confess I had not given much thought to before now."

"Yes?"

"If you walk out of here and go curl up with Carole rather than the desk sergeant at the second district precinct house—"

"—I am guilty of obstruction of justice, or withholding evidence, or something. I know. I figured that much out on the way over. I undertipped the cabbie as a result."

"And?"

"And what?"

"What are you going to do about it?"

DuBois was enjoying the moment. "What should I do?"

"You should turn me in, I suppose," he said curtly.

"Which would accomplish what?"

Hoskins ticked off the items on his fingers. "You would preserve your personal honor," he said. "You would demonstrate that we are a nation of laws and not men, and you would be richer than Croesus from speeches and book contracts. They'll make you president of LSU. After you retire, every third journalism student in the country will come around and sit with you on the front porch, and Carole will serve them lemonade while they kiss your ass."

The advisor cocked his head, pretending to consider the scenario. "Not quite," he said. "You can count Carole out."

"Why's that?"

"She wouldn't bother with a man who betrayed his friends."

Their eyes locked. The room was silent. Then Hoskins said, "Haven't I betrayed you by taking this action without telling you and then involving you after the fact?"

"You occupy this office by virtue of the individual choices of fifty million Americans," DuBois said. "They trusted your judgment. How can I not do the same?"

"Mr. President."

They looked up and saw Ned Flach standing in the shadows just inside the door. His right arm was in a sling.

"What is it, Ned?" the President said in an urgent growl. "What's the matter with your damned arm?"

"I'm sorry to bother you, sir. But there was a problem with the reporter."

It was eleven o'clock Friday night. The Saturday paper had been put to bed, and the Sunday paper was yawning and brushing its teeth. Funnies, classified ads, the magazine, and the other soft sections had already been printed and shipped to distributors. But the main news sections would be open another twenty hours, waiting for late-breaking stories and a few of the long, analytical "thumb suckers" that were read by the people they were written about, by other journalists, and even occasionally by normal readers, most of whom, however, made a mental note to go back and read them later which they promptly mentally misplaced.

The newsroom was nearly empty and nearly quiet, the loudest sound being the anachronistic clatter of the manual typewriter of an elderly, irascible, but much valued sports columnist who would later slip a copy aide a few dollars to enter his story onto a terminal. One day twenty-five years before, when the technological revolution came to the *Post,* the columnist had been given an IBM Selectric typewriter and a list of codes the writers were supposed to put in their copy to identify beginnings of paragraphs and italics to the typesetting scanners. The same evening the cleaning lady found the Selectric in the maintenance closet. The columnist's editors told the technical wizards to leave him be, and the next wave of the future—the installation of desktop terminals—left him and his antique Underwood high and dry. A hand-lettered sign pasted on the side of his filing cabinet said, "Computer-Free Zone."

Carole was at her desk, too, revising the final paragraphs of a Sunday piece slugged "Whither Fed." Stevens had assigned it to her personally. She was to decide whether the

President's new chairman was running a tight enough ship in view of the leak of his plans to the *Post,* which had caused such turmoil in the financial markets. By posing the question the *Post* would be creating an issue where before there was none. The leak had resulted not from the chairman's inefficiency but from Carole's diligent development of her sources. She liked to think she'd have done as well if the Fed were run by Andrei Gromyko. *But that's the news business,* she thought as she polished the peroration and, with a loud groan of relief, scrolled back to the beginning of the story to proofread it a third time.

She sat in a loose beige skirt and blouse with her legs crossed beneath her, her stockinged knees tucked under the arms of the chair. After six hours of uninterrupted composition and revision, she felt somebody should flip her over to prevent sores from forming. Her attractive dark features, which normally bore a bright and persevering grin, contorted as she squinted at the increasingly blurry green letters on the screen. Her hair was piled on top of her head, bolted out of her way with bobby pins.

Carole didn't care much for her story. She enjoyed reporting, not ruminating. These editorials-cum-quotes were not her style, but they were George Stevens's, and it was his newspaper.

She looked up to see the normally gregarious national editor, Herb McGraw, rush by her desk without a word or glance, apparently plotting the shortest distance to Stevens's lair. *What's* he *doing here?* She focused her attention on to the screen again. She had to finish and file in twenty minutes and get to her apartment to purge the impurities from her body. *Fat chance,* she mused as she took a sip from her umpteenth cup of sour *Post* coffee.

DuBois had called a few moments before, sounding in need of feminine comfort. Could she still make it? he'd asked.

"Count on it," she had said, cradling the receiver between chin and shoulder as she reunited a split infinitive and inserted a missing quotation mark.

"Hurray," DuBois said. "Pick you up at your place in an hour."

Pulling her hands away from the keyboard to grab the receiver with both hands, she had turned away from the screen, smiling brilliantly. "With the boys in tow?" she said in a mischievous whisper. "Can we still neck in the backseat?"

"I'll be in a cab, big shot," he said. "But we can do whatever you want, as long as we don't get one of those prudish Senegalese drivers. Hurry up. I love you, though I can't imagine why. Your kind is nothing but trouble."

Distracted by DuBois's unwontedly overt testament of affection, she assumed her kind meant women.

He continued, "Also, pack a change of shorts. I'm taking you away from all this."

"Really?" Carole said, turning back to her story with renewed enthusiasm. "For the whole weekend?"

"For the whole night. I've got to be back by two tomorrow—three at the latest."

"What do you have in mind?" she groused, spitefully deleting an anonymous negative quote that Stevens would have loved. "A sleeping bag on the Mall? Various lewd acts on the steps of our treasured national monuments? A hot dog for breakfast? Geez, Parker, how far can we get in fifteen hours?"

Sounding a little too cheery, he said, "I have in mind a pretty little bed-and-breakfast—with a pronounced emphasis on the bed—in historic Appomattox Court House, which as you may recall was the birthplace of the restored American Union. En route there and back we can engage in the kind of spirited *intellectual* intercourse the hurly-burly of Washington makes so difficult. But if you'd rather meet at my apartment for a quick—"

"Never mind," she'd said. "I surrender. See you in an hour, lady-killer."

"George."

Stevens was at his desk in evening clothes, staring intently at his VDT. He turned and cast an unsettled, irritated look at his national editor, who was standing over him. "What's the problem, Herb?" he said, clearing the screen with three expert keystrokes. "What're you doing here?"

"I was going to ask you the same question. Chuck Sampson's been killed in an auto accident in Virginia."

Stevens's head jerked back. He hissed, "When?"

"Sometime in the last two, three hours. We got a call from the local cops."

"How?"

"He wasn't drunk."

Stevens barked, "I know that. He wasn't a drinker. Answer my question."

McGraw looked at him oddly. "Apparently he skidded on some oil on the road just as he went into a curve," he said. "He hit a tree and went through the windshield." He stared at his feet and shook his head. "It's a damn shame, George," he said. "He was an arrogant little shit, but he had potential. He could've been a great reporter."

"Right," Stevens said. "No seat belt?"

"Apparently not."

"His own car?"

"Sure. Why not?"

"I meant, was he alone?"

"Oh. Yep, he was."

"What do they say he as doing out there?"

"They don't. I guess he was going for a drive. Anyway, how should we handle it? Up front?"

"Yes." Stevens paused. "No. Put it in suburban."

"George, he's one of our—"

"Dammit, Herb, when some citizen gets smushed in the sticks it runs in suburban, right? Why should we give preferred treatment just because the kid worked for us a couple of years?"

McGraw shrugged. "Whatever you say." He started to leave.

Stevens waved him back in. "Did he have parents?"

"I suppose so."

"I mean are they alive somewhere? Get me their names and number. I'll give them a call."

"I can handle that for you."

"No, I want to. I should do it. And the girlfriend, too, poor gal. Get me her number, all right?"

When McGraw brought the numbers and left for home, Stevens turned back to the computer and once again used his master password to open Chuck Sampson's personal storage area. He called up the main menu:

SEC-HHS. NTS
DEP-SEC-HHS. NTS
MEDICARE. NTS
HHS-PRESS. NTS
WALKER. NTS
1MEDICARE. TXT
2MEDICARE. TXT
SIS. LTR
JOEJACKSON. RVW
ROBINSON. NTS
OBRIENAIDE. NTS
DOD-PRESS. NTS
DUBOIS. NTS
HANSEN. NTS
RAID. TXT

He reexamined the final file, which contained the draft of Sampson's article on the upcoming raid, and then read backwards through the list, opening the files one by one to isolate those that were about the raid. After copying these six files to a floppy drive on his desk and putting the diskette in his coat pocket, he called up the original files one by one and performed the complicated series of commands it took to delete them irretrievably from the memory of the *Post*'s computer.

Then he looked at the slips of paper McGraw had brought him. He put aside the one with the names of Sampson's parents. The other said, "Girlfriend—Amanda Wilde," and gave a telephone number. He dialed it and sat back and stroked his chin, watching through the glass partition as Carole Nelson straightened her desk and strode off toward the elevators. He wondered how much Sampson had told her when he had seen them talking at her desk.

He wondered how much DuBois had told her, too.

I really can't be sure, can I? He heard a click on the line and then the electric voice of a panic-stricken woman. *"Chuck?"* she said. "Where are you?"

On the streets of Washington, Parker DuBois was recognized by one person in three; away from them, by one in three thousand. In the village of Appomattox Court House, she happened to be the proprietress of the rambling twelve-room boardinghouse where he and Carole spent the night. When he went down for the newspaper at nine-thirty Saturday morning, she intercepted him at the foot of the stairs and personally ensconced him, well cushioned by several flowered chintz pillows, on an Early American couch in the sitting room off the foyer. "We normally don't serve downstairs," she said, "but in *this* case. . . ."

By the time he was into his second cup of coffee, DuBois had promised her autographed pictures of the forty-first president of the United States for an assortment of children, siblings, and friends, all undying adulators of Eugene Hoskins and all his works. He also said he would arrange a VIP tour of the White House for her entire delegation. Satisfied, she withdrew, leaving DuBois with the unhappy reflections that had kept him awake most of the night.

The Secret Service's elaborate but hasty cover-up of the circumstances of Sampson's death had changed the complexion of the situation he and the President faced so dramatically that it had proved to be quite beyond them. After Flach left, the President announced he would call off the raid and resign. He said he would go through with the raid and *then* resign. He said he would go through with the raid, announce what had really happened to the reporter, see what the reaction was, and then *probably* resign.

Finally, they had decided nothing. On Saturday afternoon, the President would give O'Brien the final go-ahead. If it succeeded, DuBois knew they would not want to dampen the thrill of success, so a decision on the Sampson matter would probably be postponed. It would no doubt be postponed again when DuBois told the President that full disclosure would doom the arms treaty in the Senate. Then there would be some other reason to postpone it, such as the realization that they had made the matter infinitely worse simply by already postponing it twice. The worse it got, the more reasons there would be to postpone a decision. And there was still the election.

DuBois hoped the Virginia police were as dumb as they looked.

He considered Sampson's actions unconscionable and Hoskins's justified, at least in the long run. The accident couldn't have been helped. Still, the enjoyment had suddenly gone out of the practice of government. He didn't feel guilty, but he felt sick, tired, and cheap.

He had planned this trip as his and Carole's last hurrah. The secret between him and Hoskins would loom too large between him and Carole, or so he had believed on his way to meet her Friday evening. She might be ambivalent about the business she was in, but she wouldn't be about his role in the death of a fellow reporter. Before, he had lied to protect her from knowledge she would find needlessly burdensome, and she had known it. It was the critical element in the compact that made their unnatural association possible. But now, by expressing mild surprise at the news of Sampson's death, he would be lying to protect himself. That he could not bear. If he told her the secret, she would not understand it and could not keep it. She was too honest a woman and too good a reporter. It would mean the end of them anyway, followed by the end of everything else. So he took her away for one more night together before he told her it was over. To protect her, to protect him, to protect the sanctity of what they had shared together, he would have to think of *some* damn reason to tell her they were through.

But by the time his cab pulled up outside her building, he had not figured out what to say. She was waiting on the curb, and his heart began to ache at the sight of her. A favorite song came into his head:

For suddenly I saw you there
And through foggy London town
The sun was shining everywhere

She climbed in, bringing along a gust of air full of the smells of perfume and brushed teeth and damp, scrubbed hair. After she hugged him and kissed his cheek, he pointed out she had brought only a purse. She smiled demurely and said, "Mind your own business, General Lee." They took the cab to National Airport and rented a car, DuBois declining the standard government discount because he would be paying the bill—a tiny gesture of ethical purity he found comforting.

After a Roy Rogers dinner eaten en route, they reached Appomattox in the wee hours. Mrs. Tiggywinkle, or so Carole had dubbed her, showed them their room, brought extra towels, cracked the window, closed it again, pointed out the thermostat, and finally bustled butt first out the door, flashing a matronly though vaguely salacious grin. While DuBois watched, Carole unpacked her purse like a magician pulling animals out of her hat: a toothbrush, a pair of panties, and then, with an elaborate flourish, a long, sheer, fitted nightgown not of DuBois's previous acquaintance.

He helped her into it and then helped her out of it again.

They flung open the window and sank deep beneath the patchwork quilt and then kicked it off as the heat of their bodies repelled the cool night air. As he kissed her, he reached up and, uncharacteristically, turned off the light by the bed. She slid from underneath, pushed him onto his back, and rose over him, turning the light back on again so she could see his strong chest and arms and he could see the movement of her shoulders and breasts. Usually they hurried each other, afraid the phone would ring. Tonight they lingered and stalled, certain no phone would ring because there wasn't one in the room. The adolescent intensity of their lovemaking surprised and delighted them but ignited a small spark of worry, too, in Carole because it reminded her of Parker's unusual behavior and moods over the previous few days, in DuBois because he was guilty that the most intense expression of his love was merely physical.

His hands brushed her hips, stomach, and nipples, then reached up along the ridge of her collarbone to her tensed, long neck. He lightly touched her closed eyelids and her parted lips, and she grasped his wrist and kissed his fingers as she rose and fell on him. But the position was two for him and one for her, so he reached down again and caressed her to help her reach an orgasm. When she had, he sat up, encircled her with his arm and, staying inside her, lifted her up and lay her down on her back. Just at the end he put both his hands around her face and kissed her as hard and as deeply as he could.

That was theatrical as hell, he thought a while later as she nestled against him and he covered them with the quilt. A lot of effort for nothing. He would sacrifice his career for Eugene Hoskins. He already had. He could even contemplate going to prison for the sake of what they had tried to accomplish together. But he wouldn't give up Carole.

He was amused by the thought that he'd always believed it would be a miracle if he and Carole managed to get out of town together. He and Debbie had had everything going for them, having built their marriage on the twin pillars of a healthy, enlightened mid-fifties high school courtship followed by residency within the same zip code, at least until he went off to Indochina. In contrast, he and Carole partook of each other the way a marathoner drank water, in a few brief, desperate gulps every five miles. Having been raised in the sixties, Carole at first seemed better suited to a less structured relationship. But over time DuBois discovered that people's emotional needs did not change the way tastes and fashions did. She didn't necessarily expect a dozen roses on Valentine's Day, but she also didn't expect his attention to drift into the arcana of warhead sublimits while she was trying to describe her own worries and crises. DuBois soon realized that a successful romance still required a certain properly balanced sufficiency of sack time and face time. While they rarely achieved it, DuBois and Carole discovered another of life's little secrets, which was that the proof was in the trying. Their spirits were strong, their flesh was willing, and they exulted in the scarce, rich pleasure of each other's company. Eventually they came to love each other with all the open-eyed certitude of two mature, capable adults who recognized quality and comfort when they saw it.

Even the small things about her that he once found irritating had somehow become endearing—certain exaggerations of voice and gesture, such as the way she flipped her hair back and overenunciated during an argument, or the drawn-out "ooh-kay" she used to force an end to a telephone call. He was, of course, dimly aware that there were things about him that got on her nerves. But the unendurable thought of giving her up made him realize that her idiosyncrasies were like the ornaments and variations in a favorite sonata, the moments of variety the listener anticipated to keep from being lulled by the plain, pretty, familiar melody. He guessed he was hooked. So he would have to improvise, he had thought, stroking her hair as she dozed. The months ahead were draped in looming shadows. He couldn't possibly face them without this one source of absolute contentment.

In the morning he had slipped out of bed, dressed, and begun his plot by coming downstairs ahead of Carole so they wouldn't read the paper together. He asked Mrs. Tiggywinkle to take a tray to her with the *Post* tucked under the edge of the plate. He knew if Carole found the inevitable item about Sampson while in his presence, his deceptive powers would be overcome. But if she discovered it alone and then mentioned it to him, he might be able to wing it.

As Mrs. Tiggywinkle struggled up the stairs with Carole's tray, Parker glanced at the front page, then the second, then the third. He looked in Metro and on the front page of the suburban section. It was on page five, below the fold—a routine four-paragraph police story under a one-column headline. DuBois was simultaneously pleased and miffed. The *Post* obviously thought it was an ordinary accident, or it would have played the story bigger. On the other hand, Carole would probably miss it. But when she did learn about it, he could just say he had overlooked the story, too. *Fine. I'll worry about it later.* His orderly, ethical life had become *ad hoc*.

"Come in," Carole said at the knock on the door.

"Good morning, young lady," Mrs. Tiggywinkle said briskly, shoving the door open with her rear end and thus entering the room as she had left it the night before. "Mr. DuBois asked me to bring you some breakfast."

Carole noticed her hostess was getting more pleasure out of speaking Parker's name than was entirely fitting. Glancing at her nightgown on the floor, Carole pulled the sheet up in time to hide her naked shoulders but not the deep blush spreading over her face. She smiled shyly as the woman put the tray on the bed. "Parker sure knows how to treat a lady, doesn't he?" Carole said.

"I wouldn't know, *miss,*" said Mrs. Tiggywinkle, bending laboriously to pick up the nightgown. She shook it out and draped it carefully over the end of the bed, like a deputy marshall serving a summons. Again presenting her hindmost aspect, she swept out the door and, after glaring at Carole over her shoulder, pulled it shut.

Carole lodged a pillow behind her and sat up, reaching for a Danish with one hand and for the *Post* with the other. Her eyes caught the date on the top of the front page, and she automatically made the rapid, routine calculation women made on the morning after if they had forgotten to the night before. She stopped chewing, put down the paper, and counted again on her fingers.

"Oops," she said.

Seven hours later, Carole sat in front of George Stevens's desk, willing herself not to erupt in tears of white-hot rage. She had been summoned by a message left on the answering machine in her apartment.

It appeared she was being fired.

"So you didn't even know about your colleague's death?" Stevens said. "Don't you read your own newspaper?"

"George, don't be ridiculous," she said. "It's buried in the back of the Virginia section, which I normally don't even see. I would venture to say that you don't see it much, either. And besides, I wasn't aware you'd started giving spot quizzes."

"There are other ways to find out what's happening on a newspaper besides reading it *in* the newspaper," he said. "Where were you all night and morning?"

"Until eleven last night I was right over there," she said, gesturing toward her desk with her chin and then setting her jaw. "After eleven I was minding my own business."

Stevens came from behind his desk and leaned against the front of it, just a few feet from Carole's chair. "Last night," he said, as if speaking for the record, "one of my reporters died in a lonely, ugly way after spending two days knocking his head against the wall trying to write the most important story of his career. He came to you for help. You refused. He told me yesterday he hadn't been able to pin it down. I told him not to sweat it. He left here just before seven. I guess he couldn't sleep, so he went for a drive." He grunted, glanced at Carole with distaste, and then looked away again. "If you had decided once—*just once*—to put this newspaper ahead of your sex life, Chuck Sampson might be alive today."

Carole's eyes grew wide, and her mouth fell open. "That's outrageous!" she said. "It's insulting, and it's obscene. I'm sorry about what happened. But whatever he was working on, it was appalling for him to suggest that I call DuBois. That's not honest reporting, it's a lousy, cheap trick. I get my stories through good hard digging, not by insinuating myself with people's sex partners. Anyway, if you had a problem with my refusing, why didn't you take it up with me?"

As Carole spoke, Stevens rose and walked to the window facing the street. If anyone had been looking in, they would have seen he was smiling like a gambler with a pile of chips on the winning number. *She doesn't know shit.* "Because I knew it wouldn't do a damned bit of good, sweetie," he said. "Because I knew that at heart you're not a newspaper reporter. You're a mistress."

She fought successfully to retain her composure. "I am one of the best reporters on this newspaper," she said firmly.

"You're not on this newspaper anymore," Stevens said, still looking away from her. *But how did they manage the bit with the car?* "You're out of here tonight. You have two weeks' severance."

"George." She waited for him to turn and look at her grim face. "I won't need two weeks."

Captain William Bentley DeMuth, his curly, jet-black hair barely disturbed by the fifteen-knot Mediterranean breeze, stood on the deck of the *John F. Kennedy* in the dark, which was precisely where his sketchy orders had left him. For nearly twenty-four hours, since just before midnight Saturday, assorted navy and marine commando units had been arriving from all over the Middle East, though fewer than he would have expected for a major operation.

Ten of his precious fighters were fueled below deck, their crews standing by. Now a Sea Stallion helicopter containing General Robert O'Brien was ninety seconds out, or so reported his communications officer via the short-range receiver with earplug that DeMuth carried in his shirt pocket.

At least now he would get some answers. With feet planted well apart and arms folded across his chest, DeMuth stared into the darkness from which the helicopter would come. A half-dozen senior officers clustered a few feet behind him, speaking quietly to one another, aware of the old man's pent-up frustration and sympathetic enough to let him alone.

In front of him, the landing pad flooded with light just as he heard the faint buzz of the rotors. Reflected light illuminated DeMuth's face, which was craggy, handsome, and uncharacteristically sullen. A man entrusted with one of the most powerful and sophisticated pieces of war-making machinery in the world was not a man for whom it was necessary to paint a lot of pictures. He could guess why he had been ordered to delay shore leave for 5,600 officers, sailors, and airmen and proceed to a spot just over the horizon from Beirut. But guessing was for enlisted men. In seven years of command, DeMuth had grown accustomed to more or less knowing what the hell was going on.

He had never met Bob O'Brien, and yet here he was turning over an eight-ship battle group to him and his motley collection of shoe-polish-streaked irregulars for some sloppy Chuck Norris feature in Lebanon. O'Brien's three-year-long accumulation of money and power had been the talk of every wardroom and mess in the navy, a bureaucratic soap opera of historic proportion. But it had never occurred to DeMuth that he would be providing the stage for O'Brien's first production.

The helicopter came in low, its running lights appearing to skim the deck. Just before the noise made conversation impossible, he heard one of his officers yell, "Wonder why he didn't just stroll across the water from Alexandria?"

DeMuth smiled to himself and lowered his head for an instant to acknowledge the gesture of commiseration. The chopper touched down, and the door opened immediately. Not waiting for the staircase to be cranked out, O'Brien hopped to the deck and reached up to retrieve a duffle bag and briefcase, which he carried himself. He walked directly to DeMuth, dropped his bags, and saluted, an unnecessary but graceful gesture of deference to the ship's commanding officer. DeMuth returned the salute, and the two men shook hands.

"Permission to come aboard, Captain?"

"Welcome aboard, General," said DeMuth, turning to face his officers. "Meet my XO, Commander Turnbull."

O'Brien shook hands with him and then turned back to DeMuth. "Captain, I appreciate that this mission has already put extraordinary demands on you and your outstanding crew," he said, "in spite of the fact that you have been told damn little about it."

DuMuth's voice was as flat as a drunken bugler. "Don't mention it, General."

"But I should mention it, Captain. If you were less of a gentleman, you'd say it was a royal pain in the ass. In the world we live in, this kind of cloak and dagger business is necessary, but that doesn't make it easy for honorable men such as you and me. All I can do is promise that throughout this operation, the safety of your men and this vessel will be uppermost in my mind."

"Thank you, General," said DeMuth with genuine surprise and appreciation.

"Would it be convenient for you, and whichever of your senior officers you might designate, to receive a briefing in fifteen minutes?"

"I'd be delighted," said DeMuth. He nodded at one of the officers and gestured toward O'Brien's bags. "Meanwhile, let's show you your quarters."

"Thank you, Captain, but I won't need any," O'Brien said, picking up his luggage again. "Just a conference room and a pot of coffee. But may I borrow your Mr. Turnbull for a second?"

"Of course."

O'Brien turned to the executive officer. "Commander, before we go any further, I wonder if you might open a line to the situation room in the White House. They're standing by. I'd appreciate it if it was kept open for the duration."

A few hours later, the deputy metropolitan editor of *The New York Times* was dressing for Saturday night at the theater when his wife told him his boss was calling. She held the cordless telephone to his head while he continued to struggle with his clip-on bow tie.

"Yeah, Sam," he said. "What's up?"

"I just got a call from an old friend at the *Washington Post.* George Stevens fired Carole Nelson."

"The Fed reporter? Why? She's good."

"I don't know why, and I don't care. Just get hold of her for me. See if she'll come up for lunch Monday."

"Okay," said the deputy. "But how?"

"Come on, Nick," said the editor, "you used to be a reporter, right? Try information. But get on it quickly, would you, please? I want to make her an offer before the *Journal* gets wind of this."

SIX

AT 10:00 A. M. SATURDAY, AS HE WATCHED THE SEQUENTIAL, super-high-resolution images form, dissolve, and re-form on his CRT screen, U.S. Navy Lieutenant Ralph Daniels was enjoying a microwaved hoagie from 7-Eleven and a tiny moment of jingoistic satisfaction. He had no doubt the radical Shi'ites and their Iranian masters knew the United States, with its Lacrosse spy satellites in geosynchronous orbit over the Middle East, could watch convoys, small groups of men, and even individual vehicles gleaming against dusty desert roadways. But did they realize that seven thousand miles away, in a reconnaissance installation inside a mountain somewhere in Maryland, Ralph Daniels could watch a man walk out onto the parapet of the old Basta prison in Bas Beirut, stretch and crane his neck toward the setting sun, and urinate off the side?

Daniels laughed quietly. *I wonder whether the National Security Agency analysts can confirm that he's circumcised.* A fresh image came up, showing the jailer's bald spot, which given the angle of the shot probably meant he'd lowered his head briefly to admire himself as he shook off the last drop of moisture and retracted. A moment later he turned and began to wander back inside.

As he noted the event in his log—thus creating a record that, since it was written on acid-free paper, would endure for centuries in the archives of the Department of Defense—the lieutenant felt a nostalgic tingle. He and his Lebanese friends had shared many such moments. Soon he would go off duty. After preparing to transmit the electromagnetic imagery record of his four-hour shift to Washington, he made a final, unofficial notation: "Ape's Last Piss."

"Good night, Beirut," he murmured as his friend passed out of sight. "And good-bye."

The Summerland Hotel, a four-times-rebuilt, currently pastel and Art Deco oasis on the Lebanese coast two miles south of the old prison, was what the whole town used to be: chic, sexy, and prohibitively expensive. In a city riven by twenty years of civil war, it was a ferociously guarded enclave of fun, sun, peace, and quiet for anyone who could afford it. Its customers were diplomats, businessmen, and those Christian and Moslem warlords who were willing to leave their gunsels at the door, Dodge City style.

In the summer, the wide, curved beachfront along the inlet was decorated with well-to-do young people whose oiled, olive colored bodies glistened like the sand under their soft feet. Its five restaurants, one beneath a giant glass dome that was one of the city's few remaining unviolated landmarks, were among the best in town. They were also the only restaurants whose clientele was never inconvenienced by assassination attempts or the purely culinary disruptions experienced by the cafés that depended on the city's power supply, which supplied no power at all as many as eighteen hours a day. Private generators kept the steaks sizzling, and a crack private militia made sure they were the only dead meat in the place.

But at 2:00 A.M. on Sunday, May 31, the Summerland was as barren as the rest of the benighted city after hours. A statistically insignificant portion of Bob O'Brien's four-year, $10 billion budget had persuaded the owner to instruct his private soldiers to turn people away at the gate beginning Friday afternoon. These disappointed would-be revellers, along with a few overnight guests from Thursday who were transferred to other, less decorous and more dangerous lodgings, were told that the generator was down. All Saturday night and into early Sunday morning the private beach, normally aglow from giant spotlights that illuminated the foaming Mediterranean surf and the faces of wandering lovers, was pitch-dark. Guards, reinforced and supervised by a half-dozen of O'Brien's frogmen, were posted to the north and south of the hotel and kept the beach clear for a mile and a half.

Even they were surprised by the suddenness and silence with which the two JEFF-B hovercraft appeared. Running without lights, gliding as smoothly and stealthily against the horizon as mice along the edge of a kitchen floor, making hardly more noise than the waves and breeze, they were guided by sonar and a signal from a transmitter that O'Brien's men had carried ashore. The first vessel rustled against the sandy bottom of the inlet and soon had accomplished a feat virtually unprecedented in the recent annals of American industry: the successful exportation of U.S. made vehicles to a Third World country. They off-loaded a fleet of thirty Jeeps, some bearing Syrian insignia and the others grainy photographs of the Ayatollah Khomeini and Musa al Sadr, the Lebanese Shi'ite martyr, which were attached to hoods and fenders with strips of masking tape. The second ship slipped in beside the first and off-loaded 120 men resembling Syrian soldiers and Shi'ite militiamen. Then the vessels pulled away from shore and were gone.

The commander, Colonel Arch Smathers, was dressed as a Syrian army sergeant, his skin darkened by six months of ultraviolet treatments, his light beard and thick, droopy moustache seeming to bespeak an uneventful, discipline-dulling, eight-month tour in President Assad's weary peacekeeping force. He had only a few whispered exchanges with his men as they found their vehicles, checked out the equipment concealed on them, and made sure the sea air hadn't loosened the portraits of the heroes of Islam. Within fifteen minutes, they had formed a column that with headlights off threaded through the grounds of the hotel, past the front gate, and up a small hill to the main road, where it turned north for a half-mile.

At the first fork in the road, the ersatz Syrians continued north, toward Basta prison, where Ali Rahmi's information promised ten Americans and two West Germans were being held. The rest made for a hide-site in a verdant triangle northeast of the airport. Here Beirut was as it had been centuries before, thickly forested and fragrant with jasmine and cedar. A sixty-man squad would wait there for the signal to proceed to Shiya, the squalid labyrinth where eight hostages were held under guard by forces loyal to Immad Mughniye, the leader of *Hezbollah* and one of Iran's principal surrogates in Beirut.

Since their arrival, Smathers's group had exchanged no radio messages with Bob O'Brien aboard the *Kennedy,* which waited a hundred miles offshore, and he would not, unless something went wrong. The mission was running according to a clock that had started ticking several hours before when the President of the United States had turned from the window behind his desk and nodded to Parker DuBois. Since midmission adjustments could not be made, the schedule would not withstand a single element falling behind. O'Brien had insisted on this policy over his advisors' objections. For fifteen years, Beirut's Shi'ite cells had been thwarting Western intelligence agencies by simply not using the telephone, and in his planning, O'Brien had torn a page from their playbook. His men would make no sound until they wanted to be heard.

Many unfriendly ears were listening. While Damascus was cooperating, Moscow was not. The technicians aboard its warships in the area, and their counterparts on assorted Soviet-manned fishing trawlers and commercial vessels, had been logging every radio message and virtually every sound aboard the *Kennedy* since it arrived on the scene thirty hours before and began steaming in a thirty-mile-long north-south circle. Increased radio traffic or other activity might well be reported to Teheran, and Captain DeMuth was making sure that all the *Kennedy*'s noises were routine. His 2,500-man air wing was unspread, and his radio operators sent short, unremarkable messages to Sixth Fleet headquarters in Naples. He had even arranged for them to spend seven minutes receiving the Friday evening and Saturday baseball scores and standings.

Meanwhile, the hovercraft had stolen a march on the watchful Russians with their fifty-knot, 350-mile voyage from Alexandria. A separate commando force would soon arrive aboard a C-141 transport and parachute into the Bekaa Valley to rescue the nine hostages at the Shi'ite stronghold near Ba'albek. This operation would be backed by four AC-130U Spectre helicopter gunships, which would disrupt any organized resistance the Iranian Revolutionary Guards stationed there attempted to mount. The Syrian-manned SAM sites in the valley, which had given United States flyers trouble before, were supposed to remain unmanned this time. Thirteen hundred miles away, at NATO's newly expanded air base on Sicily, American pilots were climbing into F-16Cs that had been given desert camouflage paint jobs to make them look like they belonged to the Israeli air force. At 0600 hours, after making their leisurely way across the Mediterranean and refueling in air off the coast of Egypt, they would plunge to an altitude of 300 feet, enter Lebanese airspace ten miles south of Sidon, and then veer north toward their target. The Soviets would surely notice them penetrate Lebanon, but by that time, they would be moments from Beirut. Teheran would not be able to notify the Shi'ites that it was an American strike until the operators now hiding in the park had taken full advantage of the appearance that it was an Israeli strike.

During O'Brien's briefing for DeMuth and his officers, in a conference room off the Captain's cabin, the XO had asked how the commandos in Beirut would know when to move without using their radios.

The general said, "Because there'll be the most awful clatter you ever heard when those boys take out Beirut International Airport. That means 'go'."

The command master chief, whose business it was to sympathize with the men who had to execute officers' grand schemes, was appropriately skeptical. "Do you really expect it to go that smoothly, General?" he said. "Don't get me wrong. The radio silence bit is dramatic as hell. Peter Jennings is gonna love it. But you could safely say we're prone to screwups in this part of the world. Wouldn't it help to have a little coordination among our units?"

"I can see your point, son," O'Brien said patiently. "But the operators are trained to avoid only *unnecessary* communications, not if they or the mission are endangered. To answer your specific question, the quality of our intelligence is such that I have a reasonable expectation of success. What we also have in our favor is plenty of time written into the plan for unanticipated delays and plenty of cooperation from the Syrians, who are delighted we're finally going to kick *Hezbollah* in the hind end."

"Why haven't *they* done it?" asked the chief.

"How many Syrians are blindfolded and chained to a basement wall in Beirut?" snapped O'Brien. "An American problem requires an American solution, don't you think?"

DeMuth, who an hour before had been miffed that his ship might be imperiled under another man's command, was now dogged by the perverse fear that it was now extraneous. He cleared his throat and said, "General, what exactly are we here for?"

O'Brien had anticipated the question, and he tried to field it gingerly. "You'll get us home," he said. "The *Kennedy* will stage the retrieval of the operators and hostages at dawn Sunday, both in Beirut and at Ba'albek. If something goes wrong on the ground, I have units aboard that can assist. You are also providing a base for command and control, though admittedly they'll be very little of either once the President lowers the green flag." He glanced at his watch. The call from DuBois was due in thirty-seven minutes.

O'Brien looked across at DeMuth, who was proud of his ship, his men, and their capabilities and remained suspicious they weren't going to be tested. He continued, "Captain, as you well know, at this moment there's a giant blinking yellow arrow pointing straight down at us saying, 'Here are Americans. Look sharp.' As this ship's own experience showed ten years ago, when we lost two planes and Lieutenant Mark Lange trying to take out this same installation in the Bekaa Valley, it's difficult to mount an effective strike from a vessel that every military authority in the world is watching."

DeMuth responded quickly, his voice laden with sarcasm. "As *you* well know, General," he said, "that mission failed after our friends in Washington suddenly moved up the time five hours and increased the size of the strike force. The JCS have got to have something to worry about besides whether we're going to use twenty-nine planes or thirty-eight and what color shorts the pilots are wearing."

"And what would that be?" said O'Brien with his best grin, which softened DeMuth's fierce expression somewhat. He continued, "The ship's capabilities aren't at issue. Nor is micromanagement. What is at issue is the advisability of trying to run a multifaceted surprise operation from four and one-half acres of aircraft carrier that you can see from the planet Mars." He looked around the table at the sullen faces of the other officers, who weren't used to loose talk about what their ship couldn't do. "What we've always lacked out here," O'Brien said, "and what Hoskins has managed to get for us, is the active cooperation of other nations in the region. Five years ago the role the Italians and Egyptians are playing, not to mention the Syrians, would have been inconceivable. In the 1980s, most of the Delta Force's problems were purely logistical. We could never get them on-site from Fort Bragg fast enough to engage the enemy because we had to spend forty-eight hours begging the A-rabs for landing rights on Malta."

O'Brien caught himself, cooled down with a sip of ice-cold coffee, and continued more temperately. "In contrast, the men going in tonight have been out here for two years at bases in Egypt, Jordan, and Saudi Arabia, training in this climate, eating the food, and learning the language. Say what you will about this President, but for my money, he's the first politician who's given us what we need, besides money and hardware, to defend our country against these bastards." He rubbed his hand back and forth through his crew cut, squinted at the captain, and said, "Damned if he hasn't extended the boundaries of the civilized world just a tiny bit."

Once a president had approved an operation such as the Beirut raid, the standard drill was for him to go about his normal business to avoid giving the impression that something was afoot. Eugene Hoskins's normal business on a Saturday was to sit around the White House and call aides away from their weekends for urgent meetings that could probably have waited until Monday, so no one much noticed when he spent the late afternoon and evening with Parker DuBois in the Oval Office.

Pat Robinson and Felix Mendez were in the situation room, but because of O'Brien's no-news-is-good-news policy, by 4:00 P.M. Saturday, with the hovercraft still hours away from the beach, the only thing Hoskins had learned from the *Kennedy* was that everything was "apparently copacetic." This didn't sit well with the man in the hot seat. Hoskins had led troops in Vietnam and knew that military decisions were best made by military commanders on the ground. He didn't want to interfere, but like DeMuth on the carrier, he sure as hell wanted to *know*. He had had DuBois call downstairs several times "just to check," but had finally gotten the message. The next definitive word would come from Sicily and Cairo, where O'Brien had generously permitted air controllers to tell the commander-in-chief when his F-16s and the C-141 were wheels-up.

So they waited and fidgeted. At the cocktail hour—Reykjavik time—Hoskins had called for a steward.

As DuBois sipped his beer, their usual weekend libation, and watched the President gaze distractedly into thin air, it occurred to him that the decision to adopt a meticulous but flexible plan and automatically abort if it went sour relieved them both of a tremendous burden. Twelve Aprils before, during the Iran rescue mission, another president had been alone with his NSC advisor in the tiny study a few steps from the Oval Office when word was flashed that only five helicopters had made it through the sandstorms to the refueling point at Desert One. The plan for storming the embassy and freeing the hostages required six. Zbigniew Brzezinski, tempted to urge Jimmy Carter to press ahead, instead suggested he find out what the commander on the scene advised. Delta Force's legendary Charlie Beckwith advised they come home, and the exhausted, discouraged President agreed, put down the telephone, and lowered his head to the desk.

Carter, reluctant to commit military forces to begin with, saw the seeds of political oblivion in their humiliating failure. Brzezinski suspected he could have persuaded Carter to order the men into Teheran. Nagged by guilt about the opportunity that might have been lost, he sought out Beckwith and asked him what would have happened if the mission had gone ahead with only five helos. The gruff Georgian had said, "It would have been a disaster." This had struck DuBois as a dramatic example of the practical limitations of civilians' theoretically unlimited authority over the military. Soldiers would live to try again, but Hoskins, like Carter in 1980, had an election campaign to wage. An unanticipated result of O'Brien's fail-safe planning was to insulate the mission from extraneous political pressure.

DuBois winced as the memory of Friday evening's potentially deadly political disaster flooded in. *What the hell are we going to do about Sampson?* He glanced at the President, who was looking into his glass as he swished the liquid around the rim. DuBois considered raising the subject, then put it aside. *He's got enough on his mind.*

"Parker, what are we going to do about our dead reporter?" said the President, looking up.

A moment before, DuBois had been feeling smug about not having to make any tough military calls in the next six hours. Now he was faced with the toughest political call of his life. He had wrestled with it through a sleepless night and this long, weary day, wrestled so strenuously that when Carole called and said she was leaving the *Post*, the information had barely registered. Finally he'd changed his mind and decided to urge the President to make a clean breast of it. But he hadn't expected to be asked the question so soon.

"Honestly, Gene," he said, "I don't know." He felt suddenly Mephistophelian as he took a deep breath and added, "I do feel we can't reject the option of just letting it ride."

Hoskins didn't seem very surprised. "You mean not say anything more?" he asked. "Let the impression persist that he was driving by himself?" DuBois nodded. The President said sharply, "You realize the risk that runs, of course."

DuBois smiled to himself, remembering that the night before he had been doing the maximizing and the President the minimizing. "Sure I do," he said. "I was the one who didn't think we could beat it if he was alive. Now that he's dead I'm convinced we couldn't." The President didn't answer. *He's already come to the same conclusion.* DuBois remembered something that had bothered him all night, and it permitted him to refocus his frustration. "How the hell did it happen, by the way?" he asked. "Those guys are at least supposed to know how to drive."

The President lowered his head and tried to massage the weariness from his brow with the heel of his palm. "I called in Ned Flach this morning to ask him just that," he said.

"He told me the kid had been badgering him ever since they left the White House."

"I can't blame him," DuBois said. Hoskins looked away. *He's sorry about the accident but still hates the little bastard's guts. Come on, Parker; you're paid to sympathize with the man, not the boy.* So DuBois went on, "Can't you just hear him? 'You muscle-bound son of a bitch, just wait till I get to a telephone'!"

"That was about the size of it, actually," Hoskins said. "Ned can take the abuse, of course. Remember when we went to the University of California at Santa Barbara during the '88 campaign? It was like Kent State, with those kids screaming 'war criminal' at us. There weren't many, but they sure gave the Secret Service a hard time."

"As I recall, it was the other way around."

The President, ignoring DuBois's remark, took a sip of his beer and went on. "The problem, Park, was that the kid tried to climb out of the car. Ned was distracted by trying to keep him from getting the door open and didn't see the curve." Hoskins drained his glass and set it down so hard on the table next to his chair that his friend thought it would break. "*Damn* it," he muttered.

DuBois could see the pain in the President's eyes. He'd had a dead American on his hands less than two days before he would send two hundred more young people off into the night. There were grieving parents and shocked friends, and he couldn't even write them a letter or invite them to the White House. Instead, he had tacitly lied about it and was now seriously considering never putting it right.

While Hoskins had ordered men to their deaths for principle's sake before, DuBois knew it had been a monumental struggle for him to do it in peacetime and especially in relativistic times, when principles—involving national and spiritual ones—were déclassé, even suspect. DuBois knew the final decision to approve the Beirut mission had not been made in Hoskins's mind until the last possible moment. But Sampson's death had queered his calculations before the fact and soured the contentment he deserved to feel afterwards. It was a portent, like the rotting entrails of an augury. Ned Flach, standing in the shadows Friday night, cradling his broken arm, and telling his horror story in his maddeningly bland way, had presented Hoskins with an unfamiliar dilemma: making a choice that he believed was the right one in the long run—because he believed in what he was doing as President—but that would also save him grave personal travail. In his own mind, DuBois felt the dividing line between the two contrary motives becoming indistinct. That meant Hoskins felt it, too. On top of that, there was the unmentionable, unbearable possibility that Sampson had died to protect a mission that would fail.

To Arch Smathers, driving the lead Jeep in a twelve-vehicle convoy, the sweetness in the air was reminiscent of the desert in his native Arizona after a spring rain. Each place was more lush, more full of life than visitors expected. Most of his attention was focused on the road and on peering at the buildings they passed, looking for lights and dark figures in windows. But he couldn't ignore the primary stimuli of smell and the way the damp air felt against his face. It reminded him of driving through the night at home with far prettier company in the other bucket seat. The memory communicated Lebanon's tragedy as he'd never understood it before. Here the roads belonged to the guns.

"Post Abel in five hundred yards, sir," mumbled the lieutenant next to him, his eyes darting back and forth between the odometer and the printout in his lap, both lit by a penlight he held in his teeth. They were approaching the first real test of President Assad's cooperativeness. The two operators in the backseat gripped their AK-47s a little tighter.

Two figures blocked the road. They separated, and Smathers stopped between them. "Good evening, Sergeant," he said in flawless Arabic. "We're here to relieve you."

The Syrian met the eyes of every man in the Jeep. In

spite of himself, he produced a small, approving smile. "You are late three minutes," he said, in mock testiness and busted English. Then he switched to Arabic. "We made you some Turkish coffee, which I fear you will find unappetizing enough when fresh and far more so if it's allowed to age any longer." Everyone relaxed. Within ninety seconds the four Americans in the second Jeep had replaced the soldiers in the guard post. "You boys go with Allah, all right?" Smathers had said, shaking hands with the genuine article before he and his unit melted into the night.

By 0400 every post along the coast road between the hotel and Basta prison was held by American commandos. An hour and a half later, all the men except those at Post Abel moved north, like the curling tail of a scorpion, to gather on the rocky headland at the western tip of the promontory where Bas Beirut was built. Here they were a minute and a half from their objective. To the east, past the empty black skeletons of the great downtown hotels, they searched the tops of the mountains that swelled behind the city for dawn's first faint glow. And they peered south, too, back toward the airport, straining to hear the thunder of the F-16s.

At 0550 hours Lieutenant Emilio Stewart, waiting behind the wheel of his Jeep in the pines two miles southeast of Smathers's force, was trying to clear the decks. Others had responsibility for securing the perimeter of the hide-site and confirming what they already knew from the satellites, that the *Kennedy*'s helos would have two clear acres in which to land. His assignment was just to sit with the engine running and try to relax before the fury began in exactly seven minutes.

It was hopeless. He was trained to empty rooms. But every time he tried to empty his head, he was deafened by his wife's quiet voice.

Two nights before, when they had last spoken, he had

been in the rec room of the staging base outside Cairo. With their daughter in her arms, she had been sitting next to her bed in the Long Beach naval hospital. When Cecilia was born three days earlier, the doctors said they thought something was wrong with her heart. After a while they took her out of ICU, wrapped her in a blanket, and gave her to her mother. Stewart had called that night, praying for a miracle. In a tone of desperation that frightened him out of his wits, his wife had said to him, "Our baby is dying."

If he had shared the information with Smathers, he would have been instantaneously scrubbed—guaranteed. The psychological profile of the optimal special forces operator did not include fresh, sudden grief. So he didn't share it, and it didn't find its own way from California. *Gracias, Tomasita.* She could have pressured them to bring him home. His going wouldn't help his darling child or his wife very much, and staying meant the world to him. Life was trying to beat him down, to make him old before his time. Not going to his family until he'd done his job was youth's last selfish defiance of the inevitability and persistence of suffering.

He put his hands on top of the steering wheel and rested his head against them. When he did go home, his job would be to help repair their violated dreams. He was prepared for that, but only after he'd finished the rescue he'd been sweating over. It didn't occur to him what would happen to his wife if he didn't come home at all. That, too, had been left out of the operator's psychological profile. *Surprise, speed, success.*

"Would you take a look at him?" said a voice. "The GBU-15's are chewing up the airport, we're about to drive into hell's basement, and Emilio's asleep. Talk about *cajones.*"

"Hey taco face," said another. "You there?"

Emilio looked around. The shaggy heads of his three buddies were framed by a burning glow in the southern sky. He could hear the jets screaming up and away, back out to sea.

I missed the opening credits! "Hell, I've been ready to go, assholes," he said, for the last time feeling under his shirt for his .45 and under the seat for the gleaming twenty-pound steel pole that they all called the key to the city. He gunned the engine and yelled, "You gonna get in, or should I just pick you up on the way back?"

They got in. His partner, a skinny, dark-haired Kansas farmer's son named Evan Saunders, took the right-hand seat as everyone tightened the grimy checkered *kaffiyehs* around their heads and faces so only their eyes and noses showed. They were wearing green combat pants and black T-shirts bearing assorted anti-American slogans. The two men in the rear sat up on the backs of their seats with the butts of their machine guns anchored against their thighs.

When the caravan hurtled out of the park onto the main airport road, it looked every inch a contingent of militiamen setting off to awaken their Shi'ite brothers to the latest Israeli banditry. They drove a mile south and then screeched off the boulevard and into the twisting alleys of Shiya, a rat's nest of crumbling tenements and shanties. Massing at the first intersection, they leaned on their horns, fired in the air, and screamed at the empty doorways and windows.

"The Zionist entity has struck the airport," shouted Emilio Stewart in gutteral Arabic. "Their commandos are coming ashore to attack Bourj Al-Brajneh. Rise and defend our Palestinian brothers against the Hebrew swine!"

They loaded up again and pressed further east, confident that scores of groggy, angry Moslems were even then making their way west toward the giant refugee camp near the airport, where the tower personnel—if the pilots had managed to follow the plan and keep them alive to tell the tale—were already confirming to anyone who called that in the first light they had seen the birds were from Israel. Every few hundred yards the Americans repeated the drill, stopping long enough to attract plenty of attention but pushing on before anyone could come out into the street and ask any uncomfortable questions. Shi'ite discipline and its imperviousness to infiltration was based on patterns of Shi'ite housekeeping. Everyone within the various sects knew everyone else. O'Brien's Paul Revere gimmick would buy them the forty-five minutes their duties in Beirut required, but they weren't prepared to give names and addresses or debate the Koranic fine points.

They could succeed only by exploiting the home boys' confidence that no stranger could find his way on their turf. The driver of the lead car had spent the last eighteen hours studying the Lacrosse images of the route, and he knew every pothole between the pines and the two-story cinder block apartment house where they would find the hostages. He drove confidently and skillfully. For an O'Brien-trained operator, an unfamiliar, unpaved maze at dawn's edge was as good as a four-lane straightaway at high noon.

In moments they were there. The Jeeps circled the building, which was dark and apparently unfortified, sitting close to the street. Four two-man units took up positions at the corners of the block with HK41 machine guns to lay down enfilading fire if necessary, though O'Brien didn't really expect the militiamen in the neighborhood to rally quickly enough.

Before Stewart's Jeep had completely stopped, he'd grabbed the steel pole and somersaulted to the ground, looking up at the first-floor windows. *No bars. Hot damn! We can save the A-bombs for next time.* He didn't look around for the other three men because he knew exactly where they were. He leapt up and plunged the bar through the lower-right corner of a window, dragging it around the frame and pulverizing the glass in two seconds. While two men jumped through the opening, he dropped the bar, pulled his sidearm, and lifted his right arm so Saunders could drape a 9mm submachine gun over his shoulder. The air was full of the sound of gunfire, all friendly, all inside. He ripped the black patch off his right arm, exposing the American flag stitched on his T-shirt, and shed the scarf so he could pull down his infrared, heat-sensing goggles. Then he and Saunders went to see if any bad guys were still breathing. They were only four seconds behind the first two men.

They didn't identify themselves or speak. Anyone alive where hostages weren't expected was doomed.

The front room was already clear. Three Shi'ites were down. One had been lying on the couch, his weapon resting beside him on the floor, and hadn't even begun to get up. The bullet holes in his forehead looked like a vampire bite. The first pair of Americans had automatically gone through a doorway on the right, and Stewart led the way to the left, down a narrow hallway. He saw a shadow in front of him and put two rounds from his .45 into its head. It sank to the floor. He passed a closed door on his right and heard a scraping metallic sound, a weapon being dragged from under a bed. He holstered his handgun and nodded to Saunders, who attached a small C4 charge to the door, stood back, and blew it. Stewart plunged into the smoke with his machine gun blazing and took out three shapes that were still gasping and staggering from the shock.

The five teams that had entered the building simultaneously were to clear the upper two floors and then converge on the basement, where intelligence indicated the hostages would be. Stewart was about to follow his partner down a stairway when he saw another closed door. An unpainted plaster wall ran from the door to the front of the building. He hit a switch on his goggles and studied the readout, which showed two upright figures on the other side and another near the floor. The scenario, suggesting two terrorists and a hostage, required him to fire chest high through the wall, and he did. The wall turned to sawdust. He shoved the door open with his shoulder. What he saw on the other side turned his guts to water.

His training was supposed to have prepared him for the shock of discovering he'd killed women and children. But here was a young mother in her nightgown, a necklace of blood across her neck and chest, draped with the laundry over a clothesline that had been strung along the back wall of the long, narrow room. *Dios mio.* Stewart stared and gagged. Her husband lay at her bare feet, which were splattered red from his wounds. The weapon leaning in the corner was a small kindness, but not enough to mitigate Stewart's rage at monsters who housed families with prisoners of war and at himself for not *just going down the damned stairs*.

Family? Mother? He was suddenly conscious of a sound that he realized he'd been hearing since he walked in. The crying infant was wrapped in a dirty blanket on a crib-sized mattress on the floor in the corner. When Emilio Stewart saw it, something snapped.

The landing zone sounded like the end of the world, but it looked like heaven to Arch Smathers, who stood on the edge of the clearing under a giant pine tree. Four Sea Stallions, rotors and jet engines roaring, were taking on hostages and commandos from the successful strikes on the two Beirut sites. The Jeeps were being parked in a corner as they came in, on top of a half-ton of explosives that had been buried in the sandy soil and would be detonated by radio when the helos were away, *maybe with some of our hosts standing there kicking the tires*.

One man, his hair hanging in tangled clumps around a gaunt, confused, angry face, was being led to his chopper. He stopped and stared at Smathers. He was a forty-five-year-old classics teacher from American University, who, after four years of being shuttled around Lebanon in boxes and car trunks, looked like he'd been in Andersonville. "Why did you kill them?" he yelled, with more force than Smathers would have thought him capable of. "For God's sake, you didn't have to kill them!"

An operator started to move him toward one of the Sea Stallions when Smathers lowered his clipboard and touched the man's arm. "I'm sorry, Dr. Travers," he said. "We really didn't mean to. But we wanted you to be able to come home, and things got out of hand. Please go with the man now. We can talk later." He was led away, sensing, Smathers hoped, that his grievance had been properly received.

Smathers rechecked his count, because he couldn't believe it. He had all but two hostages. One operator had a chest wound that might be trouble. One Jeep was missing, besides the one that had been loaded with explosives and used to make a fifteen-foot-wide hole in Basta's medieval masonry. He peered through the trees. *Where's that damned Mexican?*

A moment later they appeared. Smathers counted to four and began to think of home again. But then he saw Stewart was in the right-hand seat. *Who's driving? Is Emilio hurt?* The Jeep stopped, and one of the operators hopped down from the backseat, pulled the tarp off the rear bed, and helped the last two hostages out. One, the Reuters correspondent who'd been imprisoned for seven years, looked around absently, caught sight of Smathers with his pen and paper, and staggered over. He pointed at the clipboard and said, "Uh, do you think I could . . . ?"

The colonel smiled and said to the man's handler, "Lieutenant, make sure this man gets something to write on once we're out of here." There was a commotion at the last Jeep, and Smathers strode over.

"I said shut up!" yelled Stewart.

Saunders was nearly hysterical. "And I said you're a maniac!" he screamed.

Their colonel was mad. "You're four minutes late, and the mission's six minutes behind," he barked, turning to Stewart. "Get this vehicle—" He stopped when he saw a bundle in Stewart's hands and his alert, sullen face.

"Don't touch it," Stewart said menacingly.

"Don't touch what?"

"It's a *baby,* Colonel," cried Saunders. "He took it out of the site and just about shot my balls off when I tried to get him to leave it. Maybe there's a funny farm in the neighborhood where we can drop them both off."

"Shut up," Smathers snapped at him. "I think you'd better get ready to move out." As the confused commando stalked off, the commander looked back at Stewart and tried to suppress his anger enough to sound civil. "What are you doing, Emilio?" he said.

"I'm taking it out of this hellhole, sir."

He was holding the baby against his gut like a football; Smathers wondered if it was still alive.

Wait a minute. "Your wife's pregnant, isn't she?"

Stewart looked away. "No," he said.

"Was there a problem?"

Stewart appeared embarrassed and changed the subject. "We left about twenty satchel charges in that building. It's nothing but dust by now. How could I have left it in there? Could you have, sir?"

A small crowd was gathering, some eager to hit the road, others amused by the sight of a Syrian cowboy reprimanding a Moslem Mexican. Smathers yelled out, "I want every man on his chopper *now.*" As they broke up, he yelled out to a sergeant who was in touch with the perimeter posts. "Any sign of assholes?"

"Not yet, Colonel."

He turned back to Stewart. "Emilio, we're paid to kill 'em, not adopt 'em." He edged closer. "If you leave it here, I'm sure someone will look after it. But if we stay any longer you'll be risking the whole group. You should be thankful these guys don't have artillery or armor." He began to reach out for the bundle.

Stewart's right hand drifted toward his holster. Smathers looked into his burning black eyes and stopped cold. "I'm sorry, sir," Stewart said, "but there's just no way."

In Washington it was 1:00 A.M. Sunday. The President was alone upstairs, sitting in his easy chair with his face resting in his hand.

The Bekaa Valley team was en route to the *Kennedy* with all hostages safe. The gunships had lingered to destroy the Iranian training installation, Assad's *quid pro quo* for giving his SAM units the day off. Now they were on the way home, too, and Hoskins was waiting for word that the main force was away. The word was twelve minutes late. He kept catching himself holding his breath, trying to make time pass slower.

DuBois knocked and came in. Hoskins lifted his head. "Problem?" he said.

"All units are at the LZ," DuBois said. "All the hostages are okay. One of our guys is injured."

"So? Why don't they move?"

The advisor explained. He concluded, "Smathers says bringing a live foreign national out requires a political decision he is not empowered to make, and O'Brien has bucked it to us."

The President looked at DuBois with an expression that could have made a snowball in hell a winning proposition. "Can't they overpower him?" he said. "They just killed about a million guys."

"Mr. President, I've told you all I know."

Hoskins stood and looked at DuBois. "Recommendation?"

"We should burn rubber."

Hoskins reached down for the phone and asked the operator for the situation room. "Is this Robinson?" he asked. "This is the President. I want those choppers in the air in thirty seconds or else. Let the kid bring the baby. Let him bring a rhinoceros if the chopper can lift it." He slammed the phone down. "Let's go," he said, heading for the door. "I want to talk to O'Brien."

By the time Hoskins reached the situation room, a conference room and communications center in the basement, Smathers's force was over water, forty-eight minutes away from the *Kennedy*. Robinson and Mendez were seated at computer terminals, processing information pouring in from all over the eastern Mediterranean and beyond. Iran had scrambled a few of its aging F-14s, which were heading toward the carrier group but would be utterly impotent once they reached it. The Soviets contacted the United States embassy in Moscow and requested information about scattered, contradictory reports it was receiving about Israeli and American military actions in the region. Israel had put two and two together and didn't like the answer. The government of Lebanon was apoplectic about the obliteration of its airport but invigorated by the blow the United States had dealt the Shi'ites, who were a constant irritant to the new Maronite Christian president. The Syrian foreign minister had summoned the American ambassador, lodged a formal protest, and then invited him to stay for an informal breakfast.

The President absorbed all this quickly. There was nothing he hadn't anticipated. Then DuBois pointed to the open line to O'Brien's command, and the President picked it up. DuBois went to an extension. "Bob?" Hoskins said. He listened for a moment. "Calm down, ensign," he said mildly. "Just see if the general can come to the phone."

"Mr. President," O'Brien said.

"Bob, I want to congratulate you on a splendid mission. Every American is in your debt. What the hell's going on with that kid?"

"I gotta apologize for that, sir. Our psychological screening process is evidently flawed. It will be corrected."

"What are you going to do?"

"We have a team ready that will subdue him on arrival."

Hoskins flashed DuBois a pained look. "For God's sake, is that necessary?"

"I believe it is. He threatened a member of his team with his sidearm and was apparently prepared to do the same to Smathers."

"Why?"

The line was silent for a moment. "They simply suggested that he leave the—" he hesitated, and DuBois and the President exchanged mild grins. "—the infant in question inside Lebanon."

Mendez had passed a printout to DuBois, who read it and handed it to the President. Hoskins scanned it and said, "We just got word that Lieutenant Stewart's week-old daughter died yesterday morning. Could that be the problem?"

"I suppose it could, but—"

"I don't want you to jump him. Do you understand?"

"Yes, sir."

"Hold on." The President pressed the telephone against his chest and turned to his staff. "Felix?" he said.

Mendez said promptly, "I recommend the child be separated from him as soon as possible and flown to Cairo, where it can be turned over to the International Red Cross and returned to its family."

DuBois, appalled, looked at Mendez and slowly shook his head. *There is no family anymore, Felix.* Then he looked at the President. An instant before, he'd been vibrant, flushed with his greatest success; now his face was ashen and uncomposed. Instantly aware of his blunder, Mendez added, "Of course there are other options, Mr. President."

Hoskins turned to Robinson. "Pat?"

As she swiveled around in her chair, her stark, pale face was in turmoil. All three assumed at first it was because no woman could possibly deal with a baby-related issue dispassionately, strictly as a matter of national policy. But she said in a calm voice, "My advice would depend on what Lebanon does. If the government files a formal protest, we would have a problem. But I doubt whether the Shi'ites will even discover the baby is missing. Still, even in the event no protest is made, returning the child would be interpreted as a laudable humanitarian gesture. In the long term, we would run the risk of political damage if it was ever discovered we had essentially kidnapped a citizen of a foreign country."

Hoskins, impressed by Robinson's display of ethics-free practicality, though not particularly pleased by the absence of a final recommendation, looked at DuBois. "So what do we do with it?"

DuBois shrugged. *Your call, big guy.* The President grunted in mock disgust and then stood for a while and looked at the telephone receiver, which he still held in his hand. Finally, he lifted it and said, "Bob?"

"I'm here, sir."

"My orders are that Stewart has custody of the child until I say different. I take full responsibility for the consequences. See that it . . . what exactly is it?"

With obvious irritation, O'Brien replied, "I'm told it's a male, Mr. President."

"Have the medics look at him on board ship. Stewart can stay with him at all times if he gets nervous about our trying to swipe it. As soon and as quietly as possible, get them to LA. I'll handle the legal bullshit in the morning. I happen to know the immigration commissioner. Finally, nobody else in your operation is to say anything to anybody about this. You with me, Bob? Great. Thanks again."

After hanging up, the President looked at his friend. "Am I even now, Parker?" he said quietly. DuBois returned a weak smile. Mendez didn't notice the exchange. Robinson, unnoticed, turned sheet white. There were more than two people in the room who weren't sleeping at night because of Charles W. Sampson.

PART TWO

SEVEN

IT EXPLAINED A LOT ABOUT WASHINGTON THAT IT followed the same calendar as elementary school. When the speaker's and vice-president's gavels fell in mid-September after a month's summer break, more than a few representatives and senators expected a stern voice with an Akron, Fargo, or Savannah accent to say, "Take your seats, class." Autumn's chilly, brilliant sunshine evoked memories of the clatter of Pop Warner shoulder pads and the smells of burning leaves and freshly printed textbooks. Old grudges were forgotten as sides were picked for new campaigns; summer-camp crushes fizzled and black-tie romances ignited. The city resonated with the power of perpetual youth. The only thing ending was the fiscal year, and even this impelled secretaries to order plenty of school supplies in order to use up their office budgets.

History may have marched inexorably, but in Washington it definitely straggled in the summertime. Hardly anything of real importance was permitted to happen in August. If it did, its historical standing was as ambiguous as the sound of the tree falling in a deserted forest, since journalists as well as officials were discharging their constitutional responsibilities in Kennebunkport, the Vineyard, or the wine country. Everyone returned tan and fit and ready to do battle with the popular belief that life was a long gray line, impervious to the efforts of men and governments to make it brighter without making it shorter. Washington may have been a free-fire zone for ambition, hunger, and covetousness, but it was also the last running wellspring of pure hope. If the world would ever be a better place, the path would be illuminated by a beacon lit here.

This year the city's rites of renewal—culminating in Eugene Hoskins's landslide reelection and the Senate's ratification of the arms treaty—had not touched Parker DuBois. He had once enjoyed fall in Washington, but as he was driven to work at six in the morning on this Monday before Thanksgiving, his thick daily briefing book open on his lap, he felt as empty and cold as Connecticut Avenue.

Glancing out the window as the car passed through Dupont Circle, he saw a pretty jogger with a ponytail, and for a moment his throat tightened. His plans to get away somewhere with Carole during the summer had fallen through when she said she couldn't take the time. For the last few months, she had sounded distant and distracted on the telephone. She dissuaded him when he offered to come up to New York for a weekend or even an evening. At fifty-five, he was invested with many awesome responsibilities and remarkable secrets, but he felt as he had nearly forty years before, when a girl from Lake Charles he had taken on a date kept putting off his follow-up invitations until she finally said she had Montezuma's revenge and hung up. Something smelled fishy.

Carole's departure had been sudden, and it remained unexplained. "George and I never did see eye to eye," she had said. "Let's leave it at that, lover." His efforts to prod more out of her were feeble because he felt May's events had deprived him of the moral authority to demand unconditional candor. In almost an instant, she was simply gone. On a rainy Sunday afternoon in July, he had sat down at his old portable typewriter and written a love letter, his first since a shorter and less self-conscious postcard he'd written Deb one afternoon as he sat at the bar of the Hotel Continental in Saigon. "This distance between us is more galling than any of things that kept us apart when you were here," he wrote Carole. "Even when I didn't see you, I sensed you. We were elements in the same matrix. It even made me feel good to see your byline, just as you used to say you'd talk back at me when you saw me quoted in the paper.

"I love you. I want you to marry me. It wasn't our intention to be separated, but we have to live with it for now. Please let me know if you still can." The only stamp he could find in his apartment was on the return envelope from a *Time* magazine subscription offer. He got drenched running to the mailbox a block away. A week later, she sent him a box of peanut brittle from Bloomingdale's, a reminder of a long-weekend driving trip when about all they had eaten was Pennsylvania Dutch junk food. She had written a note on the gift card: "Watch it—this stuff's more fattening than we thought. Carole XXX." *What the hell did that mean?* Twice he had decided to fly up and see her without calling first; both times he hadn't gone. Would he find her alone? *Yes*. That wasn't it. But it would be a futile exercise and somehow an unacceptable invasion of her privacy. Each partner in this laissez-faire love affair had dictatorial powers. If he tried to force the issue, he'd probably finish it.

As the car glided onto the White House grounds, he returned to his briefing book, reading over the marginalia he had made earlier. Another Italian government was tottering, Chinese troops were moving menacingly along the Vietnamese border, and the movement on the German right to deploy national nukes—*Force de frappe de Fritz!*—was picking up steam. *I hope Gene's had his Wheaties.*

That evening, Carole clutched the handrail and scrunched over, straining to read the "Tax Watch" column in the *Times* as the Lexington Avenue express lurched out of the Brooklyn Bridge station toward Fourteenth Street.

The paper belonged to the passenger seated in front of her, a young executive who, by virtue either of many years' experience or simply having the proper genetic material, was practicing the art of the vertical quarter-fold. Working-class people read tabloids, while professional people made a Savile Row crease down the middle of their *Times*es and *Journal*s, held them four inches from their noses, and read by half-pages, turning them around with insectile flips of the wrist. This was best done sitting down, which young, white professional men usually were, since they—unlike blacks, Puerto Ricans, Chinese, Israelis, Egyptians, Koreans, Indians, Pakistanis, and Malays of both sexes and all ages and sizes—were the only subway patrons in the urban polyglot who never, absolutely *never,* gave their seats to pregnant women.

Or so Carole had observed in her months as an oversized New Yorker. She viewed it as a practical issue rather than a sexual one. If the shoe were on the other swollen foot, she would give her seat to a pregnant man without a moment's hesitation. As it was, if a typical male yuppie was one of three people who simultaneously spotted an empty seat, he would be the only one who would walk on broken glass or the windpipes of sleeping infants if that was what it took, in the words of the upscale beer commercial, to go for the gold. Such was the Age of Aquarius in its maturity.

"Tax Watch" flipped out of view in favor of the upper left-hand corner of a Merrill Lynch ad, and Carole eased her sore neck into a more or less upright position. Her eyes met those of a young black woman standing next to her, whose sympathetic glance spoke volumes about the indignities women suffered in an era of selective egalitarianism.

"Your first?" the woman said.

"I prefer to think of it as my last," said Carole with a smile. "I vowed to try everything once, in order to live life to the fullest."

The woman sniffed. "Hope you got more than one try when you were making it."

Carole absorbed this with good grace. She had discovered

that by getting pregnant, a woman automatically invited full-scale invasions of her privacy by all other women, whether friends or strangers. A fellow tenant in her building on East Twelfth Street, an ethereal type in a billowy Indian gauze dress, noticed Carole and her condition one afternoon in front of the mailboxes. Without a word, she sank reverently to her knees, lifted Carole's blouse, and pressed an ear against her belly button. Carole nearly swatted her with a Macy's circular.

Nietzsche's last man switched to the sports section, brushing Carole's protruding stomach in the process and staring at it for a moment in indignation. The woman eyed it, too. "It's a boy," she said.

Carole cocked an ear. "How do you know?"

"The way it sticks out."

"My doctor knows," said Carole, "but I asked him not to tell me."

"Didn't your husband want to know?"

Carole inhaled and said firmly, "I'm not married."

The woman touched Carole's arm lightly and said, "Me neither, and I've got three babies. We're both better off, believe me. If I was married, I'd have four."

The train pulled into the station. Carole said good-bye and got off. The cheerful exchange had lightened her mood, and while she didn't exactly bound up the steps to the street, she felt a little less than usual like an old pack mule carrying two fat tourists up the south rim of the Grand Canyon. The cool night air made leaving the urinous atmosphere of the subway especially pleasant. As she started east on Fourteenth Street, she even forgot for a moment that she was ruined and abandoned in the loneliest city in the world.

Her momentary sense of well-being ended when she glanced at two derelicts huddled against each other in the doorway of a vacant storefront. *Who elected me Joan of Arc?* She was about to kick an empty brandy bottle down the street when she heard someone call her name.

She turned and saw a cab stalled in traffic. The turbaned driver looked at her without expression.

"My God, Carole, what happened to you?" The passenger poking his head out the window was Oscar Middleton, a high-level White House budget official. At the sight of a familiar face, Carole nearly burst with joy.

The cars in front of the taxi edged forward. "You are still going to La Guardia?" the driver said to Middleton.

"I'm working for the *Times,"* said Carole.

"I know, and that's not what I meant," said Middleton with a twinkle in his tired eyes. His species of Washingtonian worked fourteen-hour days and, when they really wanted to get crazy, took Sundays off to watch the Brinkley show.

Carole walked to the car and leaned against it, looking down at her friend. "How did I get like this?" she said teasingly. "Well—"

"You are going to La Guardia, or you are not?" The driver's singsong voice trembled with irritation.

Middleton said, "No, dammit. Here." He shoved five dollars at the driver and climbed out.

"What are you doing, Oscar?" She took his arm as they began to walk down the street.

"I was at a briefing at Federal Plaza," he said, "about the Emergency Management Agency's imaginative schemes for evacuating the five boroughs to the Catskills in the event of tidal waves and nuclear holocausts."

"But what are you doing now? Don't you have to get back? Won't Eugene miss you?"

His jaunty step and robust laugh gave Carole the feeling he was exhilarated by what for him was an act of wild rebellion. "I'm not sure the old man could pick me out of a police lineup of Bulgarian paratroopers," he said. "Besides, I'll just catch the next shuttle." They had reached Third Avenue. "Can I get you something?" He gestured toward a coffee shop on the corner.

A few minutes later they were huddled in a booth under an enormous wall painting of the Parthenon. Middleton had coffee, and to Carole's surprise the waiter was able to produce a cup of her favorite brand of herbal tea. It was only beginning to dawn on her that New York was just as uncivilized and primitive as she had always assumed except in marketing and commerce, in which it was state of the art. To survive in the new age, every short-order café within a two-mile radius of New York University had learned to anticipate and conform to successive refinements in nutritional doctrine. She didn't know it, but she could have chosen from among seven brands of domestic and imported bottled spring water and four unappetizing but healthy varieties of all-bran muffins.

"Does Parker know?" he asked.

Carole fussed with her tea bag, plunging it into the cup and pulling it out and then squeezing the tea out with the tips of her fingers. "What does he have to do with it?" she said with unconvincing absent-mindedness. He rebuked her by gently nudging her wrist with his spoon. She took a sip and said, "He doesn't know, and he won't."

"Why not?"

She gathered her hair from the side of her face and flipped it over her shoulder. "Because it would be an appalling situation," she said. "I would look stupid, manipulative, or both, and he'd quit, move to New York, and resent me for the rest of his life."

"Why?" he said. "New York's an hour away. He couldn't exactly fly home every night, but it'd be better than being left out of it entirely. By the way, why did you leave the *Post,* anyhow?"

She drummed her fingers against the table. "I got a better offer here," she said.

"Pretty cold, Carole."

"Back off, Oscar," she said crossly. "It was a pretty unhappy business."

Middleton contemplated his Eugene Hoskins signature tie bar for a moment and said, "Sorry." He came back with a smirk. "But how have you kept all this secret?" he said, nodding his head toward her midsection.

"Easy," she said, overlooking the implicit and familiar reference to her being as big as a house. "I didn't tell him. You don't really begin to swell noticeably until the fourth month, and by then the election and the treaty hearings were heating up, anyway. A couple of times he called and said he could get away for the night, and I just told him it wouldn't work out for me."

"You must recognize this may work in the short term but will be utterly ineffectual in the long term."

Carole luxuriated in this burst of Beltway mumbo jumbo. "Bless you," she said. "I've been covering the New York Supreme Court for eight months. Nobody talks to me like that anymore."

"Married people commute all the time," he continued, unfazed.

"The national security advisor is going to fly home to the wife and kid every weekend?" she said. "Sure thing." She looked into her cup, trying not to give in to a wave of sadness and frustration. She looked up again. "Besides, we're talking about the original square here, Oscar. Parker DuBois harbors the living essence of Andy Hardy. One hint that I am in distress, as he'd put it, and that would be that. He'd hew gallantly to my side day and night, and Gene'd be left in the lurch." She impulsively squeezed her shoes off and crossed her aching feet on the seat next to her, sighing with pleasure and tucking her black woolen dress around her knees. She said, "I don't want to make him do that, and frankly I don't want people to think I made him do that."

"Honey, we even won Arizona this time," Middleton said. "We shot so many Moslems in May we almost got the NRA endorsement. The Hoskins administration will endure without Parker DuBois."

"Why should it?"

"Because you need him more."

Her eyes drifted. "We'll get along. Listen, I'm not trying to be independent as a matter of stupid principle. I have many moments of terrible, hopeless despair. It would be wonderful to have him here. It's a comfort to know I could if I wanted to. But I can't take responsibility for depriving a man of the most enriching experience of his life."

"Maybe that's just what you're doing," he said.

"Come off it, Mr. Rogers," she said. "There are supposed to be men out there who like changing diapers, but Parker DuBois would much rather change the balance of power."

"So you're going to keep the kid a secret for four years?" he said. "You may not have noticed, but your profession attracts the world's biggest gossips."

"Next to yours."

He tilted his head, conceding the point. "Still, it's only a matter of time," he said.

"Why's that?" she said. "I hate to break it to you, but to the average New York journalist, Washington might as well be La Paz as far as the gossip mill is concerned. I haven't met anybody who mentions knowing Parker and I were an item."

"No one's even vaguely curious about who brought you to this pretty pass?"

She shrugged and said, "I hem and haw. A single woman with a baby hasn't been news for twenty years. If I said I'd done it myself with a turkey baster nobody would bat an eye."

"Still. . . ."

She rested the side of her head against the back of the booth. "I know, Oscar," she said wearily. "And at some appropriate moment I'll tell him that I need time to myself, or that I'm in love with the German ambassador to the United Nations, or something."

"He won't buy it."

"He won't have time to question it. He'll say, 'I've got a problem with that, baby, but let me get back to you. Dobrynin's on the other line.' "

"Wrong," he said. "It'll rip him to pieces."

"So will leaving the White House." She stared at him and said urgently, "You had damned well better keep your mouth shut."

He looked away. "That's a lot to ask."

"Why?"

"You want me to conspire in the unnecessary destruction of an exceedingly worthwhile thing."

"We could quibble about the language, but that's basically it. Will you promise?"

Oscar looked at his watch and then glanced around for the check. "I can't," he said. "But I'll do my best."

Carole felt her resolve slipping away. *I could pummel him into submission on this. I could make him promise. So make him promise, Nelson!* She put her feet back on the floor and poked around for her shoes. *What kind of idiot takes a man to La Guardia along Fourteenth Street at rush hour?* Awash in guilt and relief, she said only, "Please. I'd appreciate it."

Beth McGuire, the *Post*'s society editor, put down the telephone and sighed. This terse summons did not bode well. She had not been asked to George Stevens's office since before it belonged to George Stevens. Her infrequent instructions from him came by computer. He loved seeing society news and gossip in the paper, especially when it embarrassed the Hoskins administration, but like most other people in the business, he disdained those who wrote it. Whenever she was with two or more colleagues and the talk turned to *real* news, they treated her like a tart at a tent meeting.

She took up a notebook and pencil and slipped her sweater over her shoulders, pausing for a moment to cast a nostalgic look around her neat cubicle. *Sic transit gloria.* Her felt-bound Green Book, the Baedeker of capital society, was open next to her terminal. She closed it and returned it to its position between the dictionary and Congressional Directory. Then she slipped her reading glasses off and let them dangle from the strap around her neck, patted her neat, gray hair, and turned regretfully toward Stevens's office.

She must have misplaced a crucial wedding announcement, matched some eligible ambassador at a party with the wrong divorcée, or quoted a powerful hostess who now, upon seeing her boozy expostulations in cold, hard type, claimed she had not expected to be quoted. Still, it had been a good ten years. In what other job could she have dined at the White House with Cory Aquino and Sylvester Stallone the same evening?

She veered to the right to avoid the copy desk. *Of course!* She'd misspelled the nine-syllable name of the guest of honor at the previous night's state dinner! Or perhaps her description of the President-Forever's colorful attire had transgressed tribal law, causing a rupture in diplomatic relations and our supply of some obscure, vital mineral. After being sacked, would she be kidnapped and ritually sacrificed in the basement of a foreign embassy by high priests with commercial portfolios and diplomatic immunity?

She had stopped guessing whose milk she'd spilled and begun pondering the condition of her bank balance and the probable size of her severance package when she saw Stevens waiting in his doorway for her, smiling like Howdy Doody.

"Beth! Come in. It's been too long," he said.

"Yes," she said, catching herself seeming to imply he had been remiss. "No." *Now he'll think I mean never would have been too soon.* "It's always a comfort," she said, recovering nicely and taking the seat he pointed to, "to know you're nearby."

He settled behind his desk and began some casual instructions about how the owners and their family should be handled in her columns. They were not to be mentioned too often, lest it appear the *Post* was their plaything, which of course it *was*—here he winked—but she was to be sure to mention them just often enough, and especially in connection with their pet charities. This was exactly what she had been doing for years, since mollycoddling owners and publishers was the society writer's Algebra I. She took notes furiously.

"But you know all that," said Stevens.

She stopped writing. "I do my best, sir," she said.

"Sure you do. You're doing a great job." Glancing nonchalantly around his desk, he reached for an invitation. "Listen, Beth, while you're here. I don't know about you, but I'm tired of seeing the same pompous asses at every one of these White House functions, aren't you?"

"Um, I suppose so."

"Sure you are," he said. "They're like family reunions where you always know who's going to get drunk and how fast, and I'm not sure I can take another four years of it. Isn't there somebody at the White House social office you can talk to about inviting some of the assholes who do the actual work?"

She gulped. "Sir?"

He cast a speculative gaze over her shoulder. "Take that Beirut raid," he said. "There're probably two or three people in the NSC who put that sucker together. And yet when I go to this New Year's Eve reception"—he waved the invitation in the air—"all I'm going to see is Billy Wheeler with his chest stuck into the other room, even though he probably didn't even know about the thing till he read it in the paper."

Beth said carefully, "Ever since Ollie North they've kept the NSC staff very much in the background, Mr. Stevens."

"You call me George, honey," he said, smiling painfully. "I know they have, but there's such a thing as too much of a good thing. They ought to get an hour and a half off for good behavior, and frankly it'd be good for the paper if we could get to know some of them. Give somebody a call. Exploit your tremendous influence. Start with this New Year's soiree." He stood up. As she stood, too, he said, "Oh, and Beth. Tell 'em it was your idea. Then they'll owe you one." He patted her in her lower back as she scurried out. Then he looked at his watch. *Perfect.* He buzzed his secretary in the office next door and told her he was going to lunch.

Stevens walked fast, so if he wanted to be purposely late, he had to work at it, for example by calling employees to his office at the precise time he ought to have left. It took him six minutes to get to Chez Robert, just around the corner from the *Post.* He was down the stairs and standing at the maître d's station at 12:17, probably fifteen minutes after his luncheon date had arrived. Marshall Brandon was alone in a booth with his second Perrier, glancing around uncomfortably. Stevens grinned. *He can't take a piss without his staff to unzip his fly.*

Everyone in the room was staring back and forth from him to Brandon and pretending not to. He sauntered among the tables without looking at anyone and giving them the satisfaction of being recognized by him. *Why should I apologize for yanking Brandon's string in public? What are they going to do about it? I'm the editor of the damned* Washington Post! "Hello, senator," he said, sliding into the booth and signaling the waiter. "Something came up. You been here long?"

"No problem," Brandon boomed. "I just got here myself."

The waiter brought Stevens's martini, and Brandon watched hungrily as he took a sip. "Why don't you have a drink?" Stevens said.

Brandon shook his proud silver mane. "Sets the wrong example," he said.

"For who? Them?" He took in the room with a jerk of his head and then grinned. "For the press?"

The waiter came back to take their orders. When he had left, Brandon said, "What's on your mind, George?"

Stevens put down his drink and leaned forward, folding his hands on the table. "I shouldn't be telling you this," he said quietly.

Brandon slowly leaned forward, too, with the ambivalent expression of an eight-year-old who was about to spend his milk money on a dirty postcard.

Stevens continued. "We're working on the biggest story

since Watergate. Hoskins has stepped in it but good, and I want you to be ready."

"Ready?"

Dammit he's stupid. "For the investigation. To angle for the chairmanship of the select committee, or whatever they decide to have."

Brandon's chiseled features arranged themselves into a perfect expression of civic concern. "What's happened, George?" he asked.

"Can't say yet," Stevens said. "My boys are still tracking it down. It'll take another few weeks. But if I were you, I'd get set to move. Everybody else will sit on their butts for a day or so to see how long the story lasts. It'll last, believe me. So grab the spotlight as soon as you see it. Make an immediate, strong, judiciously worded statement of concern. And if I were you, I'd line up a staff counsel."

The senator considered this for a moment. "We brought in a good man for the treaty hearings," he said. "He's a generalist, but he's sharp, and he's fair."

"Fair?" Stevens spat. "In the twenty years they've been investigating Republicans do you think the Democrats ever resolved to be *fair?* This isn't a missile treaty. You want a man who acts fair in public and then stays up late thinking of ways to ream Gene Hoskins."

Dawning comprehension lit the stark planes of the senator's face as he said, "Is this as serious a matter as it sounds?"

"I said it's as big as Watergate. Hoskins will go down."

"And John Jeffreys," Brandon said drily, "will go up."

"He can't govern, and he can't be elected," Stevens said, rapping the table twice with his knuckle. "Hoskins's insistence on having a weak man as VP will doom the Democrats in '96. Whoever runs this investigation can be the nominee. Against Jeffreys—if he's dumb enough to run—you'll win. The integrity issue in the wake of this scandal will be gravy." Stevens emptied his glass. "It's our best shot, Marshall."

Lost in thought, Brandon had reverted to their old college

pastime of trying to balance a salt shaker on a single grain. "They went after Nixon and Reagan like Apaches," he said.

"Damn right," Stevens said.

"The Democrats are the biggest thieves in politics, but since we've almost always been in the minority against them, we've never landed a solid punch."

"Never have."

The salt shaker fell over, and Brandon looked at Stevens keenly and asked, "Is it money?"

"Worse," said Stevens, reaching over and picking the shaker up.

"You have somebody in mind?"

Stevens nodded. The tip of his tongue slipped through his teeth as he concentrated on holding the shaker steady.

"He's a Republican?"

The editor shook his head. "Doesn't need to be. Bipartisanship and all that." He grinned again. "And fairness." He reached into his pocket with his free hand and pulled out a card with a name and telephone number. He put it on the table between them. "He's just a mean, tough son of a bitch."

Brandon tucked the card away. "Should I call him now?" he said.

Stevens flashed a contemptuous glance at his friend before refocusing his attention. "What will you tell him?" he said.

"All right, all right. But how will I know when to call him?"

"You still get the paper, don't you?"

"On occasion," grumbled the senator. "The kid who delivers my neighborhood isn't going to win a new wagon this year."

"We haven't used kids out there since 1968, Marshall," Stevens said. "It's probably a redneck in a Chevy van."

"Whatever. But sometimes I don't see the paper till I get to the office."

Stevens edged his hand away from the balanced salt shaker like a retracting rocket gantry. "So sue me," he said.

"How do you do that, George?" Brandon said plaintively. "I never could do that."

The next day, Tuesday, DuBois asked for a fifteen-minute appointment with the President in the early afternoon. When he appeared in the anteroom Irene, evidently overcome by the spirit of the season, smiled with frank affection and opened the Oval Office door. She announced him and patted his arm as he walked past. Hoskins was at his desk staring at two memoranda in front of him, his face creased with worry. DuBois took one of the side chairs, and the President turned to face him.

"Parker," he said, picking up one of the memos, "I don't expect any President will be able to accomplish much in the next century."

"Why is that, sir?"

"It's a simple matter of diminishing power and lowering expectations. Let me give you some examples. On one morning in 1863, Lincoln freed three million slaves living in states that no longer even recognized his authority. Nixon spent a full year knocking heads with bureaucrats just to get the old navy building on the Mall torn down, bless him." He rolled the memo up, crushing and twisting it and then tossing it over his shoulder in the general direction of the wastebasket. "And in 1992 I cannot get my own staff to agree to cancel the damned annual Thanksgiving photo opportunity."

"You mean the turkey," DuBois said.

"Every year they find a sixty-pounder for me to wrestle with in the Rose Garden." He looked at his watch, swore quietly, and continued. "The reporters make the same stupid turkey jokes while the photographers wait until it nearly knocks me on my rear, and that's the only picture they use."

"It depends," DuBois said. "When the President's riding

high the way you are, they sometimes use a better picture. They only kick a man when he's down."

But Hoskins was disconsolate. "What I said was: 'We don't need this. Let's just skip the thing. I don't go to the Gridiron Dinner and kiss the press's ass. Does the sky fall in? Hell no.' "

"What'd they say?"

"They told me about the poultry growers. They told me about humanizing the President. They told me how mad the press is already because I don't go to the Gridiron."

DuBois smiled in spite of his own glum mood. "I'd apply one of your own lessons," he said. "When someone wants something and you don't, repackage it so they'll end up not wanting it, either."

"I fail to see how that applies." The President's tone was grim, but he looked interested.

"Tell them you'll do it if they kill the turkey."

"Say what?"

"The turkey that gets to come to the White House is never eaten. The photo caption always says, 'White House officials promised that the official national turkey would live out his days on the turkey farm.' In view of all the turkeys that aren't so lucky, that's darned hypocritical. We don't like hypocrisy. Nor do our friends in the media. So we say we're establishing a new tradition. Install a stump on the South Lawn. After the photo, the senior correspondent, Henson McMasters. . . ."

The President broke into a wide, winning smile.

". . . takes the ceremonial ax and chops its head off on national television, and we send the carcass to the Newark Boys' Club."

"You of course mean Henson," Hoskins said.

DuBois grinned again. "And that will be the end of the Thanksgiving photo opportunity."

Hoskins picked up the other memo. "Parker, your abilities have been misapplied."

"Thank you, sir." He shifted in his chair. "Mr. President—"

Hoskins interrupted. "Read this first, please."

DuBois took the paper.

November 23, 1992

MEMORANDUM FOR THE PRESIDENT

FROM: Oscar Middleton

A sensitive personnel matter has arisen that has put me in a position of having to choose between my public and personal responsibilities. After careful thought, I felt it was crucial that I raise the matter with you.

Parker continued reading. At the bottom were the usual option boxes, which in this case read, "Tell Mr. DuBois," "Do not tell Mr. DuBois," and "See me." The President's thick black check mark was in the first.

When DuBois had finished, the President said, "Is that what you wanted to see me about?"

"Yes, sir."

"When did Oscar tell you?"

"This morning."

The President stood and looked out the windows behind his desk. "You can't leave her alone in New York City with a child," he said.

Parker lowered his head. "No."

"She won't quit and come back here, will she?"

"No."

"So what are you going to do?"

"Remember when the Ford Foundation approached me last month and asked if I was staying on board for the second term?"

"Fine," said Hoskins. He turned around. "But I want you to stay in touch. I mean it, Parker."

"You've got a good team at NSC, sir. I'd suggest you look to Mendez to replace me."

"We've already spoken." DuBois looked surprised, the President smug. "I've known you twenty-five years," Hoskins said. "You're not exactly an imponderable." His expression and voice hardened. "But I have to be able to get hold of you any time I need you."

"I've already told them I'll need the flexibility to get down here whenever you say, for extended periods if necessary."

Hoskins looked at his watch again. "Damn," he said.

DuBois stood and walked with the President to the door. "You're going through with it?"

The President shrugged. "I hate to disappoint the kids," he said. "They look forward to this darn picture every year, you know."

DuBois opened the door. "Bull, Mr. President," he said.

Hoskins smiled sadly at his friend, made a limp salute with his left hand, and went to face the turkey.

EIGHT

LOUIS CAMARE, VETERAN POLITICAL COLUMNIST OF THE *Washington Post,* exuded spiritual as well as sartorial composure as he doffed his Aquascutum raincoat and took his seat on the set of "King's Capital Round Table." His white-flecked brown hair was as sleek and well-tended as a mink collar on Madison Avenue. His scarlet and blue paisley bow tie was nestled comfortably beneath his Adam's apple, set off by a discreetly monogrammed, all cotton tattersall shirt, cashmere herringbone blazer, charcoal gray trousers, and argyle socks. A pair of tasseled loafers would have been the expected touch, but instead Camare had chosen Bass's laced, buttersoft leather walking shoe in a rich reddish brown.

He was fifteen minutes early, so after picking up the microphone by his place and pinning it to his shirt, he reached into his double-gussetted Coach briefcase for something to read. To maintain his standing as Washington's most erudite columnist, Camare made a practice of using every spare minute to absorb other people's periodic prose. This afternoon he'd brought the current *Nation* and a new analysis by the Institute for Policy Studies of the impact of U.S. sugar price policies on the struggling economies of Latin America. To better match task to available time, he took the magazine, crossed his legs at the knees, and began to scan the editorials, highlighting particularly impressive passages by making neat check marks with a .05 mm mechanical pencil. The studio technicians had thoughtfully left the bright, hot spots off but bounced some light off the ceiling so he would be able to see properly.

He was halfway through a predictable but pleasing excoriation of the Hoskins administration's continued countenance of Zionist excesses in southern Lebanon when his colleagues began to drift in. First the *New Republic*'s chubby, amiable Winston Reedy tossed his dog-eared yellow legal pad onto the table, sat down, and crossed his Adidas clad feet on top of it. Camare glanced at them in mild irritation.

"Afternoon, Lou," said Reedy. "Will we see you tripping the light tonight at the White House?"

Camare turned back to his reading. "I was not invited," he said.

"For goodness sake, Louis, lighten up. He's kidding," said Alice McGuire as she sat down and began searching for a fold in her blouse's big satin bow to hide her mike. "Of course you weren't invited. Nor, I would think, was Pol Pot." She beamed at the columnist and then dug into her purse for her makeup.

Camare, now certain that his powers of concentration could not withstand further assaults, sighed and put away his magazine, surrendering to the usual asinine pretaping banter. He turned toward the Baltimore *Sun* political correspondent and said, "That, Alice, was a facile, ugly remark," he said.

She shrugged, holding out a compact mirror and poking at her shaggy blonde hair with the pointed handle of a comb. "Facile's what we get two-hundred-fifty dollars a week for, Lou," she said. Then she rolled out her lipstick, and because she was holding her lips still to apply it, her husky voice was almost all throat and tongue as she added, "You're the one who insists on lobbing genuine pearls of wisdom around Peter's pigsty."

"Alice, darling, save that kind of stuff for the program,

will you?" said the moderator, Pete King, as he settled into his chair at the end of the table. "In the week before New Year's, there's not enough news to spend a half-hour on."

"When there's no meat, we serve metaphor," said Reedy.

"Don't you mean no beef?" said King.

"No beef, no alliteration," said Reedy. "Which reminds me, Peter. Why did I draw the budget bill this week? Nobody cares about the budget in January. Besides, Comrade Camare's the economics expert."

King said, "When for the first time in history Congress leaves the omnibus appropriations bill on the table until after the election and the Christmas break, it's an issue in January. The government's been in legal never-never land since October. You'll have a ball with it."

Reedy sulked as Camare said, "Perhaps everyone's tired of hearing Reedy's affectionate justifications of Eugene Hoskins's war crimes."

"More likely," said Ethan Spravak, rushing in at the last minute, as usual, and settling next to his nemesis, "they're tired of your cryptosocialism."

Camare could hide his contempt for almost everyone in Washington except the combative conservative writer, who was now grinning at him like a gorgon. He was about to lash back with genuine hatred when King adjusted his earplug and repeated his director's warning: "Ninety seconds, kids."

Alice edged her chair into position, looking across at Reedy. "At least you don't have to deliver King's Personality Parade of the Air every week," she said.

"I resent that," King said affably. "The departure of the President's national security advisor and closest friend happens to be the most important story of the week. Sixty seconds."

"Sure," said Alice. " 'Hoskins Aide to Wed Pregnant Honey'."

Reedy looked alarmed. "You're going to say that?"

"Don't worry," she said. "I'm going to say that for a combination of professional and personal reasons, Parker

DuBois is relinquishing the reins of power to a carefully groomed successor, Felix Mendez, whose still mysterious qualifications I'll then enumerate at great length."

"Oh," said Reedy. "You mean he's 'a savvy, behind-the-scenes bureaucratic operator.' "

"Right," said Alice. "Also 'an honest broker of varying opinions, much prized for his loyalty.' "

"Twenty seconds," said King.

"One hopes that you'll also address how our distrustful President will get along without his boyfriend," said Camare blandly.

Reedy spat out, "Oh come *on,* Louis. That's—"

"Save it for the *program,* Winston," King said. "Ten seconds. Places, please." His panelists straightened up and presented their best phlegmatic but plugged-in expressions as the theme music began to play faintly through the studio monitors.

"If I'd been you," Carole called out, slamming the top onto the tea kettle and turning on the burner, "I'd have called ahead."

DuBois was leaning on the end of her living room couch, out of sight of her six-by-ten-foot kitchen. He looked around the apartment, which was bright but overfurnished, since it contained everything from her far more spacious digs on Massachusetts Avenue. He had been asked neither to sit down nor take off his raincoat, which was probably best, since the heat didn't seem to be coming up. "And you would have said what?" he said, his eyes fixing on a small wall-mounted frame containing a photograph of them together.

"Damn," said Carole.

"What?"

"The pilot light's out."

"Oh." He started for the kitchen and then thought better of it, saying only, "Do you have a match?"

She didn't answer. He heard the sound of a match being struck and leaned back again. In a moment she came out of the kitchen and brushed by him into the living room, her arms wrapped tightly around her chest. She was wearing a baggy Georgetown sweatshirt, and her hair was pulled back into a tight bun, highlighting her lustrous cheeks and turquoise and silver earrings. For the second time he resisted reaching out for her, not just because he thought she would pull away. Outside the settings where they had been lovers and friends, she seemed anomalous and strange. So he kept his hands in his coat pockets. She sat at the other end of the couch, putting her feet on the edge of the coffee table and squeezing her knees together. She shielded her swollen stomach between her arms and thighs.

DuBois moved to a bentwood rocker on the other side of the room. "What would you have said?" he asked again.

"Said about what?" she said, looking at him innocently and without evident affection.

"About my coming to New York."

"I would have said it wasn't necessary."

DuBois tried to match her bland expression. "For whom?"

She smiled for the first time, and he was startled by a flush of yearning. "You're suggesting you're here out of an unsatisfied yen to be a philanthropist and not to protect my honor?"

He shrugged. "To be honest, while I loved the old job, I'm greatly intrigued by the new one and sick and tired of working eighty hours a week," he said. "But if I'd made the move for some other reason, it wouldn't have been for the sake of appearances. It would have been because I missed you and wanted to be near you again."

She cocked her head as she considered what he had said. "That's touching," she said, tentatively.

"But true," he said, suddenly bursting out, "Darn it, why didn't you tell me?"

She looked away. "I didn't think you should have to suffer for my stupidity."

"Stupidity? Carole, people do have babies. We'd talked

about it. *You'd* wanted one. *I'd* wanted one—I think." She grinned. "So it happens, and you sneak off like an eighteen-year-old postulant to have it in the woods."

Carole let the subject pass. "How did you break it to our leader?"

DuBois chuckled. "He gave the order to break it to me," he said. "Oscar's a born bureaucrat, and I'm not in his loop."

"So what'd he say?"

"He said, basically, 'Damn your eyes and God bless.' " He paused. "He's a fine man, Carole."

"You don't have to convince me."

Someday I might. He was about to speak when the phone rang. Together with a lap-top computer, it rested on a low wicker table next to his chair. She moved quickly from the couch to answer it.

"Oh, hi, Otis," she said. She sank to the floor with a long groan and slid her feet under the table. "No, you're not interrupting anything," she said, "except a passionate interlude involving the world's most pregnant lady." She reached behind her and squeezed the toe of DuBois's shoe before calling an electronic notebook program onto the screen. "What's the jury doing?" She asked a few more questions, took rapid notes, and had the information shaped into a paragraph before the conversation was over. "Thanks," she said. "You don't think they'll report tonight, do you? No, me neither." In three more minutes she had called the copy desk at the *Times,* told them she had a new third paragraph for her story in the next day's paper, and plugged the phone line into the back of her computer.

While she was talking, DuBois went to the kitchen. The water was boiling, and she had left two mugs on the counter. He opened a few narrow cupboards until he found the tea, both her brand and an unopened box of Lipton, which was his. He poured the water, added a dash of evaporated milk from the refrigerator to hers, and left both cups to steep. Carole was just beginning to struggle to her feet when he went back into the living room. He helped her up, and their arms wrapped around each other. It was the first time they had touched. She pressed the side of her face against his chest, and he stroked her hair and the back of her neck.

"I do love you, Parker," she said in a muffled voice. Then she pushed him away. "But I regret to say," she said, dabbing at her eyes with a knuckle, "that for two people who have never lived together, the seventh month of pregnancy is probably not the time to start."

"I can't imagine why not," he said. "I've got—"

"—a riverview apartment on Sutton Place, supplied by the Ford Foundation," she said. "I know. Your reputation precedes you. But I'm getting used to my little nest here."

"Phooey," he said pleasantly. "But what I was going to say was that I'll have plenty of time. For the first year, the Ethics in Government Act places me at risk for phoning my dentist, let alone doing any serious work."

She took his hand and rubbed it between her palms, savoring the feel of his strong fingers and rough skin. "I've also gotten used to the idea of doing this by myself," she said.

He was aghast. "What, you mean here? My God, Carole!"

She laughed. "At Beth Israel Hospital," she said. "I meant without the traditional nervous dad hovering over me. A friend from work is going to be my breathing coach, and she's got her heart set on it."

"Fine," he said. "You talked me out of it. Frankly, my principal concern is that I don't have anybody to watch the Rose Bowl with tomorrow."

"Sorry, Park," she said. "I'll be downtown all day, hoping this trial ends before the blessed event. How about dinner?"

He kissed her on the forehead. "Here we go again," he said. Then he went to the kitchen for the tea, tossing the bags away and bringing the cups back to the living room. She was still standing and watching him with a coy smile. He put her cup on the coffee table and sat down. She sat, too, a respectable distance away. During the friendly but cagey conversation that followed, he resisted mentioning the room temperature. When he looked at his watch and said he should be going, she rose, took him by the hand, and walked him to the door. *I guess I should be going.*

On the way out, DuBois stopped at the mailboxes in the lobby and got the super's apartment number. Introducing himself to the amiable Hungarian who answered the door, he explained over the blare of "The Honeymooners" that his lady friend on the second floor didn't have enough heat. Would he please look into it? The super grinned and nodded and slammed the door, immediately forgetting the conversation and settling in front of the television again. DuBois left the building, inhaled deeply of the night air, and then stood in the middle of the deserted sidewalk with absolutely no idea where he was. In a moment the door opened behind him and Carole emerged, bundled into a knee-length quilted jacket. She said, " 'Ex-Hoskins Aide Meets End in Avenue C Drug Shootout.' "

"What's that?" he said.

She took his arm and pressed her body against his. "How did you get here?" she said.

"My driver brought me. I told him to head on home. I thought I could get a cab," he said.

"Your driver," she repeated, rolling her eyes. "I always knew I was in the wrong business."

"Me, too."

"Thought you'd get lucky, huh?"

He looked down at her. *I am.* "It crossed my mind," he said.

Her eyebrows danced. "Have you ever—"

"I have not," he said firmly.

"Then I would suggest you go back to your riverview apartment, Parker DuBois, and practice balancing on a beach ball. Then give me a call." She began to walk west toward First Avenue, pulling him along. "In the meantime, let's find you a cab," she said, "so you can live to continue rescuing me tomorrow."

As he followed his wife and this year's riffraff up the driveway to the north entrance of the White House, George Stevens vowed to make sure that when Marshall Brandon took office as president, he never read books about his predecessors, a vice that inevitably led to preposterous exercises in one-upmanship. In Hoskins's case, it had nearly ruined the practice of having the capital's most powerful men and women to a New Year's Eve reception every year. Somewhere he had read that on New Year's Day in 1907 Theodore Roosevelt stood in the Blue Room and shook the hand of any citizen willing to wait in line for the privilege. TR's record—8,150 handshakes, 8,150 "Dee-lighted"s—had stood unchallenged for eighty-six years, and a month into his first term, Hoskins had told his staff he wanted to see a plan for reestablishing the tradition. Then he leaked it. "The President is said to believe," the *Post* had reported at the time, "that throwing open the doors of the White House to the general public once a year would have a salutary effect in an era when the increase in terrorism has turned most of the world's leaders into virtual prisoners of their massive security apparatus." In 1989, Stevens's predecessor, Ben Bradlee, had not yet ascended to dwell among the colossi at the Columbia Journalism School. Stevens smirked. *If it had been my watch, I'd have used that story to make Hoskins's name forever synonymous with "bozo."*

But the President had made the mistake of giving the Wizards of No in the White House social office and Secret Service ten long months to practice their sorcery. When they had finished, Hoskins's exciting plan called for supplementing the usual New Year's Eve guest list with a hundred so-called average citizens gathered painstakingly from around the country and subjected to background checks, metal detectors, random frisks, and constant surveillance by uniformed and plainclothes centurions and rooftop snipers who matched the intruders virtually one for one. Hoskins bitched but bought it, figuring it was the closest he could get to a populist gesture in the nineties. It appeared there simply were things a President could not do. Once he had suggested casually to Ned Flach, the head of his Secret Service detail, that he might like to ride the Washington subway, and Flach looked at him as if he were proposing to expose himself in front of the Women's Democratic Caucus.

Stevens guided his wife around a yahoo in a plaid suit who had stopped to point at the window of the Family Dining Room and explain to his rapt wife that it was actually the Lincoln Bedroom, where Kennedy took the mobster's moll. "Excuse us, please, sir," Stevens said with icy contempt.

"You bet, my friend," said the excited guest. "Happy New Year!"

The Entrance Hall, usually intimidatingly barren, was lush with fragrant pine boughs, and someone was playing carols on the ornate Steinway in the East Room. The President had invited just his daughter and son and their children to join him in the receiving line, which Stevens appreciated since it saved him having to grip and grin with the Cabinet. It took him only a few moments to reach Hoskins, who gave him a broad, empty smile as he extended his hand.

"Happy New Year, Mr. President," Stevens said obsequiously. "Do you remember Ruth? We want to thank you for having us to your home again."

"And let me thank you, George, for that supportive editorial this morning on the budget," the President said in a loud voice. "If we can put this unseemly little tussle behind us, you deserve all the credit."

The remark was, of course, calculated to gall him. The *Post* had been forced to reprimand the Senate for bottling up the appropriations bill in the last Congress. Hoskins was so popular that the blame for the delay was falling squarely on the Republican leadership, including Brandon, and Stevens had had to pull the rug out from under them to prevent further damage. But under the circumstances, he could afford to be kind. "Well, I hope it helps, sir," he said. "It's going to be an exciting four years for you, and in view of your triumph at the polls, you deserve to have old business behind you."

Hoskins, off balance because of Stevens's graciousness,

patted his arm absentmindedly and greeted his next guest, and the editor turned to the final person in line, the aloof, graceful former senator who served as chief of protocol and the President's official hostess. But he heard Hoskins call his name again, and he turned back to see him with the man in the plaid suit. *Why, you son of a—*

"George, I want you to meet someone," Hoskins said. "Mike Donahue, here, is the biggest auto parts dealer in San Diego."

Donahue said, "Now, Mr. President, that's not quite—"

"And *this* lovely lady is his Betty," the President continued, pulling her forward and holding her hand in both of his. Stevens grimaced and shook Donahue's hand and nodded at the smitten wife, who did not take her eyes off Hoskins. "Mike, you've heard of the *Washington Post,* haven't you?" the President asked. "Well, this is George Stevens, the editor. That makes him the second most powerful man in town—the first being the commissioner of Internal Revenue, right, Mike?" Everyone laughed boisterously, though the President and Stevens were regarding each other with deadly calm. "George," Hoskins said with a wink, "why don't you introduce Betty and Mike around?"

"Of course," said Stevens, pleased with the mechanism Hoskins had unknowingly afforded him for extricating his wife from the chief of protocol and himself from his wife. He introduced her to the Donahues, excused himself, and then plunged past the pack of Secret Service agents into the East Room crowd. He expected to find her on the periphery, since she would be uncomfortable and unwelcome among the VIPs, and he was right. He recognized her lean and serious face from the mug shot the *Post*'s photo lab had sent him. Only a moment before, she had been standing with the new national security advisor, Felix Mendez, but he had been seized by the secretary of state, who was ferociously saddle soaping him on the other side of the room. Now she was alone and lost, a tiny presence under a massive portrait of Martha Washington. Her black cocktail dress hung on sharp, thin shoulders. She glanced nervously toward the cluster of people around the President. Then she sipped her white wine and through the bottom of the glass saw Stevens's hand snaking toward her.

"Pat Robinson?" Stevens said. Her eyes widened as she nodded. "George Stevens," he said.

"Yes," she said in a little voice, shaking his hand. "Hello."

He paused, letting her search his face for a clue to how he knew her, why he had approached her, why he didn't speak. He had expected wariness. He sensed terror. He took a drink from a passing waiter's tray and then said, "Didn't you know Chuck Sampson at Harvard?" She sagged, as if he had thrust an icy steel spike into her stomach, and her features dissolved and reassembled into a picture of a private holocaust. Stevens could see that there was nothing she would not tell him, because her face already said she understood that his power over her touched the fundamental questions of her survival and sanity. The sound and joy of the season and promise of the New Year cascaded around them, and Stevens was so happy that he was tempted to take her in his arms and whirl her across the shiny parquet floor. He expected great things from this promising new source.

Three hours later, he was at the small conference table in his office with two of his top editors, whom he had just called away from their holiday celebrations. Herb McGraw was in black tie. The head of the *Post*'s special investigative task force, Alton Jennings, who had been celebrating at home with his wife on the living room floor, was wearing jeans. Stevens knew both were hiding their irritation, and he was savoring the rich anticipation of hearing their jaws clatter onto the table. *Lazy bastards!* He said, "I've just learned that on the night he died, Chuck Sampson had a meeting at the White House." He looked at one, then the other, before adding, "With Hoskins. Alone."

"What?" said McGraw.

"I've also learned that he knew about the plans for the raid on Beirut and was going to file a story."

"I guess he'd somehow stumbled off his beat," said McGraw dryly. His eyes narrowed as he added, "You didn't know?"

"No," said Stevens. "Did you?"

McGraw looked down and shook his head.

"That's what the Hoskins meeting was about?" Jennings said.

Stevens nodded.

"Holy shit, George," Jennings said.

McGraw said, "Who says?"

"Same person who told Chuck about the raid."

"Who is?"

Stevens shook his head. "This source is to be protected at all costs. The only person who needs to know is me, at least for now. You guys are going to have enough to do, anyway." He stood and went to his desk for a notebook and two felt pens, which he tossed onto the table. McGraw tore off a few sheets and handed the notebook to Jennings while Stevens sat down again. "I want you to get on the Secret Service like mud on a pig. We know they brought him to the White House. How'd he get out again? And the hell with their usual 'We don't discuss security' line. Get the accident report from Virginia. Did the cops find it, or did someone call it in? If someone did, do they have a tape of the call? Where's the car he was killed in? Did they do an autopsy? Will the White House confirm Hoskins saw him? What did they talk about? But be careful. Do as much digging as you can at lower levels. We don't want to alert the brass, and especially the White House, until we have to."

McGraw stopped writing. "Are you suggesting," he said, "that the White House was involved in his death?"

"I'm not suggesting a damn thing," Stevens snapped back. "I'm saying that the night a reporter was going to write the story of the year, he got a one-on-one with the President and then got killed."

Jennings looked at McGraw. “If that story had run,” he said, “Jack Kemp would be ironing his morning suit for inauguration day, not Gene Hoskins.”

“Sure, but—”

“Damn it—” Stevens calmed himself. “Herb, listen. You agree it’s an interesting coincidence? So we’ll see where it leads. I figure we owe it to the kid.” He stood, and the two men filed out. He went to the door and called Jennings back, and they sat down again. “You know and I know that Herb’s a pussy, right?” Stevens said. Jennings grinned, and Stevens went on. “Right. So without making a big deal about it, I want you to take the lead oar on this.”

“Will do,” said Jennings. “Remember, all these bastards were in Vietnam—Hoskins, O’Brien, DuBois, and about half the senior staff at the White House. There’s no question they snuffed Chuck for getting in the way of their little war.”

“I agree.”

“But do they have the thing wired so well that we can’t get at it?”

Stevens shook his head. “Not likely. We’re not talking about the KGB here. But we’ve got to work on more than one front. Remember the hints we got about ballot irregularities in Cook County in November?”

“Sure,” said Jennings, chuckling contemptuously. “Herb shot it down. As I recall he said, ‘Why cheat when you’re going to win forty states?’ ”

“So I recall. Put a man on it now. What about that Amnesty International bullshit about the innocents that got killed in the raid? Can we get a new angle on it?”

Jenning said, “I’d give that kind of story to the national desk. It’s more Herb’s style, and it’ll keep him busy.”

“Agreed. Al, this could be big.”

“I know.”

“So keep the pressure on your kids. They’re good, but some of them aren’t mean enough. They’ve got to know that this one’s for keeps. We nail them or they nail us.”

Jennings chewed on the end of his pen. "May I ask when and how this came up?" he said.

"That's the strangest thing. The source came up to me tonight, in public, inside the damn White House."

"At some point, don't you think we're going to have to interview him properly?"

Stevens glared at him. "You're saying I didn't?"

"I'm saying you couldn't, not in that setting."

Stevens shook his head. "Maybe later," he said. "But not now. It's too delicate. Anything you want me to ask . . . to ask them, I will."

Jennings barely suppressed a smile at the editor's coyness about using the singular pronoun, which strongly suggested his source was a woman. Stevens easily suppressed his. He knew Jennings thought he'd tricked him into saying more than he'd wanted to. Thus were legends made. Now Jennings would never doubt the *Post* had been fed the story that destroyed the President of the United States in his own front parlor on New Year's Eve.

NINE

WASHINGTON WAS A JUNGLE OF CRISSCROSSING TELEphone lines that sometimes formed a welter so thick it repelled light and fresh air. Regimes were threatened, reputations cheapened, orders issued, ambitions advanced, dreams disrupted, and hearts broken, all by people who throughout long, busy days never touched or laid eyes on one another. The telephone permitted everyone to act quickly, decisively, and above all abstractly, without having to go across town and accept someone's greeting and hand and drink his coffee before getting down to business.

On Friday, January 8, 1993, journalists punched the phones in their own special way, collecting statements from surprised officials as the concluding ritual of the process known as investigative reporting. A reporter had to be able to say he had "covered that base" before writing what he was going to write anyway. In person he might have to watch a man sweat and stammer and to wonder what the family in the picture frame on his desk would feel, once the next day's paper hit the doorstep. He was best kept on the other end of the line, where he was just spokesman or malefactor, thoroughly divorced from such details as his motives and guiding principles as he produced the reaction to impending disclosures required by propriety and, of course, by the slim body of law that grew from the First Amendment.

Once he had it, the reporter could say thank you, hang up, and immediately chuckle with his editors and colleagues about what the sneaky bastard had said. If it was too artful, it could be rebutted in the next paragraph or simply abridged. If it was too sparse, the reader could be reminded of what the man did not say and which charges he did not deny. If he hadn't been in, perhaps because he was visiting his aunt, attending Good Friday mass, or even out committing further offenses against the commonweal, the story would say, "A reporter's calls were not returned," and the reader would be left with no doubt whatsoever. All in all, the getting of statements generally accelerated rather than impeded the investigations the press conducted on behalf of the American people.

If the story was about a specific wrongdoer, then his loyal wife, solemn children, and stubbornly supportive neighbors all emerged later, in the color story or movie script, long after the public had been helped to make up its mind. By then they would be the paraphernalia of a character from tragedy, or more frequently farce, described by commentators whose amused expressions and tone informed the listener they were conveying the epitome of irony. The approach was like that taken with the acquaintances of the quiet man in whose backyard the sheriff had just found twenty-seven bodies in shallow graves. They all still believed in him; they said he was a good father, a hard worker, a churchgoer, a Scoutmaster, a player of Brahms on the piano. They had no idea that downtown every day he had been subverting the Constitution and their way of life!

This process of sifting and straining a man to expose the essence of his evil was what made journalism society's great simplifier. It blended words with pictures to turn people into totems that could either be venerated or abominated. Two decades before, during Watergate, there had been a man from the White House named John Ehrlichman. He was accused of involvement in illegal espionage against another man, Daniel Ellsberg, who had stolen thousands of pages of top-secret Pentagon documents during wartime and given them to the newspapers, which were delighted to have them. The newspapers made the right and wrong of the matter perfectly clear, but they couldn't have done it without the long-suffering photographers. They squatted in front of John Ehrlichman's witness table with their long lenses, tripods and bulky equipment bags for hour after dreary hour, trying to keep their legs from falling asleep as they waited for the witness to tilt his head back and pull his lower lip so far over his upper lip that it touched his nostrils. When he finally did, producing an expression of singular malevolence, the photograph moved on the national wire, and editors in all fifty states said, almost simultaneously, *"There's* the son of a bitch!" They knew it would have confused people to see John Ehrlichman smile. Thus in complicated times did the American media help the American people to be absolutely sure of things.

That Friday, the Sampson crisis began at about 10:00 A.M., when one of Alton Jennings's reporters called the spokesman of the United States Secret Service, who had been eating his yogurt and reading the funnies in the *Post*.

"Good morning," the reporter said. "Tomorrow the *Post* is going to run a story saying that on the night of reporter Charles Sampson's death last May, he was brought to the White House by the Secret Service for a secret meeting with the President. Apparently no one ever saw him alive afterward. We also have sources and witnesses who say he did not leave the White House alone, that his car was taken from in front of his apartment building by two men, neither of whom was Sampson, and that the Fairfax County police department received an extraordinary number of anonymous telephone calls that night and early the next day inquiring about the accident. Would you care to comment?"

"That's preposterous," said the spokesman.

"What is?" said the reporter.

"The obvious suggestion that the Secret Service had something to do with somebody getting killed."

"Then you're denying that the Secret Service was involved in Sampson's death."

The spokesman gasped, "Good God no! Hold on. Off the record for a minute, okay?"

"I'm not authorized to go off the record."

"Since when?"

"Do you have a comment for this story? We're running it whether you do or not, but we wanted to give you the opportunity."

"I have no idea what you're talking about. What does the White House say?"

"Who do you think I am, Ask Andy?"

"I think you're a son of a bitch. Print that."

"If that's all you've got, hey, I'll go with it. But keep in mind, the son of a bitch is filing at two."

"Dammit, I'll have to call you back."

At 10:10 the spokesman called the aide to the director of the Secret Service.

"You're kidding," said the aide.

"The hell I am."

"Did you talk to Flach?"

"Do you think he'd return my call?"

"Actually, no. I'll call him."

"Do you think he'll return yours?"

At 10:45 the director called the President's chief of staff, Donald Hendricks.

"That's ridiculous," Hendricks said. "What did Ned Flach say?"

"He said, 'I answer only to the President.' "

"But he denied it, right?"

"Nope. He said, 'I answer—' "

"All right, all right. I'll get back to you."

At 10:50 Hendricks called the President's press secretary, E. Ephraim Perkins.

"You got any calls from the *Post* about a wild story having to do with that reporter that got killed?"

"Which reporter?"

"The one that hit a tree in Virginia last spring."

"Never heard of it, Don."

"Then I take it, E. E., that you don't have any calls."

"That's what I said. What's up?"

"Just listen. If anybody calls, say you'll get back to them and call me immediately. If I'm with the old man, get me out."

"Sure, boss. Sounds pretty silly, though."

At 11:15 Perkins called Hendricks back. The chief of staff's secretary said he was with Mr. Flach but that she would interrupt them.

"The *Post* just called about that story," Perkins said. "What should I say?"

"Don't say anything. In fact, don't take any more calls. Have your girl say you're in meetings."

"The guy sounded pretty sure of himself. I should really get back to him with something."

"You've got nothing to get back to him with. Just sit tight, will you?"

"Sure, but—"

"Good-bye, E. E."

At 11:45 Perkins called Hendricks again.

"Don, I got another call from the *Post,* something about ballot stuffing in Chicago and Texas."

"Damn it, I thought you were going to be in meetings."

"I don't get invited to meetings, and the entire Washington press corps knows it."

"Same guy?"

"Nope. Same irritating air of self-confidence, though. What's going on?"

"Just don't take any more calls. That's an order."

At 2:30, Alton Jennings called George Stevens.

"The wagons are being drawn in a circle," he said. "Everybody in town is referring us to the White House, where Perkins is apparently hiding under his desk and no single other top guy is taking calls."

"No denials?"

"No denials."

"What's Hoskins doing?"

"Keeping to his schedule, which means nothing."

"I'd say we're in business, wouldn't you?"

Jennings laughed. "Did you ever doubt it?"

Stevens paused a moment and then said, "Keep me posted."

At 2:35, Stevens called Herb McGraw for a progress report.

"The foreign desk's still angling for a piece of the cover," McGraw said.

"For what?"

"Pakistani A-bomb."

"Did they explode the damned thing?"

"Not yet, but—"

"Then it goes inside. Tell the copy desk to put an index box in the lower right-hand corner that says 'Other News' or something. I want every story on the page to be about the conspiracy."

At four, Jennings called Stevens again.

"They're going to make a statement."

"Great," said the editor. "Won't change a thing."

"I'm talking about a formal statement, in the briefing room. It won't be an exclusive anymore, George."

"Everybody'll know it's ours. This late no one will have time to do anything besides take down the statement and then get the details out of our early edition. All that matters now is nailing these bastards."

"The George Stevens I knew and loved would've sent a sniper to the press room to keep E. E. Perkins from giving away a *Washington Post* story."

"The mantle of public service sits heavier on my shoulders these days, Al," said Stevens. "What's more important, the search for truth or the search for scoops?"

"Scoops, George. Scoops."

At 4:45 Don Hendricks called Perkins.

"Take this down," the chief of staff said.

"Hold on. Let me get the girl in here."

"You got a pencil? Just take it down. 'Statement by the President—' "

"The President?"

"Isn't that what I said? 'On the evening of Friday, May 29, 1992, I asked Charles Sampson, a reporter for the *Washington Post,* to come to the White House for a meeting with me, during which I unsuccessfully attempted to discourage him from revealing details about our plans to mount a surprise military operation—' "

"Oh, no, Don."

"Write, E. E. '—operation to free American and West German hostages being held in Beirut, Lebanon. I believed then, and I believe now, that had Mr. Sampson written his story, it would have been impossible to conduct the operation safely and return our hostages to their families. When Mr. Sampson refused, I made the decision to detain him—' "

"Oh, *no,*" said Perkins.

" '—until the operation was over, a period of time of thirty-six hours at most. I took this action in my capacity as commander-in-chief of our armed forces. Mr. Sampson was killed in a tragic automobile accident en route to the location where he was to be held. Acting on their own but with my subsequent tacit approval, agents of the United States Secret Service concealed the exact circumstances of the accident, making it look as though it had occurred in Mr. Sampson's own automobile and as though he had been alone at the time.

" 'I know this matter raises more questions than can be answered now,' " Hendricks concluded. " 'I will cooperate fully with those officials of the executive and legislative branches who may undertake investigations. Obviously, a special prosecutor should be empowered. In summary, however, I believe I acted properly in protecting the integrity of a military mission that was necessary for our national security. There is no question but that I acted improperly in permitting the public's misconceptions about Mr. Sampson's death to persist after the mission was successfully completed.' End of statement."

"Holy mackerel, Don! What a disaster. You got a hard copy of that?"

"He just dictated it to me. Do you have it all? Better read it back."

After he had, Perkins said, "Did you know?"

"E. E., that's the problem with having an actual human

being as press secretary, especially one with a steel-trap mind such as yours. I didn't know, you didn't know; apparently nobody knew. But at this point it is not profitable for you to be answering the inevitable question, 'Who knew?' by saying, 'Not us, fellas. Must've been something the boss cooked up all by himself.' Just go out at five, read it, and leave. Do *not* take questions."

At 5:30, the President called Parker DuBois in New York.

"Did you hear?" Hoskins said.

"Just before you called. My secretary had her radio on to get the traffic report."

"I'm sorry I didn't let you know."

"I imagine you had a lot on your plate this afternoon. What's it like down there?"

"Like a stag party just before they show the dirty movie. The whole town is anticipating something absolutely grand, but they're not sure if they're going to see full penetration."

"How did they find out?"

"Damned if I know. It was definitely the *Post,* though. I saw George Stevens at New Year's, and from the evil glint in his eye, I figured he had something in the oven. The weak link in this dirty little business has always been the Secret Service. Maybe the guilt got to be too much for somebody to bear."

"Maybe," said DuBois. "What's next?"

"I've already admitted the whole thing, Park, so it's just a matter of how it plays."

Then we're history. "How's the staff holding up?" DuBois asked.

"I'm not sure. Don Hendricks has been a bit austere. Not much eye contact. He thought the statement should have contained an element of contrition. I told him that I wasn't feeling contrite and that it ought to be enough for the President to freely admit kidnapping and conspiracy without also having to put his meat on a block in Lafayette Park."

"I'm afraid all your loyal aides are going to be doing some vigorous ass covering, Mr. President. Many high administration officials will be quoted tomorrow as saying they were nowhere near the place during the fateful events in question."

"Speaking of which, Park, there's no need—"

"Sir, it's too late. Ned Flach knows I knew from the beginning, for one thing. Also, I'm the linchpin, as it were, since I invited the poor guy to the White House. I'll own up if anyone asks me, which is not to say that I'm exactly going to wait by the phone."

At 5:37, DuBois called Carole at work.

"Nelson," she answered curtly.

"Carole."

"Parker, did you know about this?"

"I did."

"That's a little too much for even me to swallow. I didn't know you were killing reporters."

"It was an accident, Carole."

"We're remaking the paper, and I've got to go. Of course I get to write a heart-wrenching sidebar about the life and times of my poor dead former colleague, who was a pluperfect shit but didn't deserve to die for the sake of the reelection of Eugene Hoskins. But don't worry. I'll leave your name out of it."

DuBois closed his eyes as Carole hung up.

At 8:30 the phone rang at attorney Stewart Bryant's house in Bethesda, but he didn't hear it. He was stretched out on the floor wearing his new digital-ready headphones and listening to *Santana Abraxas*. His wife had given him a copy on compact disk for Christmas, but not until tonight had he been in the mood to replay the soundtrack of 1969's glorious fall and winter. It was the year of the November Moratorium and the march on Washington, and he would always associate Carlos Santana's crystalline guitar playing with the smell of tear gas on the cold wind and the exquisite sensation of enraged, tottering authority. Alien rhythms helped propel subversive times. He found it just the thing to play out his dormitory window at Dartmouth's startled faculty wives in their plaid skirts and knee socks:

I got a black magic woman . . .
A black magic woman,
Tryin' to make a devil out of me.

In 1975, when America's attention had turned away from Saigon and Hanoi's troops rolled in on Russian rubber, Bryant finished law school and again set his 1967 VW van for Washington, this time as a $15,000-a-year lawyer for an international human rights lobby. Jimmy and the Hayseeds set the tempo for his halcyon years. Watergate had left government timid and eager to please. Lacking any coherent sense of what it was supposed to do, it was especially receptive to what various organized interests wanted it to do. Bryant was delighted at the swiftness with which sixties street wisdom became national policy. The Senate eviscerated the CIA, the UN ambassador took tea with the PLO, and the president quoted Bob Dylan. Only ill-timed moves by Brezhnev into Afghanistan and the Ayatollah into the United States embassy compound in Teheran brought to an end what Bryant considered the most promising trend in American government in decades.

During the Reagan darkness, Bryant took refuge in one of Washington's big Democratic firms, but as the conservative movement began to spend itself in inept adventures, he emerged briefly to serve on the Iran-Contra prosecution force. Fewer people showed up for the hanging than during Watergate, but he took comfort when the most anti-Soviet president in a half-century was driven to spend his last year in a flurry of superpower summitry.

"We want the world, and we want it now!" Jim Morrison had screamed in 1968 before being arrested. In 1988, GM used Marvin Gaye tunes to sell Pontiacs, and Bryant had assumed that with the help of the baby boomers, Reagan's successor would make some serious progress tugging the country left to stay. But he watched in horror as a brokered Democratic National Convention extruded the Louisiana Sidewinder himself, Eugene Hoskins, a protégé of Russell Long who'd led men in battle in Vietnam and wasn't even ashamed of it. *And then he won! Son of a bitch!* There was no room in his administration for Stewart Bryant and his maturing generation of Port Huron Democrats; Hoskins had preferred to hire *Republicans!* Republicans and Rambos; that escapade in Beirut had been keeping him awake nights. An American President had once again done exactly what he pleased in the world, flailing around like a drunken bully, only to become the first Democratic President to be reelected in nearly half a century.

Bryant used the remote control to turn up the volume for the quiet "Samba Pa Ti," and his fingers began to wander over the strings and frets of an imaginary Gibson Standard. But this afternoon, as he drove home, National Public Radio had brought glad tidings. The anchorwoman couldn't quite disguise the pleasure in her rich, sensuous voice as she described Hoskins's announcement and the ensuing uproar. He had felt the same nearly sexual tingle when Alexander Butterfield revealed the Nixon taping system and Ed Meese announced the diversion of funds to the *contras*. There were high times ahead!

He felt a nudge, a stockinged toe at his hip. He glanced up at his bemused-looking wife, who was holding the phone out to him. He took it and doffed the headphones.

"Mr. Bryant?" said a woman's cool voice. "I have Senator Brandon for you."

At one o'clock Saturday morning, Parker DuBois was sitting by his patio door in the dark, sipping a Scotch and water and watching the Pepsi-Cola sign across the East River. He was worried about his legal and professional situation. He was in a near panic about Carole's hostile, hurt reaction to his telephone call. But he was also relieved, *still* relieved, that the secret of Charles Sampson had been bared, though after flipping back and forth among the five major network newscasts, he'd decided his relief was at best perverse. Instead of news, he had witnessed a cathartic spasm of institutional outrage. His side had consisted of E. E.'s terse reading of the President's *mea culpa* and a vigorous statement of support from Lyndon LaRouche, who called for "further and massive state action against the Jewish-dominated media conglomerates." No other prominent administration figure appeared before the cameras, while the Senate Democratic leader's efforts to mount a defense were so frequently interrupted by reporters' hostile, shouted follow-up questions that he never managed to utter a complete sentence.

Their side was Sampson's parents, Sampson's schoolmates, Sampson's political science teachers, George Stevens—*in a blue suit and with his hair combed, no less!*—various outraged journalism professors and press-lobby lawyers, and a wide variety of congressmen and senators from both parties. The usually docile Marshall Brandon had delivered seemingly extemporaneous remarks about "a heinous, heartless, savage blow struck against the freedoms for whose sake so many other young men, in the full flush of their vigor, wetted foreign fields and furrows with our sweetest, dearest blood." All five network commentators expressed grave concern; all five anchormen felt moved to add somber personal notes at the close of their broadcasts. All in all, it was a PR wipeout.

DuBois sipped his drink and chuckled quietly, hopelessly, and, he thought, foolishly. Matters being as they were, he was becoming agitated by his preternatural calm. The coming firestorm, an iron triangle of carping, courts, and clink, didn't delight him. But he found his psychic territory miraculously unconsumed with worry or shame, and he was surprised. Despite the hay the 1988 Hoskins campaign had made on the sleaze issue, he now realized he must always have secretly sympathized with the predicament of the accused White House pol, studying optimistic, impossible lawyer- and staff-prepared scenarios and culling friends' private letters of support, with luck protected by these small comforts from the knowledge shared by the most harried tabloid reader and every homemaker glancing at "Live at Five" while making dinner—namely, that the jig was up. But DuBois was not good at self-deception. He'd been present at the beginning of this scandal, and he could easily foresee the end. For a soiled politician, oblivion was inevitable, and due process just a mechanism for postponing it and making it really hurt.

The trick for a man wanting to put down roots in Washington was knowing that the muck wasn't evenly spread. In the 1980s, hundreds of ex-congressional aides had earned handsome sums by openly and routinely performing services that were earning White House aides docket numbers and charges of influence peddling and conspiracy. The public's reaction to this, were the public to have learned about it, would have been a shrug: "Some get caught, others don't." Actually, some just weren't pursued. DuBois understood that the press, and the prosecutors who so often took their cues from the press, didn't crave the demise of congressional aides or minority whips the way they did presidents and their men. There was neither much pleasure nor opportunity for professional advancement in laying low a man who at the very pinnacle of his power could single-handedly close an army base in Alabama and distribute free tickets to the Senate gallery.

DuBois decided that liquor and cynicism were dulling his conscience. The liquor came from a bottle of forty-year-old Ambassador Scotch the President had given him on a dimly remembered election night. The cynicism came from knowing that Hoskins was absolutely right in stopping Sampson from filing his story and that he would have absolutely no chance of making the point stick. DuBois felt less like a criminal than a man who, having lived many unmolested years in the same cave as a sleeping beast, one day decided to rap it on the snout with a stick and thumb his nose when its eyes opened, just to prove once and for all that it could eat him for breakfast.

"Parker," Hoskins had said whenever someone on his staff proposed an aggressive response to a story that wasn't fair or right, "taking on the press feels good, but it's a nonstarter. It doesn't work because they always get the last word. Anyone who tries is going to die lonely." In this law of nature, DuBois had found the answer to a question that had recurred for months: *Why didn't I make Gene come clean?* The answer was that he had believed full disclosure would have meant the defeat of the ticket in November. Since he also believed that Eugene Hoskins was the best man available for the office he occupied, the cover-up had become a noble act.

DuBois smiled again, glancing over the arm of his chair at the empty glass dangling from his fingertips. *Time for another slug of Old Rationalizer.*

Of course the public would be told—*No, they'll grasp it intuitively*—that Hoskins's men had acted solely to keep their power. A politician's "I want to serve my country" had become an anachronistic notion, even though a journalist's "I'm just interested in the truth" for some reason had not. People had become utterly jaded about the motives of every institution in modern society except the one that had so persuasively educated them about the others. *Should people be less trusting of the press, or just more trusting of everyone else?*

To help himself over this philosophical dilemma, DuBois was planning to draw further nourishment from Hoskins's historic jug when the phone rang for the first time in an hour. It had been ringing when he came home and had stopped just before midnight. Until now, he had ignored it, preferring to deal with press inquiries through an interposed secretary. Now he looked at the telephone. He wondered if it could be a reporter this late. Impulsively he picked it up. It was.

"What are you doing up?" Carole said.

"That's rich," he said. "You through with your labors?"

"Oh, my, yes, and I must say it's a tearjerker. You guys are really in for it. This story is only eight hours old, and tomorrow it'll have two-thirds of the front page, the whole op-ed page, the whole Washington Talk page, and the lead editorial, which incidentally will be the *only* editorial."

"I figured as much. I saw the news. What do you suggest?"

"That you not take this lightly."

"I never have."

The line was silent. Finally, she said, "My main problem is that you knew about it when we were together and yet kept it from me."

"It wasn't the only thing I kept from you. And I'm not sure it's more important than things you've kept from me."

"I had my reasons."

"So did I."

She said, "I know."

He was loathe to endanger this fragile moment of concord, so he took a breezy tone. "You'd better get some sleep, kid," he said.

"Sounds wonderful. But it's a little chilly out here."

"Where are you?"

"In a phone booth at Fiftieth and First."

In three minutes he'd taken the elevator to the lobby and rushed past the dozing guard at the vast marble desk in front of the gargantuan bank of security monitors. He could see Carole striding toward him, a checkerboard muffler trailing behind and a few shiny wisps of hair showing under her beret. They reached the door at the same time. He stopped and pressed the sides of his hands against the glass, peering out skeptically between them. She crossed her arms and flashed a wicked and promising smile. Then he threw the door open and grabbed her.

TEN

PARKER DUBOIS'S FEW HOURS OF SLEEP AND DREAMS ended when a sliver of sunlight fell across his face. All he could ever remember about dreams was whether they were good or bad. Anxiety about phantom crises in the bad ones made him eager to get out of bed and turn on the shower and the all-news radio, filling the bathroom with steam and distractions. But today his drowsiness and contentment were potent enough to repel all his waking demons, which presently seemed to be taking numbers and lining up in the hall.

Ah, a warm and familiar smell. *Carole.* His face was a few inches from her, his breath ruffling the hair on the nape of her neck.

Who cares how history rates me
As long as your kiss intoxicates me?

Trying not to wake her, he reached around her hip and lay his hand on her round, taut belly, exploring, less intrusively than a few hours before, the contours of a peculiar but pleasant landscape.

DuBois hadn't taken time to think about being a father. *Where's her bellybutton? Guess there's not much time left. Names, furniture, clothes, insurance. Where do we live?*

Here? Can you raise a kid in New York anymore? Deborah's poor health had finally forced him to accept that children would never be a part of their lives. It had taken much longer to put them out of his mind as well, but he had. *Getting married again.* With Carole he had revisited the question of children only fitfully, spinning their small-town, Norman Rockwell fantasies to blunt the meanness of Gore Vidal's big city. But he never quite got past expecting something—his age, her age, their Age; their jobs, their ridiculously complicated lives—to snatch her away. *Going to jail might do it, too.*

Now he had Carole again, and there was going to be a baby after all, landing smack in their laps, as it were, at the worst possible time. *Or the best.* He pressed closer against her back and stroked her stomach paternally and—*ah ha!* The sex had been splendid. DuBois zestfully fastened onto the first element of impending fatherhood that was actually solid enough to grasp. Was this entirely proper? He dismissed the thought. His hand crept forward, down one steep, smooth slope and up—

She was awake after all. "Are you mapping your next assault on the summit," she said into her pillow, "or getting sentimental?"

Her tone was . . . discouraging. He pulled away and lay on his back, clasping his hands behind his head. "Just wrestling with my conscience," he said.

"About what?"

"Can you send a severely pregnant woman out to get the papers on a frigid morning in January?"

She rolled over to face him. Her eyes and cheeks were wet. "What the hell do you want with the papers?" she said. Surprised, he pulled her up so her head was on his chest. She cried for a little while, her body shaking with spasms under his hand, and then rolled away again and sat on the side of the bed. He got his shirt from the floor and put it over her shoulders and sat beside her, his hand on her knee, while she stared vacantly at the rug under her outstretched feet.

He wanted to comfort her, but he couldn't. He wanted to promise everything would be all right, but he knew it probably wouldn't be. So he didn't have anything to say. Despite their hungry lovemaking, they still weren't back in sync; her palpable disappointment in him made him feel childish and embarrassed. Their affection for each other had been founded on a mutual trust she obviously felt he'd violated. He didn't agree, but he had never discounted her feelings before, and he couldn't start now. He reached up and took a strand of brown hair from the side of her face and tucked it behind her ear. She misread his gesture and his silence and gave him a harsh look. "If you'd been in the newsroom yesterday," she said, "you wouldn't be quite so sanguine about this."

He wasn't so much sanguine as resigned. But he let her remark pass. "I take it they smell blood," he said.

"Yes," she said. "Ours."

"They don't believe it was an accident?"

"Why should they?"

DuBois let his irritation show. "Has Gene ever exhibited the outward characteristics of a cold-blooded murderer before?" he asked. "Have I?"

She put her hand on his. "Parker, he arrested a reporter," she said. "He's sacrificed his constitutional right to getting the benefit of the doubt."

"On the contrary," DuBois said. "The commander-in-chief detained a man who was about to destroy a crucial military mission and endanger our hostages' lives. We sure screwed up later, but on the fundamental question of whether Gene acted properly in gagging Sampson, I'm with him. The kid was way out of line."

She took her hand away. "You could have gone to court for a restraining order," she said.

He shook his head. "It couldn't have been done quietly enough. But what irks me is that people aren't going to get a balanced picture of this. The press is not even going to try to be objective about it. Your self-interest is going to get in the way."

"Can you blame us?"

"I can, and I do," he said. "If he'd locked up a ham radio operator who'd intercepted messages about the raid while puttering around in the basement, you'd probably see his point. But since it's a reporter—"

"—Make that a *dead* reporter."

"But it was an accident!"

She took a pillow and leaned against the headboard. DuBois drank in the welcome sight of her while trying to keep his mind focused on the argument. In a lighter tone of voice, she was saying, "What exactly was your role in all this, Mr. DuBois?"

"I invited Sampson to the White House. Within a few hours of his death, I knew what had really happened. I advised the President to keep it quiet."

"Did you know what Hoskins was planning to do?"

DuBois paused. Would it be disloyal to say no? He decided to equivocate. "It wouldn't have mattered if I had," he said. "I probably would've concurred in it."

"You going to tell anybody?"

"If they ask."

Her eyes wandered. "What're we in for, I wonder? Obstruction of justice?"

"I suppose so. Why?" She looked sad, patted her stomach, and then leaned forward to hold him. "Oh," he said, leaning toward her. Her shirt fell open, and in the process of consoling her, he slipped it off one shoulder to kiss her there. For the sake of symmetry, she slipped it off the other shoulder, and he kissed her there, too. As the shirt came off entirely, she wrapped her strong legs around him and drew him back into bed.

Before pressing her mouth hard against his, she whispered, "There's something you should know about pregnant women."

A half-hour later, they were maneuvering around each other in the kitchen, exchanging satisfied smiles and making an enormous breakfast. No one had gone for the papers. Carole had suggested he put on a record, perhaps the

Rolling Stones greatest hits package she'd given him for his birthday the year before as an experiment in cross-generational acculturation. "Sorry, baby," he'd said after a few moments. "I can't seem to find it. I'm still getting settled here." Instead he'd put on Ella Fitzgerald singing some Gershwin songs.

Carole smiled. *You can't always get what you want!* It was just her luck to fall in love with an older man who was musically retrograde even for his own generation. She was going to say that at his age he at least ought to be spinning "Jailhouse Rock," but she thought better of it. She had begun to crack an egg on the edge of a bowl when her hand froze. *"You* invited him to the White House?"

Poking around in the refrigerator for a jar of marmalade, DuBois stopped humming "Embraceable You" long enough to grunt yes.

"Where was he when you talked to him?"

"At the *Post.*" He looked over to see her slowly put the egg in the breast pocket of her shirt, turn around, and lean against the counter. "Carole?" he said, alarmed.

She gave him a strange look. "Did I ever tell you why I was canned?"

"Basically, no."

"Stevens said Chuck told him I refused to pester you about a story he was writing, which turned out to be the Beirut thing."

"Did you?"

"Of course, but that's not the point. Isn't it strange Sampson would tell Stevens I wouldn't call you but not tell him he was going to the White House, at your invitation, to see the President?"

DuBois shrugged. "Don't ask me," he said. "I find the rules governing what reporters tell other people and under what circumstances to be more confusing than Mendel's sweet peas. Coffee or tea?"

"Coffee." She fished out the egg and hit it so hard against the side of the bowl that it exploded. "And another egg, please."

On most Saturday mornings in Washington, DuBois had watched "King's Round Table," handicapping it and the other weekend political shows so Hoskins wouldn't have to watch them or depend on E. E.'s staff's bland summary, though he knew the old man really did watch them and just feigned amusement or outrage during DuBois's Monday morning replay. Having strong opinions about the damage done by television to the political process and the beta patterns of children's brains, Hoskins was ashamed (DuBois thought unnecessarily) that he sometimes found it as seductive as everyone else. Every few weeks he would ritualistically describe trying to find the Sunday afternoon football game—Hoskins thought sports redeemed the tube, a little—only to "stumble onto," and nonetheless watch in its entirety, an MTV heavy-metal survey or some poorly dubbed Japanese movie. He had to admit it because he wanted to talk about something he'd seen. His roaming, hyperactive mind couldn't dismiss a thought until he'd heard it aloud. And there was more. DuBois had learned about it from the President's young personal aide late one tipsy night in the Hotel Oriental bar during a state visit to Bangkok. The aide was immediately aghast at himself, and before they parted, he made the national security advisor swear never to disclose what he had learned: The President watched "Barney Miller" reruns.

Sealed in his cocoon with Carole, DuBois skipped the King show this morning. The pretaped, prefirestorm program had been scrapped; today's panel was live and cooking. For fifteen of the twenty-seven air minutes, everybody talked at the same time, although every once in a while a single voice sounded above the tumult.

"All that remains to be learned," said Louis Camare, his face and eyes seeming to glow as never before, "is the full extent of this President's contempt for our most basic freedoms. Those few of us who questioned the propriety of last spring's sneak attack in Lebanon failed to ask ourselves why we should expect such lawlessness to be confined to the administration's behavior abroad. We see now, in our own country, the tactics of Pinochet and the Brownshirts."

"Or Ho Chi Minh and Lenin," cut in Ethan Spravak, "if you'll excuse me, Louis."

"That's outrageous, both of you," Winston Reedy burst out. "Mind you, I hold no brief for what Hoskins did to the reporter. It's beneath contempt. It's—"

"Criminal," interrupted the grinning Spravak again. "It's criminal, it's impeachable, it's downright jailable." His grin widened alarmingly. "And he's a Democrat!"

Alice McGuire's irritation seemed genuine. "It's unbecoming to the memory of this martyred young man," she said, "for you to take so much pleasure from his and our nation's misfortune. We're about to go through another Watergate, another disgraced president, another national nightmare. Do you relish that?"

"What a joke," Spravak said. "During Iran-Contra, I didn't hear you lecturing Ben Bradlee for saying he hadn't had so much fun since Watergate. I didn't hear you lecturing the entire liberal press corps for having so much fun *during* Watergate. But now we have a Democratic crook, and Alice has a long face. Well, I'm sorry, little lady, but on my side of the aisle, it's Miller time."

Camare looked witheringly at Spravak. "Somehow, Ethan," he said, "you manage to oversimplify, distort, or cheapen every subject you touch."

"Cheapen?" taunted Spravak. "What do you think this is, *Julius Caesar?* It's another D.C. soap opera, no more, no less. Do you really think Hoskins was out to repeal the First Amendment? Then you're nuts. He screwed up, and he'll pay, as he should. But that's all there is. Anything more is just a product of an ideologue's fevered, conspiratorial imagination."

Camare sputtered, "The only ideologue in this—"

"But he's right about the press, Lou, in a way," said Reedy. "We're most content and also most competent when we're on the offensive. But I *don't* agree we'll be less enthusiastic about this story just because the President's a Democrat. Nor, as Americans, are we any less dismayed by a tragic development such as this."

Spravak moaned. "Winston, my friend," he said, "you were going great for a minute there, but then you let that sanctimonious note creep in. This kind of story is what we all came to Washington for. It's nothing to be ashamed of."

Then King asked Reedy to explain what was going to happen next.

"That depends largely on Congress," said the columnist, smoothly slipping from the hortative mode to the informational. "Many observers were surprised to see Marshall Brandon, Pennsylvania's usually low-key senior senator, get out in front on this one this quickly. The crisis seems to have struck a chord in him; his aides say they have never seen him so energized. Because he's chairman of the foreign relations committee and a trusted member of the Republican leadership, the smart money says that if the Senate conducts an investigation, which it certainly will, and he wants to spearhead it, which he apparently does, it's his for the taking."

To wrap up the show, King asked his panelists to predict whether the administration would survive.

"Doubtful," said Alice.

"No way," said Spravak.

"No," said Reedy glumly.

Camare said, "Eugene Hoskins will be inaugurated and impeached, convicted by the Senate, and buried." King signed off while everyone looked concerned about the future of the Republic.

When the red lights on the cameras blinked off, Alice slumped back into her seat and groaned. "Shit, Pete," she said, looking morosely at her host. Then she saw the time on a studio clock and leapt to her feet. "I've still got to file my Sunday story. See you."

"Get used to it," King called after her. "We'll probably have to be live most weeks for the duration."

Camare, who, despite his virile commentary, was the

only panelist whose brow hadn't glittered with sweat by the end of the broadcast, calmly stowed his notes. "Speaking of the press," he said, "I'm surprised no one mentioned the friendship between the Senate's white knight and the founder of our new feast, my able colleague George Stevens."

"I'm not," said King. "You know how this town operates as well as I do. If we started getting into that kind of personal nonsense, we'd confuse the hell out of everybody."

The cozy restaurant in the basement of One Washington Circle Hotel had recently become popular with people who didn't go to lunch for the sake of being observed eating lunch. People sat in groups of two or three talking rather than performing, which was the practice at the capital's more fashionable restaurants. Lovers met there and also—even more scandalously—those husbands and wives who still enjoyed each other's company enough to experience it in the middle of a working day. Sometimes reporters met there with sources. And sometimes old friends met for fond reunions, as Alton Jennings of the *Washington Post* and Stewart Bryant, majority counsel of the newly empaneled Senate Select Committee on the Alleged Illegal Activities of Eugene Hoskins, were doing this afternoon. It was Tuesday, January 19, the day before Eugene Hoskins's second inauguration. The last time they'd seen each other was backstage at a no-nukes concert some years before. Jennings had been free-lancing for the *Village Voice,* and Bryant had been a volunteer advance man for Ralph Nader, who spoke between musical sets by Jackson Browne and the just-paroled David Crosby.

After their food had come, Jennings grinned at Bryant's pinstripe suit, silver cuff links, and sixty-five dollar haircut. "If the old gang could see you now," he said.

"They do," Bryant said. "I married one, and half the rest appear to work in town. As for you, pal, what happened to

Ramparts, New Times, and *Mother Jones,* the magazines on the cutting edge of advocacy journalism? The only kind you said, admittedly in a drug-induced stupor, that you'd ever work for?"

Jennings took a dripping bite of his blue cheese mushroom burger. "Two out of three fell off the cutting edge," he mumbled, wiping his mouth with his cloth napkin. "But I've been able to work some great stories at the *Post.* The mainstream press has loosened up a lot because of Vietnam, Watergate, and generational attrition. The old farts in their short-sleeved white shirts are dying off."

"Don't forget the complete vacuum of fundamental respect among reporters, editors, and most readers for any organized authority in modern society," Bryant said, digging into his shrimp salad.

"There's that, yeah. But what's happening with you? How's Sheila?"

Bryant shrugged and took a gulp of his Bass Ale. "She wants a kid," he said.

"You don't?"

"I never have, and Sheila used to say she never would." He scratched the side of his head vigorously and nervously. "And it pisses me off. Our generation's vigor is being squandered on rug rats. Georgetown's starting to look like "Romper Room." Go into Olsson's bookshop on Saturday and all you hear is the dull roar from the kiddie section."

"It's not that bad, Stew."

Bryant laughed sarcastically. "Spoken like a true father. How many?"

"Up yours," said Jennings. "Two."

Over decaf, the reporter asked, "What's Brandon like?"

"What do you think? Like most politicians, he's a dumb turd with his beady eyes on the main chance."

"When I read you were going to work for him, I just about fell off my stool."

"Turkey called me up cold one night and said he'd heard of my work for the Iran-Contra special prosecutor."

"Your party affiliation wasn't a problem?"

"It appears to have cinched it," Bryant said. He tucked his chin in and mimicked Brandon's slow, deep voice: " 'The American people must be reassured this is not a vindictive, partisan exercise'."

"Right," said Jennings. "Speaking of which, what's up?"

"Off the record? Or rather, no attribution?"

"My middle name."

"We've begun to investigate possible widespread campaign abuses and vote fraud going back as far as Hoskins's first gubernatorial election. Buying votes, voting the graveyard, quid pro quos for contributions, the whole down-home ball of wax."

As Bryant continued, Jennings took some notes in a notebook he held in his lap. When the check came, he put away his notes, leaned back, and drained his coffee. "You realize, Mr. Bryant, that I need two sources for serious allegations such as these," he said with a twinkle in his eye.

Bryant tossed a gold credit card onto the plastic tray with the check. "Fine," he said. "I'll have Sheila give you a call. She'll confirm everything, after which you can tell her about baby diarrhea and anything else that might get her off my back."

The next afternoon, the President tossed the *Post* onto the ottoman in his third-floor study. There were three stories about him above the fold. The first said that a leaked draft of his inaugural address "contained no apology" for his role in Washington's latest scandal. The final draft, which the President had delivered four hours before, hadn't contained one, either. The second story, headlined "Senate Hoskins Panel to Probe Abuse Charges in '80 Governor Race," was the one the President wanted Parker DuBois to take a look at.

"I read it in the cab on the way from the airport this morning," said DuBois, who'd flown to Washington to see his friend take the oath of office on a dais with a dozen empty seats and give his short, low-key second inaugural address to a subdued but curious crowd. "I got a free copy on the shuttle."

"You remember Spike Henderson, don't you? Warren Hess's campaign manager the first time we beat him?"

"Sure do."

"Then you'll remember this is the same crap he peddled to the *Baton Rouge Times and Advocate* after the election. It played well in what we used to call the post-Watergate era. But damned if I wanted it hanging over my head the rest of my life, so we had the state attorney general appoint a special counsel."

"Who found that there was nothing to it."

"Right. A few pissed-off Republican precinct captains with no evidence. But Brandon dug out the old clips and dug up Spike, who's been practicing law in Bossier City or someplace and was delighted to take a first-class plane ride to Washington to be paid attention to by a committee of Congress investigating the bastard that whomped his butt twelve years ago. And, of course, ten minutes later it landed in the papers."

"I saw E. E.'s statement about it."

"Sure you did," huffed the President. "About thirteen words in the fifth paragraph. Parker, I know it won't stick. So do Brandon and Stevens. But once you get it into print, it doesn't die, especially in a situation such as ours, when everything coming out of the White House is automatically tainted. It'll become part of the 'pattern of abuses.' " He made quotation marks in the air with his fingers. "Speaking of which, can you believe Stevens is recycling that crap about the Beirut operation? We know—and *he* knows, the slimy son of a bitch—*precisely* how many rounds were fired and where just about every one of them ended up. No unarmed Lebanese was killed or injured except that woman who was living right in the middle of the hostages." He again gestured in disgust at the folded newspaper and went on. "Every source they have is either corrupt or fictional. All the so-called evidence was faked by the Shi'ites and fed to every gullible goody two-shoes who showed up at the Beirut Greyhound station."

Parker got up and walked to a tea cart by the window for more coffee. "I notice you haven't been taking a very aggressive PR posture on this," he said, collecting the President's cup from the table next to his easy chair.

"Two reasons," Hoskins said. "First, we don't have the firepower, since almost everyone on the staff is more interested in proving they weren't involved than in protecting the President."

"What about the Cabinet?"

Hoskins chuckled. "Gone fishing. But second, I decided it was better to hunker down, anyway. No way we're going to get a fair hearing now. Our only chance is to wait until the harpies catch their breath and then mount our defense."

DuBois gave the President his refilled cup and stood over him for a moment. "Which will be?"

Hoskins looked up and said, "The President's extraordinary powers as commander-in-chief in wartime or a moment of imminent hostilities."

DuBois winced and went back to his chair.

Hoskins caught his friend's expression and smiled wryly. "That's what the lawyers said."

"It won't be easy, Gene. First, we've got to begin thinking about this as two distinct problems: your initial action, then the cover-up. For now, the focus is on the kidnapping—"

The President interrupted. "Around here we've been saying 'temporary detention'."

"Oh. Sorry. But if we ever begin to win on that front—and we just might—then the media will shift to the cover-up, which is going to be a lot tougher for us. So if I were you, I'd cut your losses on the second front immediately."

"How?"

DuBois looked somber. "By hanging everyone who was involved, and everyone who advised you to keep it quiet, out to dry."

"We've been over this already," the President said in a clipped voice. "It's one thing if a President's staff takes actions that damage him without his knowledge. Then it's their little red wagon. But this was my baby from the beginning. And as far as the agents who fixed the accident were concerned, if I'd wanted to own up, I could've easily gotten them off the hook. No one's going to blame a bunch of relatively unsophisticated guys for doing what they thought was best for the old man. But I approved their actions after the fact and then enjoyed the benefit of them. I'm not about to abandon them now, especially when it would only make me look like an even bigger jerk. And as for you—"

DuBois said, "Taken care of, Mr. President." Hoskins tilted his head inquiringly, and his friend went on. "On the plane this morning that cute NBC reporter, the one with the frosted Dutchboy haircut and the eyebrows, came up and asked if she could ask me some questions."

Hoskins frowned and said, "Parker, it wasn't necessary. It won't help me, and you've screwed yourself."

"Won't hurt you, though, will it?"

The President reconsidered for a moment. "No," he said, "and in an odd way it might help just a little." He paused and sniffed, folding his hands over his stomach and adding drily, "I might catch some of your reflected glory."

"Impossible, sir," said DuBois formally. "Things may look a little dark at the moment, but this administration and this President will shine a light down the ages." He paused to steady his voice. "It's been an honor to be your friend."

Hoskins looked troubled by DuBois's overdramatizing but said only, "Thanks, Parker. Can you stay to dinner?"

DuBois said no. Looking at the President carefully, he asked, "How are you holding up?"

Hoskins shrugged. "All right." Then he got the point and got irritated. "Why? Did you expect to find me squatting in the corner, giggling and drooling? It's only been two weeks, and so far it's at least three-quarters a media story. Damn ugly one, that's for certain. But our polling's not as bad as you'd think."

"Try me."

"Down twenty-five points, to thirty-seven percent approval."

DuBois rolled his eyes. "Nixon resigned at twenty-nine, and it took eighteen months of Watergate plus the Arabs and a recession to get him there."

Hoskins stared. "And Harry S Truman was at thirty-one when he left office. Look at *him* now. When did you become such a pessimist?" DuBois started to speak, but the President raised his hand. "Never mind. But it's a hell of a lot more depressing than it used to be."

DuBois said, genuinely, "I'm sorry."

DuBois tarried on the way out, walking slowly through the hallways and smiling at the alert faces of each of the guards who watched him pass. After tonight's revelations he did not expect to be back, and he wanted to savor the pleasure of being in this bright, quiet, white and crimson house his friend seemed to suit like okra suited gumbo. He did more than suit it; he *defined* it. The President swept around corners and in and out of rooms with a confident American majesty that made his flashy predecessor seem celluloid thin. He enjoyed interrupting White House public tours and popping into the kitchens to thank the cooks for dinner, but he never tried to force ordinary people to pretend he was ordinary, a status to which no effective president dared aspire. The rap that he was awkward on television had actually pleased DuBois, who distrusted any man with the capacity to look natural in the unnatural presence of a hundred million other souls and yet of none.

Hoskins didn't play tennis, sail, climb mountains, or chase women. He governed, which meant that people said he was one-dimensional, although he did a thousand small things most would never know about and none could fully appreciate. With the help of his weary, once-devoted staff, he steeled himself for every meeting, delighting foreign ministers with his grasp of events in their countries, 4-H'ers with stray details about grain hybrids, a widow of a political foe with affectionate insights about a man he'd never much liked. His news conference answers far exceeded the substantive capacity and the interest of his glib interrogators. His toasts for visiting leaders of countries large and small were always apt and delivered without notes. This was not done to impress the public, for few state dinners were extensively covered by the press, but because of his old-fashioned belief that it was the business of a national leader to appear to feel personally honored when other national leaders came to sit at his table.

On flights home from his own foreign visits, Hoskins wrote out notes and searched for nuances. It didn't occur to him to leave such details to subordinates, since policy was built with them and principle empty without them. He drove his staff nuts by talking so much about difficult subjects; raising and discarding options; deciding, undeciding, and redeciding; goading obsequious aides into saying they disagreed with him, even if they didn't, just so he could hear an opposing view; announcing that he had made an irrevocable decision, only to distribute a memo on Tuesday countermanding Monday's orders. His enemies said he was indecisive, even irrational. In fact, he feared overconfidence and smugness. Sensing either in himself, he immediately deduced he was on the wrong track and threw the switch. Whatever track he was on, he never stopped stoking. If an aide was resting on his laurels at the end of some successful project, Gene Hoskins took special pleasure in personally lighting a forest fire under his butt.

These were only the outward expressions of what DuBois had always taken to be Eugene Hoskins's greatness. Its essence occupied a space behind those seemingly cold slate eyes. DuBois had seen it for the first time nearly twenty-five years before, in South Vietnam in the middle of the night after a firefight seventy miles northwest of Saigon, when the jungle in front of the company he was leading teemed with hidden terrors. The press was in the capital, compiling stories about dope-smoking soldiers that became fodder for the protests of dope-smoking students, who didn't understand the forces at play in Indochina until half a million people died fleeing Hanoi's blitzkrieg and the stacks of skulls from the Cambodian holocaust touched the porcelain-blue Khmer sky. Captain DuBois's units had taken 30 percent casualties that day. Colonel Hoskins learned of these sacrifices, and although the area wasn't secured, he came up the line and walked among the huddled soldiers and junior officers, sharing their coffee and his cigarettes and listening to them bitch about an enemy who wouldn't show himself, who observed no rules and knew no honor, who had made such a hard science of cruelty that anyone raised in a free, good country like theirs couldn't cope or survive.

DuBois took the elevator to the first floor and walked down a long corridor toward the West Wing. He passed Clark Mills's sculpture of Andrew Jackson at the Battle of New Orleans, the President's favorite. *Not much glory for Gene that night.* No photographers recorded the moment as they had when MacArthur risked death wading ashore at Leyte Beach. There was no glory for anyone when the Viet Cong's failure in the Tet offensive the next year was reported as America's, when the Communists' ordinary savagery didn't make the papers while the isolated tragedy at My Lai was made into an ink-black mark on the soul of man.

Before going back to headquarters on that night so long ago, Hoskins had stood and smoked with the nervous, grateful captain from his own home state. The yellow flash from Hoskins's match lit his eyes and revealed a warming, calming light behind them. DuBois had seen it a hundred times since then, including tonight in the White House, when in one brief, emotion-charged moment, the President had been more worried about his friend than himself.

A guard held the door as DuBois went out the side door of

the West Wing and headed for the northwest gate. He treasured that moment with the President and also regretted it. Hoskins's most valuable staffers honed their imperturbability, trying never to complain or otherwise involve him in unessential matters. If an aide mentioned a new baby, the President might paralyze the maternity ward with his fifty-man entourage. If a secretary referred to a laid-off father-in-law, he would spend half the morning finding him a job in the government. *You act tough so he can, too, and everyone gets their work done.* The ever-present risk was activating Hoskins's compulsion to stand alone against the general disintegration of spirit, will, and civility in the West at millennium's end. DuBois had often feared that if the President ever lost his capacity to pick his fights carefully, his compassion might use him up.

Hoskins ate alone and watched "NBC Nightly News." The lead story was Tammy Glindy's exclusive airborne interview with DuBois, which contained the shocking admission that he had counseled the President to continue the cover-up of the true circumstances of Charles Sampson's death. DuBois denied knowing Hoskins was going to kidnap him, though he said he believed it was "the proper decision under the circumstances." (Here Glindy arched her trademarked right eyebrow.) When she quoted unnamed Brandon committee sources as saying their preliminary investigation had implicated DuBois anyway, Hoskins laughed out loud and then used the remote control to turn the set off. He sat for a long moment with an unfocused expression on his face. Then he hit the intercom button. Usually the Secret Service answered after hours, but tonight he got Irene.

"And why aren't you home, young lady?" he scolded.

"I preferred to be here," she said in her confident, friendly voice. "I had some work to catch up on. What may I do for you, Mr. President?"

"Three things. First, get me the list of the agents who

were involved in our little situation last May. Second, see if Walker Smith can come by at eight-thirty tonight, assuming we promise to sneak him in the coal chute so nobody knows he's associating with the criminal element. And third, get yourself home before your husband hauls me into court for alienation of your affections."

"Yes, sir," said Irene. "You really do have quite enough legal troubles at the moment, don't you?"

"You ain't seen nothing yet," Hoskins said, grinning and slamming down the phone. In a few moments Irene brought up a sheet of paper with the names of Ned Flach and six other agents. He wrote Parker DuBois's name on the bottom and then went to pour himself a drink and wait for the attorney general.

Scrubbing her bathroom mirror before the reporter came the next day, Amanda Wilde stopped in midstroke, just as her hand whisked over the reflection of her face. She was finally looking well again, even after a harrowing day at the office. Her eyes were clear and untroubled, and her skin had lost the horrible pallor that for months after Chuck's death had caused her worried friends to ask so persistently if she was getting enough sleep. She hadn't been, because she'd been getting up every two hours to look out the window and see if someone were there.

She'd always known that someone had come and taken Chuck's car away that night. It had been there when she came home. Then it was gone. After she'd talked to George Stevens, she'd tried to convince herself it *had* been Chuck who took the car. But she was sure he would've come inside first to tell her. Anyway, they never came back. *He never came back.* In the mirror she saw the corners of her eyes crinkle and felt a familiar hot lump of anxiety forming in her stomach. *No. Damn it, it's over.* She tore her eyes away, put the window cleaner in the cupboard under the sink, and ran her cloth over the fixtures. She glanced at the bathtub, deciding it was clean enough to leave the shower curtain open. Then she looked at her watch, went to the hall closet, hung up her raincoat, and changed from pumps to slippers.

She wandered into the living room, which was still faintly lit in the dusk, and looked down at Prospect Street. *But it's not over.* Wasn't that the reason she'd rushed home early? Wasn't she hoping the doubt that had sharpened and prolonged her loneliness might finally end?

On the night it happened, she remembered telling George Stevens, who had been nice enough to call, that she thought something was strange about what had happened to Chuck, but he had assured her it was nothing. "He was working on a big story that he couldn't pin down," he had said. "I suggested he get some fresh air, maybe go for a drive to clear his head." He had paused. "I really feel terrible about that aspect of it, Amanda." Then she told him about the way the car had disappeared. It wasn't like Chuck not to tell her where he was going. Stevens didn't say anything right away. Then he said she should just put that out of her mind. It had been a bad day, and Chuck probably didn't feel like talking. "I'm sorry it had to end so senselessly," he said. "He was a very special young man. Knowing him has meant a lot to me." She did as Stevens suggested. She tried to put it out of her mind. She *ached* to. But she couldn't.

Months later, in January, the *Post* reporters started coming, bothering her neighbors and taking pictures of the building. None of them had talked to her. When she saw the paper and heard the news, she knew why: Something *had* been wrong, and Stevens was ashamed he hadn't looked into it at the beginning. He must have told them to leave her alone. She opened the refrigerator to make sure she had something to offer her guest to drink. *Weren't newspaper editors supposed to be born skeptics?* She slammed the door, making the spice jars on top clatter. *What suspended his fabled disbelief in the case of his own reporter?* After the story first appeared two weeks ago, there were even more reporters, pushing her and everyone else's buzzers at all hours and standing out front with their cameras and lights and their absurd trench coats. She wanted nothing to do with them. She had always disliked people who made a public spectacle of their grief. So she tucked her collar around her face and glided around and behind them, quietly and anonymously, the dead reporter's unnoticed ex-live-in lover with a bag of groceries. She'd been keeping her home phone off the hook, and at work her secretary rigorously screened her calls.

Amanda went back to the front door to collect her briefcase and put it next to her desk in the living room. She closed the curtains, turned on a lamp, and spent a few more moments straightening up. She'd just finished when the doorbell rang. She'd gotten the call at work this morning. First she said no. Then she said yes. *This one's going to be different.*

That was for sure! When she opened the door, she was astonished. "I had no idea!" she burst out. "How soon?"

Carole Nelson smiled. "It's nice to see you again," she said cheerfully, reaching out for Amanda's hand. "How soon? I'd say about twelve minutes. But if you'll just position me near the door so I can exit quickly if necessary, I guarantee no one will get hurt."

As Amanda closed the door and looked back at her, Carole was startled by the sudden way her pleasant features had become a mask of anguish. She realized it was the baby that had upset her, and regretted her joking. She touched Amanda's arm. "How have you been?" she asked. After staring at Carole for a few seconds, Amanda grabbed her hand with both of hers, pressed it to her chest, and began to sob. Watching the woman trying to stanch her tears, feeling the desperation and loneliness in her iron grip, Carole despised herself, her mission, and her business.

At about the same time, George Stevens was sitting in his well-appointed, little-used study in Georgetown, staring at the Associated Press flash he'd just called up on his PC.

The telephone rang. Someone answered it. Stevens kept staring.

"George," called his wife from the living room.

He stared.

She poked her head through the doorway. "George. It's Marshall Brandon."

He slowly rotated his head in the direction of the sound and looked without seeming to recognize her.

"George!"

"Does he know I'm here?" he whispered.

"Of course."

He turned his head again and looked at the telephone the same way he'd looked at his wife. After a while he picked it up and placed it beside his head as reluctantly as Beethoven must have the first time they handed him the ear trumpet.

"George?" said Brandon. "You there?"

"Yes."

"George, great news," Brandon said.

"Great news?" Stevens repeated contemptuously.

"I just played three sets with the Speaker at Burning Tree, and he's going to play ball," said the senator, proud of his unpremeditated epigram.

"What?"

"He's going to let us have a full run in the Senate before the Judiciary Committee gets started. He said we could take eight weeks, George. Eight weeks of televised hearings, eight weeks of the first fifteen minutes of the network newscasts and the first half-hour of MacNeil-Lehrer." He waited. "George?"

Stevens stared through the wall of richly bound and never opened Heritage Library books that happened to be in front of his face. "Where are you?"

"I'm at home. I dropped the Speaker on the way."

"You didn't listen to the radio?"

"No. Why? What's happened?"

Stevens smiled a smile of helpless despair. "He pardoned them," he said.

"Who did?"

Stevens let the receiver fall to his lap for a moment while he dragged his hand back and forth across his forehead. Then he lifted it again and said, "Who the hell do you think? *Hoskins!* He pardoned them all—DuBois and all the Secret Service agents."

"He can do that?"

Stevens's face flushed with pleasure. He had never enjoyed his friend's guileless stupidity more than he did in this moment of their ruin. He found it life-affirming in the way it seemed to justify his contempt for every other living creature.

Meanwhile Brandon was slowly reasoning the question through. "But that's good, isn't it, George?" he said. "It makes him look bad, doesn't it?"

"Marshall," Stevens said, patiently, almost gently, "let me tell you what happened. The pardons were handed down forty-five minutes ago. The attorney general and White House chief of staff and a variety of other officials have resigned in protest. The special prosecutor said that since Hoskins is his only remaining indictable target, he's closing up shop two days after opening it and leaving the matter to Congress. The Speaker must have learned about it right after you dropped him, because he's already got a statement on the wires saying he's asked the chairman of the Judiciary Committee to propose a schedule for immediate impeachment hearings. The majority and minority counsels are already in conference. There aren't going to be any Senate hearings, and you are never going to be president."

Then George Stevens hung up.

PART THREE

ELEVEN

WATERGATE WAS SHAKESPEARE AND THE IRAN-CONTRA affair was Gilbert and Sullivan, complete with the very model of a modern lieutenant colonel. In journalistic argot, they were both "great political theater." At curtain's fall—as Nixon flew his living, breathing, bruised family to their Orange County Elba and Reagan's shaky hand reached out for his smiling new Russian friend and his newest prop, a pen for signing treaties—many Washingtonians were strangely wistful as they filed back out into the neon-bright real world.

The Midnight Massacre of 1992 was strictly cinema verité. The greatest human cost of political history's most celebrated massacre in 1973 was Archibald Cox's having to take his autographed photo of JFK off the wall of his Washington office and put it up again in Cambridge. This time, there was real blood on the hands of the prince. Pundits who once built columnar cathedrals to show why offenses against the Constitution were infinitely worse than ordinary felonies felt colder and meaner than ever before as they set their jaws and bore down on their word processors. Like George III at the hands of Thomas Paine and the czar at the hands of the Bolshevik pamphleteers, Eugene Hoskins was feeling the fatal sting of poisoned print. No president had endured worse since Woodward and

Bernstein investigated the First Lady's sex life and the Democratic *New York Herald* called Lincoln an ape. In the prestige press, Hoskins had no friends, no defenders, and absolutely no chance.

Print reporters were an exclusive and superior-feeling clan, and Chuck Sampson had been one of their own, so most wrote from the heart and perhaps the spleen. Elsewhere in the mass media, other body parts were calling the shots. The day the *Post*'s story broke, before the sun had set on his Malibu deck, the first screenwriter had sent the first mini-series treatment ("In Cold Type") by messenger to agent Swifty Lazar's Beverly Hills office. In New York, book queries began arriving at Scott Meredith's Fifth Avenue office by the sackful. And in Washington, TV host Peter King had been working the phones in his Crystal City headquarters for a solid week. The Iranian hostage drama had made Ted Koppel's "Nightline" the hot news show of the eighties. King had decided that if he was going to become a living legend in the nineties, the dead reporter was his best shot.

The "Round Table" was broadcast on an ad hoc network of 150 independent television stations. But since it appeared at different times in each major market, it lacked the bonding, national-village effect of the major networks' Sunday talk shows. So King had been lobbying his stations to take a special live feed during the same half-hour of prime time on Thursday evening. He goaded his producers into spending hundreds of thousands of dollars on advertising in the key cities. When the White House on that very evening issued its incendiary two-paragraph announcement of unconditional pardons for DuBois and the others, King couldn't believe his good fortune. As his director pointed to him at precisely nine o'clock, his expression was grave, but his glittering eyes revealed even more profound sentiments: *Fifty million damn people! CBS, here I come!*

King had dropped the usual theme music and introductory graphics, so the first thing viewers saw was his ashen face. His tense voice was the first thing they heard. (The

Post's TV critic wrote afterward, "In an era of pulse-quickening John Williams scores and computer visuals, King's stark, primitive approach to the news was breathtakingly dramatic.")

"Good evening," King said slowly, as if trying to penetrate static like Churchill on the BBC in 1941. "I am speaking to you from Washington, D.C., which tonight finds itself plunged into the greatest political crisis of modern times. After fifteen years in broadcasting, I never thought I would be reporting a story such as this. Just this evening, the President of the United States, in an action universally condemned as a naked abuse of the democratic process, pardoned seven men known to have been involved in the death of a young *Washington Post* reporter. Charles Sampson was killed in what the White House claims was an accident after he learned of Hoskins's secret plans to attack Beirut last spring.

"Within two hours of the White House announcement, the President's chief of staff and attorney general and over twenty other top administration officials resigned in protest. Forty members of the Senate and two hundred thirty-seven congressmen have already called for the President's resignation. More are certain to follow. The House will begin impeachment hearings in two weeks.

"And yet from the White House there is only a brooding, foreboding silence. The President has not been seen in public since his sparsely attended inauguration. His remaining aides do not return telephone calls. The daily press briefing has been suspended until further notice." King paused and then continued, his voice low and tremulous. "There are even rumors tonight—terrible rumors—of an impending military coup. According to this morning's *Washington Post,* an unnamed source, a former member of the White House staff, has revealed that within the last forty-eight hours, the President spoke by telephone with General Robert O'Brien, the swashbuckling head of Hoskins's controversial irregular forces and the leader of last year's bloody attack in Lebanon."

At this moment, viewers at home heard a short eruption of background noise—Ethan Spravak slamming his palm on the table in front of his dead microphone as a gesture of hopeless exasperation. King's eyes flicked to his left momentarily and then found home again. "I have asked your local station for this special time," he continued, "so your thinking during these troubled days can be guided by the insights of our panel of veteran Washington observers." He turned to his right. "First, the *Post*'s own distinguished columnist, Louis Camare. Louis, what is this President thinking? What is he doing? For God's sake, what is happening to our country?"

To match the gravity of the proceedings, Camare was observing a new no-fop policy, looking every inch the freshman Republican congressman in his navy blue suit, white shirt, and red foulard tie. His delivery made King's earnest solemnity sound like a Letterman monologue. "Tonight our country is in the hands of a maddened tyrant," he said. "With his midnight killing and midnight pardons, Hoskins has made it midnight in America and brought our democracy to its darkest hour."

Spravak's voice could be heard taking vigorous exception, but his microphone stayed off and the camera held on Camare, who went on. "These are hard words, and they come hard to me. Regrettably, they are true. And yet those of us at this table"—he nodded to his unseen colleagues—"bear a measure of the responsibility. In two weeks we have learned more about Eugene Hoskins than in the previous sixty years." Ticking off his points on his fingertips, he looked directly into the camera and said, "Kidnapping. Involvement, some suggest, in a homicide. Destruction of evidence. Conspiracy to obstruct justice. The pardon power once again used to cover up crimes. There are serious new charges about atrocities committed by our troops in Lebanon and about illegal campaign practices in both presidential elections and indeed throughout his political career. And Peter, do we dare credit these startling new disclosures about a possible coup d'état? One shudders at the very thought."

Camare looked at the table for a second and shook his head minutely; then his face took on a reproachful expression as he looked back at King. "But I submit that it's as much our fault as his," he said. "This man has been in the public eye for over two decades, beginning during the tragedy of Vietnam. Why have we failed to show the American people the real Eugene Hoskins? Why did we wait for him to show himself to us?" Camare sat back in his seat as he reached his peroration. "My friends, we must make a pact with one another that no one will ever again be permitted to assume the vast powers of the presidency until he has endured the most rigorous possible examination of his record, his qualifications, and, most importantly, his character. We do not deserve to have a free press unless we can prevent a man such as Eugene Hoskins from reaching positions of such authority."

King thanked Camare, turned to his left, and said coolly, "And now, syndicated columnist Ethan Spravak."

Dignity had never been the most salient characteristic of "King's Capital Round Table," and tonight Spravak felt strangely off balance. Camare had obviously prepared carefully, and since he had not, he was thrown onto the defensive. "I am no fan of Gene Hoskins," he began, "but—"

Camare interrupted him. *His* mike was still live, and the camera trained on him went live as soon as he spoke up. "You are more useful to him than a fan, Mr. Spravak," he said. "You are a consistent and dependable apologist." He looked back at King. "But more is at stake here than the fate of one man or one administration," Camare intoned. "Mr. Hoskins and his defenders represent an anachronistic but stubborn strain of undemocratic, Wild West lawlessness in the American character. You'll remember Nixon's crimes against the people of Cambodia, Reagan's against Grenada and Libya. Both certainly had their domestic scandals. But neither stooped as low as this President. Neither took the lives of their own people as blithely as they took those of

Asians and Arabs." He looked across the table at Spravak and concluded, "No President ever took the American people for saps the way Mr. Hoskins has."

King retook the floor and steered the conversation around Spravak, who sputtered in unseen, unamplified rage. "Now we'll turn to our resident neoconservative, Winston Reedy of the *New Republic*. Any words of wisdom, Winston? Any predictions?"

Reedy's cherubic face was composed but grave. "The annual State of the Union address is scheduled for next Monday," he said. "As you point out, we've heard nothing from the White House on this or any other subject, but congressional leaders tell us they have no reason to expect that Hoskins won't show up to give the speech as scheduled." He stopped; his face signaled a real sense of having been betrayed, cheated. He sounded tired when he spoke again. "Perhaps then we may hear some statement or apology about his actions of last year and last night," he said. "Or we may hear something else. We may get an explanation of his bizarre and under the circumstances gravely inappropriate back-channel contact with the man widely regarded as his favorite in the military. I just don't know what's going to happen. No one knows."

The next morning, Bing "Bytes" Billings was playing "War in Europe" on the Macintosh SE in his corner office at Programmic Music Software in Palo Alto, California, his glasses propped on his nose at a forty-five-degree angle as the time-honored home remedy for an outdated prescription. His secretary ducked her head in and said a reporter named Carole Nelson was on the telephone. As he moved a West German armored division along the Elbe, he touched a pedal with his toe to activate the speakerphone perched on top of his monitor.

"Yo," he said with the breezy self-confidence of an unreconstructed nerd who had made $3 million the previous tax year. "Who's Carole Nelson?"

"I met you at a *Washington Post* party last year when you were in to install our new program. A business writer," she said, leaving the verb out of her second sentence to avoid telling an explicit lie about her current employment. "We were all exceptionally sweet to you, since you were the man who was going to stop the machines from swallowing our copy."

He prepared a tactical nuclear strike. "I sure remember the party," he said. "I don't remember you, but I won't hold it against you. Hey, you guys sure are shaking them up back there again. I can't wait for the movie."

"Thanks. We try."

"What do you need?"

"Tech support."

"On that *Post* system? Excuse me for saying so, but that's one of my transcendent accomplishments. Do you use the overlapping windows for note taking?"

"Best I've ever seen. This is a user problem, not a system problem." A white lie was now unavoidable. "About eight months ago, I erased some files that I want to try to retrieve. Is there any way to do it?"

Zap. Two crack East German divisions disappeared. "Zip," he said. "They're gone forever. Ironically, you all used to have something akin to the White House PROF setup that got the Iran-Contra crew in so much trouble by rolling out to tape all the memos they thought they'd erased. Dump something on your current system and it stays dumped, except for the record of the transaction."

"There's a record?"

"Sure. The operating system notes everything you do to a file and then stamps it with date, time, and terminal number."

"You know, Mr. Billings—"

"Bytes."

"What?"

"Call me Bytes." Paris disappeared. *Bastards must have*

kept some intermediate-range nukes hidden away somewhere. "Damn," he muttered.

"What?"

He typed "Exit," which at this stage of the confrontation was akin to a man who'd just been fired telling his boss, *Oh, yeah? Well, I quit!* "Sorry. What were you going to say?"

"Just that it'd even be useful to see the names of those files. Frankly, I'm not exactly sure what's missing and what I've still got."

"No problem. You at the office?"

She said casually, "I'm working in New York today."

"Then just log on from a PC and type OPSYS.DIR, space, and the date you want. It's not double passworded. It'll be a gigantic file, but you can scan the right-hand column for your terminal number."

"Bytes, you're a prince."

"Thanks." He paused. "You get to California very much?"

"Sometimes," she said. "I'll give you a call, and we can get some enchiladas. But while I've got you, there's something else I want to ask, just for fun. It's a running joke at the *Post*. Who's got terminal number one, the publisher or his arch subordinate George Stevens?"

"The publisher," said Billings.

"Oh," said Carole, disappointed that her gambit had failed. The search would be easier if she knew what terminal number to scan for.

But before she could speak again, Billings added, "Stevens asked for number zero."

On the same Friday morning, Pat Robinson had just put on her coat and tucked her ears under her white knit cap when the phone rang. "Darn," she said. She put her purse and briefcase down, took her hat off, and went to the wall telephone in the kitchen.

When she had answered a voice said, "Hey, sis."

Absorbing such an enormous horror took a long moment.

There was a tightening and buzzing in her cheeks, as if her blood had suddenly congealed and started to numb her flesh from the inside. She stared straight ahead and reached out with her left hand, groping for the counter like a blind woman in a treacherous new place. Finding it, she edged over and put all her weight against it. "What?" she said in a small, terrified voice.

"It's me," he said.

"Why are you calling?" she said. "What do you want?" She swallowed, pressed her eyes shut, and added, "Where are you?"

"I'm still in town," he said. *Ominously?* It was ominous news; it didn't matter how he said it. "Still in town, Pat." He laughed pleasantly. "You won't get rid of me that easy."

She couldn't figure out what he meant. Did he have some idea of what she'd done? Or did he have no idea of what he had done to her? Anger and hatred, fear and helplessness knotted together inside her and expelled a sour liquid that burned her throat and mouth. She was pressing the receiver so hard against her face that her knuckles ground on her gums. *First that awful Stevens, and now. . . . Good Jesus, please help me.*

"It's just that I saw you the other night at the White House, at New Year's," he went on, "and I realized how long it had been since we'd talked. I feel I've neglected you."

Despite that bitter irony, she felt a tiny warming sensation of relief. "That's all right," she said. "It really is." It even emboldened her a little. "You've certainly been in the news lately," she said.

He chuckled. "Don't ever try it yourself," he said. "Anonymity is a lot more fun. Listen, Pat, I left you alone. That's what you wanted, wasn't it?"

"Yes."

"Still?"

"Yes."

The line was silent. Then he said, "I understand. I just wanted to see how you were."

"Thank you. I've got to go to work now."

"I've got to go, too. Maybe I'll give you a call again sometime."

Oh God no. "All right. Good-bye." When she had hung up, she stripped her clothes off and took a scalding shower to try to wash away the sweat and terror. *How did he get my number?* After wrapping herself in a bath towel, she checked the locks on all the windows and doors in the apartment and called in sick to the office. *He can get anybody's number he wants. He can do anything he wants.* She turned on the television in her bedroom, pulled the covers over her head, and started to cry. Routine was her greatest solace and her only company, and its disintegration left a yawning, terrifying sense of hopelessness. The certainty that the disruption would recur enveloped and suffused her with an inconquerable despair. She couldn't imagine tomorrow or later today or getting out of the bed. What was the use?

In New York, Parker DuBois was listening to some Mozart divertimenti and slicing tomatoes to put on buttered toast, his favorite solo breakfast. His few years as a bachelor in public life had taught him to treasure solitude, and even though the rest of the day promised to be miserable, he was enjoying the morning's small, pleasant routines. A relatively new element was the more or less constant contrapuntal bleeping of his telephone, which he ignored. Those he wanted to talk to knew how to reach him.

It actually calmed him even further to think of the mounting frustration of the various parties on the other end. He could imagine editors wearing green eyeshades standing over them, waving their metal pica poles menacingly and screeching, *You get me a DuBois quote or you're going to be covering church bingo in Tuckahoe!*

He dropped two slices of pumpernickel into the wide-slotted toaster Carole had given him as a housewarming gift. *I've got to ask her if they still have green eyeshades and pica poles*. She'd been on the run on a story of her own and had made a couple of mysterious trips to Washington on the Amtrak Metroliner, Eastern Airlines having deprived her of her First Amendment right to fly because she was eight months pregnant. Meanwhile, he had become a focus of national curiosity, the nation's principal query—inscribed by his secretary on two dozen pink slips importuning him to engage in the masochistic act of calling reporters back—being whether he would accept the President's pardon. The subject left him almost speechless with irritation, but not completely. He was afraid that if he did get into a conversation about it, he would say that the President of the United States was a damned fool. "No comment" was more polite and patriotic. But recognizing the issue had its legal as well as its PR dimension, on the day before he had gone to the Madison Avenue office of his lawyer, Stanley Hersh, to ask what he should do next.

"Far as I can tell," Hersh had said, running his hand through his tightly curled black hair and peering over his glasses at a short brief prepared by one of his young associates, "one neither accepts nor rejects a presidential pardon. One simply contemplates its pristine beauty."

DuBois, seated in front of Hersh's cluttered desk, posed the inevitable question: "What did Nixon do?"

The lawyer shrugged, flipping to the back page of the brief and reexamining a long footnote. "He accepted it," he said. "But we feel that in view of the weight of public opinion against him, he and his people decided he had to take public note of Ford's gesture in some way. It wasn't legally necessary."

DuBois got up and began some desultory pacing. "It's damned humiliating," he said. "I'm inclined to call Gene up and tell him to rescind it."

"Would he?" DuBois didn't answer, and Hersh continued. "As your attorney, Mr. DuBois, I'd suggest the humiliation lies in spending a million bucks on my outstanding services and getting convicted, which is the certain alternative."

"It's not the money, Mr. Hersh." *Because I don't have it.*

"No," Hersh conceded. "But there's no shame in benefiting from a gesture from someone you've served so loyally all these years—especially when in making it he's worsened his own position." He absorbed DuBois's sharp look and said, "I'm sure that's the aspect that disturbs you the most. But the resulting impression from the recent actions of both of you, at least the one I get, is of two people with the highest possible regard for each other."

DuBois, who in his reverie had found himself in the unintended position of appearing to study Hersh's framed Columbia Law School diploma on the wall, walked back to the lawyer's desk and sat down. "You don't think people see it that way, do you?" he asked.

Hersh had leaned forward and taken off his glasses. "You read the papers too much, Mr. DuBois," he said. "You guys were dumb, sure. Nobody applauds what you did. But nobody likes the press, either." He added conspiratorily, "There are a lot more people than you think who're glad you gave them a good swift kick in the can."

Thus fortified, when the phone rang yet again, DuBois went on fixing his breakfast. But when it stopped after two rings and then started again, he wiped his hands on a dish towel, picked up, and extended the antenna. "Missed me, didn't you?" he said. "If you come up right away, I might be able to fit you in."

"I didn't call to be propositioned. I get that every morning on West Forty-third Street."

"In your condition?"

"You bet, sweetie. This isn't Bethesda. Parker, I've got to interview you."

DuBois frowned. "You do?"

"I phrased that incorrectly," she said. "May I interview you for a story I'm writing?"

In spite of himself, he couldn't help feeling suspicious. "About what? Not me?"

"Of course not," she said, offended. "Not directly, at least. It's about George Stevens."

"How intriguing. Hold on a minute." He poured himself

some coffee and took it and the phone into the living room, where he turned down the music and settled on the couch. Lifting the phone again, he said, “On or off the record?”

“On, preferably.”

“How are you going to explain that?”

“That’s my problem,” she said, sounding miffed. “What do you say?”

“I’ll listen to the questions and then let you know how you can use the answers.”

“Fine. There’s not much, but it’ll help the story. Remember the day you called Sampson?”

“I do.”

“Would you please describe why you called and what happened when you did?”

“Gene—uh, strike that.”

“You brute. Oh, all right.”

“The President said he wanted to see the reporter who had called saying he was going to reveal the plans for the raid, and he asked me to make the call myself.”

“When did you call?”

“About five.”

“Did you use his direct dial?”

“I didn’t have it,” he said. “I called the *Post* switchboard and asked for him.”

“Why didn’t you have your secretary or the White House operator do it?”

“I hardly ever did,” he said. “I suppose it was a reverse status thing. The most tiresome game in that town is trying to force the other guy to get on the line before you do. Besides, this call was somewhat delicate.”

“Okay,” she said. “This is where it gets important. How did you ask for him?”

“By name.”

“Did you give yours?”

“I said it was Parker DuBois.”

“Did you say, ‘At the White House’?”

“Well, why not?” he said defensively. “I suppose it’s a bit

pushy, but you tend to get your calls a lot quicker. One learns to say it automatically."

"It's nothing to be ashamed of. As a matter of fact, darling, I could kiss you. I *will* kiss you. And more. Did he come on immediately?"

"There was the usual delay. It took a moment or two."

"You don't remember an exceptionally long wait?"

"Well, there was a little wait, then the operator came back on and said she'd connect me."

"She came back on? Isn't that odd?"

"Maybe his line had been busy."

"She didn't say it had been?"

"No, I guess she didn't."

"Thank you, Mr. DuBois."

"What's this all about, counselor?"

"I shouldn't say."

"Oh," he said, hurt. "All right."

She relented. "I'll put it to you in the form of another question," she said. "Had you ever heard the silly rumor that George Stevens has left standing instructions at the switchboard that he wants to be informed, and that he wants to listen in, whenever someone from the White House calls the newsroom?"

"Holy smoke," he said. "You're kidding."

"Nope."

"You're saying he must have known all along that Sampson was going to the White House that night."

"You'll keep this under your hat, of course."

"Of course."

"So, Parker. Are we on or off the record?"

"What are you going to write if I say off?" he said. " 'Sources close to DuBois—' "

" '*Mr.* DuBois.' I work for a classy organization now."

" '—say that the operator came back on the line'? If you want to quote me, quote me. But I still don't know how you're going to get away with it."

"If you were the alpha and omega of this story," she said, "you'd have a point. But you're not. *The New York Times* is going to like this one so much that it'll pop for our honeymoon."

DuBois had been sipping his coffee, and at her last comment he spilled it down his chest. "What?" he yelped, in pleasure and pain. "Does this mean—"

"Oh, maybe," she said. "Got to go. What're you doing today?"

"Probably getting fired," he said, brushing at his singed, wet skin with the belt of his terrycloth bathrobe. "The chairman is taking me to Lutece."

"He's going to fire you at Lutece?"

"I work for a classy organization, too."

Early that evening, in a conference room off the *Times*'s third-floor newsroom, Carole sat across from the managing editor, the executive editor, the Washington bureau chief—who had just arrived from LaGuardia and looked crabby as he tossed his rumpled coat over the back of his chair and sat down—and a swanky libel lawyer from *The New York Times* Company. When he had entered and Carole rose to shake his hand, he glanced at her swollen stomach and smirked.

"All right, Carole," said the managing editor, pleasantly but coolly. "What've you got?"

She had a reporter's notebook and a pile of file folders containing her notes in front of her place. It was not comfortable to lean forward authoritatively, but she did. Folding her hands on top of her materials, she said, "I can show that the editor of the *Washington Post* knew on the night of Charles Sampson's death that Sampson had an appointment alone with Hoskins. He also knew that Sampson was ready to file a story revealing the plans for the raid in Beirut. Only a few hours after Sampson's death, he erased the relevant files from the reporter's private computer storage area."

As the lawyer took notes, a band of sweat appeared just below his hairline.

Carole continued without looking at her notes. "Told by Sampson's girlfriend that she thought something was fishy, Stevens calmed her fears, telling her Sampson had just been on a wild-goose chase. After the November election and several weeks before the *Post* actually began its investigation in January, he told Senator Brandon that the *Post* was working on a dramatic story that would bring down the administration. The majority counsel Brandon hired for the select committee was a college friend of Stevens chief investigative guy and was suggested to Brandon by Stevens." She paused. "Learning Sampson had discussed some details of his Beirut story with a fellow reporter, Stevens fired her."

The lawyer looked up. "Who was that?"

"Me."

"Oh." He carefully positioned his felt pen along the pale red left margin lines on his legal pad and sat back in his chair, crossing his arms. "Why," he asked sarcastically, "would Stevens do all this?"

"It's widely known in Washington that he has political ambitions," she replied.

He taunted, "Widely known? I've seen that construction before. You mean *you* think he does?"

The Washington bureau chief, whose expression had softened as Carole talked, answered for her. "It's universally known, Mel. He and Brandon have been soul mates since they were fraternity brothers at Penn. Everyone knows George wants Brandon to be president so Brandon can put George in the Cabinet."

"So the idea is that Stevens held off until after the election so he could turn Brandon into a nationally known scandal buster, Sam Ervin style," the executive editor said.

"Right," said Carole, pleased at the bureau chief's mellowing attitude. He was number three in the pecking order but number one in influence. He reminded her of the sardonic, dissipated reporter who spent most of *Mr. Smith*

Goes to Washington lying around on Jimmy Stewart's office couch making time with his Girl Friday. He had also been Carole's kind of reporter. Thirteen years before, he'd been on vacation in San Diego when two 727s collided over the harbor. He told the wife and kids to go to Tijuana without him, left them in the third lane of Interstate 5, and hitched back downtown. Two hours later he called New York and dictated a twenty-three-take story he'd written on a borrowed typewriter perched on an overturned trash basket outside the local FAA office. It was California, so the copy desk slashed it to six inches and put it inside, but the legend persisted nonetheless. He caught Carole's eyes lingering on him and winked.

"That's preposterous," said the lawyer.

Carole snapped back to attention and flipped her hair over her right shoulder. "In what precise aspect?" she said in a steely voice.

"Do you have any idea how ferocious newspaper people are about even the tiniest errors about them in the newspaper?" he said. "He'll sue Punch Sulzberger before the close of business the day the story comes out."

The ME reached over, lifted Mel's legal pad so the pen clattered onto the table, and put it in his own lap. The lawyer had been glaring at Carole; now he glared at the ME.

"So for our publisher's sake, let's talk about sources," the ME said, taking out his own pen and studying Mel's list. "How do you know he knew about the Hoskins meeting?"

"He listens in on every call his reporters get from the White House."

The heads of all four men jerked up. The ME said, "Source?"

"For the specific call to Sampson, the operator who was on duty that afternoon, on background. Corroborated by Parker DuBois, on the record. For the general practice, two former operators, on the record."

"How did you get DuBois?" the ME asked. "Nobody's gotten to DuBois."

She eyed him evenly. "He's my boyfriend." The lawyer

rolled his eyes. The executive editor smiled at her candor. She added, "And I don't really need him, even for this element of the story. I was just triple checking the phone call procedure. If the operator had put Parker on with Sampson without a delay, it would suggest she hadn't signaled Stevens. But the long pause he described to me is consistent with what I knew already from the operators."

"Agreed," said the executive editor, with a peremptory glance at the ME. "Go ahead."

The ME moved down the list. "What about the computer stuff?"

"This afternoon I got a printout from the *Post* system's memory showing that six files, all of them with titles clearly connected with the Beirut story, were deleted just before midnight the night Sampson died. It was done from Stevens's terminal."

"How do you know Brandon was primed before they started working on the story?"

"He bragged to his administrative assistant, who told me, off the record."

"Couldn't he just have been slipping his old pal some political intelligence about a work in progress?"

"You mean insider trading, Washington style?" She shook her head. "I checked the timing carefully. Brandon's aide says his conversation with Brandon occurred in late November. He's got notes, too. Stevens first briefed his team on the famous East Room leak on New Year's Eve."

"Why did the aide talk to you?"

"He resents Stevens's influence with his boss." Carole felt guilty about this source. She added, "I don't think he quite realizes the awkward position this story will put his boss in."

The executive editor cut in. "I don't suppose you turned up this famous source of Stevens?"

Carole looked vaguely at the center of the table and spoke softly. "As a matter of fact, I did. And I'm not naming or using him."

The tension in the room increased palpably. The *Post*'s

source was the most notorious since the alleged Deep Throat. The scuttlebutt said no one but Stevens knew who it was.

"Why not?" asked the ME.

"Because he believes his life is in danger. I believe him, and he's only peripherally relevant, anyway."

"In danger from the White House?"

"No."

"You said *he,*" the bureau chief barked. "It's supposed to be a she."

"I'm not saying who or what it is," Carole said tersely, looking at each of her colleagues in turn. "I'll resign first, so please just forget it."

The ME looked at the executive editor, who nodded, and then turned back to the reporter. "Not necessary, Carole. The buddy of the investigative guy—who's that, by the way?"

"Al Jennings."

"Oh, great," said the lawyer, slapping the table with the end of his legal pad. "Now we're going to libel a Pulitzer Prize winner."

Carole sensed she was on a roll, so she went easy on him. "I can understand your concern, but it wasn't really his doing," she said. "Stevens knows more about his reporters than they do about themselves. He planted one of Al's old antiwar buddies with Brandon, knowing that Al would approach him and he would probably leak."

"Hence all the other stories the *Post* beat us on," said the executive editor, drumming on the table with the eraser of a pencil.

Carole noticed the competitive glimmer in his eyes and reeled him in a little more. "They had an exclusive deal, those two," she said. "Nobody else on the committee staff was permitted to give us anything good."

"Back to reality, folks," said the ME. "Source on the Jennings stuff?"

In spite of herself, Carole cracked a wide, self-satisfied grin. "The national editor, Herb McGraw, on background."

The executive editor and the ME looked at each other uneasily and then both fixed on Carole. "What the hell's going on down there?" the ME said. "If there's something personal between McGraw and Jennings, should we really get in the middle of it?"

"It's true they don't get along," Carole admitted, "but if they were in government that wouldn't be an issue for you, would it? As a matter of fact, if everybody got along we'd be out of business." They said nothing, and she continued. "Herb's a good editor. He just feels the *Post*'s campaign against Hoskins is taking on the trappings of a—" She grasped for the word, then realized she'd already used it. "—of a campaign."

The ME made another check mark. "I assume you have Sampson's girlfriend on the record."

Carole nodded. "On the night of the accident, she told Stevens that Chuck's car had disappeared from in front of their apartment building. He lied and told her he'd suggested Chuck go for a drive. As you know, the car the Secret Service stole was a key element in the story."

"How do you know he lied?" asked the bureau chief.

"Because Sampson never returned to the *Post* from the White House," she said. "In fact, Sampson and Stevens never even spoke that day. Amanda told me he was ducking Stevens until the story was tied down."

"You trust the girlfriend?" asked the lawyer. "What's her state of mind?"

"Troubled because of months of uncertainty about Sampson's death, but basically stable. She showed me her journal, which confirmed everything she told me. I think we can rely on her."

The ME tossed Mel's pad onto the table and said, "Sounds good to me."

The executive editor turned to Carole and said abruptly, "You realize you have a problem on this story."

She took a deep breath. "Actually, I have three," she said. "The first is DuBois. While he has only a rough idea of what I'm doing, he did inadvertently provide certain insights. I care for him a great deal, but I'm not in the business of fighting his battles for him. And this isn't a 'what if?' exercise, since even if the story had broken when it should have, the cover-up would've already been approved and Parker's goose would still be cooked.

"The second problem is that Stevens fired me. But I like it here, and I'm not a vengeful person.

"The third is the most important one, since we all share it: George Stevens, who's an embarrassment to journalism." They were all silent and grim—even Mel. *Bingo.* "This story will expose him. The other two problems are inconsequential unless the story's wrong. It's not." She sat back and crossed her legs as gracefully as she could. Professional pride and personal satisfaction warmed her aching muscles like a bucket of Ben-Gay.

The executive editor had found a fourth problem: It was a good story but a bad one, too. "You realize this will be a hell of a shot in the arm for Hoskins," he said, his face twisted by the struggle between two contrary instincts.

"And a hell of a blow to the newspaper business," said the ME.

Carole smiled confidently to herself. *But a hell of a boon for* The New York Times.

The room was silent for a few moments. Then the Washington bureau chief stood, put his jacket on, and said to the executive editor, "I kicked and screamed when you said you wanted to do this story from New York. I still wish you'd let us handle it. But your gal's done a hell of a job." He waved his hand at her. "Don't try to get up," he said with a twinkle in his eye.

When he'd left, the executive editor looked at Mel, who waved both hands in the air and said, "It's your paper."

The irritated editor said, "Six figures a year, Mel, and all I get is this?" He mimicked the hand waving.

Mel took his legal pad back from the ME and ceremoniously tore the top sheet off, which he handed back. "I can only urge extreme caution and assiduous attention to detail," he said, tucking the blank pad into his briefcase.

"Great," said the executive editor, shaking his head and gazing at him in wonderment. "Mel, you're a total fraud. You realize that, don't you?"

The ME folded the paper and put it in his shirt pocket. "Give him a break," he said. "We should count our blessings. You'll recall the lawyers were against printing the Pentagon Papers."

"It happens to have been against the law," Mel said haughtily as he stood up.

"It happened to be a shitty law," the ME shot back.

Buttoning his suitcoat and heading for the door, the lawyer said, "I imagine G. Gordon Liddy felt the same way about the D.C. burglary statute. See you."

"Thanks for staying after five," the executive editor said blandly over his shoulder. Then he turned back to Carole. "How long do you need?"

"I won't finish for Sunday." Cocking her head toward the door the lawyer had just used, she said, "Assiduous attention to detail and all that."

"No problem. We'll look at your copy Monday."

In Washington that Friday afternoon, two troubled men took long walks. Each could have driven but needed time to think.

One was E. E. Perkins, the President's press secretary for a term and a half in Baton Rouge and a term and two days in Washington. In the face of a brutal Manitoban wind, he set off from the White House for the half-hour walk down Pennsylvania Avenue to the Capitol, where he had a ten-minute appointment with the Speaker of the House.

The other walker was Pat Robinson's half brother, bound for a round of Nautilus at his health club a half-mile from his apartment in northwest Washington. Against the same brutal wind he was warmed by the memory of his sister's terror. It was important she know there was nowhere on earth she could go where he couldn't find her. He grinned, thinking of her pathetic little voice on the telephone. He had plenty of time on his hands now because of her. Soon, one way or another, he'd have his hands on her again.

Perkins simply felt he had lost control of his life. As he left the grounds, the uniformed Secret Service officers at the northeast entrance nodded respectfully and looked back at their clipboards and TV monitors. But the fat, bald aide could feel the odd second look they cast at him as he hurried through the guard post and out the heavy iron gate. They couldn't figure out why such a big cheese was rolling out by himself, without a White House car and driver. Because it would buy him another hour outside the bunker, that was why. Leaning into the wind, he dug into the pockets of his grimy Botany 500 and headed up the street, grasping his hands together in front of him through the fabric to compensate for the missing button he kept forgetting to tell his wife about.

In the ten years since Hoskins had plucked him out of the Baton Rouge press corps and appointed him press secretary, E. E. had never had the kind of advisory and policy-making role he had taken on in the last two weeks. Don Hendricks and the others who'd resigned in high dudgeon over the pardons were relative newcomers. Now just a few loyal Louisianans remained, and the President was reaching out to them. So finally Perkins had real power. He had status. Everybody returned his calls, as long as there was an official still occupying the office in which the telephone was ringing.

Unthinkingly propelled by his quickened thoughts, Perkins trotted a few steps as he left Pennsylvania Avenue for the three-block walk down Fifteenth Street. He didn't care for the new regime one bit. He was becoming executive officer just in time to help guide the boat to a permanent berth on the bottom. *Take this job and shove it.*

The other man was most conscious of his immediate mission: to do a full cycle, but especially to concentrate on the right arm. He'd been putting more weight on it than he should, and it hurt like hell, but he needed it strong again.

He was also conscious of the barely arrested animality in his walk and the graceful swing of his thick arms. He passed a well-presented redhead carrying a shopping bag. He scanned her breasts and legs and then fixed on her eyes. Didn't they brush his shoulders, his chest, the little swelling under the waist of his leather jacket? *They all love it. Pattie sure did.* The woman smiled at him, and he smiled back pleasantly. *Bitch.* His hair was longer than he liked it, his clothes looser, but he couldn't help it. When you're well built and your hair's short and you wear clothes that show your muscles, people think you're a faggot. Once he was leaving the all-night drugstore at Dupont Circle and one of them touched him. He smiled again. *Bastard had to pick his teeth out of the toilet.* As he stepped off the curb at New Hampshire and R, he saw another woman with straight blonde hair like his sister's. His hand tingled. He remembered reaching down and laying it against her young, smooth white neck to hold her head steady in front of him, anchoring it like a clamp up against her jawbone and chin. Pleasant reminiscences faded as he dwelt on his recent troubles. He could see now that they were all her fault. His brawny hands folded into fists as he fixed on the image of her talking to George Stevens at New Year's. He needed the right arm strong again.

The press secretary passed the Hotel Washington and glanced enviously through the window of the lounge, where lobbyists were flashing their congressional cuff links and quaffing overpriced imported beer. *Lucky bastards.* At the moment he would have paid $7.50 and kissed the bartender full on the lips for a warm Coors Light, a bowl of pretzels, and a ball game, even Ivy League football. His loyalty and affectionate respect for Eugene Hoskins persisted, but he had never counted on working for the least popular public figure since Abraham Lincoln—*speaking as a southerner.* The year before, when the administration was riding high, the media—with their unerring sense of what the antiestablishment market would bear—were all sweetness and sunshine, but when the downturn came, he didn't have a lot of chits to call in. Together he and Hoskins had revolutionized the concept of the presidential press secretary by transforming him into a creature who professed to serve no one's interests except those of the President of the United States. As a result, E. E. Perkins was history's most loathed presidential press secretary.

Four years before, while formally introducing himself to the press corps in the briefing room, E. E. had told them he hadn't been in the decision-making loop in the statehouse and wouldn't be in the White House, either. On most key decisions, he said, he would learn the details about fifteen minutes before the press did.

Expecting (unrealistically, as it turned out) this administration to leak as torrentially as the previous one, the reporters had taken this well enough. There had been see-no-evil spokesmen before. But then the correspondent of the *Philadelphia Inquirer* had mentioned the L word. He called out, "Will you ever lie to us?"

E. E. had leaned against the podium and flashed what he hoped was a boyish, engaging smile. "Not unless the President tells me to," he said gamely.

The stunned silence was broken only by the whirring of video cameras and motor drives and the humming of klieg lights, which made the assembled press sound like a giant insentient mechanical beast slouching down a corridor of the starship *Enterprise*. All of a sudden, every reporter in the room was on his feet and in full cry. Finally one managed to yell loudly and persistently enough to be heard above those who either couldn't yell as long or wouldn't yell as loud. "Isn't it your responsibility to tell the truth to the American people?" she gasped.

"My responsibility," said E. E., stating what he felt, though with rapidly failing self-confidence, was perfectly obvious, "is to serve the President. If a time comes when he believes the interests of the American people would best be served by certain facts not being made public, especially in the foreign policy or military area, then it's my job and that of everyone else in the White House to see that those facts are not made public. If it takes a lie to do it, so be it."

"But what about your credibility? How can we believe anything you say?"

"My credibility will come into question immediately where it most counts," he said, gesturing over his right shoulder with his thumb in the general direction of the Oval Office, "if I begin to promote somebody else's interests besides the President's. I don't work for you. I work for him. If you don't like what he decides to tell you, you are free to investigate further and inform your readers of your displeasure. But the idea that I'm here to make your life easier is a myth."

The resulting headlines—"New President a Liar?"; "Truth Inoperative at Hoskins White House"—stirred up two more days of heavy weather in recent history's least tranquil presidential honeymoon. Without any public outcry outside Washington or a specific example of presidential dishonesty, the story soon faded. But among journalists it left a sour residue the capital had not known since Nixon, too, treated the press not as a sacred fraternity but as just another powerful, self-promoting Washington institution. And then, a whole term later, the other shoe dropped—*right on their own damned head. Four years they've been sitting there like a hungry gator with its mouth open, and we had to sashay right in.*

E. E. had reached the United States Capitol. Skirting the white-streaked statue of U. S. Grant, he entered the Longworth building and began to make his way through the musty hallways to the Speaker's office. He passed a group of young congressional aides chatting in the corridor, who when they recognized him stopped talking and stared as if he were a traffic accident. He grinned weakly and tipped an imaginary hat.

The truth about Chuck Sampson's death and the cover-up had been like a match thrown on an oil slick. The fires of the media's pent-up outrage lit the facades of the city's marble monuments and the face of the nation with a sickening yellow glow. But E. E. thought it was all happening too fast. It was hard to tell for sure, since Washingtonians depended to a large degree on the press to tell them what the public was saying and thinking, but the American people did not yet appear to be caught up in the frenzy. While Hoskins's reputation and popularity had been hammered down to an astonishingly low level, the crisis still had a forced, unmanageable feeling to it, like a freshly hard-boiled egg sunk into a glass of cold water too shallow for the job.

The classic pattern of White House scandals in the press was a gradual process of getting the public's attention and guiding it from indifference to dismay and finally to ridicule and condemnation. But this time the press hadn't taken the time to prime the pump, and it seemed to E. E. that the people were still biding their time. The White House's overnight polls now showed Hoskins's general approval rating at 25 percent, driven down one small notch by the pardons, which didn't seem to bother people as much as the press had apparently expected, and another hefty notch by the military coup story that had been saturating the country for two days. In spite of it all, Hoskins was still rated highly for competence and strength. And two-thirds of the people said they were still interested in hearing his side of the story.

E. E. arrived at Fred McCarthy's office and opened the door to the reception area. His message for the Speaker was simple: The President wished to be invited to arrive at the traditional time next Monday to give the traditional State of the Union speech. No text would be available beforehand, because the President was not yet sure what he would say. But E. E. was authorized to reassure McCarthy that, yes, the President would indeed address what the genial, ruthless California Democrat referred to in private as the "Sampson matter" and in public as "Lady Liberty's nightmare."

E. E. took off his raincoat and handed it to the receptionist, who held it well away from her dress as she motioned him toward the inner office. All he knew was that in three days, Hoskins would get his first chance, and maybe his last, to put his thumb on the scale of public opinion. *I hope that madman O'Brien can deliver on his promises.*

At about the same time, the other man arrived at his health club and ran into a former colleague who was holding his gym bag and racquetball racquet in one hand as he reached for the door. "Ned!" said the agent. "Good to see you."

"Hi, Charlie," Flach said in his smooth, dispassionate voice. "How's the vice-president?"

"I'm on the missus's detail now. It's my day off. Otherwise I'd be at the Trump Tower in Manhattan with nineteen other guys, watching her buy shoes. How're you doing?"

Flach shrugged. "All right," he said. "I could be better, but then again I could be a whole lot worse."

"Newsies still bothering you?"

"Not anymore. It didn't take long for them to get tired of taking pictures of me walking down the street with my mouth closed."

Charlie studied him closely. "What're you going to do now?" he asked. Flach could tell what he was thinking: Why had he been stupid enough to throw away the best retirement plan in law enforcement for a protectee, even if it was the President?

Flach smiled. "I'm going to work out, Charlie. Say hi to the guys for me." As he waved and turned toward the men's locker room, Flach's hand tingled again. *Bitch.*

TWELVE

DUBOIS'S LUNCH THAT DAY IN NEW YORK WENT EXACTLY as he had predicted. Leaning over his goose-liver terrine and fillet of St. Pierre, the chairman of the board quietly admitted great sympathy for what the administration had been up against with the press but said that he hoped Parker could see the awkward position in which his legal situation put a philanthropic organization such as theirs, "which has really got to smell sweet as a baby's behind."

Recoiling inwardly from what he suspected he would soon discover was an oxymoronic simile, DuBois said that he of course understood and that, as a matter of fact, the chairman would find a letter of resignation on his desk when they returned to the office. After suggesting they both try the julienne of orange rind for dessert, the chairman added that the foundation felt it could offer a twelve-month severance package to give DuBois some flexibility.

DuBois thanked him but said it wouldn't be necessary. Just before lunch a top New York book editor had called to offer him $2.5 million worth of flexibility for an intimate biography of Eugene Hoskins, plus, in the editor's words, "a guy to crank it out for you if you want." He had continued, "We're talking about an off-the-shelf, stand-alone, full-service quickie memoir here, Mr. DuBois. Eight months from signing to number one in the *Times*. You don't need an agent. Who needs an agent? You keep first serial, we keep the movie rights, justice and truth are served, and everybody makes a little money." DuBois said he'd write it himself in a year and a half and would take a couple of PCs and printers instead of the ghostwriter, whereupon the editor reduced his advance offer by $1 million and DuBois accepted. He figured they could use the money they saved to buy slop for their new pig in a poke.

Late Monday afternoon, after a long Sunday brunch with the editor, he visited the publisher's offices to sign the contracts, collect the first of his advance checks, and raise a glass with the publisher and a few of his top executives. Afterwards he asked if he could use a telephone. His editor stopped gazing at the completed instruments on the conference table and rubbing his palms together long enough to point to a small adjoining office. DuBois closed the door, sat down, and dialed Carole's number at the *Times*.

"I got it," he said.

"Ill-gotten gains," she said, "although a little summer place in the Hamptons does sound nice."

"They came to me, you know, not the other way around."

"That's what Dustin Hoffman said about Mrs. Robinson. You could have said no. You could have said, 'The American people have suffered enough for my misjudgments. I choose instead to take my wife- and child-to-be to rusticate in Nova Scotia, where I shall chop wood and examine my conscience and soul.' "

"Piffle. You'd last fifteen minutes and then bury the ax in my head." When she didn't demur, he smiled into the receiver. *So much for our pastoral fantasies.*

Instead she asked, "Did you talk content?"

"Oh, it was all very highbrow, but there was a lot of nudge-nudge, wink-wink. They're obviously hoping for Don Regan, but they're going to get Carl Sandburg. I'm thinking of calling it *Eugene Hoskins: Rail-splitter, Patriot, President.*"

"That'll really take off, Parker. Before you leave, see if they'll buy an option on *The Quotable Kurt Waldheim.*"

"You're about to talk yourself out of dinner."

"I don't have time for dinner. I'm on deadline."

"Not even a half-hour at Miyako's?"

She sighed. "Okay. I'll meet you in twenty minutes."

The crowded restaurant on West Forty-fifth Street off Seventh that Carole and some of her friends from the *Times* had discovered had managed to avoid being discovered by the restaurant reviewers at *New York* magazine or the *Village Voice* and was still mainly patronized by Japanese businessmen hunched over steaming bowls of ramen and week-old Tokyo newspapers. On their one previous visit together, DuBois had excitedly ordered *oyako don,* a mixture of scrambled eggs, chicken, and rice he'd relished ever since discovering it in a Bangkok noodle shop during R and R in 1968 but couldn't always get in pricier places. Carole took one look at it and turned green. He in turn couldn't abide the music on the PA system, which was tuned to a New York station that ran to Billy Joel and Madonna—which, as Carole pointed out, made Japanese visitors feel right at home.

When he walked in, suffused with a sense of well-being that radiated from the check in his jacket pocket, he saw she was already there, nursing her weekly beer and staring through the dirty window onto the street. DuBois thought she looked beat.

He bent to kiss her and then sat down facing her, folding his raincoat on the seat next to him. "Did you order?" he said.

She nodded.

"How's the family?"

She edged her glass across the table so he could take a sip. "I used to hear that every pregnant woman had moments where she despised the man who did it to her," she said, "but I never believed it." She took her glass back and lifted it to her lips, and as she looked at DuBois over the top, her eyes narrowed. "I've changed my mind."

DuBois patted her hand. "And here I thought you'd be

braced by the prospect of changing political history tomorrow," he said.

"Actually I'm pretty ambivalent about all this. Mauling other journalists doesn't come naturally to me."

"Shouldn't it?"

She gave him a knowing look. "I suppose you expect me to be bowled over by this provocative moral equivalence of yours," she said. "But why should the same rules apply to us as to politicians? We don't spend public money, we don't seek public favor, and we don't have the power."

"Oh, come on," he said, picking up his side of an argument they'd had before. "You've got a lot more influence over the everyday course of events than people in government. You can rally public sentiment a lot easier than public figures, even as you interfere with their efforts to reach the public directly. You insist that every element of a politician's life be subject to scrutiny, yet you resist all inquiry and criticism of your own activities. You ever see a reporter in the witness box during a libel trial? He acts like a guerrilla under interrogation in the basement of a Chilean jailhouse."

Carole grinned as she slid her chopsticks out of their paper sheath and broke them apart at the bottom. "A vigorous exploration by the press of the character and morals of this reporter would have been a little embarrassing to a certain old-world southern gentleman named DuBois last December," she said. Her expression turned serious. "Even if I granted your points, which I don't," she went on, transferring the fried onions from her tempura platter to his bowl, "it's the only system we've got. There's no solution to the problem—if it is a problem—that doesn't give the state power over the press. That isn't what you want, is it?"

He shook his head as he pumped in a few tablespoonsful of soy sauce. "Of course not," he said. "The only answer is for journalists to completely rethink their mistrustful, malignant relationship to society and the state. For that reason, I sometimes despair for our country. Someday an American government might really move against the press and succeed."

Carole smiled her most winning smile as she took back one of the onions and popped it into her mouth. "Oh, come on, Parker," she said. "You sound like a paranoid thriller writer. No wonder they gave you such a big advance."

"I'm serious," he said. "Think of it this way. In their wisdom, the framers assumed that if any branch of government had too much power, the people who held those positions would abuse them. Checks and balances flowed entirely from their understanding of human nature. If you look at the way American public figures behave, you'll see the socializing effect of the system. One can't imagine the Secretary of Defense calling troops into the street. He could, but he just wouldn't. But what about journalists? Aren't they as likely to abuse their power as the rest of us? You can admit that possibility, can't you?"

Carole, chewing a deep-fried shrimp, shrugged noncommitally.

He went on. "Isn't that human tendency going to be encouraged by the absence of constraints? I think it is. So you have respected columnists freely admitting that they make up anonymous sources to throw competitors off the trail. As editorial writers are so fond of telling us, unaccountability breeds abuse. And one day they'll go too far. Take this bizarre story about Gene's impending coup. For God's sake, Carole, you don't believe that, do you?"

"It wasn't our story," she said, flipping her hair over her shoulder.

"You ran it after the *Post* did."

"We haven't played it anywhere near as big."

"A meaningless distinction to the average reader."

"And *I've* never invented a source in my life, Parker DuBois," she said harshly.

It was his turn to shrug before plunging further into his rogues' gallery. "Then what about the new generation of reporters who say that if they'd been covering World War II and learned when D-Day was going to be, they would've printed it?"

"But I—"

He interrupted. "But Chuck Sampson intended to do precisely that. Remember, Carole, that you're an exception to the rule."

She set her jaw and glared at him, as if he'd suddenly become a real adversary. "A reporter doesn't like to be complimented by—" She caught herself, but her flashing eyes finished the sentence.

He let her moment of instinctual distrust for anybody in authority, even her out-of-authority fiancé, pass without comment. "You're a talented, honest journalist," he said softly. "I respect and admire you almost as much as I adore you. You're a credit to your business, and you're a member of a distinct, dwindling minority."

She jabbed angrily at a yam slice with her chopsticks. "Stevens is in the minority, not me."

"On the contrary. Stevens is the undistilled essence of modern American journalism. You just normally don't get such a concentrated dose in one bottle."

"You've made quite a study of the subject, I see."

He grinned. "I stole most of my material from Gene."

DuBois had sensed the discussion was becoming too heated, and Carole cooperated in his disengagement initiative. With a smile, she asked, "Does he carry around clippings about press atrocities the way Reagan used to with welfare horror stories from *Human Events?*" Then she noticed the time. "I'm sorry, sweetheart, but I've got to go," she said, tucking her napkin under her plate and reaching behind her chair for her coat.

He signaled for the check. "You going to watch Gene's speech at the office?"

She nodded. "I've also got a couple more calls to make before I close out the story."

He walked around the table and extended his arm so she could pull herself up. "I'll guide you through the bowels of hell," he said. She was about to tell him not to bother. She'd long since come to terms with Times Square's squalor, and even felt a little proprietary about it. Then she remembered he didn't have anything else to do.

He helped her on with her coat, squeezing her shoulders affectionately in the process. As she looked into his kind, strong face, a specter that had been nagging her suddenly loomed: the indomitable DuBois, finally singed by his proximity to power, retreating into domesticity like John Lennon, raising the little one, baking bread, and tapping away desultorily on his book of memories and dreams. She knew she would always love him. She was giddy with excitement about their having more time together. *But . . . but.* So as they stepped into the night and turned toward the *Times,* she said, "I worry about you, Parker. Are you really in the mood to write a book? Wouldn't you rather teach or something?"

"Ugh," he said. Then he added, with genuine enthusiasm, "I'm delighted to have a chance to spend some of my creative energy on myself. Do you realize I've been Gene Hoskins's third arm for twelve years? Spinning in the orbit of such an overpowering force has its dangers. You begin to wonder where his consciousness stops and yours begins." Sensing what she was getting at, he added, "I think I'm going to establish a small office, probably in my lawyer's suite, and maybe hire somebody to answer the phone and look up facts and figures. I might even make some speeches and do some consulting. Heck, look at Liddy on the lecture circuit and Agnew working for the Saudis. I should've gone bad years ago."

At Forty-third and Broadway, a discreet half-block from the *Times*'s main entrance, they stopped to kiss good-bye, lingeringly. Afterwards he looked down at her and said, "I'll bet you thought I was going to ask you to type it, didn't you?"

"It crossed my mind," she said, smiling as she turned away and went back to work.

One of the modern era's enduring anachronisms was the gathering of the entire United States government, save one junior Cabinet officer who stayed home for succession's sake, in the same room in the Capitol each year for the

President's State of the Union address. In an age when someone could have obliterated almost every official above the level of deputy assistant secretary of state for Far Eastern affairs with a missile launched from behind the Urals or beyond the continental shelf or with a tactical-nuke-bearing public television tote bag concealed in the lady's room, this was a massive, defiant act of nonviolent resistance. It was admirable, even awe inspiring, but probably pretty stupid.

The senators and representatives grumpily squeezed into their hard, leather-upholstered seats and squinted into the TV lights that were a few notches brighter than comfort allowed. They rubbed natural, custom-tailored shoulders to make room for the diplomatic corps, the Joint Chiefs of Staff, the commandant of the Coast Guard, the Cabinet, senior White House officials, and the justices of the Supreme Court in their somber, custom-tailored robes. The justices observed an unwritten code permitting them to show up and hog the front row but not to applaud any portion of the President's remarks, even a vigorous endorsement of the laws against child labor and wife beating. The place was so chockablock there wasn't the elbow room for much legislative arm-twisting. A legislator's primary mission, especially if he was a member of the President's party, was to try to get a seat on the aisle so he could lay a hand on the mystic vessel of American democracy as he was borne by.

But not tonight. Tonight they would have rather squeezed a rotten banana than the strong right hand of Eugene Hoskins.

The dynamics of the Sampson scandal were unique in Washington's annals, having almost nothing to do with traditional politics. Congresswide, constituent mail was running about two to one against the President. This was a decisive margin, but normally not enough to provoke the nation's representatives to treat the visiting President like a worsted-wool cannister of nerve gas that had been accidentally rolled down the center aisle. Most congressmen of both parties still secretly admired him. He was strong, competent, and personally likable. On domestic and economic issues, he had been a pragmatist, taking the substantial risk of sending up as his first budget a judicious mixture of spending cuts and new taxes that the members, afraid to take the initiative on revenue themselves, embraced like Moses' tablets. The Republican majority in the Senate kept trying to edge to his right on foreign policy. But after his predecessor sat down with the Soviets and decided that—despite enslaving a hundred states and ethnic groups across thirteen time zones—they were really just folks after all, Hoskins's hardheaded neo*realpolitik* had been a welcome relief to most savvy Washingtonians. The Beirut raid had legitimized his Middle East initiative, a tiny tilt to the Arabs that was little more than an effort to get the United States and its moderate friends in the region to talk to one another in public as civilly as they did in private.

So Congress liked Hoskins, and his forty-state landslide in 1992 proved the voters did, too. But in post-Sampson Washington, the last thing these congressmen were concerned about was offending voters. The handful who had defended Hoskins had been roped into a pen the press labeled "those few supporters of the Hoskins administration's anti-First Amendment actions and policies." For all but the most powerful legislators, this was not a comfortable brand to bear. Worst of all, it was a small enough group that everyone was receiving individual attention. Some correspondents had even taken to calling them a "cadre."

In short, the media had gone ballistic, and the President's friends in Congress had gone underground.

Who could blame them? Few people realized how dependent the average congressman was on press largess. Only those with the safest seats could afford to risk their access to relatively friendly coverage for the sake of shaking hands with a politically leprous president within sight of the unblinking eye. So most of those coveted aisle seats contained members who were scanning the chamber for someone who might abandon his landlocked position by going to the restroom.

Everyone was in his seat well before the President's precisely timed, slightly tardy arrival. Just as professional football was run according to the networks' clock, so was professional politics. Starting the speech exactly on time would mean either beginning the broadcast at 7:59 and deleting a commercial or skipping the President's arrival, which was the most dynamic part of the show. Both options were unthinkable. Thus the ultimate collective ritual of Washington's public life always started late, so the five private corporations that covered it could have time for their trumpet fanfares, "special report" graphics, and a brief anchorman's invocation.

Under new procedures promulgated by Speaker McCarthy, all five networks were using the same pool cameras trained on the podium from four different spots in the House chamber. In a new control room directly beneath the chamber, each network's news division had a producer observing the House technician who radioed the cameramen their instructions.

At one minute after eight, the President, wearing a gray suit and a navy blue tie, arrived outside the chamber. With the help of two pages pulling from inside, the doorkeeper opened the double main door and walked down the aisle to announce the guest's arrival. From here, backstage, the room lacked its familiar orderliness. Hoskins could see backs of heads and crowds of aides and security guards lining the rear wall, peering and grinning at him in the odd, off-balance way people peered and grinned at presidents and other celebrities. He looked toward the two seats behind the podium and saw his amiable vice-president, John Jeffreys of New York, listening as hard as possible to something McCarthy was urgently telling him. Just then Jeffreys looked up, met Hoskins's eyes, and made several rapid, panicky time-out gestures at McCarthy before leaning back and attempting to look like he was waiting for the Constitution Avenue bus. A careful study of the President at that moment would have revealed a twitching in the lower half of his ruddy, tired face, a protracted but successful effort to prevent his solemn expression from erupting into a grin as broad as the mouth of the Mississippi River. He could guess the presentation he'd interrupted: "John, you should stay at arm's length *for the President's own good.* It's what *he* would want you to do."

"Mr. Speaker," the doorkeeper said in his high, grating voice, "the President of the United States."

E. E. Perkins, the press secretary, had been given only one assignment that day by the President. He had called the Secret Service, the House majority leader's office, the Senate Democratic leader's office, the Speaker's office, the office of the Clerk of the House of Representatives, the sergeants-at-arms of both houses, and anyone else he could think of and tried to make sure that no other human being even *thought* about walking down the aisle with, ahead of, or behind the President. This required the Senate and House to forego appointing the usual escort committee. Under the circumstances, the Senate and House were pleased to comply. But for good measure, E. E. was standing near the door, intending to forcibly restrain anyone who attempted to mount an impromptu posse.

No one did. The President walked alone.

Virtually every legislator had cleared some time in his schedule earlier that day to mull over giving the President the customary standing ovation. Some had asked their staffs to do a memo, which had resulted in 127 requests to the Congressional Research Service for analyses of the videotape of Nixon's last SOTU speech in January, 1974, when he'd dragged the iron chains of Watergate to the Hill for the last time. "They *all* stood up for him," concluded 127 earnest young aides, many of whom added that some network commentators had taken special pains to emphasize that the gesture was purely a matter of tradition and in no way was to be construed as a sign of personal respect for the embattled President. Most members had read these studies, initialed them, and then decided to see what everybody else did before they made a final decision.

After the doorkeeper's announcement, there was a delay as the members began to applaud halfheartedly and look around frantically. A few daring souls were on their feet, but their courageousness went unnoted, because all eyes were on the President. In two important respects, he was just about the only man in the room.

A president normally elbowed his way in like a celebrity wrestler at the end of a long night's card, being nudged along by his handlers, shaking a hand every few steps, and stopping every once in a while to be massaged by some particularly ardent admirer. He would throw his head back and roar at jokes he hadn't had a hope of actually hearing over the din. But tonight Hoskins barreled down the aisle without company or a hint of a glance to right or left, his eyes boring into the American flag hanging on the wall between the startled faces of Jeffreys and McCarthy. His face wore an expression of almost frightening intensity, and in his determined, measured stride there was a hint of self-consciousness, as if he wished people to understand that his speech had already begun.

The five network anchormen watching on television from their Washington or New York studios began to comment excitedly about the departure from tradition and to ask their mystified correspondents, who were outside the chamber watching on television, what was going on. It was one of those transcendent moments when newsmen knew nothing more than the millions of other people watching on television, but could not bring themselves to do what propriety and good sense demanded and be quiet.

Meanwhile, the congressmen fixed on Hoskins's empty hands. "No copies for McCarthy and Jeffreys?" they whispered to one another. They hadn't been surprised when an advance text failed to arrive at their own offices that afternoon. They had assumed the White House either didn't want any leaks or was still desperately searching for a formula to get Hoskins off the hook. But to refuse to pack in copies for the vice-president and Speaker was unprecedented.

Then they looked at the podium for the two transparent monitors, the device speakers used to impersonate the audience at a tennis match. *And there's no TelePrompTer!* What was the poor bastard up to? Some members, worried about the *Post's* coup scare, sneaked glances at the doorways in the back of the room, half-expecting to see them darkened by green-clad soldiers. They were more guilty for looking than relieved over finding no one there.

Hoskins arrived in front of the two-tiered clerk's desk, which was fully stocked with the usual officious-looking assortment of congressional bureaucrats. He walked past his Cabinet and senior staff—they, at least, were standing—without a glance or gesture, and then mounted to the podium.

"Good evening, Mr. Speaker," he said to McCarthy, who stopped clapping long enough to reach down for Hoskins's hand. "Thanks for having me down."

"It's an honor, Mr. President," McCarthy said formally and distantly.

Hoskins turned to the vice-president. "Hello, John," he said, in a warmer tone. "I know you're under a good deal of pressure, and I appreciate the way you've been bearing up."

"Thank you, sir," Jeffreys said, at a genuine and typical loss for words.

Hoskins turned and faced his audience with an utterly blank expression, and in a moment the applause died down. McCarthy stood and uttered the usual introduction with somewhat less than the usual verve: "Members of Congress, I have the high privilege and distinct honor of presenting to you the President of the United States." The second ovation was more enthusiastic, because Hoskins was watching them with his deep, dark eyes and because they sensed in his bearing a measure of hauteur, even contempt, that as political animals they were compelled to acknowledge, since they themselves were contemptuous of supplicants and respectful if only rarely capable of displays of conspicuous courage. After a few seconds, though, Hoskins raised his hand. It was an order. They stopped, and an expectant silence settled over the chamber and the nation.

Standing two feet behind the podium, he moved his head a notch to his right to acknowledge Jeffreys. "Mr. President," he said in a powerful but flat voice, refusing to milk the irony of addressing the Senate's presiding officer in this way. Then to the left: "Mr. Speaker." Then the front: "Mr. Chief Justice, members of the Cabinet, ladies and gentlemen of the United States Congress, honored guests.

"The charter under which we serve together specifies that from time to time the President should give Congress a report on the state of the Union.

"This evening I must therefore report that the state of the Union is troubled. Not because we are not at peace, for we are. Not because our people are not by and large prospering and secure, for they are.

"But because the fabric of our Union is strained by a crisis which results—and here I wish to be very precisely understood—which results from my own inexcusable misjudgments regarding the unfortunate death of a young reporter from the *Washington Post*."

The audience was stone silent. Few had expected him to capitulate so quickly, and speculation shifted from revolution to resignation. *Was he going to quit? Not right here, right now?*

Since he had no text, as Hoskins spoke, he kept his eyes trained on individual members of the audience, moving his gaze every few phrases, avoiding the cameras' eyes completely. "Because the misjudgment ultimately was mine," he said, "last week I relieved seven former officials and employees of the executive branch of any legal responsibility.

"Those who have called this an abuse of power should remember two things.

"First, the Constitution places no limit on a president's pardon power. While our nation's editorial writers and commentators seem to be aware of limitations on that power that are not specified in Article Two, Section Two or anywhere else, save in their own overheated prose, I think even the strict constructionists on our high court"—here he nodded his head toward the nine robed figures in front of him without looking at them—"would have to concede that I was fully within my authority to take the action I did." The sound of mumbling and squirming descended from the press gallery above and behind him. *Press bashing! What gall!*

"Second, the critics will note that while I could also have pardoned myself, I did not. And I shall not. These loyal subordinates were in essence carrying out my policies. All I have done is to relieve them from suffering for misdeeds for which I automatically absolved them by giving my complete approval after the fact."

Done with that subject, Hoskins paused. He put his hands on the side of the podium and leaned against it. "It is my understanding," he said, "that in eight days the House Judiciary Committee will begin hearings on proposed articles of impeachment of the President." He smiled, for the first time. "I know a couple of you are lawyers"—here quite a few in the audience smiled, too—"and you probably wouldn't advise a client to reveal his legal strategy before the fact. But that's exactly what I'm going to do.

"First, there is the cover-up"—he emphasized the word, and at the sound of it, hundreds in the audience caught their breath—"of the circumstances surrounding the automobile accident in which the reporter died. I did not order the cover-up, but I approved it immediately afterward. By making this distinction I do not intend to shirk blame. Given the opportunity, I might well *have* ordered it if it had been necessary to protect the Beirut mission. Accordingly, neither I nor anyone representing me will contest this charge. I shall respond immediately and fully to all requests and subpoenas for information and materials and to all subpoenas of current and former employees of the executive branch. I expect to face a cover-up article in a Senate trial, and frankly I can think of no conceivable legal reason why

I should not." The tension in the room was giving way to curiosity. If he was going, it wasn't going to be quietly or quickly.

He continued. "Second, the media are airing charges of campaign irregularities. So far as I am aware, neither I nor anyone with whom I came into contact in either of my presidential campaigns has committed the illegal acts attributed to them in the media. I do intend to contest this charge, and I expect that my colleagues and I will be fully absolved.

"Third, I am charged with interfering with Charles Sampson's civil and legal rights as a journalist and a citizen of the United States." His eyes lifted toward the crowded visitors' gallery, drifted toward a pair of figures who were just being seated in a roped-off area to its right, and then focused on the floor again. "It is my contention," he continued, "that in the face of Mr. Sampson's refusal to abandon his irresponsible plan to reveal details of an impending use of American military power, I had no alternative but to detain him." Most of the faces before him were blank, but their eyes bespoke amusement, amazement, fascination. They were damned glad *they* weren't up there. "Further," Hoskins said, "I believe that *not* detaining him, and thus permitting his story to appear and putting in greater danger the lives of our imprisoned countrymen, would have been an inexcusable and possibly criminal abrogation of my responsibilities as president.

"On this issue, I expect and hope for a vigorous debate on the role of the press in our national affairs. It is an article of faith that the media's inherently adversarial posture is healthy and constructive. But we live in a time when it is the fashion, perhaps even the compulsion, to question articles of faith. Is it therefore not appropriate to ask whether the media's adversarial posture cannot at times be harmful to our country? I consider this not only our generation's greatest unanswered question but also its greatest unposed one. It is my hope that the one positive outcome of these unhappy proceedings will be an examination of what I consider to be modern democracy's greatest dilemma."

Again the President paused. Since he had no pages to turn or electronic crib sheets to read, his audience had no relief from the intensity of his gaze.

Then, bluntly: "Some have proposed that I resign. I shall not resign. One resignation a century is enough. Our Constitution specifies a means for removing presidents. The American people deserve to see that process carried through.

"President Nixon resigned before the House could vote to impeach him and at least six months before the Senate trial could have been properly conducted. Whether he could have prevailed in a proceeding conducted according to our legal system's rules of evidence instead of our media's, I do not know. I do believe that his voluntary relinquishment of the vast powers and privileges of this office saved our nation further anguish. But if I were to follow his example, an exception could become a pattern, and I believe our nation's anguish would be far greater for it."

John Jeffreys, perhaps the first vice-president in history to say he didn't care to be president and mean it, was visibly relieved. He now looked down at Hoskins with some of the respect and affection that many others in the room felt but still found it impolitic to express. Ten minutes had passed, and he had not once been interrupted by applause. As State of the Union addresses went, so far Hoskins' fifth was a disaster. He had scored early by walking in without a machine gun over his shoulder and by speaking in coherent sentences. But he had only shown the way toward months of controversy and paralysis. Congress's attitude was perfectly expressed by the empty expression on Fred McCarthy's face. Congress wasn't looking for a national debate on the media. It was looking to get this extremely awkward matter behind it as quickly as possible.

But he wasn't finished. His face and tone were darker when he spoke again. "There is another charge made by the media, one which I have difficulty speaking of without emotion. But I will try.

"It is suggested by some in the media that our men at arms conducted atrocities during military operations last May in Lebanon. I cannot permit this lie to go unnoted.

"Some of you served with me in Vietnam," Hoskins said, meeting the eyes of several fellow veterans. He met other eyes as he added, "Others opposed the war. I do not exaggerate when I say that our politics is still characterized by a sharp division between those who went and those who did not. That division is a wound in our society that has still not healed. By speaking so bluntly, I will be accused of reopening it. So be it.

"We came home from Vietnam accused of savagery against an enemy whose own savagery was so profound that our training left us wholly unprepared. Also, our leaders failed to give us, not to mention the American people, an adequate explanation of why we were there. In spite of these handicaps, Americans in Vietnam fought honorably and well. Those few exceptions, hardly more than the exceptions in previous American wars, stand in stark contrast to the actions of the enemy, for whom atrocities were an everyday tactical option."

Hoskins returned his hands to the sides of the podium and looked down. After a while he looked up and, with pain and anger etched on his face, said, "I have always believed the American press betrayed our men in Vietnam while they were there and when they came back. This may be a weakness in me. It may be a strength. I don't know. But I do know one thing: I will not permit them to betray the men who risked their lives in a noble cause last spring in Beirut."

He straightened and gazed into the middle of the room. "Last year two investigations, one by the department of defense and the other by this Congress, found that the Beirut mission was conducted entirely within the laws of our country and the laws of war and that all charges by various international organizations of so-called atrocities were unfounded. Both those commissions had full access to this administration's papers and personnel."

Now he looked toward the row of uniforms to his right, the joint chiefs of staff. "Accordingly, so long as I hold this office, I intend to use the authority embodied in the concept of executive privilege to block all further requests and subpoenas for information relating to our operation in Beirut. I shall *not*"—he smacked the podium with his palm, and the noise echoed through the room like a gunshot—"permit the men and women of our armed forces to be further harassed for the sake of my opponents' need to build a political case against me." Here there was a smattering of applause that Hoskins immediately quashed by raising his right hand.

He went on in a conversational tone that relieved some of the tension he'd just created. "Some members of my staff urged me to ask our former hostages to come up to the Hill with me today," he said with a smile. "I am a politician in trouble, ladies and gentlemen, and frankly I was tempted. But I decided it would be wrong to extricate them from the greatest misery of their lives only to embroil them in mine.

"But then I got a call last week from General Robert O'Brien. He said there was one man on that mission who insisted on coming forward. Bob said that if I refused to tell the story, he would. So I agreed. Incidentally, some have a more sinister interpretation of that telephone call that I won't dignify with further comment." As this mild rebuttal of the *Post*'s military coup allegations settled on the audience, there were the sounds of chairs squeaking and throats being cleared as members took a moment to convince themselves they'd never believed it, anyway. A few stretched their well-coifed heads to look up at the press gallery, where the reporters were scribbling more intensely in their notebooks than they had to when they had been given an advance text.

None of the press felt remorseful. Some felt skeptical. "So *he* says," muttered a *Post* reporter to a colleague. Most felt temporarily outflanked. Their confidence level remained high until Hoskins spoke again. Then a score of felt-tipped pens stopped scratching as the combined Capitol and White House press corps stared in befuddlement at the man so many of them abhorred and had therefore completely underestimated.

"This story is about another kidnapping and another cover-up," he said. "I'll gladly plead guilty to both if I have to. And it is about the humanity and courage that are the real essence of the American soldier.

"As I think you all know, that raid was not a pretty thing. In any successful antiterrorist operation, innocent people can be hurt, and some can die. It is a risk a president resists but must ultimately accept. Last May the casualties included a terrorist and his wife who lived in one of the buildings where hostages were imprisoned. You may have read something about that, but what you don't know is that they left a child behind. One of our men found him. At great risk to himself and in spite of some pressure from his colleagues, who reminded the young lieutenant that regulations strictly prohibited what he was proposing to do, he insisted on carrying the baby out of the combat zone."

Hoskins smiled again. "Of course, Bobby O'Brien, being a by-the-book soldier, bucked the problem to me. Soon we found out that the lieutenant and his wife had just lost their own infant daughter. So I decided, as I think any one of you also would have, to permit the young officer to bring the baby out. I contacted the president of Lebanon, who was able to learn that the child had no immediate family in Beirut. After obtaining his consent, I persuaded our own immigration authorities to arrange an adoption as quietly as possible, so this new family would have a fighting chance."

The United States Congress was restive. Was he nuts? Was this some kind of gimmick? So much ground was being covered that many wished they could toss the whole thing around a bit with their staffs.

Others glanced toward Pennsylvania's distinguished, stately, white-topped mountain of a senior senator, Marshall Brandon, who had been watching the President from a seat near the center of the chamber. A number of his leadership colleagues—all outwardly sympathetic to his disappointment about missing the opportunity to lead a major Senate investigation, most inwardly amused at how suddenly the spotlight had left him in the shadows—were gathered around him, forming a wedge of silent contempt for the slippery southerner who was now posturing so bathetically for the camera.

But the expression on his Rushmoresque features and the periodic nodding of his massive, silver-shrouded head told an unexpected tale. He was impressed. *Darned if Gene Hoskins isn't making good sense. Nobody has a right to impugn our young men and women in uniform!* If George Stevens had been there, he would have whispered, "It's the wrong party, you idiot!" But he wasn't. In the absence of Stevens's influence, Brandon's own began to spread through the crowd.

Eyes shifted from the senator back to the President. "Bobby O'Brien said this young couple insisted on coming forward," he said. "I told them they might lose their baby and become part of another article of impeachment to boot, but they only said, 'When do you need us there?' " He looked up at the two figures in the gallery again. "So here they are. Lieutenant Emilio Stewart and Tomasa, why don't you two kids stand up?"

When the President gestured to the gallery, everyone in the television control room except the House technician started to squirm. They couldn't see what was happening, but their instincts told them they'd better find out.

"Who's he pointing at?" whispered the Fox representative.

"What's going on?" asked NBC. "Can we get it?"

"I'm supposed to keep it on Hoskins," said the technician, staring stubbornly at the four monitors.

ABC had headphones on and had heard the noisy rustling of eleven hundred men and women turning in their seats to look into the gallery. She whipped them off and nearly yelled, "We've *got* to get that shot."

"We want the shot, asshole," said Fox in a clipped voice.

The technician protested. "The Speaker's staff said—"

"The Speaker can eat my shorts," said Fox. He reached over and tore the technician's headset off. The technician started to stand; NBC and CNN sat on him. Fox put on the headset and said, "Camera two, get the gallery. *Now!*" The monitor showed a dizzying, blurry pan from the President up to where two figures stood. As soon as the image zoomed in and steadied, Fox pushed the lit "2" button on the control panel.

Viewers suddenly saw a closeup of a handsome, serious-looking naval officer in his dress blues, standing at attention with glistening eyes as he saluted his commander-in-chief. His small, startlingly young wife, wearing a red dress with big white bows on each shoulder, was looking back and forth from Hoskins to the dark, doe-eyed baby boy she held in her arms, smiling affectionately at both. Tears of excitement and joy coursed down her face.

From Concord to San Diego, 50 million hearts reached out for them instantly. Such was the brute force of television. On the House floor, it took only one. Such was the magic of politics.

For a long moment Marshall Brandon stared over his pinstriped right shoulder at the couple in the balcony. In a sea of confused whispers, he was a well of quiet. Then, to the astonishment of his colleagues, he faced front and stood up. He squared his shoulders, fixed the President with a respectful stare, and began to applaud, slowly at first, then faster and more insistently. "Hear, hear!" he shouted, his deep, musical voice filling the chamber. Instantly his ramrod-straight six feet became the new axis along which the political world began to spin.

The *Post*'s George had never quite understood that inside his dumb old buddy beat a heart as big as that of Steinbeck's Lenny. That was why Brandon had not yet mastered the fundamentals of politics: The fool kept calling them as he saw them. And when everyone else saw him on his feet—the President's most eloquent critic, cheated out of his moment of glory only because the President's contempt for the American people ran deeper than anyone imagined—then they, too, were moved to reexamine what they liked to call the state of play. This calculation took about two seconds. A few others stood and applauded, and it sounded at first as if Brandon's own clapping was richocheting wildly around the chamber. Then hundreds of right and left legs pumped up like pistons and right and left hands began to pound together, and before anyone knew what was happening, the man who fifteen minutes before could not have borrowed five dollars in this room was getting the most deafening standing ovation of his life.

The noise shook the control room below like a depth charge. While the technician's slack-jawed captors stared at the screen, he managed to squirm free, and after gazing for a few more seconds at the screen, he reached out to hit the button for the center aisle camera. When it came back on the main monitor, they could see the President with his hands at his sides, standing a few steps back from the podium, looking not at the raucous audience but up at the mother with a small smile on his face. The technician hit camera two again; she was looking right back down at him, gratefully and adoringly. The technician switched back to camera one just as the President returned the lieutenant's salute.

The network observers knew a "defining moment" when they saw one. They also knew one hadn't been scheduled this particular evening. Their scenario had called for Hoskins to act out a demonstration of public humiliation and disintegration or, even better, a dramatic fit of rage. Instead, he was giving them the bird. CBS, made uneasy by the ease with which Hoskins had turned the tide, or at least contained it, spoke for countless of his colleagues when he muttered, "Son of a *bitch*."

In New York, Parker DuBois had been packing books and records, which he'd unpacked only a couple of weeks before, when Hoskins's speech began. At first he continued to work while he watched a portable set he'd propped on a bar stool. The Ford Foundation had offered him the apartment until it found a new president, which could take as long as six months, but he preferred to move. Hoping to lure Carole away from Greenwich Village with a commanding view of Long Island City, he'd put a deposit on a three-bedroom apartment in a new high-rise on Third Avenue.

Thirty seconds into Hoskins's address, he'd wandered over and sat down on the next stool and stared at his friend with growing excitement. *He's sure got his chops tonight!* Fifteen minutes later, he was still sitting there with a smile spread over his face, still absentmindedly holding a volume of Eisenhower's presidential memoirs in each hand. Hoskins normally wasn't one for show-biz gestures or human visual aids, preferring to persuade through obstinacy and the sheer force of reason and will. But then DuBois thought back to May. He had been with the President when, for reasons that had everything to do with humanity and nothing to do with PR, he had decided on the problematical option of letting Stewart have his way and bring the child out. It seemed a relatively small thing that had become a big one, big enough to improve Hoskins's prospects dramatically. It was a gimmick, DuBois guessed. But he finally decided the American people were entitled to see the essence of Gene Hoskins in living color.

Across town at the *Times,* a dozen reporters and editors, including Carole Nelson, were gathered around a set that was mounted on a support column in the middle of the newsroom. They had watched the speech silently until the exchange of salutes and the ovation, which triggered an orchestral suite of groans and oaths.

"Katie bar the door," said one writer, looking grimly at the bemedaled Stewart. "Here comes Oliver *Norte,* America's equal-opportunity war criminal for the nineties. Too bad Checkers wasn't stuffed. They could've rolled him out, too."

"Does Hoskins think anyone's going to buy this?" said another. "You can't swing a dead archbishop's envoy in West Beirut without hitting somebody's relative. They must not have looked too hard."

The first reporter responded, "Don't worry, it'll play. Never underestimate the simpleminded, jingoistic sentimentality of the American people." He warmed to the scenario, setting his stance and making blocking-out gestures with his hands. "Here's what'll happen," he said. "On the first day, there'll be outrage and marching in the streets as various goody-goody groups condemn the misappropriation of a helpless foreign national. On the second day, Hoskins has Emiliano—"

"Emilio," said the other reporter.

"Whatever. He'll have him and his cute little wife to the White House, which means two-minute spots on all five networks and four-color art on the cover of *USA Today,* around which they'll wrap the *USA Today* poll showing that 75 percent of the people think the tyke will have a better life being raised by *Americanos* rather than unwashed crazies in the Middle East. By the fourth day, voluntarily deporting it to Beirut will add to Hoskins's troubles, not detract from them. Meanwhile, the evil media will camp out on Emiliano's lawn, harassing the wife and the baby and once again earning the public's contempt for not being able to leave good, innocent people alone. In the end, even if Hoskins is somehow forced to repatriate it, he still wins."

The two reporters' attention returned to the screen. Carole, her features blank as she watched the broadcast and their exchange, said nothing. Since the pardon, word had gotten around about her and DuBois, and, in the last couple of days, about the story she was about to tell on George Stevens and the *Post*. Newspaper people were as clannish as cops and Teamsters, and while no one had said anything to her about either matter, she sensed a cooling in her colleagues' attitude toward her.

She shifted her weight from one overtaxed leg to the other. *Who cares?* This was a *New York Times* story, not a Carole Nelson story; otherwise she wouldn't have gotten past the editorial conference last Friday. So they should freeze out her editors, too. They also probably thought she was carrying water for Parker, an assumption she hoped would evaporate when they read the story. It was true she had developed it out of a stray, tiny detail he had inadvertently provided, but it wouldn't have gone any further without a big hunch of her own and a lot of digging. And why *should* she have turned it over to the Washington bureau, as some of her fellow reporters in both towns seemed to think she should have done? So Punch could save on long distance? *I know my way around that town as well as anybody in the bureau.*

The speech ended, and one of Carole's two colleagues, irritated either by the applause or the awkward ad-libbing of the startled commentators, reached up and turned down the volume on the television set. Hoskins was making his way back up the aisle, this time flanked by the smiling House majority and Senate Democratic leaders, stopping every few feet to shake hands with members in aisle seats who had been blown to their feet by the sudden change in the political winds. She looked at her watch and lumbered back to her desk. She had to touch one more base before letting the copy desk have her story.

Back on the Hill, the network producers were huddled around one of the monitors, watching a tape of the end of the speech. When they came to Hoskins's ragged little ex-colonel's salute, Fox said, "How the hell did he know when to do that?"

"Simply, revoltingly perfect," said ABC.

Added CBS, again summing up, "We are *screwed.*"

This was not exactly the way it was. Along with everyone else, he had been caught up in the drama of the moment. But even in the cold light of morning, few disagreed with the veteran national correspondent of *The New York Times,* who grudgingly opined in a front-page "news analysis," which was to say a front-page editorial: "The Louisiana Sidewinder has slithered back into the ring."

Hoskins's speech was like a cluster bomb lobbed into the middle of the *Washington Post* newsroom. A task force of fifteen reporters and editors was working the State of the Union address, and they had their hands full preparing a half-dozen articles and news analyses for the next morning's paper. The promise to defy Beirut-related subpoenas was story number four; the refusal to resign was number three; the admission of "inexcusable misjudgments" was number two.

But the baby was story number one, and it wasn't going down well at all. Herb McGraw, the national editor, yelled out at one of his reporters, "Can't we get one of those human rights outfits to condemn them for stealing it?"

"I've got two," said the reporter from his desk fifteen feet away. "But we've also got twenty congressmen and senators, from McCarthy on down, praising it. And they've got a point. You realize they blew up the building after they pulled out, don't you?"

"How's the speech playing in general?"

"Damn well," admitted the reporter. He scrolled through the notes on his computer screen. "We've got a lot of guys appreciating his honesty and candor, his cooperativeness—"

"Cooperativeness?" interrupted McGraw. "He said he'd defy subpoenas!"

The reporter shrugged. "What can I say? Since Beirut, the promilitary stuff plays again. And frankly, a lot of them like the bastard, and maybe now they figure it's not the end of the world to say so. If the House were held by the Republicans, it'd be different; they'd be aching for the payback for Nixon and Reagan. As it is, they're going to bend over backwards for the guy. Some will even be inclined to say, 'He's admitted his mistake. Just so long as he promises not to kill any more reporters.' "

McGraw was surprised. "You don't think he'll beat impeachment, do you?"

"I didn't say that. This was his best shot, and he made the most of it. While he's got a fighting chance again, remember that the man destroyed evidence to save his own skin. We'll wear him down."

McGraw looked away from the reporter and glanced through George Stevens's picture window. The senior editor, who normally would be in the thick of planning the coverage, seemed to have lost interest in his historic scoop. He was sitting alone in his office, watching the network postmortems that were still underway. McGraw had watched from his own desk on a Casio portable, and he had sneaked a glance at his superior when Brandon was shown coming to his feet. Stevens was giving the screen the finger. Now he could see the senior editor smiling a little as the various panels of stunned correspondents applauded the President's guts and showmanship but politely cautioned their viewers about the "many unanswered questions."

Just as McGraw looked away, the editor's phone rang.

He picked up. "Stevens," he said, still fixed on the television.

"This is Carole Nelson—"

Bitch wants to come back. Well she can—

"—of *The New York Times.*"

"I know where you work," Stevens snapped. "How's it going? Congratulations on your old man's pardon."

"Thank you," she said. "I'm calling to offer you the opportunity to comment on a story we're running tomorrow."

THIRTEEN

SO EUGENE HOSKINS LIMPED SAFELY BACK UP PENNSYLvania Avenue to the White House with restored measures of honor, dignity, and, most important, breathing room, thanks to his boffo performance and *el dios de la maquina* that had appeared in the House balcony. Like Terry Malloy stumbling back to work on the docks in the last reel of *On the Waterfront,* the President had reestablished his foothold on the premises, though it remained to be seen whether the beating he'd taken would permit him to do any heavy lifting.

And on Friday, columnist Ethan Spravak came blazing back during the taping of "King's Round Table," in the wake of the astonishing report in *The New York Times* three days before. He'd been virtually muzzled during the special prime-time broadcast the previous week, when there had been no market for any line of analysis that didn't paint the President as the enemy of every enlightened democratic development since the Greek *ostrakon*. But Hoskins's gritty eloquence and George Stevens's audacity restored Spravak's substantial capacity for both, and he promptly sank his blunt rhetorical fangs into the tweedy arm of his archrival, Louis Camare.

The severity of Spravak's attack was perhaps intensified by the *Post*'s having dropped his syndicated column in 1989, leaving him with 430 major dailies but none in the Washington market, which for a Washington columnist was to say none, period.

"Who's abusing power now?" he taunted the patrician, white-lipped *Post* columnist. "Who's violating the public trust? Who's lying, who's covering up, who's putting his own political interests ahead of the truth?" He turned to their extremely flexible host, who studied his conservative panelist with renewed interest. "Now we *do* owe our listeners an apology, Peter," Spravak said. "This entire crisis has been cynically manipulated to serve the interests of the *Post,* its ambitious editor, and his Senate pet, Marshall Brandon." Returning his gaze to Camare, Spravak said, "Stevens hasn't apologized to the American people yet. Should he, Mr. Camare? Will you tell our listeners that you repudiate him and his betrayal of his own reporter? Or do you stand by him and support using our precious First Amendment liberties to produce fake news for you and Georgie to use?"

His iron discipline melted by Spravak's sarcasm, Camare burst out, "The pregnant mistress of an admitted felon has made unfounded—"

"Now wait one damn minute," shouted Alice McGuire, so loudly and uncharacteristically that Camare stopped with his mouth half-open and stared at her. The deep, black pupils of her eyes trained on him like a double-barreled shotgun. "Carole Nelson is an outstanding reporter, and I haven't seen or read a single convincing refutation of the basic elements of her story," she said angrily, "and that includes those of George Stevens and the *Post,* both of whom have been trying to will the scandal away by a continuous and increasingly unsatisfactory chant of no comment."

She turned her shaggy blonde head toward King, and when she spoke again, her husky voice was more under control. "But it won't go away. The saturation coverage it's had on the network news for three straight nights proves it won't. This man apparently sat on the story of the decade for seven months and then tried to ride it to power himself. This is the greatest press scandal since the same newspaper won the Pulitzer Prize ten years ago for a profile of a nonexistent teenage drug addict, and we'd better face up to it." She nodded toward Camare without looking at him. "And smearing the messenger won't help."

"I agree," ruled King, glancing at Camare. "Let's not get personal, Louis."

"We're exploring new frontiers in good taste today, are we?" said Camare coldly. "Fine. Then I'll just say that whether there's any truth to this pastiche of unnamed sources and unattributed accusations against the *Post—*" Here each of his colleagues suddenly felt the same strange mixture of amusement and foreboding. How often had they heard an accused politician use these words while scrambling for position? How often had they savored his discomfiture in the same way a fisherman smiled at the sight of his quarry convulsing desperately on the end of the line? "—that remains to be seen. But whether it is or not, it doesn't change the complexion of the constitutional crisis into which the President has plunged us. Charles Sampson is still dead. The cover-up remains. Other charges persist. This soap opera of the *Times* is but a momentary distraction from the real business of this nation, which is to get Mr. Hoskins out of the White House and into—"

"You'd better watch it, Louis," said Winston Reedy, mildly but insistently.

"Yeah. Into where, Louis?" said Spravak, goading him. Would the representative of the newspaper that had just been discovered directing a rigged trial by media have the audacity to pronounce sentence, too?

"Why, *retirement*, of course," said Camare with a thin smile. "What did you fellows think I was going to say?"

Pete King turned to Reedy. "Do you long-view boys over at the *New Republic* agree with that? Isn't this business with the *Post* essentially irrelevant to the larger issues at stake?"

"Unfortunately, no," said the columnist, without his

usual ebullience. "In Washington we see two distinct scandals, but I don't think that's how the public sees them. We like to imagine voters, listeners, and readers sitting around their dining-room tables debating the same technicalities that make Washington cocktail parties, and probably these weekend programs, so unremittingly dull. But they don't. They tend to see the big picture and the mighty clashes of great forces, which in this case are the President versus the press." A rueful smile lit his face. "And I'd have to say that at the moment the score is tied, one squalid mess apiece."

Camare was outraged. "Winston is, of course, inclined to forgive the man who fulfills all his militaristic fantasies," he said. "But I'm not. This is still the worst White House scandal since Watergate."

"Says who?" asked Alice sarcastically. "Says the press?"

"Say the American people, of course."

Reedy, who'd been shuffling some papers on the table in front of his place, came up with the one he was looking for. "That's not what this morning's CBS/*New York Times* poll indicated," he said. "It shows the President's approval rating up twelve points, the largest rise attributable to one speech in the history of the survey. And in response to the question, 'Do you approve or disapprove of the way the American media have handled the Sampson scandal?' the result was seventy-five percent disapproval." He looked up from his notes and scanned the faces of his colleagues as he continued. "You'll note it said 'the media,' not just the *Washington Post*. I hear the American people saying that before we worry any more about treachery in the White House, we'd better get our own house in order."

When King had signaled the end of the taping, he and the four writers detached their microphones and sat morosely in their seats for a few moments while the technicians doused the lights. Finally Reedy said, "Damn it, Louis, didn't you know what George was up to?"

Camare looked at him haughtily at first, but then his face fell. "No," he said, reaching for the briefcase next to his chair. "You know as well as I do that I don't have much contact with newsside."

Alice was staring into the darkness behind one of the cameras. "I was at a reception at the Willard last night for the Maryland House Democratic delegation," she said in a small voice. "I know every one of these guys. I consider some of them friends." She turned to look at Reedy. "But you should've seen the look in their eyes. It was a subtle blend of quiet loathing and supreme satisfaction."

"Nice image," said Spravak. "I don't suppose we'll see it in your story on Sunday."

She glared at him and went on. "A few of them said, 'You've really stepped in it this time, sweetheart.' I'd say, 'What do you mean, *I've* stepped in it? It wasn't our story, for heaven's sake. Go smirk at George Stevens.' But they'd change the subject or wander away." She shook her head. "Politicians are the ultimate fair-weather friends, and I guess I'd brought my own personal rain cloud to the party."

"Politicians are never friends," said King. "They need and use us; we need and use them. How many of you would sit on the biggest story of your career because it hurt somebody you were close to, even friends with?"

"I might," said Alice, pouting.

"I wouldn't," said Spravak. He grinned. "And you wouldn't, either." She glared again but didn't speak.

Camare had his briefcase on his lap but hadn't made a further move to leave. Usually eager to avoid these post-taping bull sessions, this time he appeared to take comfort from the camaraderie. "We make them squirm for a living," he said. "Their seeing us squirm is a pleasant and all-too-rare form of recreation. You can't blame them for enjoying it as much as we do."

King said, "I think it's worse than that, this time. We'd just brought another president to his knees. The combination of his counterattack at the State of the Union and the *Times* story has built a firewall and perhaps even saved him." He nodded toward Reedy. "These rubbery polls show he still has a residue of popularity that won't be easily overcome. The public's going to be watching the media now, not him. So will we keep the heat on, or let up? We'll do it like John McLaughlin does on his program. You tell me, and then I'll tell you. Alice?"

She was smiling, but her eyes looked tired. "My only question is whether we can get our crow cooked to order," she said. "But even if they serve it on the hoof, I'm for eating as much as we have to."

King grunted. Whether this indicated agreement or disappointment was unclear. "Winston?"

"If there are more Hoskins revelations, which there probably will be during the impeachment hearings, then we've got to cover and discuss them," he said. "But from now on, we've got to be a whole lot more scrupulous. Some of these stories, especially the atrocities and the campaign irregularities, have been pretty thin. I'd say the only clearly impeachable offense is the cover-up."

Camare interrupted. "What about the child the soldier kidnapped?"

"Lacking a more sinister version of the story than Hoskins's, it's untouchable," said Reedy, shuffling his papers some more. "The polls—"

"Forget it," said Camare, closing his eyes and waving his hand. "I've seen them."

"And there's now enough hostility toward the press in the Congress and in the country that *Sampson's* kidnapping is beginning to be as popular as the Emancipation Proclamation. If I were calling the shots for the press, I'd say focus on the lies and destruction of evidence, but only after putting George Stevens's head on a stake in Lafayette Park." Reedy's brown eyes flashed behind his wire-rimmed glasses. "That son of a bitch has got to go."

Camare didn't wait for King to recognize him. "I agree we've got a public relations dilemma," he said, "but that doesn't mean Hoskins is off the hook." He looked at Alice. "Besides, while I appreciated your gesture of sisterly solidarity on the show, you have to admit that Nelson's vulnerable on the simple question of conflict of interest."

She said wearily, "Louis, the story's solid, and the story has stuck. It's bad enough to go after a pregnant heroine, but if it looks like we're doing it just to regain tactical ground, we're going to be in worse shape than we are already."

King summed up. "And that's just how it's going to be. From now on, on this program, the commander-in-chief gets the benefit of the doubt, squared, while George Stevens is persona non grata and Carole Nelson our savior, her scoop and her pregnancy both acts of immaculate conception." While gathering his notes and preparing to rise, he paused, cocking an ear. "But where's the thunder on the right?" he said gamely. "We haven't heard Ethan's game plan for saving the republic and our overpaid butts."

The columnist had his chair tilted back on its two rear legs and his thumbs tucked into his vest pockets. "I'm just an informed observer," he said, with one of his awful grins, "watching the proud American press while they rig the news, with fear and favor." After he'd absorbed a final volley of insults and curses, the knights of "King's Round Table" sallied forth, bloodied and not exactly unbowed.

"So why did you become a reporter?" Pat Robinson said.

The next evening, a cold, snowy Saturday, she and Carole were in a small Bangladeshi restaurant above a real estate office, somewhat off the Bally-beaten track on a Georgetown side street. Business was good upstairs as well as down. Both condos and cuisines of desperately poor Third World countries always sold well in Washington's playground beyond Rock Creek. Long before the Reagan state department had summoned the courage to deliver Stinger missiles to the mujahideen in Afghanistan, Washington's new Afghan restaurants were delivering rush orders to the eighteenth-century townhouses of deputy assistant secretaries of state. Congressmen who had voted against military aid to Saigon had no qualms about appropriating personal funds at the many new restaurants established by those South Vietnamese refugees hearty or lucky enough to survive the gulag or the boatlift across the South China Sea.

Being overrun by Communists gave a nation and its cooking a cachet that Bangladesh, formed from a subcontinental stew that had been as confusing as it was bloody, seemed to lack. Even still, tonight almost all the twenty or so tables in the place Carole had suggested were full, so she and Pat Robinson spoke quietly, as everyone did in Washington restaurants, often only to be more intently eavesdropped upon.

This was their second extended conversation. The first had been over the telephone a week before, when Carole, on the afternoon of her editorial conference at the *Times,* had discovered what she suspected was the meaning behind the entry ROBINSON.NTS on the printout from what was left of Chuck Sampson's file in the *Post*'s computer.

Sitting uncomfortably at her desk, she had consulted the office copy of the Federal Directory and found four Robinsons in the executive branch, one of whom was listed as deputy director of Near East and South Asia affairs in the NSC. She had been one of Parker DuBois's key Mideast aides. That the name was unfamiliar she took as further proof of her and Parker's mutual, fierce, completely incredible sense of discretion.

Then she looked again. *Robinson, Dr. Patricia Kaye.* The scuttlebutt liberally spread by sources at the *Post* was that Stevens had learned key details about Sampson's visit to the White House from a *woman,* obviously one close to the center of power. As she reached for the telephone to dial Robinson's number in the Old Executive Office Building, Carole was surprised to see that her forearm was covered with goosebumps. After she punched the number, she sat back and stared across the busy newsroom, which was beginning to fill with people and an atmosphere of controlled frenzy as the first deadline for the city edition neared. *Stevens would have found her name the same way I did,* by rummaging around in a dead man's electronic remains. She wondered to what use her inventive former boss had put the information.

When the analyst answered in her small, emotionless voice, Carole introduced herself, took a deep breath, and asked politely whether Dr. Robinson might confirm for the readers of *The New York Times* that she had disclosed plans for the Beirut operation to Charles Sampson. Instead of hearing the reaction she'd expected—evasiveness or contrived outrage—Carole was shocked by the sense of frightened vulnerability that seemed to course through the line.

"You don't understand," she had said, whispering, begging, obviously near hysteria. "He might even try to *kill* me if he finds out. He's already done far worse, so I know he's capable of it."

"Who'll kill you, for goodness sake? Not someone in the administration?"

"Not anymore."

"Then who? Where? Is he the reason you talked to Chuck?"

"Please—" Carole could hear air catching in her throat, as if she was trying to suppress waves of sobs. "Please just leave me alone."

Carole spoke as persuasively as she could. "Dr. Robinson, you have nothing to fear from me. I wouldn't ever reveal your name without your permission."

"That's just what George Stevens said. He *didn't* say he wouldn't reveal my gender," Robinson said, anger briefly displacing fear. "I don't suppose I have to tell you that when you coyly imply to every columnist in town that you got information from a high-ranking female in the Hoskins administration, you are talking about a strictly finite set."

This time Carole had felt the chill blanketing her, as if someone had suddenly thrown open a window to let in the winter wind. *The evil bastard!* By somehow persuading her to tell him a tale he already knew, he'd made her his unwitting accomplice, a show source to be paraded across the country if anyone ever questioned the genesis of his story.

Pat was still talking. "I've nothing more to tell you."

"Don't worry," Carole had said quickly. Whether justified or not, such genuine anguish left her no acceptable alternative. Such deceit as Stevens's demanded recompense. She would protect this source. But was there also some way she could protect this person? A perverse mixture of fascination and compassion drew her closer, making her eager to meet the woman and try to learn more. "Please don't worry. But can I call you again later? Not for a story, but just to see—frankly, at the risk of being presumptuous, I'd like to check to see how you are. I don't understand how you could be this upset."

Robinson laughed bitterly and meanly and said, "Why should *you* want to talk to me again? If it's worth your while, then it's dangerous for me. If it's not, why bother?"

"Please."

The line was silent. Finally she said, "If it's a condition for your not using my name—"

"It's not," Carole said. "I'm asking a personal favor. I won't ever use or speak your name, whether you talk to me again or not."

When Robinson spoke again, her voice was livelier. "All right," she said. "You know, Chuck could've learned something from you."

Carole paused. "He was a good reporter," she said. "He just lacked a certain sense of perspective."

Robinson had laughed quietly but warmly. "That's like saying an orangutan tossing his dinner around the cage lacks a certain sense of dignity," she said.

Once the story about George Stevens's conspiracy had appeared and the woman could see the promise had been kept, Carole called to arrange the meeting. She took the train down to Washington that afternoon. They sat at the far end of the room, away from the entrance, at a table with a woven tablecloth and a guttering candle encased in glass and white plastic netting. As they sipped wine and waited for dinner, they pretended they were friendly acquaintances and not strangers brought together by public and evidently also secret tragedies. When Robinson asked why she was in the newspaper business, Carole was happy to have an opportunity to reveal something about herself, hoping it would make information flow easier in the other direction later. She intended to keep her word about never using Pat's name. She was equally determined, for hopelessly intermixed human and professional reasons, to find the source of the pain that seemed to be draped over Pat like her shroudlike clothing.

Of the two women, one pregnant and the other slim and nice looking, if uninviting, it was Carole who had drawn sidelong glances from the men they passed while walking to their table. Struggling against monumental odds to look reasonably stylish, Carole had on her pearls and a black knit dress with an empire waist, long sleeves, and a dramatically low-cut back. Her hair was drawn back over her shoulders, exposing silver earrings and her angular neck. In contrast, Pat wore no jewelry and a plum and navy shirtwaist dress and blue blazer that masked her figure. Her straight blonde hair was cut short. Next to Carole—next to almost anyone—she made little impression. In an upholstery showroom, she would have flickered like the candle and disappeared.

Before answering Pat's question, Carole impulsively sprinkled some red chutney over her chicken *biryani*. "I'm going to regret this in the morning," she said.

"Regret what?" said Robinson, looking up. "Having dinner?" Her eyes were troubled, her pale features empty.

"Having this particular dinner in this particular condition," replied Carole. "If I were smart, I'd stick to oatmeal and mint tea."

Her partner shrugged. "I wouldn't know," she said, looking back at her plate. "I won't ever know." Here Carole tried to catch Pat's eyes, but she didn't look up again. Such a melodramatic remark rendered so matter-of-factly deepened Carole's curiosity. Was it a signpost to the forbidden territory?

She turned instead to Pat's question. "In newspaper work, if you work hard enough, you can achieve an approximation of perfection," Carole said, reaching for a slice of buttery paratha bread, staring at it for a second, and then putting it back on the serving plate. "At least for me, the challenge is to try to communicate the essence of a person or a situation. A good newspaper story is a picture of a moment of reality, like an Impressionist painting. If you're lucky, the moment's small enough so you can get most of it right. It's harder than you think. Every story can have an infinite number of facets, often cross-cutting and contradictory; and yet the greatest weakness of our business is that we want it crystal clear. A lot of reporters decide what they want the story to say before they start making calls, and then paste in whatever facts and quotes prove their point. Whenever you read a piece where everything fits together as neatly as a jigsaw puzzle, look out. If there's no ambiguity—especially in the realms of the motives and beliefs that drive people to do what they do—then it probably isn't true."

Pat had listened carefully, but when she spoke, her face was skeptical. "How often can you achieve it? How often are you permitted to?"

Carole reached for the bread again and took a bite, then shrugged. "Good question," she said as she chewed. "I compromise a lot. Most of the time, in fact. Ambiguity doesn't win awards, and editors and publishers, not to mention reporters, do crave awards. But I do the best I can." She massaged her breastbone, took a sip of water, and pushed her plate away. As the heartburn began to fade, she went on. "I'm still attached to the notion of a public that, if it's clearly given the basic facts of a matter, doesn't need to be prodded toward the right conclusions by the snot-nosed, know-it-all, thirty-five-year-old white males who seem to write most of America's news."

Robinson smiled weakly. "Your not-so-golden mean seems to be a perfect description of Charles Sampson."

Carole looked closely at the woman. She was being invited to peel back a layer. "Had you known him long?"

"I knew him at Harvard," Pat replied. "I was an assistant professor at the Kennedy school, and he was a callow *Crimson* reporter who had dedicated himself to making the editorial board by exposing the medieval injustices of our department's tenure system." She smiled. "I had him in a class, and he began to cultivate me—you know, investigative reporter style." She looked pointedly at Carole and gestured over the plates and dishes on the table.

Carole smiled. "Touché," she said.

"He would come to office hours and promise me that we were on something called deep background and that he wouldn't reveal my name even if they got rough and took away his Adams House meal ticket and his Coop card."

"Did he expose any injustices?"

"Sort of," she said. "He revealed that a Welsh specialist in comparative government, a Marxist, was denied tenure as a result of the vigorous objections of the chairman, a conservative who'd served in the Reagan administration."

"Was he?"

"Yes, but it had more to do with his getting drunk at a party at the chairman's house and throwing up on the one-hundred year old Ottoman Empire carpet in the foyer."

"You didn't tell Chuck about it?"

"Of course not," Pat said, looking away from Carole to rearrange the salt and pepper shakers. "There are still things that don't belong in the newspaper."

The reporter felt defensive. "We're only as good as the information people give us."

A flash of light danced briefly across Pat's eyes as she said, "Since nobody forced Chuck to write about high crimes and misdemeanors at the school of government, it strikes me that the burden was on him to get it right or not print it at all."

"You're not saying that ignorance of the facts is no

excuse, are you?" Pat smiled, and Carole went on. "Did you stay in touch after you left Boston?"

"No."

"Were you surprised when he approached you last year?"

Pat took a sip of wine. "I approached him. I knew he was—" She hesitated.

"Unscrupulous?" Carole suggested. "Willing to cut corners?"

"Yes. Either one. So I called him and arranged a meeting." Before Carole could speak again, she added, "Please don't ask me why. It was an impulsive, stupid, tragic mistake. And I want you to know it had nothing to do with my great respect for Parker, who gave me the chance to come to the White House, and for what he and Hoskins were trying to accomplish."

This was a reassurance that Carole hadn't required or expected, but she still appreciated it. She absorbed it with a downcast look and faint smile, and then looked up again and asked about George Stevens.

"You've done quite a job on him," Pat said with obvious pleasure. "You're the talk of the town. There's even a fake memo floating around the White House from the President instructing the treasurer of the United States to put your picture on the five-dollar bill."

Carole looked embarrassed. "I'll have you know I've already turned down the "Today Show," "Face the Nation," "Good Morning America," "A Current Affair," and a pesistent guy at MacNeil-Lehrer who's called every day trying to get me to come on the show every night."

"Why say no?"

"Well, for one thing," she said, glancing down at her nonexistent lap, "the camera adds ten pounds." At the sight of the sheepish expression on the reporter's face, Pat covered her mouth to stifle an almost girlish giggle. Carole went on. "Pat, I do have a morbid interest in what George said to you. I promise to leave it out of my memoirs."

An expression that communicated both distaste and grim satisfaction crossed Pat's face. "I know his type," she said, drawing her cloth napkin back and forth through her clenched fists. "Smug, scheming, manipulative, cruel. He thought he had me pegged. He came up to me at the reception and said he knew I'd given his late reporter top secret information that his untimely death had prevented him from using. He said that by talking to him, I could help him get to the bottom of Chuck's death and also keep my name out of the papers. *His* papers, that is." She chuckled bitterly. "He thought I was afraid of losing a chance at promotion after Felix took Parker's job."

"While what you were really afraid of was—"

"—what had caused me to leak in the first place? Yes." Her face discouraged further inquiry.

"Did you help him?"

"I had to. He asked me if I could find out whether Chuck had come to the White House that evening. I happened to know that he had, so I told him. Frankly, I had never really believed he was alone when he was killed. But I also never thought the President had anything to do with it. He couldn't have."

Another signpost? Or a genuine testament of loyalty? If just the latter, then *why did she leak?*

"I'd always wondered why Stevens came up to me in public. I figured it out from reading your story. He hoped we'd be seen. Ironically, I don't think anyone noticed. If they did, they never said anything." She looked grim. "The office line on Pat Robinson is that she's got a stick up her butt and a cork in her box. I would never be suspected of an indiscretion of any kind."

She put her fists on the edge of the table, still grasping the napkin, and rested her chest against them. "Of course now the prevailing view is that I don't exist, that Stevens made the whole East Room saga up. I should thank you for that."

Carole reached over and covered Pat's hand with her own. "You can show your appreciation," she said, "by letting me help find a way to protect you from whomever has frightened you." *From the person who was once in the Hoskins administration. You told me that much.*

Pat looked hard at Carole's face. "It's an old story," she said. "An ancient evil." But after a moment the friendly, lonely light in her eyes blinked off, and she drew her hand back into her lap. "Thank you, really," she said. "But there's nothing anyone can do."

Ned Flach sat in his red Mazda RX-7 across the street from the restaurant and watched the front door, waiting for his bitch sister and the fat bitch she was eating dinner with to come out. He had the engine on so he could run the heater, and he turned on the wipers every few minutes to sweep away the snow. He had a rap station on the radio.

He hated stakeouts. His last had been during his stint with the Los Angeles field office five years before, when he'd been working credit card fraud. It was a dull business, a drag queen computer genius from Caltech using his home terminal to open fake accounts and get American Express and Visa cards in the names of real women and then going into boutiques on Lake Avenue to charge clothes for *himself!* The way to close that case would've been to drop by one morning and beat the shit out of him. If they had, what was he going to tell the Pasadena cops? I was just dressing up like a woman to go use my illegal credit cards to buy some red-lace underwear, officers, when these big mean men in suits came and hit me? He wouldn't open his mouth, if he *could* open his mouth, because that'd be the end of his grant money, his scholarships, and whatever else the government gave worthless garbage like him to sustain their worthless lives.

But that kind of operation did not go over well in the United States Secret Service. The whole point, they'd been told at their initial briefing, was to make a clean, detailed bust so they could study his techniques and the companies could design better safeguards for their computer systems.

For one thing, the kid had found a way to get the cards sent to him and the bills sent to the idiot ladies. So they sat in the car and watched him wiggle his skinny ass up and down the street for a day and a half until Ned thought he was going to explode from frustration and boredom. It was then, exactly then, that the call came over the radio and he was touched by destiny.

The dispatcher said some of the presidential candidates had changed their schedules for the California primary at the last minute and protection was shorthanded. He was to join the advance detail meeting the Democratic front runner, the governor of Louisiana, at the Santa Barbara airport when he arrived that evening. Ned interpreted the order literally, which was to say he obeyed it immediately, saying so long to his startled partner and leaving him sitting in the car. Halfway up the block, right in front of Bullock's, he came up behind the suspect while pretending to look off to the side and plowed right into him, digging his fist, with the knuckle of his forefinger extended, into the base of the kid's spine as they went down. Then, for his partner's sake, he made a big show of apologizing and helping the faggot up and gathering all his bags and boxes. His wig and whatever he'd stuffed under his bra had come loose, and while he stood there trying to put himself back together, Ned smiled as warmly as he could into the boy's eyes, which were damp because of the pain and the humiliation, and said in his soft voice, "Now you have a nice day, ma'am." Then he'd turned and headed up toward Colorado to try to get a cab to LAX.

Santa Barbara was a hoot, a ten-strike. In the sixties, they'd burned down the Bank of America protesting the war, and in the nineties, the first Vietnam fighting man ever to be nominated for President was coming to give a speech on campus. Fundamentally he hadn't changed, and some of them hadn't, either. What a sight! There were four thousand people waiting inside the gym for the speech and seventy outside, the Isla Vista Peoples Alliance Against Eugene Hoskins, who said they were going to keep him from getting in. Usually in such situations, especially when newsies were around, Secret Service agents like to recommend to the protectee that he avoid the area or, if he refused, to more or less pretend for public relations purposes that they themselves weren't present in the area.

But Hoskins wanted to make the speech, and so Ned called an impromptu meeting of the other agents who went ahead to the site and said that nobody was going to blame them for enabling the man to go into the gym. The shitheads had joined hands and stretched themselves across the entrance and started to sing and chant. When they got the word the motorcade was ninety seconds away, the agents formed a wedge to break the line, and at eleven against seventy, it was no contest. They walked up and put their palms on the chests of the ones in the front, two per agent, and pushed until the joined hands came loose, which didn't take much. The ones in the back pretty much scattered. The agents kept pushing until they had twenty-two guys pinned against the wall of the gym. One of Ned's was content to stay put, so he concentrated on the other, who was dressed like garbage but looked middle-aged, maybe a professor reliving the good old days. He squirmed and talked dirty, so Ned raised his hand and pressed against his neck until he shut up and began to gasp for breath, while Ned smiled pacifically, thinking about what it would be like to bring a knee between the guy's legs and jam his balls up his asshole. Meanwhile Hoskins slid in like a greased banana.

Three years later, Flach got another call. The head of Presidential Protective Detail was retiring, and the President wanted the man that got him into the University of California gym to run his detail.

Refocusing his eyes for a moment, Flach studied the reflection of his smooth, blank face on the inside of the window. So here he was, sitting in the snow with his butt unemployed and falling asleep because of some dirty-mouthed punk reporter and his own sister. He didn't care what the papers were saying now. He'd seen her talking to George Stevens at the White House, and he'd read the article in the paper a few mornings later. He didn't know how she'd figured out what he and the other agents had done. He didn't care. All he knew was that by the time he'd gotten to work that day, he was out of a job. So what if he had the pardon? Try to eat a f------ pardon. He'd been in town nearly a year and never bothered her. At first he didn't even know *she* was here until he saw her at a Hoskins speech at the Hilton one afternoon last March.

But then she nails him for no reason. *And she'll regret it.*

The door opened and the fat one came out, then Pattie. He watched as they walked up the street to the corner of M Street, where they stood for a few seconds talking and then shook hands. Fattie opened her umbrella and went one way, while Pattie put on some kind of hat and went the other way. Flach took off the emergency brake, made a U-turn, and drove to the corner, turning left to follow his sister. He had to keep an eye on her, to see what she was up to. Why not? He didn't have a damn thing else to do.

Dave Donnally, to whom the *Post*'s owners had given day-to-day control of the newspaper two years before, was one of the new generation of touchie-feelie publishers. His brown hair was bushy and tousled, his manner boyish and engaging, his door always open, his sleeves always rolled up. Layout artists and secretaries were encouraged to address their forty-six-year-old boss as "Dave." He turned up regularly in the sports department and the pressroom, smacking the pressmen on the back and getting his button-down blue oxford shirts covered with ink. When he had visitors to his office on the sixth floor, he was more likely to lean against his desk or sit on it than sit behind it. He answered all his reader mail, placed his own telephone calls, sharpened his own pencils, and every spring traveled throughout southeast Washington on high school Career Day to rap with the District's sullen young people about journalism.

The *Post* had managed to block any meaningful local competition for ten years, but its parent company still required meaningful annual increases in circulation and ad lineage. Dave had been hired two months after the paid circulation of *USA Today,* the television of newspapers, topped 10 million. He was part of a nationwide trend that hit Washington last, as nationwide trends were wont to do.

Ultimately the *Post*'s Washington proved to be just as post-literate as the rest of the country. Consumer surveys showed that thirty-inch analyses of the Burmese insurgency or dramatic exposés of petty cash voucher abuse at HUD simply were not being read, even by those who were conducting the nation's business in the nation's capital. Editors and reporters all over the country had always known such stories weren't read, but for the first time they were being asked by such as Dave why the stories were therefore in the paper. Confronted by substantial evidence that the American people didn't care, journalists' traditional reply—"the American people have a right to know"—resounded as smartly as a squash ball off a haystack. Their fallback reply was that quality, in-depth coverage in the paper won awards and had a profound influence on the direction of TV coverage and thus on the conduct of public affairs in the modern world. To this, America's newspaper publishers were saying, "The networks can hire their own newswriters, and just try to eat a plaque."

Dave liked color, short copy, big pictures, bold, witty headlines, polls about sexual behavior in the nineties, tax tips, recipes, gardening columns, and front-page stories about people helping people. If he could've gotten away with it, he would have put girls back in the paper in swimming suits with cutlines such as, "Shapely Georgetown physical education major, 19, basks in the first rays of the first day of spring. Today temperatures are expected to climb into the seventies again." But he couldn't. George Stevens, the powerful, well-connected, nationally prominent, award-winning editor he'd inherited, wouldn't have stood for it. So for two years Dave had loitered on the periphery, revamping the magazine and the other soft sections but having little impact on Stevens's editorial operation. Dave didn't like George Stevens. He was retarding journalistic evolution, and he took four hours to return Dave's calls. But he'd been stuck with him. Until now. Now it appeared the old bastard might be coming unglued.

Today Dave's door was closed. He was sitting behind his desk, elbows on the edge, fingers spread over the empty white oak surface, thumbs tapping out the drum solo from side two of *Abbey Road*. As he spoke, Dave looked at George Stevens, splayed out in a chair in front of him with his stringy white hair and newsroom dishabille, with something approaching fear and loathing.

This was their first extended conversation since the *Times* story had appeared nearly a week before. Outsiders would've been surprised at how seldom and how reluctantly the great wall that separated a newspaper's editorial and business operations was scaled, by either party. But after seeing the Sunday shows and reading the newsweeklies on Monday—in *Time* and *U.S. News* the cover story was the *Post* scandal, while *Newsweek,* which the *Post* owned, had a cover story about the newest imported dog fad headlined "America's Dingo Daze"—Dave had finally asked his secretary to call Stevens and ask whether the editor might step upstairs for a moment.

"Well, George," he said politely, his drum solo reaching a furious crescendo and then subsiding. "I hate to do the heavy boss bit, but what exactly are we going to do about all this?"

Since being ushered into the office, Stevens's manner had been confident and breezy. "I don't know what you're going to do about it, Dave," he said with the satisfied smile of a man in black tie who'd just tipped the men's room attendant a dollar and decided he'd done his bit to redistribute wealth, "but I'm going to keep putting out the newspaper."

"But what about these stories?"

"What stories?"

Dave smiled in an unsuccessful attempt to hide his

irritation at being jerked around. "The stories that have been saying for a solid week that you've been using my paper to try to get your asshole friend elected president."

Surprised at his employer's arrogance—*his paper?*—Stevens muttered, "They're a crock."

"That's not what *The New York Times* and *Time* are saying. That's not what the networks are saying. That's not what the readers—"

Stevens interrupted. "I don't give a shit about the readers. What are *you* saying, Dave?"

Dave stood, walked from behind the desk, hiked his khaki trousers up a few inches, and leaned against it. "I'm going to level with you here, George," he said. "Some aspects of the lady's story appear to be accurate. For instance, the computer stuff. His files were indeed erased from your terminal the night Sampson died. We checked."

"Of course they were," Stevens said. "I didn't want anybody messing around in them."

"Given all the safeguards in the system, who else could've looked at them? By the way, did you?"

Stevens just shrugged. He knew he had a reputation for being nosy. So what? "No," he said, "but I wish I had. I don't even remember looking at the file names."

"Besides," the publisher went on, "the *very* first thing you do when you find out you've got a dead reporter is erase his files? That seems pretty weird."

Stevens shrugged again, trying not to grin.

"Do you really listen in on your reporters' phone calls?"

Stevens was pleased, though he continued to hide it. This was going about as he'd expected. "From the White House?"

"Yes."

"On occasion I do. My reporters aren't permitted to have secrets from me, anyway."

Dave didn't hesitate. "Did you listen to the one in question?"

"No. I must've been away."

"Oh." Dave continued smoothly. "I talked to Herb McGraw this morning." Suddenly it wasn't as hard for Stevens to keep from grinning. "He told me you asked him for Sampson's girlfriend's and parents' phone number so you could pay your respects. He talked to the mom and the dad at the funeral. Were you there, incidentally? I was there. I don't remember seeing you."

Stevens didn't shrug. The shrug bit was wearing thin. "I was busy," he said.

"They said they never heard from you."

"I was *busy*."

"But you called the girlfriend."

Stevens sat up a little. "Sure I called the girlfriend. Then something came up and I forgot about the other call. Listen, Dave, I don't appreciate your manner or your questions. If Herb wants my job, he can have it."

Dave's bright young face brightened some more. "Is that so?"

Stevens, momentarily alarmed, straightened up in the chair. "Who the hell's side are you on?" he said. "Nelson's sleeping with DuBois. *You* figure it out. She's got no proof, just Hill gossip that she could very well have made up. This won't last beyond the start of the impeachment hearings next week. Then the spotlight will be on Hoskins again, and that's where it'll stay." He stared at Dave, but his eyes seemed to be looking elsewhere.

Dave was smarter than he looked. "You're not to touch Herb McGraw, by the way. He has my support and that of the owners."

Stevens's eyes snapped back. "I've won them seven Pulitzers. I'll do what I choose with my editors."

Dave shook his head. "The owners aren't pleased about what's being said about the *Washington Post* by its peers. Also, they aren't pleased by the fact that the company's stock is down five points, which means they're out about seventeen million dollars—"

"On paper," Stevens cut in.

"Of course on paper. That's our business, isn't it? So they've asked me to see that some coherent and credible explanation of this matter is made to the public, on paper in *their* paper, as soon as possible." Dave stood up to signal the end of the meeting, but since he didn't normally send such signals, the gesture lacked the practiced air of confident, superior authority he'd hoped to convey. Stevens slumped down into his seat again.

"Fine," the editor said. "We'll do a piece saying it's a crock of shit. But I still say it'll be forgotten in a week. What's Hoskins going to do about it?"

Dave said, "If there's any truth to the *Times* story, he does have options."

"There's not. But what options?"

Dave blanched. "Certain . . . legal options," he said.

Stevens stood, signaling the end of the meeting, and laughed in Dave's face. "He wouldn't dare."

The full complement of senior partners of Smith, Devine, Walker, and Eisenstein was seldom called together in the lavish conference room of their K Street offices. Even when they were, they seldom all appeared. But on Wednesday, February 3, all well-manicured hands were present, because the President of the United States proposed to engage them to file a libel complaint against the *Washington Post*.

No president had ever filed a libel complaint against anybody. Until now, such a thing had been unthinkable, because it had been considered hopeless for a sitting president to win. So in this room filled with warm winter sunshine that poured through a skylight and imbued with an ethereal magnificence the Monet water lily canvas that spanned one brilliantly white wall, twelve rich, worried attorneys were studying copies of the same four-page document as if it were the Boy Scout oath and their Tenderfoot test began in ten minutes.

The words had already been gone over a dozen times and honed carefully and lovingly. While they were all satisfied with its logic and structure, they couldn't help regretting its lack of mass. It wasn't called for at this stage, but they would still have been comforted by something thicker in a plastic Vellobound with a half-inch of footnotes and citations. It went against their nature to be sending so fateful a message in a mere twelve numbered paragraphs. And yet it was being proposed that before four o'clock that afternoon, a paralegal should take it to the civil clerk's office of the Superior Court of the District of Columbia on Indiana Avenue Northwest and file it for a small fee—thereby producing a six-column headline in the next morning's *New York Times* and an article that would prominently feature the names Smith, Devine, Walker, and Eisenstein.

Jim Smith, fiftyish, tan, beefy, and distinguished with his gray-black hair and gray Italian herringbone suit, broke the silence that had settled over the group as they read the document through yet another time. "Gentlemen," he said, nodding to Eisenstein, who sat at his left, "and Emily, I've been the President's personal attorney since he came to Washington and put his assets in a blind trust that I administer. I've been his friend for twice that long. I value his friendship and his business. Still, in this matter I put the firm's interests ahead of his. If any of you has any misgivings, let's hear them. We do neither him nor ourselves any good by advising him to initiate an action that doesn't have a reasonable chance of success."

As he shifted in his leather chair and raised a hand to stroke his chin, Smith's wrist and shirt cuff glistened with gold. "We're all trained not to think politically until we get to Washington, where we're quickly trained not to think any other way but," he went on. "I'm sure we all know what we'll be up against. Still, at the risk of being a bore, I say again: We will be taking on mom and apple pie here. This has never been done, and some people are going to say it shouldn't be. In short, if we go ahead, we're going to be the notorious anti-First Amendment firm, quote unquote."

Joseph Tully, at forty-two the junior member of the firm's senior echelon, rubbed the shiny black top of his head and said, "Let's walk through what the opening argument would sound like again, please."

Smith nodded toward the end of the table, where a twenty-nine-year-old associate was waiting. "Mr. Michaels?"

Carl Michaels's pinstripe suit was a little too loose, and his shirt showed wear along the top of the collar. He needed a shave, and nobody cared. He was the worker bee on the case. All their collective reputations and fortunes rested on his thin, strong shoulders, so they didn't look, they listened.

"This case will be a landmark in libel law," Michaels began. By the time Smith could produce his just-the-facts-please-son look and telegraph it to the eager young man, Michaels was in the thick of them. "As you all know, to show that the President—"

Barney Walker, the firm stickler, cut in. "Let's be careful about that," he said, glancing toward both the youngster and Smith. "Our client is acting as a private citizen. There's no involvement by the White House counsel's office. Jim was engaged personally during the client's private visit to Jim's home last weekend. Much as it would appall Miss Manners, it might be best to refer to him simply by his name."

"You're right, Barney," said Michaels, sounding appreciative and feeling irritated at the interruption. "To show that *Mr. Hoskins* was libeled, we must prove that untrue statements about him were published, that these statements damaged his professional reputation, and that they were made with reckless disregard of the truth—in other words, with malice."

He spoke without consulting notes. He'd been living for three days on the facts, virtually no sleep, and a steady supply of coffee and cream-filled Ho-Hos. "The errors are easiest," he said. "Especially in the matter of the Beirut raid and the campaigns, the *Post* has published dozens of allegations made by so-called anonymous sources that do not appear to be true. We can show that most are just embellishments of accusations made and thoroughly debunked earlier."

"But if we don't know their sources," said Emily Eisenstein, "aren't we in the usual pickle?"

"Not if the allegations basically aren't new and if the preponderance of evidence already in the public record weighs against them."

"But why would they run these stories?" asked Walker.

Michaels looked at Smith, who answered, "It appears the *Post* was trying to put so much pressure on Hoskins that he'd be driven from office without having the opportunity to mount a comprehensive defense. The cover-up, which he doesn't deny, did double duty as the single worst allegation and the single indisputable one, a credibility destroyer that made fertile ground for planting these other stories in the public's mind."

Tully was skeptical. "Beirut and American politics being similarly Byzantine," he said, "I worry that the defendants will manage to convince the jury that they had sufficient cause to run the stories."

Michaels deftly avoided an argument on that point by shifting to firmer ground. "A story about which no jury could draw that conclusion," he said, "is the supposed military coup. It was sheer, irresponsible speculation, and since Hoskins's speech, the *Post* hasn't run word one about it. It hasn't run a retraction, either, despite the White House's insistence. Of all the examples we refer to in the complaint, the one saying an American politician was plotting a military takeover is far and away the most damaging."

"How do we show damage?" asked another lawyer.

Michaels's tired eyes lit up. "Tracking polls," he said with gusto. "Since the crisis began, Harris and Gallup have been polling every night. We bought the data. The coup story was alive for four days, and Hoskins's personal integrity rating fell off a daily average of three points until the story died. After the speech his general approval rating improved, but the integrity number has recovered only three of the twelve points it lost. Harris shows that sixty-five percent of the people still have some residual concerns about the story. That's concrete, lasting, laboratory-quality evidence of damage to an American politician's professional reputation."

The room was silent. The lawyers looked less worried. After a moment, Jim Smith smiled. "Now comes Carl's favorite part," he said.

Michaels smiled back and straightened the edges of his unconsulted notes. "Since *Times* v. *Sullivan* in 1964, most libel cases have foundered on the malice requirement," he said. "You've got to show that a reporter or editor had serious doubts about the truth of what he was printing. To do that, you've virtually got to get inside a man's head, which you can't do, or examine his notes, which the *Post* will never let us get. Some plaintiffs have argued that journalists operate within a generalized atmosphere of malice. You get ahead by nailing authority figures; any old authority figure will do. If none happens to be misbehaving when you're on the beat, you're naturally impelled to get creative. Juries sometimes buy it, but appeals courts don't.

"But now because of the Marshall Brandon connection we have clear evidence that Stevens had a specific personal motive, other than promoting truth and justice, for running these stories. Why did all these subsidiary stories start coming out when they did? To find out, we call these reporters and editors. We don't ask them for notes or sources; then they'll clam up and go on hunger strikes in jail. We just ask them what instructions they got from Stevens and when. Did he talk about a campaign, about a consolidated effort, about moving on a variety of fronts? Did he talk about bolstering their case? Were they pressured to produce articles by a such-and-such a date, whether or not they were tied down? Establish an organized campaign, and the jury will have little difficulty concluding that malice was involved."

"It was obviously a campaign," Tully admitted.

"Right," barked Michaels, clinching. "Everyone knows that, and I mean *everyone*." He looked down at Smith. He was about to get political. "Which brings me to our hole card, which we got at no extra cost when we bought the poll stuff." He pulled a sheet of paper from his pile and waved it in the air. "The percentage of those who think the American press is abusing its power increased dramatically over these two weeks. Overall, the media's negatives are lower than they've been in the entire history of public opinion surveys. Esteemed colleagues, the folks are *pissed*." Here his eyes unwillingly flickered toward Emily Eisenstein, who was smiling and giving him a thumbs-up.

He resisted the impulse to stand up during his summation. "I therefore predict we couldn't find a jury that would find no liability in this case unless we recruited it in the newsroom of the *Washington Post*. More importantly, I suspect that our learned appeals court brethren and the high court will take a learned sidelong peek at this same data and uphold the jury verdict." He paused again. "I predict that at the end of this process, Mr. Hoskins will prevail, and the courts may even put *Times* v. *Sullivan* in the garbage by overturning this ridiculous malice requirement and affording public figures the same protection against defamation as everyone else. In other words, when they get it wrong and hurt somebody in the process, they pay damages."

Most of the young attorney's twelve colleagues spent a few minutes imagining themselves being enshrined in the annals of jurisprudence. Then they refocused on Carl Michaels, who suddenly looked like damn good partner material.

FOURTEEN

EDDIE VAN AIKEN, TWELVE-TERM DEMOCRAT FROM Maryland, lowered himself into his chair at the center of the upper tier of the long, gracefully curved dais of the House Judiciary Committee. A cap fashioned out of the crinkly gray hair that still grew on the side of his head was molded so stiffly over his bald pate that it looked as if there were a hinge in it. An equally disciplined expression was plastered onto his face. But as his full weight settled onto the base of his spine, he expelled a quiet, plaintive sound that in his weariness it took him four or five seconds to notice and swallow.

Worried, he glanced out at the two press tables, smiling automatically, judiciously, and meaninglessly. They were still filling up with reporters and producers who perched on the backs of their chairs and generally behaved like teenagers on a school bus. The tired and discouraged van Aiken loathed them. It seemed they hadn't a worry in the world. Most still had their backs to him; apparently nobody had heard him sigh. *Thank God for that.* Otherwise: "Chairman van Aiken appeared tired and distracted this morning as he lowered the gavel. . . ." Or: "Mr. Chairman, as these hearings founder, there's talk among your colleagues that the pressure is beginning to take its toll on you. This has got to be a real personal setback. Care to comment?"

The hearings on four proposed articles of impeachment of Eugene Hoskins were entering their third and probably final week. They were affording unprecedented national exposure to a congressman who had up until now presided over nothing more controversial than amending the criminal code or the salary scale of federal judges. *With exposure like this, who needs obscurity?* A sensation like a heat rash spread over his pudgy face; he glanced up, saw the reason, and winced. To hell with proving democracy worked. Democracy's works were threatening to grind him into sausage and broil him alive. He'd rather be in Novosibirsk. *No reporters. No constituent mail. And no hot lights!*

As the technicians continued to adjust the lights, he looked back to his copious papers, making sure the questions his staff counsel had written and run off were near the top of the pile. He was more than usually aware of the portent of hours of constant physical discomfort. Hot lights did double duty, feeding crystal-clear video images to a pixellated nation and administering an exquisite trial by electric fire to its politicians. Cranking the room temperature up to a hundred and three and souring the air with hostility and the odor of the gorillas in Cuervo Gold T-shirts who'd packed in the equipment created perfect conditions for posing the critical question: Did the poor boob on the business end of the cameras stay cool? Or did he have such shortages of stamina, character, and good breeding that he couldn't help but *sweat?*

Under his left sideburn, van Aiken felt the first drops form in the artificial dawn, and he lowered his head to dab them off. Raising his hand to his midsection as if to look at his watch, he dried his fingers on the side of his suit coat. Then he pulled a pen from his shirt pocket and pretended to make some notes on the papers in front of him.

He'd diverted one raging rivulet of worry and strife, but as the day wore on, there'd be more. In this area, vigilance was always the watchword, because sweat was always potential front-page news. A shadow on the underarm of your shirt was good for an "appeared nervous" someplace in a story, which was why hypereccrinic politicians wore white. Sweat on the upper lip was even more significant, while a trickle from hairline to chin was a virtual admission of war crimes.

Van Aiken slammed one of his binders closed, prompting the UPI guy to turn and look up. The chairman beamed at him. He returned a noncommital smile with pursed lips and then looked away before the chairman could. *Smug, hypocritical bastards.* Reporters never mentioned the little blonde number in blue jeans who repaired the cracks in the plaster of Paris that masked anchormen's complexions or the team of puff packers who made sure Barbara Walters' nose sucked up every ray of light that touched it.

He flinched as another bank of miniature supernovas exploded to his right. *It gets worse every day!* He was wrestling with the angry look that was trying to suffuse his features when an aide, who was in touch with the networks and therefore aware of precisely when the chairman was required to begin, said in his ear, "One minute, boss."

Scanning his script, van Aiken was reminded again of what an embarrassing exercise his historic hearings had become. The great issues had come and gone. The article he had introduced himself, accusing Hoskins of sanctioning and covering up atrocities in Lebanon, had failed by a humiliating two to one margin. Two more, alleging campaign abuses and violations of the civil rights of an American citizen, Charles Sampson, also lost, though more narrowly.

Only one article remained: the Sampson accident cover-up. It required testimony from an endless parade of unflappable law enforcement witnesses who, with their cheap suits and impenetrable security-speak, were turning his solemn constitutional confrontation into a scene from a made for TV movie. On Friday a GOP member from Manassas, Virginia, had consumed forty-five minutes of network time giving Fairfax County's deputy police chief, who happened to be his second cousin and bore a startling resemblance to Goober in "The Andy Griffith Show," an opportunity to explain why his officers hadn't realized that skid marks on the highway, purportedly from the skinny tires of Sampson's out-of-control Honda Accord, had actually been made intentionally three hours later by an agent's four-by-four.

Van Aiken had expected that the Hoskins impeachment hearings would entail some risks, but not that they would so quickly turn into a nationwide howler. A Democratic committee investigating its own President was fine, as long as it produced a corpse at the end. Then van Aiken would have been able to say that he had put partisanship aside and proved that the party could pursue corrupt Democrats as vigorously as it had Republicans. He had hoped for a little in return. Watergate had turned Ervin and Rodino, a cranky old ex-segregationist from North Carolina and a genial nonentity from Newark, into twin icons of the Republic, the Jefferson and Washington of the first TV generation. If van Aiken had landed Hoskins, he would have been enough of a hero to have a shot at the Senate or even the vice-presidency in 1996, which was more than a baker's son from Baltimore had any business to expect.

Instead, he was beginning to worry about being reelected. Some Republicans complained he was running a cream puff hearing. Others who'd rallied to Hoskins's flag after his flamboyant State of the Union address and who probably smelled the stench of failure hanging over the Judiciary Committee were also his critics. All that, he could handle. But as the President's popularity began to edge up again, many Democrats who'd headed for the tall grass when the *Post* story first broke were beginning to stick noses, fingers, and toes back into the open and check the weather. Hoskins's bedrock supporters had opposed the hearings from the beginning, and as time passed, they began to oppose them more stridently. Fred McCarthy, the Speaker, whose brief episode of Hoskins bashing ended the moment Hoskins's speech did, had now found a variety of ways to undercut and disavow the increasingly unpopular van Aiken. Just this week there was a Washington Whisper in

U.S. News saying the Californian was known to believe that next session it might be time to get "a real heavyweight" to chair Judiciary. Van Aiken blanched—though it was hidden by the blusher he'd applied in his private washroom before walking to the hearing—as he thought of how nifty the clipping would look in the campaign literature of his opponent next year.

Normally van Aiken could have expected a boost from the reporters and commentators, but after January's antipress firestorm, it seemed most were pulling their punches when it came to Hoskins. His libel suit had made them into ferocious tigers on the editorial pages but pussycats on the front pages and the evening news. *Most of them can't write, but they can count as well as I can.* A half-dozen separate polls showed the American people thought the President's action against the *Post* both appropriate and fair. Most of the lawyers van Aiken had talked to thought it both open and shut. So since there had been no major new revelations, the press was not only being painfully fair but in fact, he thought, somewhat too punctilious in its criticism of his own investigation. It was irritating and perverse how deftly the media had slipped out of the bed they'd made, only to heckle those who'd piled in behind them on the mistaken assumption that the pillow fight would last all night.

By now most of the other members and their aides had come in and sat down, and the racket from the reporters' tables had dulled. Their arrogant faces were toward him now, ready to savor watching him dodge and squirm. *Sons of. . . .*

He pulled himself together. *No sense in that. Never is; never will be.* Turning his attention to the witness table, he experienced another sort of revulsion as he watched Ned Flach and his attorney take their places, the still photographers circling them like planets around a sun. He distrusted blond Adonis types, aware of how well they did in politics. But there was something else about the former head of the President's Secret Service detail, an artificiality of gesture and coolness of expression, even when describing the events leading up to an innocent young man's gruesome death, that had chilled van Aiken's blood.

After lowering the gavel and reading a couple of procedural announcements, van Aiken looked along the table to his left and said, "Recognizing the gentleman from Rhode Island to continue questioning this witness."

As he spoke, van Aiken regarded his thirty-seven-year-old first-term Democratic colleague, J. K. Callahan, with a blank look that hid gratefulness and, naturally, also an element of contempt. According to his staff's overnight sounding of the committee, this humorless, diligent former DA had become the sole trustee of Eddie van Aiken's family jewels.

Last week Callahan had been leaning to a no vote on the final article, which would have meant the committee would end up recommending against impeachment. All the other votes appeared solid. Over the weekend, during a seance with his family, his conscience, and his God, reported and speculated upon by the army of journalists that had occupied and despoiled his hometown of West Warwick, Callahan appeared to edge back toward voting yes. It seemed he had also been unsettled by Flach's composure. As a prosecutor in Providence, he had learned to recognize inactive consciences in men whose crimes should have spawned agonized lifetimes of guilt. His distrust of Flach was leading him in a politically unprofitable direction, away from a president he admired and whose stock was again on the rise. Such purity of motive was rare in Congress, which made van Aiken appreciate and detest his young friend all the more.

His own instincts told him it was doubtful the President would be convicted in the Senate. Whether the full House would vote to impeach was also an open question. Van Aiken didn't care. All he wanted from life was to get one proposed article of impeachment out of his damned committee.

Callahan said, "Mr. Flach, may I briefly review some details in your testimony from last Friday afternoon?"

Flach nodded but didn't speak, and so Callahan watched and waited. The agent had tried this gambit of gesturing instead of speaking aloud several times on Friday. He knew the committee needed words, not descriptions of motions of the head, for the record. He wanted to make Callahan ask him again.

Callahan didn't. Fifteen seconds passed. The loudest sounds were the squeaks of the photographers' sneakers as they jockeyed for position before the witness and the whirs of their motor drives. Finally Flach said, "Yes. Sir."

"Thank you," said Callahan. "Mr. Flach, your story quite amazes me. I will never understand how a modern police force could bungle an investigation as completely as Fairfax County's did. The idea that you and your colleagues nearly got away with secretly towing your own car, stealing Mr. Sampson's, ramming it into the same tree you'd struck, and then smashing a hole in the windshield for Mr. Sampson's body is astonishing." He let sarcasm darken his voice as he continued. "Of course that is not your problem, at least in the strict context of this or any other temporal proceeding, thanks to the President's pardon. So I will leave it aside for now."

Flach wisely said nothing.

Callahan continued, "You testified that late in the afternoon of May 29 of last year the President called you to his office and said he might have an unorthodox assignment for you that evening."

"That's correct."

Callahan looked down as he turned pages back and forth, speaking into them but not referring to them. This was one part investigation, nine parts performance. Eye contact was not to be squandered. "That was his word, wasn't it?" he asked. "A direct quote, as our friends in the press might say?"

"Which word?"

Callahan looked up. Eye contact. "*Unorthodox.*"

"Oh. Yes, it was."

"Does it strike you as adequately descriptive of that night's events as they unfolded?"

"Yes."

Callahan was playing games, too. "I was just wondering at what point in your mind *unorthodox* gives way to *illegal,"* he said.

Flach smiled without warmth. "It always seemed to me that *unorthodox* covered plenty of ground," he said. "I don't have a dictionary with me. I didn't have one then. All I knew was that the President had given me an instruction and it was my job to carry it out."

"Did that include altering the scene of a fatal automobile accident to conceal its true cause?"

Flach shrugged. "It was a judgment I made at the time. I wasn't thinking clearly. Obviously, it was wrong to do what we did. I have said that, and President Hoskins has said that."

"What did go through your mind at the moment of the accident? What exactly did you do first?"

"I got out of the vehicle."

"I meant immediately after the accident, in the first few seconds."

"I experienced dismay and pain, of course."

"Pain from your broken arm."

"Yes."

Callahan stared at his witness as he asked, "Were you wearing your seat belt?"

Flach paused for just an instant. Only someone who knew him well would have noticed the hesitation. "No," he said.

"Why not?"

"Secret Service policy. Agents on duty don't wear them. You might recall there was some controversy about it a few years ago when the District adopted the mandatory seat belt law."

"Did that apply to your passenger?"

"That's another thing I regret," Flach said. "I should've made him put it on, but I didn't think of it. Though as a matter of fact, as you know, the accident happened when I looked away from the road to keep him from opening the door and trying to leave the vehicle. Even if he'd had the belt on, I guess he would've released it by then, anyway."

Callahan's tone was cold as he said, "Oh, so you feel absolved, then?"

"Not at all," said the witness, without even a hint of testiness. "It's just speculation, prompted by your own question."

Now the congressman posed the question he'd been angling toward. "You may recall," he said in a nonchalant way, "that Agent Bill Wortley testified last week that when he was approaching your car after the accident, he thought he saw you release your seat belt. Any speculation about that discrepancy?"

"Not necessary," said Flach smoothly. "I talked to Billy about it over the weekend."

Callahan, surprised, shot back, "That's highly unorthodox, Mr. Flach."

Flach's attorney leaned toward the microphone. "But not illegal, Mr. Callahan."

Van Aiken banged his gavel and said wearily, "We will be the judge of that, counselor."

Callahan said, "And what did you and Mr. Wortley decide actually happened?"

Flach's voice sounded helpful but disengaged, as if he really didn't care but was doing everybody a favor by straightening the whole thing out. "When I saw I was going to hit the tree, I braced myself against the wheel," he said. "That's how I broke the right arm. For a moment I was completely immobilized by the pain. All I can figure out is that while I was waving around with my left arm, trying to reach over to see about Mr. Sampson's condition, I got tangled in the shoulder strap. When Billy ran up, he must have seen the belt and the arm and figured I was releasing it. That's what we came up with, anyway."

Callahan's aide had suggested the seat belt discrepancy might make a good question, and the congressman had agreed, though he assumed there was some reasonable explanation. Angry at Flach's presumptuousness but satisfied by the solution it had produced, he had already begun formulating an unrelated question while Flach spoke. Before changing the subject, the congressman, wishing to appear to be a good sport, said, "By the way, how's the arm now?"

There was a television camera hidden in the curtains behind the dais, slightly to the right of center. As Flach answered, he turned his head and looked directly into it. "Just fine, Mr. Callahan," he said. "Just as strong as ever, thank you."

That morning E. E. Perkins had announced to the press that nobody in the White House was watching the hearings. "It's business as usual around here, boys and girls," he boomed from behind the podium in the briefing room. "What Eddie van Aiken does with his time is his business. We've got a country to run." He shuffled his notes and added, "As a matter of fact, I've got an addendum to the printed schedule. On Thursday the President will travel to New York City to give a major foreign policy address to the Economic Club at a banquet that evening. The subject will be the future of U.S.-Soviet relations in the wake of the treaty on strategic nuclear weapons signed last year by the President and the General Secretary."

After the briefing, Perkins hurried back to his office, closed the door, tossed his wrinkled jacket over the back of his desk chair, and sat down. After heaving his beefy legs up onto the desk, he whispered to his deputy, "Did I miss anything?"

She was sitting in a side chair, her eyes fused to one of five TV sets while she took notes on a legal pad. A former Miss Mississippi and Yale summa cum laude, she'd joined the press staff eight months before and was now handling the weekend and holiday briefings. She shook her head. "Ned Flach is one cold dude, though," she said.

"I never did like him," E. E. said. He saw her grin at the television and protested, "I know what you're thinking. Twenty-twenty hindsight. But the fact is, I plain didn't. The old man is usually wise beyond our ken, but he was wrong about that one."

She shrugged and said, "I guess he was good enough at his job." She turned away from the broadcast, batted her eyelashes at Perkins, and went on in her sweetest cornpone voice. "I'm somewhat new at this, Mr. Perkins, sir," she said, "but that's still got to count for something." After he harrumphed, she smiled in frank admiration. "Just like you're good at yours," she went on. "I watched the briefing on cable. I hope you realize you're going to hell for your myriad deceits and evasions."

He clasped his hands behind his head and chuckled as he thought back over the half-hour session. The laugh came easily; he was happier than he'd been in weeks. Hoskins had hired a new chief of staff who, in the process of consolidating his authority, had promptly and predictably locked the press secretary out of the inner circle again. E. E. hadn't seen the President in person for a week and a half, and he was delighted. People who got to see the President had worries far bigger than his, such as counting and trying to change votes on the House Judiciary Committee.

Besides, the less Perkins saw of the focus of the press's curiosity and animosity, the better he could do his job, which was to insulate the President from both. "They probably didn't believe a word of it," he said, referring to the audience at the briefing. "I should've said, 'Sam, that's a ridiculous question. Damn straight we're watching. If Roone Arledge and the rest of the brass at ABC News were counting your chips on nationwide TV, you'd tune in, too.' "

"Why didn't you?"

"I've told you time and time again, young lady—"

She interrupted to quote him. "Never waste a perfectly good fact on the enemy when a lie will sit just as well."

He nodded his head. "That's Perkins's Law," he said. "I

think you're ready for the more subtle wisdom of Perkins's First Corollary."

She sighed. "Okay, E. E. I'll bite."

He shifted his weight in his chair so he could bring his hands into play to tick off his points. "There are only two kinds of media questions," he said. "The first is the simple, honest request for information. This you almost never get, so when you do, savor it like the memory of your first act of physical love. Since answering is more or less like talking directly to the American people, traditional doctrines of truth and fair play tend to apply."

"Within reason," the deputy cautioned.

"Yes ma'am. The second kind is the malicious tactical thrust masquerading as a question. It dishonors Lady Truth, so you hold her above the fray. Today was a minor but perfect example. 'Is the President watching the hearings?' Sam asks. You think this was on the lips of two hundred million Americans when they rolled out of the sack this morning? Hell no. It's the classic no-win question. They don't want the truth; they want our ass for lunch. If I say yes, then the government's paralyzed by the fear of impeachment. If I say no, the President is contemptuous of the legislative branch as it regretfully discharges its constitutional responsibilities.

"It's the spokeman's job to blunt such an attack by any means necessary. I said not only that the President wasn't watching the hearings but that *nobody* was watching the hearings. We're discharging *our* responsibilities, I say. And then I spring a schedule item I'd held off the printout in anticipation of this question. We spend ten minutes talking about where the President's going to stay and ducking substance questions on the speech, about which I know next to nothing anyhow. Soon Henson McMasters wheezes, 'Thanks, E. E.,' and I'm off the hook, basking unscathed in the adoration of my shapely young assistant."

Who reached across the desk and tapped the sole of one of his scuffed loafers with the eraser of her pencil. "My hero."

"By the way," said Perkins with a twinkle on his eye. "Speaking of your first act—"

Drawing her pencil back, the deputy carefully smoothed her skirt over her knees and returned to her note-taking. "Too late, boss," she said. "*Way* too late."

A few hundred feet away in the Old Executive Office Building, Pat Robinson was watching the hearings, in a conference room with two other NSC staffers. When her brother turned and looked into the camera—he was looking directly at *her*—she put her thin white hands over her face and gasped in blank terror.

Just as strong as ever, sis.

One of her colleagues looked at her. "Pat?"

She turned and saw the worry on his face and the other's, too. Was something the matter? Was she sick? Even now, the irony was not lost on her. She felt like a patient who'd been transported by news of an incurable illness to a place where ordinary concern and sympathy were so useless that they seemed contemptible. Part of her had always dwelled there. The other part had remained behind, to live at least a shadow of a life and to make excuses. Both parts of her had just joined. She got up without a word and rushed from the room toward her cubicle. At this point, manufacturing excuses would take energy away from preserving her life.

Her brother's unmistakable early Valentine was only the second thing in his testimony that had frightened her. The first had been his hesitation when he was asked about the seat belt. She knew him all too well. He had been lying.

The foreboding that had lingered ever since he called her at home that morning now hardened again into terror. The lie suggested that he could kill. The message suggested that he might kill her next. He had either seen her with George Stevens at the White House or learned that she had talked to Charles Sampson. Either way, he had concluded that she was responsible for his troubles. As victim and witness, she was also an iron link to his incriminating, unspeakable past. So he'd have two motives for removing her from the scene, one a product of his paranoia, the other of his cold rationality.

She unlocked the deep bottom drawer of her desk and pulled out a folder stuffed with photocopies of clippings. The month before, when the Sampson crisis began, she had sent a memo around saying she thought it would be wise for the department to keep a complete set of clips so they wouldn't have to count on E. E.'s weary troops in the press office. She'd survey the Washington papers, the *Times,* the *Journal,* and the newsweeklies, while anybody who had any out-of-town papers could pass them to her for safekeeping. Most she kept in a credenza behind her desk, where she encouraged everyone to consult them whenever they wanted. She only locked up copies of the ones about Ned Flach. Gathering these, culling them, comparing them, learning them, were the secret purposes of the exercise.

Most were news stories about him and the presidential pardon, which had taught her nothing except how completely the newspapers could miss the point. They described his service many years before as a homicide detective in St. Louis, quoting fellow officers who said he was efficient, if a little distant. The Secret Service said roughly the same thing. Their portrait was of an unexceptional agent who'd been in the right place at the right time, only to throw it away because he'd lacked the smarts to see the President's orders were guaranteed to land him in the wrong place at the wrong time. He had no immediate family, the articles said, quoting from his personnel file with absolute authority. Robinson's face was grim as she paged through the tear sheets. He obviously hadn't wanted to answer questions about his sister any more than she did about him.

Pat sat back in her chair for a moment and stared out the window toward the White House. She remembered seeing Chuck Sampson arrive there on a warm evening nine months before and insisting to herself that the impulsive, rash thing she'd done in leaking to him had been an imperative of psychological self-preservation, a way to end her brother's White House tour in a few months instead of trying to endure his malignant presence for another four years. Instead, Chuck died, his story never appeared, the Beirut raid was a roaring success, and the President had been reelected. It was hard for her not to sense a relationship between all these events, but her suspicions remained just that. She didn't see her brother's hand in it then. Her distress had been a result not of his actions but of hers. Had she not touched Chuck's life again, it might not have ended. Had her plan succeeded, twenty-nine other lives might have.

In June the President had invited her to a picnic on the South Lawn for the returned hostages and their families. Their joy, poured out in waves when they learned she had been part of the apparatus that had carried out the rescue, was a revelation. The wives reached for her hand, the kids grabbed her around the legs, and she dropped her paper plate and got potato salad on her shoes. By dusk, she was playing badminton doubles in bare feet against the wives of the vice-president and the Secretary of Education with the seventeen-year-old son of one of the hostages, who had flirted with her in an utterly innocent and not unpleasant way.

She angrily swept away a nostalgic tear. Her guilt about contacting Sampson had faded once she had convinced herself the accident was indeed a coincidence and her responsibility therefore only peripheral. The best salve for her wounds had always been hard work, and in the exciting months leading up to the fall election, when the whole administration had been galvanized in the drive for a second term, she had found her brother's usually unseen presence less frightful. All in all, her life had seemed comparatively secure and normal until George Stevens walked up to her in the East Room at New Year's and reminded her that she wasn't entitled to security or normalcy, in full view, perversely, of the man who had deprived her of both.

Now she had to concentrate. She turned away from the window and refocused on her clippings. At the bottom of the file were a few long, lovingly detailed and illustrated narratives about the scandal: an eight-page special section of the *Los Angeles Times* titled "Anatomy of an Outrage," a twelve-pager from *Newsweek* called "America's Final Loss of Innocence."

Every account she read had her brother in a seat belt at the time of the accident. And every one appeared to be authoritative. None of the pardoned agents had submitted to press interviews, and none of the stories mentioned sources, but they all made it clear that the FBI's transcripts of its interrogations of Flach and the others had been generously leaked. Only they could have provided the wealth of detail that was laced through the exhaustive articles.

Why would he lie now? Because an agent trained not to wear a seat belt on duty who put one on anyway was an agent who was not expecting an uneventful drive. It was unlikely that this gap in his story could hurt him now, but the impeachment hearings had offered an opportunity for filling it in that he apparently had found hard to resist. His pardon was for the cover-up; it wouldn't cover murder. So in his cool, methodical way, he was tinkering after the fact with the flaws in a plan he may not have had time to consider carefully enough beforehand. She was the other gap in his story to be filled in, and filled in with a vengeance.

The articles all agreed that Sampson had not gone quietly. He had taunted and insulted his captor, not realizing the savagery such behavior could trigger. Pat did. Years before, in St. Louis, whenever she had tried to divert his ardor that way, it had only intensified, along with his ecstasy at her anguish and hatred. When she had thought it couldn't get worse, he had thought of even viler, more degrading tortures. There was *always* something new.

Shaking off the nausea she felt whenever she let those memories flood in, Pat closed and stowed the folder, putting her keys back in her purse. With her desk and mind clear, she came back to her inescapable conclusion: *If he faked the second accident, he could have faked the first.*

This possibility had apparently not been raised by the FBI's investigators. Anyone it had occurred to in the Secret Service might not have wanted to share his suspicions; people in law enforcement didn't rat on one another. And if they had thought he'd killed Sampson on the President's orders, they might have been afraid to say anything. Besides, most investigators inclined in the direction of the likely rather than the possible. Since killing on his own initiative would have been an utterly meaningless act, suspecting him of it would have required believing a man who most people considered at worst an overachiever, a common enough Washington characteristic, was in fact capable of cruel, purposeless violence. Who in the world except her could know that?

But would the Judiciary Committee staff follow up on the discrepancy Callahan had uncovered? Doubtful. He had obviously been satisfied by Ned's answer. There was a chance someone might compare his testimony with the transcript of his interrogation, but Ned could always say he hadn't been thinking clearly when he confirmed, or failed to correct, his colleagues' contention that he'd been wearing the seat belt. Also, everyone knew the committee was not looking for an excuse to meet a second longer than minimum standards of thoroughness and professionalism required.

So once again it was up to her.

Pat Robinson stood for a moment to look around the room. No one else had come back in. Pulling her address book from her purse and reaching for the phone, she smiled at the thought that she was about to do something that had backfired abysmally the first time she tried it. The thought did nothing to deter her. The greatest evils in the world were accustomed things you detested and could escape but did not. The danger was in hesitating to act and letting familiarity dull horror's hot, sharp edge until it became bearable and even routine. Many years before, the summer between high school and college, six months after her half brother had begun having sex with her, she had left her job downtown and steered her car not toward home but across the river, out of town, and up Interstate 55 toward Chicago. She had barely known she had done it until it was done. A million times since, she had wondered why it had taken her so long. Every day she had stayed, with the front door unlocked and the road away from him beginning only a few feet outside, had been a reason to despise herself ever since.

She wanted her brother to be disgorged and vilified by the civilized world. Whether he ended up in jail, on the run, or dead, she didn't care. Going to the police with her suspicions might accomplish that . . . *eventually*. At first they wouldn't believe it. Her suspicions would mean nothing unless she exposed that dimension of his character that made them plausible. She would have to describe and catalog obscenities she still feared thinking about—times, dates, circumstances, acts. *And their consequences*. Even then, running it all down would take time. If she had correctly read the message in his untroubled eyes a few minutes ago, he would require very little time to accomplish what he now had in mind. She would have to act before he could, which meant that she could not rely on the authorities.

She would turn instead to someone who had already offered to help and who could act quickly and on her terms. Carole Nelson would have to know the whole story, too, but for some reason telling it to her would be a relief rather than an unendurable humiliation. Imagine Ned's surprise at seeing his crime exposed in the morning papers—*his revealed, mine concealed*. Embarrassment would force the police to act. Their knock on his door might come even before the thump of the morning paper on his doormat. As she dialed the reporter's direct number at the *Times* and waited for an answer, she was still smiling. Now it was a smile of vengeful pleasure.

"Newsroom," said a woman.

She froze at the sound of the unfamiliar voice. "Carole?" she said finally.

"Carole Nelson? She's on leave. Who's calling?"

"A friend," said Robinson uncertainly. "A . . . source. Can you reach her?"

The woman laughed. "I'm sure she'd welcome the diversion. She's about to have a baby. As a matter of fact, we just heard she went to the hospital this morning."

"My God, I forgot." She paused, glanced at her word processor, and continued, "I hate to impose, but it's fairly urgent. If I send her something in your care, can you take it to her as soon as she can see people? I wouldn't ask if it weren't critically important."

"Sure," said the woman. She gave her name and the street address of the *Times*. Pat thanked her and hung up. She had to shake off a moment of panic over being cut off by an accident of biology from the one person in the world who appeared to have the means and inclination to help her. But then she realized she had more flexibility than Ned. Even if he meant her harm, he would have to inflict it in some precisely calculated way. He could not cover up one murder by openly committing another. So she would just use her head and learn to be unpredictable. If he had her phone number, then he knew where she lived. Carole would be available in three or four days, and it shouldn't take her long after that to get the story into the paper. She just wouldn't go home now. That was what she did before. Today was for turning single events into patterns.

That afternoon, while running an errand on the fourth floor of EOB, she ran into an Eastern European specialist she was friendly with and mentioned in passing that the furnace in her building was broken and had to be replaced. Her colleague immediately offered her the spare room in her Alexandria apartment. Pat accepted gratefully, saying she thought everything would be all right again by the middle of the next week.

Parker DuBois jaywalked across Sixth Avenue and entered the New York Hilton, looking one way and then another for the house phones. The lobby was full of hotel guests, banquet guests promenading in their tuxedos and gowns, and other men in black tie standing alone at their posts and watching everybody else. Feeling a little seedy in his raincoat and loafers—he'd been up almost all night—DuBois edged through the crowds until he found the phones on a long shelf opposite the first bank of elevators. Picking one up, he gave the operator a room number.

"Command post." The man's voice was calm and neutral.

"Good evening. This is Parker DuBois in the lobby. I have a seven o'clock appointment with Flamethrower."

He heard the sharp sound of a page of paper being flipped. "It's not on the schedule," said the agent in his clipped voice, which was now full of suspicion.

DuBois smiled into the receiver. "I should hope not. Perhaps you could check with the staff." He paused. "Isn't this Burt?"

The agent's voice brightened a little. "Mr. DuBois? Hang on a minute." DuBois used the time to doff his coat and reflect on how extraordinary it was that he'd gotten this far without being wrestled to the floor and hauled away. He was marveling that presidential security still depended on most people being who they said they were when he noticed that six-foot tuxes were now blocking each end of the passageway and staring at him. Then Burt's voice came back on the line. "We'll meet you at the concierge desk on thirty-four and take you on up." DuBois hung up and walked around one of the agents, who was whispering into the microphone in his right sleeve, and found the appropriate elevator bank. Both men followed and rode up with him. Three minutes later, he was being escorted down the hall of the top floor, toward Hoskins's suite.

Beyond the outer door was another hallway, with mirrored walls bearing fleurs-de-lis and floors made from pink Italian marble. Two sets of double doors opened off the far end. One set was closed; DuBois could hear a radio playing on the other side while the President finished dressing. The other doors led into a vast, vaulted sitting and dining room with a glittering easterly view of midtown. There was a lot of chrome and glass furniture and a white Baldwin with the keyboard cover closed. Parker lifted it and played the first few bars of the right hand of a Bach two-part invention. The piano was out of tune.

"Parker?" yelled Hoskins through the door.

"Yes, sir," he shouted back, feeling guilty as he lowered the cover.

"Read the speech, will you? It's on the dining room table. I'll be right out."

DuBois found it in a folder next to Hoskins's open briefcase. He had skimmed the twelve pages by the time the President emerged, muttering, with his dinner jacket in one hand and a needle and thread in the other. "Good to see you, Parker," he said, gesturing with his hands to show why he couldn't shake. "Darn thing falls off every third time. I suppose I can leave the jacket open."

Smiling, DuBois took the jacket and needle and sat at the end of the living room couch. "I never understood how you became a colonel in the United States Army without learning how to sew a button," he said, knotting the bottom of the thread.

"I could do it," said the President as he wandered over to the window, "but these New York audiences like to be home by ten-thirty. What do you think of the speech?"

In the room's seductive semidarkness, the black thread was impossible to see against the black fabric. DuBois looked around, saw a floor lamp at the other end of the couch, and slid toward it so he could hold the jacket underneath. Then he shrugged. "The bureaucratic fault lines are a bit obvious," he said, speaking haltingly as he focused on his work. "First there are four State Department paragraphs about international brotherhood and the tentative agreement on various scientific protocols, leavened with some rhetoric on Soviet aggression in Africa and Asia that was no doubt urged by the White House political office, which wants to edge us to the right a bit as part of its strategy for winning back the Senate next year. Then there are three Commerce Department paragraphs about trade, followed by a stirring Pentagon commercial for constant vigilance, twenty new Midgetmen, and five more Tridents."

He snapped off the thread and wiggled the button. Then he stood up and held the jacket out so the President could come over and put it on. "Nonetheless," he said, brushing a piece of lint off Hoskins's shoulder, "it's a solid speech, redeemed by an excellent opening and finish, especially where you say that the essence of the new realism you've pursued is 'more than the sterile-sounding sum of all these incremental steps, but one single leap of the imagination to embrace the potential of a realistic, equitable peace'."

"That was all mine," said the President, turning to one of the seven mirrors in the room to adjust his tie. "You've got to give them a little lift, even a bunch of cynical tycoons like I've got tonight. I had to clear a whole afternoon to get it done. You would think that after four years, my overpaid, overstaffed writers. . . ." DuBois smiled as the boilerplate tirade continued. Hoskins loved rewriting a major address almost as much as complaining about it afterward.

In a moment DuBois cut in. "It's not their fault, Gene," he said. "You've got to build your firewall at NSC, not in the writing shop. They don't have the stroke to stand up to the Cabinet, and Felix Mendez is still feeling his way. Give him a chance to get the hang of it."

Hoskins turned and presented DuBois with a wicked smile. "His initiation begins tomorrow morning," he said. "After this speech, he's going to get more phone calls than the Jerry Lewis Telethon—from the Cabinet, from the press, from everybody in the free world."

DuBois tilted his head quizzically for a moment, and then smiled back. "You son of a bitch," he said. "You're going to announce another summit."

"At the very end," the President said, savoring the anticipation like good bourbon. "After the prepared text lets off. It'll drive the press nuts, won't it?"

"Wheeler doesn't know?"

"Nobody at State knows. Nobody in the White House

knows. Felix met secretly with the Soviet foreign minister over the weekend in Tokyo. State's almost ready for another summit, anyway. We were going to have a ministers' meeting in a month and then follow it with the summit announcement. Wheeler and his fellow milquetoasts wanted what they primly refer to as my 'political difficulties' to be resolved before I went to Moscow. But I figured we might as well get a little bang out of it now, while the hearings are still underway, and Gorbachev seemed happy to play along."

"That the Soviets think we're going to beat impeachment is the best news I've heard in weeks."

The President paused. "My thought exactly," he said mildly.

DuBois, assuming Hoskins would soon explain the reason he had hesitated, said, "But aren't you playing politics with our national security, Mr. President?"

"Damn straight." Hoskins's face darkened as, to DuBois's dismay, he violently unbuttoned his jacket and thrust his hands into the pockets of his trousers. "And so is Eddie van Aiken. I warned him about that atrocities article, Parker. He went ahead and introduced it anyway. He could have gotten away with having hearings on the cover-up and the civil rights thing. I even could've accepted that trumped-up campaign abuses bullshit. But he decided to go the whole hog, and so I'm going to fry his bacon but good."

DuBois was surprised and troubled by Hoskins's bitterness. He didn't speak right away, and as usual Hoskins interpreted the silence correctly. He walked back across the room to a fruit basket on the dining room table and yanked off a handful of grapes, gesturing at DuBois to help himself. "Doesn't sound like the old man you know and love?" he said. "I'm sorry, but I can't help it. It's hard enough to conduct this office when you're running at full power. But I have all the handicaps of the second term plus I've chopped myself off at the knees with this Sampson business. I cannot abide anyone who proposes to make my job even more difficult." He looked at his watch and then motioned

DuBois to sit down on the couch again. Hoskins sat in an easy chair next to him. They had plenty of time. One of the pleasures of incumbency was skipping receptions and receiving lines and arriving at dinners between dessert and coffee, presumably fresh from such momentous activity as precluded a president from eating more than four or five meals a week.

DuBois also sneaked a peek at his watch as he sat down. He had hoped to be on his way back downtown by now.

The President had gone on. "You want to know the essence of the advice I get from my advisors? I'm supposed to sit on my injured ass and let my political capital reaccumulate, showing myself in public now and again and squeezing a few hands to prove I haven't been replaced by a robot. Well that's not why I ran for president." He stopped, lowered his head for a moment, and then looked up at DuBois. "Which is why I asked you to come tonight. Parker, I've got to ask you a big favor."

"Anything," said DuBois.

"I need somebody I can trust to represent me in a fairly unpleasant business. I want you to go down and meet with Fred McCarthy. See, the win in Judiciary is not exactly a sure thing."

So the van Aiken obit was premature! "You mean Callahan?"

Hoskins nodded. "The boy won't even return our calls. He was put off by Ned Flach's manner and has gotten it into his head that the only way to make him pay for his crimes is to make me pay for pardoning him."

Again DuBois was silent. *Pardon* was still a painful word.

This time Hoskins missed the point. "You sympathize? I guess I do too, to an extent. I'd prefer if Ned projected a little more remorse. But not enough that I'm going to let that article reach the floor of the House if I can possibly avoid it."

"What've we got to offer?"

Hoskins paused and sighed. "The libel suit," he said with great reluctance. "I'll drop it if Fred can deliver the vote."

DuBois thought for a moment. "You sure he wants you to drop it?" he said. "I thought I was the only person in the country who did."

Hoskins was surprised. "Why you? I don't want to one damn bit, but it's the best card I've got at the moment."

"Because the suit would tie you up for two years, Gene. Because a president can't have a personal agenda, no matter how unjustly he's been treated. Because if you win, or rather when you win, all that will happen is that the *Post* will pay you a few hundred thousand dollars that for propriety's sake you'll have to turn over to the Audubon Society." He took a deep breath. "And because it would paralyze your efforts to rebuild a working relationship with the press."

Hoskins stared at DuBois for a moment and then produced the tight little smile that meant he was very, very angry about what had just been said—in this case, that he was supposed to rebuild a working relationship with people whom he knew still craved his demise—but didn't feel like arguing about it. "I see," he said coldly. "In any case, it's virtually a done deal, since the Speaker has been persuaded by fellow Californians such as the publishers of the *Los Angeles Times* and the *San Francisco Chronicle* that the suit is counterproductive."

DuBois said, "Mr. President, it would be an honor to represent you again."

Then the phone rang. Both men looked at it. In the four years they had been meeting together on the road, the telephone in the President's suite had never rung. All calls were channeled through a communications center in the basement and fielded by six aides who traveled with him.

DuBois made a motion to pick up, but Hoskins beat him to it. "Hello?" He listened for a while. Then all the tension in his face washed away. He turned and beamed at DuBois. "I'll tell him," he said. "Yes, I'm sure she is. I needed him more. But he'll be right there. Yes, sergeant, I remember the weight. Thank you." Before DuBois could speak, the President had knocked the receiver off his panic phone, an instrument without a keypad that set off an alarm in the Secret Service command post down the hall. Three seconds later, the doors of the suite burst open and four agents came in, hands buried under their jackets. "I didn't mean to scare you fellows," Hoskins said, "but I need a car downstairs for Mr. DuBois in three minutes, plus a bubbletop or motorcycles or whatever you've got. Also, hold an elevator. He'll be right with you."

Parker was on his feet. "Is everything all right? How's Carole?"

The agents filed out, and Hoskins stood and extended his hand. "Congratulations, Parker," he said. "It's a boy. Seven pounds and something, I think. She's fine, although pissed."

"She's been in labor on and off for two and a half days. I left word with the signal board that the hospital might be calling. I hope you don't mind."

"That depends," Hoskins said. "You going to name him after me?"

"Not unless your polls go up another ten points."

Hoskins laughed. "Actually, that's probably best," he said. "You're not even married, and I don't need any more trouble. We'd best not remind the press that fornication is supposed to be wrong." He put his arm around his friend's shoulder and walked him back down the mirrored hall. "McCarthy's expecting your call tomorrow morning. The meeting will be in the suburbs somewhere. Even Fred would be embarrassed by getting involved in something this sordid if word got out. Watch your back, by the way. He makes the Soviet look like Shirley Temple."

"I'll keep that in mind."

Hoskins stopped at the door and looked at DuBois with a sly grin. He had one more surprise. "There'll be another player at the meeting, by the way. Marshall Brandon."

DuBois stopped cold and stared at the President. "And what's that old bag of gas bringing to the party?"

"You won't believe it."

"I don't believe it," said George Stevens, slumped later that evening in a red leather booth in the back of a Georgetown saloon. He had just read the heading on the typewritten document his friend had handed him. "The Official Secrets Act of 1993? You're crazy."

Senator Brandon did not respond, except to gesture toward the draft so Stevens would read the paragraph summarizing the bill's purpose. Even at this stage in their ruined friendship, even though he knew what Stevens's reaction would probably be, Brandon still yearned for the embrace of support and approval that had been withheld so often in the forty years they'd known each other.

Stevens read it and then tossed it onto the table. "It's ridiculous," he said, "backwards, and tyrannical. And, especially, stupid. What the hell's gotten into you?"

Brandon leaned on the table and gathered his thoughts. It was an unaccustomed, invigorating exercise. "It just seemed to me," he said, "that in a situation like what happened last year, when your man was going to run a story on a national security matter, a president ought to have some recourse, either by being able to threaten sanctions against a newspaper or network afterward or seeking an injunction in secret beforehand. This bill provides for both." He leaned back, pleased he had managed to explain his own idea so cogently. He added an afterthought: "It works in England."

"Oh, is that what your peons told you?" Stevens spat. "Did they give you an exhaustive four-paragraph study of the thousand-year evolution of British law? What the hell do you know about England? You couldn't find the Custis-Lee Mansion in Arlington without a tourist map."

An injured look fluttered across Brandon's face before he brought it under control. He spoke in a clear, deep voice. "George, you are talking to the chairman of the Foreign Relations Committee of the United States Senate." The editor rolled his eyes. Brandon continued, "Thanks to you, the media have hit rock bottom in public appeal. I could report this bill to the floor by the end of next week. I count forty Republicans for it now, and the White House promises at least fifteen Democratic votes."

The words hit Stevens like two rounds in the chest. "You're working with the *White House* on this?" he yelped. "Marshall, they're just using you. They won't deliver anybody, and they'll probably raid your alleged yes votes if this thing ever does come up. They've just dodged a bullet, and they're not going to risk offending the press again."

Stevens stopped. Brandon could sense the workings of the fast, cold mind behind his squinty eyes. For years he had been the beneficiary of this man's scheming. It was true George had had a lot of great ideas. But now Brandon felt like the village idiot, and cheap and unpatriotic besides, because of his apparent role in what amounted to a plot against the President. Brandon looked at Stevens, who was now ordering another drink, with new understanding. *He really left me out on a limb this time.* Sponsoring his new bill was one way to redeem himself. Getting even with George was another. "I know what you're thinking," Brandon said with surprising venom. "And you can just forget it."

The editor looked innocent. "What do you mean?"

"I know you too well. You've already got the editorial written in your head."

"What if I do? I'd just be saving you from your own foolishness."

Brandon spoke as if invoking a curse. "You're finished, George," he said. "You're resigning. Tonight."

Stevens just looked at him. His expression was blank.

"I happened to talk to Donnie Graham last week, when we were writing the bill," the senator said. "They want you out. They've already told Dave Donnally to can you. I asked them to hold off a couple of days so I could give you a chance to do the right thing." He smiled. "It's a way to save face. I know that's important to you."

"Bullshit," said Stevens, draining his second drink, his face aglow from the first. "We're being sued for libel by the

President of the United States. Now would be precisely the worst time to take that kind of action. It'd be a virtual admission of guilt."

Brandon shook his head. "You're behind the curve *and* the eight ball," he said. "They want to settle out of court. Hoskins won't even consider it until you're gone."

Stevens wrapped his shaking hands around his empty martini glass, staring into it as he squeezed and rolled it between his palms. Brandon had just laid out a completely plausible scenario of the one threat Stevens had feared he could not overcome. So the *Post*'s owners didn't have the stomach for a knock-down, drag-out fight with a crooked president. Bad for business! When he looked up, his expression was ghastly. "I'll stop it," he hissed. "They don't have to settle. We can *still win,* damn them."

"Tonight, George," Brandon said quietly. "Let me tell you another reason it has to be tonight. Tomorrow afternoon, I've got an appointment with the media writer for *Time*. If you haven't resigned by noon, I'll keep it. Up until now, I've avoided talking about when you first alerted me about Sampson. But I'll tell them the whole thing and a lot more. For as long as I've known you, you've been gloating about your assorted triumphs. You're the world's best gloater, George. You've told me about people you pressured into talking to you on the basis of nonexistent statements made by others. You've hinted about manufactured sources and composites. You've told me about stories you sat on because it served your interests or just because it pleased you to do so, about others you initiated for the same reasons. You've bragged about refusing to correct errors or distortions the wronged parties didn't have the power to force you to admit." He paused. "I've had my staff working on it for days," he said. "We've fleshed out a dozen examples of abuses by the *Post*. We figure we'll have a sympathetic audience of journalists who want to show that you're not typical of the species."

Stevens, stunned, whispered, "You'll destroy yourself in the same stroke. You benefited as much as I did from a lot of those stories. Making you sound and look like a real statesman wasn't easy, you know."

Brandon shrugged. "I'm not up for reelection for four years," he said. "I've got plenty of time to repair the damage. Still, you can easily save me the trouble and yourself the humiliation." Stevens sat stiffly, grasping for some remark that would adequately convey his hatred of his old roommate. But words had finally failed him, so he slid out of the booth and left the bar. Brandon sighed with relief, pushed away his Perrier, and ordered a beer.

Bending his forehead into the dark and drizzle, Stevens walked back toward his bright, glass-walled office, back to nuzzle once more at the bosom of the beast that had carried him this far only to threaten to deposit him on oblivion's doorstep. The cold wet air penetrated the numbness he had felt during his conversation with Brandon—had felt, really, ever since Carole Nelson's story in the *Times* a month before. For the first time in weeks, he began to think clearly again.

Journalism had always been an imperfect means to an indefinite end. It was a source of influence, status, and a kind of power that over the years, even as he gathered more and more of it, even though he had more practical authority than three-quarters of the elected officials in Washington, seemed increasingly diffuse and unsatisfactory. He could kill a bill, ruin a reputation, and even help swing a close election. And there was always the delicious contrast of the outraged but silent faces of people who didn't like what they'd read about themselves in the morning paper but knew there was nothing they could do about it if they wanted to stay in the game. There was real pleasure in that, and not just for him. He had come up in the business surrounded by quiet, pipe-puffing men who were delightful at cocktail parties, cracking gentle, learned jokes about grammar and presidents they'd known, only to turn into slavering beasts at the keyboard. In a civilized society that had long ago outlawed assault and battery, the newspaper business was the last in which one could willfully inflict harm upon people and not only get away with it but thrive, assuming one could do it with sufficient élan.

The new generation—Chuck Sampson's—was less ashamed to let its darker side show. In the time between Vietnam and Watergate, a harsh manner had become the rule rather than the exception. Stevens thought it was a definite improvement. There was no need for a young reporter to fashion a civilized superego since he was expected by his peers and the public to be completely without conscience, scruples, or any human feelings whatsoever as he went about safeguarding society's democratic virtues. How often in the past had such impulses, which came when a journalist forgot that all power, save his, was corrupting, gotten in the way of a good story?

After a while, though, it hadn't been enough. Stevens wanted *governmental* power, with the planes and the titles and the cachet. That's why he had put his balls in Marshall Brandon's basket. Now deprived of it forever, running the *Post* lacked the appeal it used to have. Still, he wasn't sure he wanted to give up quite yet. His still-acute reporter's instincts were tingling. *Why would Marshall be talking to Donnie Graham about his stupid bill?* Maybe he'd work the phones some himself in the morning.

He arrived at the Fifteenth Street entrance and brushed by the night guard without a word. He should have flashed an ID, but the elderly man on the post was afraid to stop him. As Stevens got on the elevator and punched five, a great irony occurred to him. He was suffering this trial not because he had done his job poorly, but because he had done it well. His pale, unlined face lit up with perverse amusement at the thought of his unlikely nemesis, Carole Nelson. Not enough reporters had gotten killed, that was all. The notion did not horrify him except to the extent that he was angry at himself for not having entertained it sooner. He shouldn't have fired her; he should have destroyed her. Any kind of a scam would have done the trick. Accepting gratuities, maybe. He never should have let one of his *business* reporters get away with sitting on the fifty-yard line at Redskins games. *DuBois and that bitch had better seats than I did!*

In a moment he had crossed the newsroom and was behind his desk, glancing at the proof of the latest version of tomorrow's cover that a copy aide had left in case he dropped by. As he read, he swore out loud and fell into his chair like a sack of wet towels.

The head on the startling lead article was six columns, two decks: "President to Visit Moscow for His Second Summit; Aide Meets Secretly With Soviet in Tokyo." He scanned automatically for a story about the van Aiken committee. There wasn't one.

Damned wimps put it inside! He looked around his messy desk, found a copy of the bulldog edition, and spotted the story on A-5. He knew they had to be careful, but this was ridiculous. He stared out at the copy desk and was about to reach for the phone to make the change, when he stopped. He looked back at the proof page, with its four-by-four wire photo of a smiling Hoskins in black tie. Under it was a news analysis headlined, "President on the Move Again." The byline read Alton Jennings.

It was over. He looked into the President's eyes. *You win, you greasy hick.*

A few minutes later, the sound of a door slamming across the nearly empty newsroom startled him. Just a few reporters were at their desks, each no doubt delighted the boss had caught them at work at midnight. He noticed with passing interest that none was using the phone. Not like him when he was their age. The middle of the night, that's when you get your best quotes. Catch the suckers off guard. It then struck him that his interest was purely academic. While his mind was drifting, he had realized what his obvious next step was. Who needed all this trouble? Perhaps it was time to take a few months off and then get something like Ben Bradlee's setup at Columbia, teaching journalistic ethics. He had a half-dozen letters on file from J-schools offering him jobs if he ever wanted to make a change. If he really was going to be canned, there was no sense in hanging around a few extra days only to be transformed into the canniest media villain of the age by the dumbest man in the United States Congress.

He turned decisively to his keyboard, opened a new document, and typed: "Dear Dave: I hereby resign as senior editor of the *Washington Post.*" After printing and signing the letter and leaving it for his secretary to deliver in the morning, he called out to the copy desk and told them to open eight inches on page three. Then he exercised his last prerogative. He wrote the *Post*'s news article about his own resignation, including a long, laudatory quote from Dave, which he made up.

Back in Georgetown, Marshall Brandon was still in the booth, nursing his third beer. With each gulp he became more certain that he'd pulled it off. He chuckled as he drained his glass and looked for the cocktail waitress. Old George's head on a plate would be a bonus for Fred McCarthy at tomorrow afternoon's meeting. The thought both pleased and saddened him. He had finally done something his old friend would have to be proud of. After a decade in Washington, he wasn't precisely sure where *Time* magazine kept its news bureau, and he hadn't talked to Donnie Graham in six months.

FIFTEEN

ELEANOR MCCARTHY'S BEST FRIEND, SOPHIE, LIVED NEXT door to a realtor in McLean, Virginia, who was handling a furnished Tudor pile set twenty-five yards back from Old Dominion Drive on three acres of snowy woods. Even in Washington's rich market, the $3 million asking price was keeping buyers away. The owners, Hoskins's new ambassador to Brazil and his wife, had decided to rent it until the midterm elections the following year, when the inevitable new gaggle of congressional millionaires would be coming to town. On Thursday, while the President was in New York, the Speaker's always game wife called Sophie and exhaled a few breathy confidences about how hard it was to get together discreetly in the District with a certain prominent unnamed party. Sophie said she'd see what she could do and swore not to name any names herself. In a few hours, she called Eleanor back and said her Realtor friend was delighted to be a part of such a romantic enterprise and had offered the house as an ideal rendezvous, so long as Sophie promised to keep her in mind for her future real estate needs and Sophie's randy friend promised not to get anything on the bedspread. Sophie said she'd leave the keys in the McCarthys' mailbox that evening. "After that, Ellie," she said with a naughty laugh, her bracelets rattling against the receiver, "I never heard of the place."

The House of Representatives adjourned Friday morning. After lunch, the Speaker had his driver drop him at home and then headed for McLean in his son's supercharged '85 Camaro, which made the meeting all the more worthwhile, once he got the five-speed under control. Arriving before the others, he carried in a large thermos of coffee that Eleanor had prepared and began looking for the thermostat so he could turn the heat up. Marshall Brandon docked his white Lincoln Town Car a few minutes later. Parker DuBois came last, in a Buick he'd rented at National Airport after flying in from New York. The sight of this motley convoy in the circular driveway sparked only mild curiosity in the neighborhood. Even if one or more of the men had been recognized, people would have wondered not about how low the mighty had fallen but how low the price had.

"Coffee, senator?" the lanky, boyish Speaker asked, bustling around the living room in his Harris tweed and gray slacks, laying out Styrofoam cups and Coffeemate, playing the genial host, plotting the cynical swap.

"Thank you, Mr. Speaker," boomed Brandon. "How did you arrange such palatial surroundings for our little convocation?"

"My wife's supposed to be getting laid upstairs," said McCarthy, pouring a cup for Brandon and then rubbing his hands together against the chill that still hung in the air. "Cream and sugar?"

"What?" the bewildered senator said.

"We told the— oh, never mind, Marshall. It's not important." He looked over at DuBois, who was pouring his own. "How did the old man sound last night? I understand he dazzled them, as usual."

DuBois sat down on the other end of a couch where Brandon had already settled. He had read the speech before the world had heard it, but over the years he had trained himself to soft-pedal his entrée with Hoskins. Now this discipline was changing from a principle to an imperative. Hoskins needed him for this one mission but knew it would not be in his best interests for either the public or official

Washington to believe he was still consorting with a man who had had to be pardoned for his crimes. Not that DuBois didn't think the boss would still call him on the sly and at all hours. *I'll need a secure line more than I did when I was in the White House.* "I missed it," he said, "though I thought the papers gave it a good run, especially because of the summit announcement." McCarthy knew damn well the speech had been a triumph and was just sending a little make-peace smoke signal. DuBois needled him a little. "Do I take it you're back on the reservation despite our Gestapo-like tactics?" DuBois asked.

"Did I say that?" the Speaker said in a mild voice, choosing an Empire armchair across from the other two men. "An uncharacteristic overstatement. I regret it. But you've got to admit, Parker, that we didn't exactly have a model for this particular crisis. Besides, if you expected us to weigh in on your side against the media, you've been reading too much Daniel Webster and too little Marshall McLuhan."

DuBois smiled. Who could hold a grudge against a politician who simply admitted he was a coward and a hack? "What we expected to happen is exactly what did," he said, granting absolution, "which is why we opted for our own deal with the devil."

McCarthy's genial face lit up as he looked over at Brandon. "Speaking of the Prince of Darkness," he said, "I read this morning he's forsaking hell's acre and a half on Fifteenth Street for—did I read it right, Marshall?—the halls of academe?"

Brandon managed a vacuous and unknowing look. For him this was always a breeze. "It certainly was a surprise to me," he said. "I haven't seen too much of George lately. I will confess to having a drink with him last night and suggesting that for the good of the country, he might consider making a change. But he gave no indication—"

"We ought to give you a medal," said DuBois, cutting off the windy oratory with some impatience. So the odd couple had broken up, with Brandon managing to evict Stevens before Stevens could evict him. DuBois assumed both the estrangement and whatever leverage the senator had over the editor stemmed from their most recent, most disastrous collaboration. He went on, "I wish I'd seen his face when he got a load of your new bill." Brandon looked surprised that the news was out, so DuBois explained, "The President mentioned something about it." He turned to McCarthy and added, "Sounds intriguing, doesn't it?"

The casual expression on the Speaker's long, tan face didn't change. But DuBois had characteristically sunk his scalpel near the heart of the matter. Delivering Callahan's vote against impeachment in exchange for the President agreeing to drop or settle his lawsuit had been McCarthy's initial plan. But then he had learned of the White House's flirtation with Brandon on an official secrets act, which was not a piece of legislation McCarthy wanted to have to handle in the House. It wasn't that he cared much about either the free press or the press's feelings on the issue. He just didn't think he could keep enough Democrats in line to beat it in the current antipress climate, especially with the White House on the other side trying to lure votes away from him. And that would make him look bad.

So when he and the President had agreed on a meeting, McCarthy had suggested Brandon also be invited. The President's quick agreement meant that he, too, understood that the bill might end up being more trouble than it was worth, no matter how good it would feel to stick it to the press. McCarthy's position would now be that poor Callahan's vote would cost one settled suit and one ex-bill. The remaining question was whether Brandon, a Republican and apparently also a patriot, favored impeaching the Democratic President of the United States. Even if he didn't, was he so enamored of his brainchild and all it could do to rehabilitate his damaged reputation that he would be willing to let impeachment go forward to save it? In that case, it was McCarthy's job today to remind the senator that the less said about the events of the last few months, the better for the senator.

He would be bluffing, of course. Not only was McCarthy prepared to kill the last article in exchange for the lawsuit, he would have done it for nothing. Impeachment would paralyze the House for two months, whether it had a chance of passing or not. Virtually no other business could be transacted in the meantime. But his tactic was to try to get something extra for the price he was going to pay anyway for peace and progress in Congress, and so he had to make Brandon believe he was willing to put up with an impeachment debate. The question then became whether impeachment, and all it would do to spotlight Brandon's role in Stevens's calculations, was also an unacceptable risk to the senator.

McCarthy shrugged at DuBois's parry. "I think the events of the last month will have a greater restraining effect on the media than any legal sanctions or punitive legislation could," he said. "The public has made clear, probably for the first time, that not only does it see the need for some secrecy in government, but that it is also offended when the press takes it upon itself to expose sensitive information in its own interests. They've been slapped down but good, gentlemen. If the President's suit and the senator's bill go forward. . . . Well, frankly, I'm afraid the pendulum will swing too far." He focused on Brandon as he aimed a shot across the old tub's bow. "Besides, a floor debate on impeachment will attract even more publicity and will be less strictly confined to the legal questions at issue. *Every* aspect of the crisis will be a matter for debate."

Brandon fidgeted. "I get your drift," he said.

DuBois said, "Subtle, isn't he? I think it's why they call his office Death Valley."

McCarthy's smile was pleasant, his eyes neutral. "They had better," he said. "It adjoins my district. My point is only that the whole matter has reached an informal resolution, at least in terms of public opinion. The President has paid a price. So has the press. We can consider the matter closed, or we can have another year of open warfare. It's a decision the three of us can make today."

DuBois spoke now, essentially reading a script McCarthy could probably have predicted word for word. "The President has authorized me to say that in the event the House Judiciary Committee ends its deliberations without recommending for impeachment, then he will indeed consider the matter closed and take appropriate action as regards the contemplated libel complaint."

"How easy will that be to accomplish?" asked Brandon. Typically, he had not paid close enough attention to know the state of play on the committee.

McCarthy indulged him. "We have a young zealot in our midst," he said. "A prisoner of principle."

"I see," said Brandon, nodding, his expression revealing that he didn't, yet.

For expediency's sake, DuBois had let himself pass into the perfect moral void that threatened to seduce anyone who came within the sound of McCarthy's friendly, good-humored voice. "It's a Mr. Callahan goes to Washington problem," DuBois said. "The sprout pops an extra hair on his chest every time he reads the second inaugural address on the wall of the Lincoln Memorial."

"He's *my* problem," said McCarthy peremptorily. "Holier than thou is easy during your first term, but only if you don't care that it's your *only* term." He gave the two men a sunny smile. "I'll just explain that he owes me."

"For what?" said the senator.

"Oh, for keeping him off the Post Office and Civil Service Committee," McCarthy said. "For letting him walk the halls without a homeroom pass. For letting him use the men's room. For letting him *exist,* Marshall." He paused. "So it looks as though we have two factors in the equation. What do you say, old pal? Can't that bill wait until next year, when passions have died and reason reigns anew?"

Brandon's handsome face contorted as he mulled the question. "The thing is, Fred," he said, "I'm not sure it would pass next year. I was thinking I had better strike while the iron is hot, as it were."

McCarthy suppressed an impulse to glance at DuBois,

shake his head, roll his eyes, and maybe laugh out loud. Instead he leaned forward and said, "What I'm suggesting, frankly, is that your bill would be awkward for the Democratic majority on the House side, not to mention for a nation that's already sick of this story. You could solve a problem for me by shelving it, just as I can solve a problem for you by stopping impeachment."

DuBois and McCarthy watched in fascination as Brandon wrestled with this more direct proposal. The varying expressions that blew across the great planes of his rugged face sang a heroic epic of the clash of mighty forces—simple forces, to be sure, but fundamental ones, too. He was balancing self-interest against public interest. His eyes were far away, narrow, wide, then finally, suddenly content. Synthesis had occurred. It was a great day for the people of Pennsylvania, because their senior senator had come to a conclusion. He rose, Zeuslike, and the other two men rose with him. Buttoning his suit coat and smoothing it over his hips, he reached for the hand of the Speaker of the House. "Fred," he said, "I appreciate what you're trying to do, and I think the country owes you a vote of thanks."

"Thank you, senator," said McCarthy humbly.

"But to be honest, I see the opportunity here to do something for my state and nation that I may never have again. Some people say I haven't been the best senator I could. Perhaps they're right. But I'm proud of this bill. I think it's good for our people. And assuming I am honored by the proper number and quality of co-sponsors, I intend to introduce it at my earliest opportunity." He looked at his watch and, as he shook DuBois's hand, added, "Please excuse me. I promised Mrs. Brandon we'd try to get an early flight to Philadelphia this afternoon."

"Of course, senator," said McCarthy. "Thank you for coming." The moment the door closed behind him, McCarthy turned to the grinning DuBois and whispered urgently, "What do you think the dumb bastard's up to? Does he figure we have a deal whether he plays or not?"

"We do, don't we?"

"Sure, but how's he know?" said the Speaker, his eyes now afire. "Is he playing us for saps?"

DuBois leaned over the coffee table and started to help clean up. "He'll probably put his grandson on his knee this weekend and tell him you're the greatest Democrat since FDR," he said. "A little goodwill ought to do you good. Didn't I read somewhere that you said Fred McCarthy's Western omelette contained only three ingredients: debt, fear, and revenge?"

"I was misquoted," McCarthy said, an uncharacteristic sulk hardening his voice. "Some guy on my staff said it anonymously to a reporter."

"What'd you do?"

McCarthy used the edge of his hand to sweep back into the jar some Coffeemate Brandon had spilled on the table. "I found out who it was," he said, "and fired his ass."

A few minutes later, while McCarthy locked the front door, DuBois asked, "Do you think Marshall's bill will pass?"

The Speaker turned and squinted at the sun. "No question about it," he said. "It'll pass sixty-forty in the Senate and probably two to one in the House, whether the White House weighs in or not." He smiled coldly as he reached for DuBois's hand. "It's a funny thing," he said. "You kill a reporter, and in the end the press gets screwed. Wish I'd thought of it."

Representative J. K. Callahan entered the Speaker's office the next morning with spring in his step and left an hour and a half later with a pallid face and clammy hands. As he wandered toward the exit, broken, disillusioned, and punch-drunk, the sound of his soles echoed down the dark, deserted corridor like the hesitant steps of a high school student on the way to the principal's office between classes. Fred McCarthy had just explained American politics to him. After nearly a month in national office, Callahan finally knew what it was all about. He was sick to his stomach. He also felt anger and embarrassment and a profound sense of humility.

Callahan had a funny feeling the meeting had been called on Saturday so his weekend plans would be disrupted. He was right. The Speaker had also stolen a lick from Stalin's henchman Beria by making Callahan wait in the anteroom for half an hour while he trimmed his fingernails, chatted with his wife, and called over to the White House for a tennis court reservation. While only Callahan and McCarthy knew what actually happened when the world's most powerful legislator and one of Washington's weakest finally came face-to-face, the imagination more than sufficed. For instance, a member in Callahan's comically inferior position who chose to stand on principle against this Speaker's wishes might well find himself standing for reelection with only token support from the Democratic National Committee. His bills and any he cosponsored might never find their way onto the House calendar. The President, vice-president, and all presidential surrogates could easily be persuaded to bypass his district like an interstate looping around a forgotten country junction. His reservations at the House television studio and print shop could be lost. Covert aid and comfort could be given his likely Republican opponent. His staff would shrink if the Speaker chose to reinterpret what he was permitted under the House's complicated staff allotment formula. The General Accounting Office could suddenly begin paying scrupulous attention to whether the subject of Callahan's reelection was ever raised in government-stamped correpondence or on government-funded telephone lines.

And that was just for starters.

By the following Tuesday, when the Judiciary Committee met to vote on the remaining proposed article of impeachment, Callahan's digestion had fully recovered. He made lengthy remarks—somewhat too lengthy for a freshman—that were coldly critical of the President. "But if it falls to this congressman," he concluded, looking out over the hushed chamber, "and to this congressman alone to say whether our nation will in the months ahead look to the future or remain convulsed by its recent past—and by my count, it now appears that it does fall to me—then I can choose no other course but to cast my vote for healing and progress rather than more rancor and paralysis."

When the roll was called an hour later, Callahan voted against the article, and it failed by just one vote. The greatest political crisis since Watergate was over.

As Callahan mulled these events during his remarkably successful political career, it became easier with each passing year to convince himself that he had not really changed his vote because of Fred McCarthy's bullying. Late Saturday evening, just as Callahan returned home from Washington to warm his chilled soul in his family's embrace, events had caught up with the principal target of his righteous ire. All the more reason, Callahan had told himself on the way to the dais the morning of the vote, to let the whole distasteful business end.

Pat Robinson was a guilty and discontented houseguest. She spent her day and a half in Alexandria in voluntary servitude, throwing away any newspapers, stacking magazines, buying a green plastic trash pail for storing the deposit bottles her hosts had been tossing out. When they went out to dinner Friday night, she stayed home and scrubbed the bathroom floor.

On Saturday evening she decided they needed some privacy. She took their grocery list, which was stuck to the front of the refrigerator with a cheeseburger magnet, and said she was going to the Safeway.

While Pat had been washing the dishes, her friend, after pleading with her to leave them for the man of the house, had changed into a flannel nightgown and pink fuzzy slippers and pinned up her curly red hair. When Pat announced her shopping trip, the friend looked back in horror. "You are *not,*" she said. "Your evening's already planned. I rented *Lethal Weapon,* that old Mel Gibson movie. You can see his cute bare butt, remember?"

"I never saw it," Pat said, taking her overcoat from the closet while she read over the list. "Are you sure you don't need eggs?"

Her friend threw some couch pillows onto the floor in front of the television and waved her hands over the scene, smiling invitingly. "You'll like it," she said. "I personally guarantee it. Come on. I'll make us some popcorn and we'll watch the sweat on his chest glisten."

"Wonderful," called the husband, coming down the hall from their bedroom in his Nike sweats. "You don't mind if I go for a run, say up to Baltimore and back? As I recall, there isn't much in that one for me except the naked girl who jumps off the building in the first three minutes."

"You *would* remember that," his wife said in a cross voice.

He smiled at Pat. "Welcome to the nineties," he said. "She's hot for some guy's butt, and I'm in hot water for noticing a girl's—" Then he saw the list in Pat's hand. "Hey!" he yelled, lunging at her and trying to snatch it away. "Would you please just sit down?" Pat whirled on the balls of her feet, and he overshot. "You've got to save your strength to plow the south forty in the morning," he said, grabbing at her from the other side.

He missed again, staggering back into the living room, and she tucked the list away in her purse. "You've both worked hard all week," she said, chiding them. "You deserve some time to yourselves. I won't be long."

The couple exchanged dejected smiles. They'd been either living together or married for eight years and were getting a big kick out of having somebody new on the premises, especially since she wasn't a visiting relative who planned to drag them out the next morning to examine Lincoln's bloody pillow or wait in the latest endless line for the hottest new exhibit at the National Gallery. The woman turned back to Pat and said, "Just watch a little bit. There's this one part where Mel—" But the door was already closed. Pat's good-bye rang faintly back up the hallway.

In the elevator she thought about what she would do next. Carole had probably received her letter at the hospital the day before. How would she react? Would she be able to focus on it? Would she want to? The elevator opened again on the ground floor, and the chill in the lobby was sharpened by the fear that she had too much riding on someone she barely knew, someone whose own life was being turned upside down. She tightened her muffler around her neck, buttoned her coat, and pushed the glass door open.

The air bore the cheerful smell of burning firewood. *Could I be imagining all this?* Here she was, camping out in somebody's guest room, enmeshed in ridiculous fictions about broken heaters, and because of what? An inadvertent glance in the direction of a television camera? An inconclusive telephone call from a man who might yet be capable of guilt and even affection toward her?

As she turned down the block toward her car, she terminated this line of analysis. Her dialogues with herself were becoming frequent and tiresome. She had not come so far from such hopeless straits to start second-guessing herself now. She would continue to trust her instincts. She would call Carole first thing Monday; by then, the baby might not be so much of a novelty. She reached the car and opened the door on the driver's side, getting in and setting her purse on the passenger seat. She turned back and reached for the automatic door lock, then stopped and gasped. There was already a hand there. It was extended from the back, between her seat and the door. She heard the locks snap shut like four nails in the edges of a coffin and his voice say, "Where are you going, sis? Want some company?"

She saw her friend's husband leave the building and begin to jog in the other direction. She tried to roll down the window, but one icy hand grabbed her arm while the other covered her mouth. She recognized the sweet smell of his soap and cologne. "Easy," he said in his soft voice. His warm breath brushed her ear. "Damn, it's cold in here. I've been waiting for two hours. How about a drive?" He took his right hand from her mouth and used his left arm to pin her against the seat while he climbed forward.

When the hand fell away from her mouth, she could have screamed, but she didn't. If she had, he would have struck her or worse. In any event her fear had already been subsumed by a sense of inevitability. As she looked into his sleepy, friendly face, its robust complexion masked by the neutral light from a streetlight, she had a single clear, astonishing thought. In all the years she had been reliving her months with him, she had ached for a chance to repay the agony she suffered. Was it possible that part of her actually relished what was to come? Whatever else was about to happen, and no matter what price she would pay for it, she would find some way to inflict pain on him—savage, shattering, enraging physical pain. In hatred she found strength and calm. She found her keys, started the engine, and said evenly, "Where do you want to go?"

He pointed straight ahead, and she released the emergency brake and pulled way from the curb. A few blocks away, he made her stop, and they switched seats. So they wouldn't have to get out of the car, he pressed his backside against the dashboard and had her slide in front of him, and she couldn't help brushing against him. She knew he was excited, and for a moment her eyes widened. That was one degradation she had never expected to suffer again. As he moved over behind the wheel he held her eyes and smiled. She forced a resolute expression onto her face. "Ned, I swear to God," she said, her voice low and calm, "I'll bite it off."

His smile vanished, and he jammed the car into gear. Then he put on his seat belt. She made an automatic motion to put on hers, and he said, "No."

He entered the Beltway, staying in the right-hand lane so she wouldn't be tempted to gesture to other cars. She tried to ask him what he was doing and why, but he would not listen or answer. Signals she remembered from years before—the veins on his temples standing out, his cheeks pulsating like membranes in a bloodstream—suggested he was in a carefully, barely controlled rage. Finally he cut her off in a cold voice. "We're going for a drive, that's all. Please just be quiet."

They drove west and then north, past Springfield, Annandale, Falls Church, Vienna, and McLean, and after about twenty minutes crossed the Potomac River and entered Maryland. The second exit was River Road. He drove west past the town of Potomac and turned north on a dark two-lane road, driving just fast enough so she couldn't jump out safely.

By staring a little to her left through the center of the windshield, she could watch him out of the corners of her eyes without his noticing. He kept looking down at the instrument panel. At the speedometer? No, the *odometer*. He must have known the precise distance to a certain place. *A certain bend in the road, a certain tree?* He was holding the wheel carefully at ten and two o'clock, his fingers drumming against the rim. She thought about the clamplike hands, the powerful arms, the *broken* arm. He'd said he had braced his hands against the wheel. But if the seat belt operated properly and prevented his weight from bearing down on the arm, how could it break? And why just the right arm? It had to have been braced against something else when the car hit the tree. Just as the thought came to her, he steadied the wheel with his knee and reached over and grabbed her by the shoulders, twisting her around and pressing her against the dashboard. "My God, no!" she cried. "Please stop, *please!*"

His self-control was pierced by a flash of madness. "*Shut up*!" he shouted. "You're just a *dead bitch*!" Taking the wheel with his left hand, he put his other hand under her jaw and jammed her head between the top of the dash and the windshield, locking his arm straight. She cried out in pain. But she knew what he was doing, and her mind was still clear. He was strong enough that when the impact came, he could drive her head through the glass. *Just as strong as ever now*. By straining her eyes to look down, she could see him. She fought panic, pretending to flail her arms but really sensing distances, finding his chest, his arm, his lap. She saw him fix on an object straight ahead and felt the awful pressure against her jaw increase. He sped up. *Any second now.* The tips of her fingers found the belt across his chest and followed it down to the buckle. She felt the wheels leave the pavement. *Now!* She pressed the release button. An instant later, the pressure on her neck was gone. As she slid from the dash toward the seat, the last thing she saw was the fear in his eyes.

Parker DuBois was in Carole's room at Beth Israel Hospital on First Avenue by nine o'clock Saturday morning. He brought a bouquet of flowers, a stuffed bear, a gym bag containing some provisions she'd asked for—knee socks, a clean nightgown, three newspapers, four women's magazines—and an unwieldy, foot-square, quarter-inch-thick plastic pass issued to visiting fathers downstairs. Carole, her long hair in braids, was wearing a regulation gown and her threadbare blue terrycloth robe and sitting on the bed with her legs stretched out in front of her, their son in one arm, asleep at her breast. She was watching television, using her free hand to flip through the channels with the remote control. He arranged the goods on her nightstand and sat in a chair. She kept flipping. "Good morning," he said after a while.

She turned and gave him a narrow look. "Did you bring the papers?"

"Sure did." He nodded toward them on the table.

She looked back at the television. "Good morning," she said. "*Damn.* No CNN." She turned it off, leaning over and grabbing the *Times*.

"Where did you get the pigtails?"

"My breathing coach did them. She just left." She glared at him. "She's been keeping us company."

"And how is junior?"

"Sleepy," she said, looking down at him with a fond smile. "Wonderful. Want to go see Daddy?" DuBois stood, and she wiggled the baby a little to rouse him and then handed him to his father. She returned to the newspaper. "Did you hear anything about an accident?" she said. Then she stopped turning the pages and became stern. "Where's your smock?"

DuBois was gently twisting back and forth. "My what?" he said, keeping his eyes on the bundle in his arms.

"You're supposed to get a sterile smock at the nurse's station."

"You go get it," he said. "I don't want to owe those iron ladies a thing. I stopped at the nursery on the way in to see if he was there and saw one of them changing somebody else's poor howling infant. It looked like she was packing a parachute." He tried without success to make the baby hold his new stuffed bear.

"Just talk to him," she said. "You have to bond." Her voice became icy. "You have some catching up to do. Except for last night, you haven't—"

"I told you, it was a matter of national security," he said. He cooed, poking the baby in the cheeks, trying to make him smile. His son gazed at him without a hint of cognition. DuBois was enraptured.

She gestured toward the window, where a massive plant on the heat register blotted out the morning sun. " 'Where eez father?' they say. 'Gee, nurse, *I* don't know,' I say. 'Uptown at a banquet, I think—' "

"I didn't go to the banquet."

" '—or on the way to Washington, or on the way back.' Nope, there's no father to be found for my child, but I *do* have a twenty-gallon cymbidium orchid from the President of the United States." She couldn't suppress a smile. "In your persistent absence, that particular delivery raised quite a few eyebrows. Talk about pregnant glances."

He finally tore his eyes from the baby and looked up at the plant. "What—"

"What are we going to do with a giant cymbidium orchid? Exactly, Parker. There in a nutshell you have the problem with Eugene Hoskins. Does he have any *idea* what a pain in the neck an orchid is to take care of? This is a man who has *never* had to worry—"

He said, "The new place is full of light. Light is good for all beautiful things. So I hope you and Gene's orchid will manage to peacefully coexist." He leaned tentatively over the bed. She pouted a little but turned her face toward him. They kissed, and she reached for the baby again. "I'm really sorry, Carole," he said. "It won't happen again."

"You bet it won't," she said, nuzzling him between his shoulder and neck. "You are looking at your only issue." She paused, caught by her son's hazy blue eyes. "I think."

He smiled. "I won't quote you." He put his arm around her and brushed her shiny hair with his cheek. *Why does she always smell so good?* Then he remembered something she had said. "What accident?" he said, straightening up.

"Oh, right," she said, sitting back. "There was a new mother's seminar this morning down the hall, and—" She stopped. "What are you grinning about?"

He shook his head and chuckled. "It's just that there was a contingent on the way to the nine o'clock class when I arrived," he said, "and to judge by the speed they were making, they must have left their rooms at eight-thirty to get there. I couldn't keep the phrase 'walking wounded' out of my head."

"You'd better watch it," she said in a near whisper. "There are twenty-three very sore ladies on this ward at the moment, and if you don't lower your voice, I guarantee you're a dead man. We may be slow, but we're tough. All we really need out of you at this point is gifts, worship, and absolutely no references to private parts. That subject happens to be closed until further notice."

"Sorry," he said again, genuinely.

"Accepted. Anyway, I was walking past another lady's room when I heard the tail end of a news item that I could've sworn was about a Secret Service agent who'd been killed."

He was suddenly alert. "It's not in the *Times?*"

"Doesn't seem to be." She turned back to page one and looked in the upper right-hand corner. "Geez, Parker, this is the home delivery edition," she said. "It closed at about noon yesterday. You got anything with this year's news in it?"

He'd hurried out of the apartment without listening to the radio and collected his *Times* from the doorman on the way out. He'd bought the *News* and *New York Post* in the hospital gift shop, along with the magazines and the bear, folding the skinny Saturday editions in half under his arm. Now he picked up the tabloids and saw that the cover of the *Post* said, AGENT OF DEATH. The story was on page three. As DuBois read it, his face turned ash gray.

"What is it?" she said.

The story was based on wire service reports, woven together in the wee hours on South Street with the *Post*'s customary panache. He read the lead out loud:

"The emotionless presidential bodyguard whose fanatical devotion to duty led to the death of a *Washington Post* reporter and the scandal of the century died himself last night the same way Charles Sampson did—from head injuries suffered when his car lost control and struck a tree in northern Maryland, police said. His passenger, a pretty, thirty-seven-year-old White House aide who was apparently his lover, was critically injured."

"Good Lord," Carole murmured. "It's Pat."

DuBois's head jerked up. "How did you know?"

Her brown eyes gleamed with understanding and, to DuBois's alarm, tears. But she just shook her head. "Keep reading," she said. "Why do they say they were lovers? That's absurd."

He read quickly through the story again. "She said so herself," he said. "She was unconscious by the time she got to the hospital, but it says that when the police got to the scene, she kept asking over and over again how her boyfriend was. They weren't wearing seat belts, and the police said he probably just lost control." He stared at the page, shaking his head. "Poor girl," he said to himself.

"Call them now," Carole ordered. DuBois looked up but didn't understand. "Call the *hospital,* Parker. Find out how she is. *Please."*

Tears were now running down her cheeks. He extended his hand, and she grabbed it and squeezed it hard. He paused for a moment, then picked up her phone, dialed the White House, and asked for an operator he knew worked Saturdays. "Betty, Parker DuBois," he said. "I'm fine, thanks. Yes, them too. Seven pounds fourteen, I think. Thank you. Listen, honey, I wonder if you have anything on Pat Robinson's condition?" He listened for a moment. "Well, that's encouraging, isn't it? Maybe I'll call again later to check, okay?" He hung up. "They've been calling the hospital every hour," he said. "She's no worse, and her vital signs are strong. They think she'll make it." His tone hardened. "I guess you know something I don't."

She handed DuBois the baby, pressed the call button, and then sat back and dried her eyes and face. When the nurse came in, Carole asked her to take the baby back to the nursery for a while and to close the door on the way out. The four-foot-nine, highly intimidating Filipino looked back and forth accusingly from DuBois to Carole, but then shrugged and did as she was told. When the door closed, Carole said, "They weren't lovers. Anything but." She opened the top drawer of her nightstand and took out an envelope. "Read this. It's from her."

The letter was printed on computer paper. "Dear Carole," it read:

> I'm sorry to impose on you at a time like this. I do hope that all is well with you and the baby and also with Parker. I am intrigued by the thought of him contending with the demands of fatherhood.
>
> When we last saw each other, I wouldn't tell you why I had talked to Chuck in the first place.

DuBois cast a sharp look at Carole. *Pat* was the leaker? And *Carole* knew? He knew she had uncovered Sampson's original source, and while he never thought to ask who it was, he also never thought it was somebody in his own shop. His first impulse was to feel cruelly betrayed by them both. His second was acute embarrassment because of his absolute assurances to the President that everyone on his staff was trustworthy. But Carole didn't absorb the reproach; she was gazing at the Mary Cassatt poster print on the far wall and dabbing her eyes. He went on reading.

> I told you it was an impulsive, irrational act and that I was ashamed about it, but it did have a rational purpose. It had to do with Ned Flach, my half brother. The reason I am contacting you now is that I have come to the conclusion that Chuck's death was not an accident, that Ned killed him, and that he might also try to hurt me.
>
> When I was seventeen, my parents died in a plane crash. I knew my father had an older son by his first marriage who lived in St. Louis and served on the police force, but I'd never met him, and his name rarely came up. For some reason—the self absorption of a much-loved only child, I suppose—I never wondered why.
>
> It had been years since Dad and Mom had written their will, and Ned inherited the bulk of their estate, including the house. He moved in, urged me to stay, and really made me feel quite welcome and safe. All our neighbors and my parents' friends were delighted that someone would be looking after me. My world, of course, was completely shattered, and he had a quiet, comforting, nonthreatening way about him that made him a perfect companion. We became quite close. We went to dinner and movies together. He told me about his plans to take the Secret Service test. One night he heard me crying. He came into my room and sat on the end of the bed and talked to me until I stopped. He hugged me and stroked my head and neck. Then he had sex with me.

"My God," said Parker. When he looked up, Carole was staring at him. He now understood everything, including the pain he saw in Carole's eyes.

Carole, I didn't do anything about it. I could've told someone, but I didn't. No matter how much I learned about these cases—and I've become something of an expert—I have never gotten over the feeling that I am somehow responsible, somehow permanently soiled, because I let it happen. I just prayed he wouldn't do it again, but he did. It continued for months, and it became worse and worse every time. Sex seemed to be a catalyst for the evil dimension of his character. Because he *is* evil—a sociopath, capable of existing and even excelling in the everyday world and yet also capable of the most horrible acts and incapable of conscience. He became more and more ingenious in his demands. When I complained, he threatened me. When I cried, he hit me. And yet I still did nothing! I went to school every day, I played the flute in the band, I went home, I filled out my college applications, I did my homework, and then I went to his room and let him rape me. I thought I would die of the shame. I hoped I would.

That June I graduated from high school. He bought me a car so I could get a job in an office downtown. One day, I got in the car and drove away, to Chicago. The car was in my name, and I sold it and used the money to rent a studio apartment. I got a job and parlayed my acceptance to two good schools on scholarship into a place in the freshman class that fall at the University of Chicago. From there my life went about the way I told you and Parker—graduate school at Yale, the teaching job at Harvard.

Since I am telling all, there is one more thing. I found out later that first summer that I was pregnant. Of course I immediately had an abortion. If I did it to put the past behind me, it didn't work. I have had a pretty lonely life and have sometimes wondered what it would be like to have at least the companionship of my child—even *that* child. So even that was a reason to loathe myself. I had no other choice. It wasn't my fault, none of it. And yet only I suffer for it.

Pat described her horror at learning that the President had brought Flach to Washington and her current suspicions about Sampson's death. She didn't want her relationship to Flach publicized; that she couldn't bear. Instead, she was urging Carole to goad the impeachment committee staff into pursuing the discrepancy about the seat belt and to get the Sampson autopsy report, to see if there were any inconsistencies with a routine passenger death in a head-on collision.

DuBois finished and folded the letter back into the envelope. With a sigh he said, “Too late. He got to her.” He paused, cocking his head as another thought came. “Or she got to him.”

Carole’s voice was small, defeated. “I guess she overestimated me,” she said, looking into her lap and playing with the ends of her hair. “I could tell she was frightened out of her wits when I met her. I should’ve kept after it, Parker.”

“Nonsense,” said DuBois sharply. “She didn’t tell you any of this. What could you have done? Where would you have started?”

She shrugged.

He pursued the point. “I won’t have you assuming that burden. It’s not your fault.” He paused. “Besides, look on the bright side. You’ve got the last piece of the puzzle.”

She stared at him.

He continued, assuming incorrectly that she had missed his meaning. “You’ve got the story of the year: the reason for the leak, the truth behind Sampson’s death, the real story of Flach’s death. Fame shall be yours yet again, and riches besides. Better get on the horn, my dear.” He watched her carefully.

Her stare drifted over his head. She thought about what she’d said to Pat. *I won’t ever use or speak your name, whether you talk to me again or not.* She thought about what Pat had said last night, lying crushed on a highway, trying desperately to keep her dignity intact. *How is my boyfriend?* She took the letter from DuBois, put it in the drawer, and closed it. “What purpose would it serve? What good would it do if I wrote it?”

“None whatsoever.”

Though she managed a weak smile, DuBois thought she suddenly looked exhausted. He resisted getting up, wrapping his arms around her, and holding her until she fell asleep.

"Well then," she said, resting her hands on her knees, "I guess we'll just have to live on my stellar court reporting and your million and a half."

He smiled. "So the cover-up continues."

She shot back, "Certainly not for your sake, or for his." She jerked her head toward the plant.

He looked modest. "Oh, of course not."

She edged away from him and patted the space she had created on the bed. "Speaking of cover-ups," she said, "get up here and hold me for a while. The nurse thought that was what you had in mind, anyway."

DuBois sat next to her with his back propped against the headboard so she could rest her head on his chest. "I admire what you're doing," he said, "but you realize the story might come out anyway."

"But it won't be my problem." She looked out the window. The view was lousy. *Speaking of my problems.* "On the way home," she said, "you'd better buy some orchid food."

Epilogue

THERE WAS NO PRETTY WAY TO GET A MODERN PRESIDENT into Manhattan. LBJ had the right idea when his party arrived for Bobby Kennedy's funeral in three choppers that dropped right into Central Park like Texas water bugs. Then he transferred to a motorcade for the brief but regal eight-block procession down Fifth Avenue to St. Patrick's Cathedral. Soon the Secret Service became so exercised over snipers in tall buildings that it insisted on using the heliport on the southern tip of the island and paralyzing the city getting the man all the way uptown to the Waldorf-Astoria or the United Nations. They bought a five-ton armored limousine with a light in the ceiling so the fourteen people waiting along the unannounced route could see him.

This irritated Eugene Hoskins. He thought it was wasteful to use three hundred highly trained people to get him the 225 miles from Washington to New York. He thought it was bad politics to inconvenience thousands of New Yorkers just to get one guy eighty blocks. Reagan, Ford, and Nixon hadn't had to worry about winning the East Side, because they knew they never would. As a Democrat, Hoskins had to. But he couldn't make his guardians or Congress give an inch. The age of terrorism had produced a security high priesthood who, when they appeared on the Hill or before OMB analysts, could say, "Cut our budget? Fine. But when the vice-president's nine-year-old gets *taken out* on the way home from school, don't blame us."

Hoskins had spent his first two years in office intriguing against this theocracy of threat levels, but then he realized it was counterproductive. He was using his valuable time and energy to debate a mere principle. People didn't care anymore. They had gotten so used to seeing their presidents either on television or encased in distant blue-serge gauntlets that they assumed they would never get near one again. Security was becoming a velvet coffin. It was *convenient* to be whisked around without having to deal with anybody. Ten out of forty presidents had been killed or shot at, and Hoskins figured anybody who really wanted to take a pop at the President would be hard to stop. But his angry memos demanding his detail be cut, his motorcade routes publicized, his two-hundred-man advance team reduced, his fifty-man pre-advance team eliminated—well, finally, he stopped writing them. It didn't matter whether he had or not, because only one had been obeyed, the one ordering them to remove the bright interior light from the limo. He said it made him feel like an organ on the way to a transplant operation.

They were pleased he had given up. Another president had been shanghaied by his security. When his staff sent him a memo detailing the arrangements for his private solo visit to the city one sun-drenched Tuesday morning in April, he approved it. During the forty-five-minute flight from Andrews to JFK, he occupied himself with state papers. He climbed without complaint into the little bulletproof wagon they made him use for the twenty-yard voyage between his new Boeing 747 and the marine helicopter that would take him into Manhattan.

His route from the Battery to City Hall and then to his second stop in midtown was already secure. If he had hopped a cab to the airport and a shuttle to La Guardia, he would have been safer than he was today, with his plans known throughout official Washington and by every law enforcement agency in the tri-state area. Thousands of agents, detectives, and uniformed officers lined the streets and rooftops, police choppers circled, Coast Guard patrol boats chugged, and civilian traffic was backed up all the way to Coney Island. In the sixties, would-be revolutionaries swore they'd close down the city. Where they had failed, the President now triumphed.

When his chopper touched down, it was surrounded by agents and police. In a moment the door opened and he came down the six steps. This instant of exposure could not be helped. His limousine was thirty feet away, and a tall young agent with red hair and freckles touched his elbow, trying to nudge him toward it.

The President, the spray he'd just applied to his thick gray hair barely holding against the fury the rotors kicked up, paused and gazed north across the FDR Drive, which at nine forty-five in the morning was empty for a half-mile in either direction. He looked at his watch. The man in charge of the follow-up car in the motorcade witnessed these developments and radioed the communications center a mile away in the World Trade Center. "New York, this is Flamethrower trail," he said. "Flamethrower has stopped."

Hoskins turned to the agent who was trying to haul him off. "Listen, son," he shouted over the chopper noise, "I'm a little early. You mind if I take a walk? I've never seen the Vietnam memorial over there."

The agent, recently transferred to PPD from Lady Bird Johnson's detail, stammered, "Uh, I wouldn't advise that, sir. We—"

The President smiled warmly and began walking. "Your name, son?"

"Mike Reilly, sir. I think—"

"Were you in Vietnam, Mike?"

"No, sir," said the agent. "My dad was. He—" He stopped. New York and Flamethrower trail were screaming in his earpiece. "Sir, the car—"

"Let's go," said the President, taking the youngster by the arm and guiding him past the limousine and through the gate, the ubiquitous officer bearing the nuclear codes trailing a few steps behind him. A score of agents watching them were momentarily paralyzed. Mike radioed the new destination.

A tense voice came back. "Reilly, New York. The walk is a negative. Would you just put Flamethrower in the car. Over."

"New York, Reilly," he said. "He won't cooperate." It suddenly occurred to him that he was an employee of the protectee. "Recommend we just *do* the walk. Over."

Youthful inexperience and naïvete? Perhaps. But it was an idea, after all. "Flamethrower trail, New York. We concur. Let's do the walk. Reilly, you copy?"

"New York, Reilly. Roger that." He helped Hoskins over the cement barricade between the empty traffic lanes and pointed to a stairway leading up to the memorial plaza. By now all the other agents were bounding ahead, preparing to join the two men already stationed there in rousting the veterans, tourists, derelicts, and other innocent passersby. As he climbed the steps, the President noticed this activity and asked his escort to send an additional message. "New York, Reilly," he said tersely. "I have an order from Flamethrower."

"I do not copy, Reilly. A what?"

"An *order,* New York. He says he understands this is unorthodox and that we are just doing our jobs, but he says if we don't leave the people alone, he'll have our badges."

There was a long pause. "Reilly, New York. Copy that. Flamethrower trail, New York. Do you copy? We're going to keep it low-key."

Hoskins greeted a few stunned people and then led Reilly over to the memorial, a long glass monolith covered with inscriptions taken from soldiers' letters home. Hoskins read a few. One, written by an infantryman to a father at work, asked him to find a way to break the news to his mother that he would probably never make it home. Another wrote a friend that there were no heroes in Vietnam, just kids trying to stay alive. A few people tried to approach Hoskins as he read, but by now the agents had formed a low-key barrier of humanity two bodies thick.

After a few minutes, Hoskins looked at Reilly, an anguished expression on his face. "Don't you think there were letters like this from all wars?"

Reilly wasn't supposed to be reading the letters; he was supposed to be keeping an eye peeled. He scratched his bushy head nervously and scanned the wall. "I don't know, sir," he said. "I guess so."

"Do you think the war was wrong, Mike?"

"I don't really know for sure," he said. "My dad was there, though."

The President stooped to read an inscription near the bottom. He was having trouble with it. "Are there light bulbs behind there?" he said.

Reilly bent to look. "I think so, sir."

The President straightened up and pointed. "They must be burned out at the bottom. See about having them replaced, will you?" Reilly gulped and nodded. Hoskins turned and walked the length of the monument, the agents reluctantly letting him pass. Near the other end was a man who had walked up from his shoeshine station around the corner to see what the commotion was all about. The President shook his hand. "And where do you live, sir?"

"Bed-Stuy, Mr. President."

"Really? I campaigned there in '92."

"I know, sir. I saw you. That was the second time."

"When was the first?"

"Sixty-six, outside Da Nang. I was honored to serve under you, sir."

Hoskins looked at the man for a long moment and then glanced over his own shoulder and leaned forward. "Listen, my friend," he said quietly, "can you tell me where the Whitehall Street station is?"

The man's eyes grew wide. "You mean the subway?"

"*Sh!* Yes, the subway."

The man pointed down a couple of stairs. "Down there and around to your left. But listen, Mr. President—"

"Thanks." He pounded the man on the shoulder. "Come

on, Mike." He reached into his breast pocket, pulled out a map, and unfolded it as he walked.

"New York, Reilly," the agent said, falling a few steps behind and whispering frantically up his sleeve. "I think he's going to the subway. I think he's got a subway map, New York. What do you want me to do, New York?"

"*Shit.* Reilly, New York. Stall him. Flamethrower trail, New York. Get the limo around to Water Street. And find out who gave him the map! Over."

Reilly came up beside the President to try to stop him, but Hoskins said, "Mike, I want you to relax. It'll be fun. I used to ride the train when I spent a summer here during college. Piece of cake." He trotted down the stairs, reached into his pocket, and slid three dollars into the slot under the window at the token booth. "Two, please," he said. The clerk, a white-haired woman who had been working a crossword puzzle, lay her palm against her breast and stared. "It's all right, ma'am," he said. "Just give me two." He smiled. "That's a pretty blouse."

Reilly described the latest events to the dispatcher. The voice in his earpiece was frantic. "Flamethrower trail, New York. *Screw* low-key. I want everybody on that platform. I want two agents in each car, one between each car, and everybody else in the car with Flamethrower. Somebody get in front with the motorman and tell him to drive that son of a bitch as slow as it will go. Also, find out who gave him the money."

The clerk slipped the crossword puzzle onto her lap, smiled nervously, and slid the tokens under. "It's on us, sir. Please," she said, trying to poke the bills back through the slot with her shaking hands.

A train was coming into the station, and Hoskins held his hands up. "No way. You come see me in Washington, all right?" he yelled over the clatter. She was nearly in tears from the excitement, and just nodded and waved.

Hoskins handed Reilly one of the tokens and pointed toward the turnstiles. "Don't worry, boy," he said. "We've spent a lot of federal money down here. It's marginally cleaner and safer than you think."

By now a half-dozen of the most seasoned agents had gathered around the President, the rest fanning out along the platform. Nobody else had bought a token. The train stopped and the doors slid open, and although the conductor's voice instructed boarding passengers to stand aside to let people off, the President's party barreled through like Pickett's Virginians at Gettysburg. Inside, a man was playing the saxophone. His gig was playing as loudly as he could and promising to stop if he collected enough money. He saw the President and stopped. The President gave him a big grin. So he played "Hail to the Chief," after a fashion.

If Hoskins had expected a sentimental bonding with the salt of the earth, he'd picked the wrong city. "Hey, Clean Gene!" yelled a hardhat standing at the other end of the car. "Where's the press? You guys push them in front of the train?"

"I think they took the bus," said Hoskins, getting a big laugh. In fact the press pool, which had come in on a second chopper, was waiting at the first stop and just now getting the word that the President of the United States was on the northbound BMT, which was probably the photo opportunity of the year, second only to the one they were now hoping to get at the Municipal Building. This was not going to contribute to Parker DuBois's healing process. But Hoskins was having the time of his life. Grabbing a pole as the train lurched gingerly forward, he bent to ask a guy in a muscle shirt and sunglasses, "Where do I get off for City Hall?"

"City Hall," he answered. "Can I have your autograph?" This set the agenda for the rest of the ride. Hoskins kept a pocketful of business cards that said, "Eugene Hoskins, Washington D.C." for those rare occasions when he expected to meet the public. As he dug them out, a French family took his picture. They left town the next day, unaware the *Daily News* would have sent them home on the *Concorde* with five thousand dollars for the negatives.

At Mike Reilly's suggestion, Hoskins leaned against one of the doors so he could write more easily. He'd done about a dozen when Reilly was designated to approach him. The other agents watched him intently. "Mr. President, sir," he said uncomfortably, "we're glad that you've had a chance to do this. But the guys wanted me to say that when you do something of this nature, it puts both you and the public at risk because we don't know what to expect. They were wondering, sir, if. . . ."

Hoskins smiled. "If I'll just get in the damn car from now on?"

Reilly brightened. "Well, as a matter of fact, we've secured the walk across City Hall Park from the station, if you'd like. But we were hoping you'd promise that we'll just follow the schedule after the first event."

"Sure thing, son," he said. "I'll behave. I've had my little fling." He patted Reilly on the arm. "It was a toot, though, wasn't it? I've given you boys a whole new contingency to run exercises on."

The conductor's voice said, "This is the double-R presidential local, making all stops to Astoria, Queens. Next stop is City Hall. God bless America!" The doors flew open, and as Hoskins left, the platform filled with cheering passengers. The President waved, walked through the turnstiles, and bounded up the two flights of steps to Broadway.

The park was indeed secure, which meant it was empty, though the steps and windows of City Hall were full of people. The mayor, who'd just gotten word that the President was a straphanger in his city, was stuck in the President's traffic jam on the FDR at Eighty-sixth Street, howling at his driver to go faster and cursing himself for deciding to work at Gracie Mansion that morning. Hoskins waved again and smiled at the crowd but kept walking. He'd fooled the Secret Service by telling his staff the ceremony was an hour earlier than it really was, but he'd almost used up his stolen time, and he was too much of a gentleman to keep a lady waiting on a day like this. He crossed Centre Street and walked under the magnificent arch of the Municipal Building, where an agent stood waving him toward a side door. Some photographers were waiting; he waved at them, too. He went up one flight and down a dark hallway, guided by agents scattered along the route like violet flower petals at a wedding. He was pleased to see no sign of the press. A sign on a door said "Marriage Licenses."

Inside, sitting in the second row of a long grubby room full of brides- and grooms-to-be, were Parker DuBois and Carole Nelson. They were talking quietly to each other when they heard the room go completely silent.

DuBois stood up. "Gene," he said, trying to keep the emotion out of his voice.

Hoskins reached past him to Carole, his eyes glowing with affection. She was wearing a hat with a veil and a rose-colored silk suit, her thick brown hair flowing over her shoulders. A wide, knowing smile spread across her face. She stood on her toes and leaned forward and let the President take her hand and kiss her on the cheek. Her bouquet pressed against the front of his suit.

He stood another moment, holding her hand. "Were you surprised?"

She paused for a moment and then nodded yes, her eyes gleaming. *Sure I was,* she thought. *You don't think I noticed the twenty gorillas in the hall, do you?* She reached over to take DuBois by the arm, keeping her eyes on the delighted Hoskins.

Several agents were explaining to the clerk why it was now DuBois's and Carole's turn. The crowd was beginning to heat up and move in on them as everybody realized how having the President in their snapshots would spruce up a City Hall wedding. The party let the agents lead them into another room, where the justice of the peace was waiting. He looked up and dropped his Bible. Then Hoskins noticed the party contained two other people: a friend of Carole—her matron of honor—and a man DuBois introduced as Stanley Hersh.

"Oh," said Hoskins. "You must be—"

"Parker's attorney, Mr. President. And best man."

"Oh," said Hoskins again. He looked a little cross.

Hersh looked from DuBois to Hoskins and back again, then cleared his throat and said, "Listen, Parker, what if I, uh—"

"The rings," Carole chimed in. "You can hold the rings, Stan."

"Great," said the President. The JP had slipped out to change into his other black suit, which was in better shape, and so Hoskins had a moment to take Carole aside.

"I appreciate what you did for Pat Robinson," he said quietly. "And for me, too, I guess." She looked surprised. "After the accident, Felix found the letter in her computer."

Carole's face darkened. "Sir, he had no right—"

The President shot back, "Indeed he did. I assure you he wasn't looking for it. But she had been working on some critical documents and was going to be out of action for so long that they ran off all her files. I'm told it's routine."

Carole seemed to accept this. "How is she?"

"A lot better."

She watched him closely. "What are you going to do about her?"

The President's expression was just as pointed as Carole's as he said, "What do you propose I do? Not keep her in the White House, I hope."

Carole broke her eyes away from him and looked at the floor. "I suppose you can't." She looked up again. "But you can't abandon her, either."

Hoskins grinned and lowered his voice. "Young lady, we're lucky to have kept this thing quiet so far. I want Dr. Robinson safely and comfortably established well outside Washington even more than she does herself." He leaned forward. "When she's better, I'm going to have her in to get her picture taken with the President, and then she's going back to Harvard. We've checked; they're willing to give her her tenured slot back." His eyes took on a competitive gleam. "They didn't even do that for Kissinger." He looked over her shoulder; the JP, resplendent in new vestments, was swaying back and forth nervously and looking over at them. Hoskins offered Carole his arm, and she smiled and took it. He felt strength and vitality in her eyes and her touch, and as they walked back to the others he suddenly wished he were swapping places with Parker instead of Stanley.

Without his staff present, Hoskins's press relations fell to the Secret Service, which made E. E.'s reasonably hard-nosed operation seem like the Waffen SS. Saying no to reporters and photographers was not as easy as some people thought. As the ceremony ended, a harried agent rushed in and said, "I'm sorry sir, but the media's getting pretty worked up, especially since they got stuck sucking hind titty on the subway thing." After consulting with Carole and Parker, Hoskins permitted photographers from the two wire services to come up.

While everyone smiled for the cameras, Hoskins whispered to Carole, "Your name's going to be mud at the *Times* after this."

She whispered back, "I'll live. They just nominated me for a Pulitzer Prize."

To avoid his exquisite captivity on the way out, Hoskins would have had to sprout wings. A hundred agents and officers formed a narrow passageway that began at the door to the Municipal Building and ended at the right rear door of the limo. In a few moments, Flamethrower was in his car and all was right with the world as he hurtled uptown in the traditional blur and blare of a presidential motorcade. It went up Park Avenue to Fifty-first Street, turned right, and then pulled into the well of the Waldorf Towers. The President swept through the revolving door and into an elevator that had been held for him. As the door closed, he waved to the half-dozen members of the press pool who were scurrying behind him. "See you in a couple of hours," he said.

They looked up and watched the numbers above the elevator door as the car ascended. They decided it was a private meeting with a visiting leader and began pressing the tight-lipped agents to tell them which foreign delegations were in the hotel. Nobody noticed the technician in front of an open panel a few feet away, fiddling with the controls. The numbers were going up, but the President had gone down. He got out in the basement, was handed sunglasses and a hat, and then was rushed through the laundry room, up a flight of stairs, and out onto Fiftieth Street, where a sedan was waiting. In fifteen more minutes, he was on the way up in another elevator in a seedy hotel on the West Side.

An agent waiting on the fourteenth floor escorted the President to a door at the end of the hall and opened it. Inside, a bearded man sat talking with a White House aide. He stood and stared as the President entered.

"Mr. Rahmi? I'm Gene Hoskins. It's a pleasure to meet you. I'm sorry it's taken so long to arrange."

The aide, Felix Mendez, also stood. The NSC advisor was there to serve as notetaker. The President had certain notions about helping effect a change of government in Persia, the West's once and perhaps future bastion in East Asia, but there was no sense in letting word about them get around town prematurely. By persuading the President that he could more easily keep his meeting with the Iranian secret from the State Department if he staged it away from the White House, Mendez had won another round in Washington's longest-running bureaucratic duke-out. He smiled faintly as Hoskins reached for Ali Rahmi's hand. If keeping the secret had the added benefit of bolstering Mendez's own power and stature, so much the better. In Washington, as anywhere, motives were never pure anyway.

Rahmi's voice was rough with emotion. "The pleasure is mine, Mr. President. To be honest, I never would have thought you would, or should, take time to so honor a traitor."

"Was de Gaulle a traitor, Mr. Rahmi?"

The Iranian smiled, though his eyes were still wary. "You Americans have a talent for exaggeration." He paused, then added, "It is one of those American qualities I never much appreciated until recently. I thank you, sir."

"You're welcome. Now let's look ahead rather than back. We've both been burned, but here we are." He pointed Rahmi back to his chair and then sat down himself. "Have a seat. We've got a lot to talk about."

Afterword

ON AUGUST 7, 1974, WHITE HOUSE AIDE BRUCE HERSchensohn wrote an eloquent, impassioned memorandum to President Nixon urging him to abandon his plan to resign and instead schedule an address to a joint session of Congress. He said the President should walk alone down the aisle of the House chamber, vow before the Congress and the nation to let the constitutional process run its course, and then walk alone back up the aisle and out of the chamber. For borrowing Bruce's scene, I owe him thanks. But no one should think I am suggesting President Nixon should have followed Bruce's advice or indeed that he or anyone else should have taken any other action that might appear to have an analogue in this story.

Other thanks: to Janet Warner, Toni Sortor, and especially Bill Thompson at WYNWOOD™ Press; to Jeanne Nahill Kempthorne and Marin Strmecki, for advice and suggestions; to RN, for his support and his wisdom, both of which he has manifested in countless ways; and to Marcia Brisbois Taylor, whose careful reading saved me from many pitfalls.